# PRAISE FOR NAN ROSSITER

"Sinking into a Nan Rossiter book is like coming home."

—Robyn Carr, *New York Times* bestselling author, on *Promises of the Heart*

"A gripping story of three sisters, of love lost and found, and a family's journey from grief to triumph. A sure winner."

—Debbie Macomber, #1 *New York Times* bestselling author, on *More than You Know*

"Eloquent and surprising. . . . I love this story of faith, love, and the lasting bonds of family."

—Ann Leary on *The Gin & Chowder Club*

"A multileveled, beautifully written story that will glow in readers' hearts long after the last page is turned."

—Kristan Higgins, *New York Times* bestselling author, on *Promises of the Heart*

"Full of family, friends, and faith, Rossiter's novel depicts a couple and a community who may sometimes struggle but ultimately find the positives in life. Readers who enjoy Lisa Wingate and Melody Carlson will enjoy the depiction of a southern beach hamlet where love and family thrive."

—*Booklist* on *Promises of the Heart*

"With a winning cast of characters and compelling plot, Nan Rossiter's *Promises of the Heart* is a story that will warm your heart, lift your spirits, and renew your faith in humanity and the hope of happy endings."

—Marie Bostwick, *New York Times* and *USA Today* bestselling author

"Another trademark Nan Rossiter story, crafted with the tools that sustain us: heart, hope, and family! A touching novel that explores the meaning of faith and family as one couple's search to complete their home merges with one child's need of a lifesaving second chance. Once again, Nan Rossiter weaves together a multilayered tale of the endurance of love and a reminder that the things we most wish for can come true, if we're open to receiving them in unexpected ways. These characters stayed with me long after the last page was turned!"

—Hannah McKinnon, author of *The View from Here*

"An intimate portrayal of a family in crisis, with good character development and a bucolic setting."

—*Publishers Weekly* on *Words Get in the Way*

"Nostalgic and tender . . . [*The Gin & Chowder Club*] summons the passion of first love, the pain of first loss, and the unbreakable bonds of family that help us survive both."

—Marie Bostwick, *New York Times* bestselling author

"The setting, with its sea breeze and quaint charm, is immediately inviting, adding to the overall sense of familiarity that the author so beautifully evokes. . . . To read this book is to feel like you've come home."

—*Hartford Books Examiner* on *Summer Dance*

"Rossiter accurately captures the nature of life's fleeting passage and offers a meditation on the need to capture and hold on to every precious moment."

—*Connecticut Muse* on *Under a Summer Sky*

"I am never disappointed with Nan Rossiter's wonderful tales and her ability to include the love of animals. The delicious recipes included are just a plus in *Under a Summer Sky*. It's refreshing to read a story of this caliber and be left with contentment and faith in the lasting bonds of family."

—*Fresh Fiction*

"This captivating and emotional novel tells a heartwarming story about love lost and found, family secrets, and a lot of truth. The author's true grit and honesty are a real eye-opener, and readers will enjoy the different time frames of flashbacks and future casts between the siblings and how they have grown. When tragedy strikes, we're not quite sure what happens in between; it takes more than several factors to digest everything. But, the four very different sisters are now well past their fifties, and it's amazing that their memories remain, as if the good ole days in Cape Cod just happened yesterday. This is the perfect book club pick."

—*RT Book Reviews* (starred review) on *Firefly Summer*

"Real and touching . . . *Firefly Summer* makes a charming, ideal summer read."

—*The Recorder*

"Nan Rossiter is at the peak of her storytelling abilities with *Under a Summer Sky*, which is told with the kind of compassion, grace, and wisdom that is nearly unrivaled in contemporary fiction."

—Examiner.com

"Rossiter examines the effects of war, loss, and secrets in this coming-of-age book-within-a-book. There cannot be triumph without failure, or happiness without tragedy. Steadily paced and with a protagonist one can only root for, this is a great read for summer at the pool or beach. Fans of Elin Hildebrand and Nancy Thayer will enjoy this Nantucket tale."

—*Booklist* on *Nantucket*

"There are moments of pure gold in a story that will touch readers' hearts. With wonderful characters and a charming idyllic setting, *Nantucket* does pack an emotional wallop along the lines of a good Kristan Higgins book."

—*RT Book Reviews*

"Rossiter returns to the characters from her novel *Nantucket* in this coming-of-age story. Sally Ryan, the proud owner of Nantucket coffee shop Cuppa Joe, is publishing a book about her life story. As readers learn, Sally had a very unremarkable childhood, living with her widowed father in Medford, Mass. Her life forever changes when she meets Drew McIntyre, gets pregnant, and marries him at a young age. Fearful of Drew and encumbered by Catholic guilt (she believes her miscarriage resulted from one of her misdeeds), Sally believes that the marriage can't be dissolved. She travels to Nantucket, finds a place to stay, and begins working at a local coffee shop. After meeting Coop, a Vietnam vet, Sally enjoys their close friendship, which evolves into an on-again, off-again romance they try to keep secret. While the story of Sally's life is a page-turner, it's the manner in which she is finally able to reconcile her faith with her relationship with Coop that will resonate."

—*Publishers Weekly* on *Summer Dance*

# PROMISES TO KEEP

## ALSO BY NAN ROSSITER

*Promises of the Heart*

*Summer Dance*

*Firefly Summer*

*Nantucket*

*Under a Summer Sky*

*More Than You Know*

*Words Get in the Way*

*The Gin & Chowder Club*

# PROMISES TO KEEP

*A Novel*

NAN ROSSITER

HARPER

NEW YORK • LONDON • TORONTO • SYDNEY

HARPER

This is a work of fiction. Names, characters, places, and incidents are products of the author's imagination or are used fictitiously and are not to be construed as real. Any resemblance to actual events, locales, organizations, or persons, living or dead, is entirely coincidental.



HarperCollins books may be purchased for educational, business, or sales promotional use. For information, please email the Special Markets Department at SPsales@harpercollins.com.



FIRST EDITION

Library of Congress Cataloging-in-Publication Data has been applied for.

ISBN 978-0-06-291775-1 (pbk.)

21 22 23 24 25 LSC 10 9 8 7 6 5 4 3 2 1

*For Bruce*

*At least there is hope for a tree:*
*If it is cut down, it will sprout again,*
*and its new shoots will not fail.*

JOB 14:7 (NIV)

# PROMISES TO KEEP

# 1

Balancing a tray of lemonade and warm sugar cookies, Maeve Lindstrom stepped onto the wide front porch of the old farmhouse that had, in its heyday, been home to one of Savannah's most prominent families. But when the last Atherton—a daughter of whispered ancestry—suffered an untimely death under questionable circumstances, the house, which was already in a steady decline, accelerated that decline into utter disrepair. It was years before the abandoned property was purchased by a wealthy anonymous buyer, but it continued to sit empty, and except for the sounds of squabbling raccoons running down the halls, and bullfrogs plucking on loose banjo strings, eerily silent. Finally, after several more years of neglect, a young company that specialized in designing alternative living spaces for seniors saw its potential, bought it at auction, and began the lengthy process of restoration and repurposing. Ben Samuelson and his crew, when they worked on it, jokingly called it "A Place for Dad," but when the beautifully carved wooden sign was installed, its official name became known: Willow Pond Senior Care; and the advertising campaign that followed caught everyone's attention. The hip, young marketing team—a group of tech-savvy millennials—knew just how to target their audience. After all, they'd been promoting state-of-the-art facilities up and down the East Coast for several years by then, and with the baby boomer generation only getting older, homes for seniors were becoming a booming market. They used words like *private*, *bright*, *airy*, *family setting*, *plow-to-plate dining*, *on-site cafés*, *individualized professional care*, and *free Wi-Fi*, and with high-resolution JPEGs to match, their campaigns resulted in long waiting lists, even before online applications were available.

"Here you go, ladies and gents," Maeve announced, as she navigated the long line of walkers and canes. Willow Pond was one of the few facilities the group opened that didn't have an on-site café, but it did have Maeve, who, with her friendly smile, sprinkle of cinnamon freckles, and copper-red hair, was a ray of sunshine and a blessing to everyone who met her. It also had Tallulah, an affectionate orange tiger cat who swished between chair legs, stretched out in sunny spots, and when she seemed to sense a lonely soul, curled up on the owner's lap. Willow Pond had the slow, easy, lowcountry charm to which its residents were accustomed . . . *and* it had fresh-baked cookies every afternoon.

Ninety-three-year-old Adeline Hart, who preferred to be called "Addie," was not a baby boomer but a proud member of the Greatest Generation—and parent of the two baby boomers who'd convinced her she'd be happy at Willow Pond. Addie looked up with a start, and then tried to hide the fact that she'd dozed off. "Well, bless your heart. We thought you got lost, dear," she said in her soft Southern drawl.

Maeve held out her tray. "I didn't get lost, Miss Addie."

Gladys Warren, who was sitting next to her, cupped her gnarled hand behind her ear. "Who's lost?" she asked, frowning.

Maeve looked over. "Where're your hearing aids, Gladys?"

"I don't know where the maid is. She probably ran off with that handsome beau of hers. Have you seen that boy?" she added with raised eyebrows. "*He* is a catch!"

Maeve bit her lip, trying not to laugh. "Gladys," she said, more loudly this time, "I didn't ask where the maid is. I asked where your *hearing aids* are."

Gladys touched her ears and then scrunched her face into a scowl. "I don't know where the damn things are. Somebody musta taken 'em . . . *again*!"

Maeve didn't argue—she knew it was late in the day. The setting sun was making the old willow tree near the pond cast a long wispy shadow across the lawn, *and* it was making long confusing shadows cross the minds of some of the seniors. Maeve affectionately referred to her charges as "the Sundowners' Club," and lately, it seemed as if only Addie, Aristides, and the Olivetti twins didn't suffer the memory-stealing effects of the setting sun.

Addie reached for a cookie. "How come you're bringing our snack today, child?"

Maeve smiled, appreciating Addie's moniker for her—it made her feel younger than her thirty-five years, and it softened the blow of her self-imposed status as old maid. "Pam had to leave early. Her kids are in a play."

"Oooh, I *loved* being in school plays," Addie mused, her mind taking a turn down memory lane. "Did I ever tell you that's how I met my Theodore?"

"I don't think so," Maeve lied. She loved when the residents regaled her with their favorite old stories, even if she'd heard them before. It made *them* happy and it made her smile, and besides, she'd recently read an article touting the mental health benefits of sharing one's past.

"Well," Addie said, giddy to have fresh ears to which she could relay one of her fondest memories. "I was assigned the song 'I'm Wishing'—you know that sweet melody from *Snow White*?"

She started to sing in case someone on the porch was unfamiliar with the famous Walt Disney song, but Gladys interrupted her. "Yes, yes, we know."

Addie nodded and continued, "Well, my Theo—who was two grades above me—was assigned the prince's part, 'One Song.' You know that one?" Again, she started to sing but, worried that she wasn't doing the melody justice, stopped. "Oh, what a lovely tenor voice he had . . . and such a gentle timbre. It was no wonder I fell in lo—"

"I can drink a *full* glass," Gladys interrupted, eyeing the half-filled glasses on the tray.

"I know you can," Maeve said, "but why don't you start with half? You can always have more."

Gladys rolled her eyes and mumbled something inaudible, but then took a glass from the tray. "When's dinner?" she huffed.

"In an hour, so don't spoil your appetite," Maeve warned, as she made her way around the porch.

"Thank you, miss," Aristides Lincoln said, nodding politely, his dark eyes sparkling.

Maeve spied Tallulah curled up in his lap. "I see you're the chosen one today, Aristides."

"I am," he said, grinning as he stroked the cat's soft fur with one hand and took a cookie with the other. "Did you make these?"

Maeve shook her head. "No, I'm afraid I can't take credit. Sal made them."

He took a bite. "Well, tell *him* thank you."

"You can tell him at dinner tonight."

"What *is* for dinner?" Gladys asked, holding her glass out for a refill. Maeve started to pour more lemonade, but when the liquid reached the halfway mark, Gladys clucked. "All the way up, missy!"

Maeve filled the glass and wondered if Gladys was truly hard of hearing. She certainly seemed able to follow a conversation when she wanted to. "Well, it's Friday, so some form of fish, I imagine. Probably sole."

"Sole *again*?" Gladys sputtered, spraying lemonade. "I'm Protestant, you know. I don't *have* to eat fish every Friday. And, my word! I'd like to know why Catholics get to dictate the Friday menu for all eternity! I'm tired of sole. How come we never have catfish or trout? My daddy and I used to catch rainbows and brownies off Ossabaw Island . . . and big ole catfish from the Savannah River.

My mama used to fry them up in cornmeal and butter . . . mmm! My mouth waters just thinkin' 'bout it. When in heaven's name are we gonna have us some catfish?"

"You'll have to ask Sal, Gladys. I'm sure he'd be happy to make catfish for you."

Gladys took a bite of her cookie and closed her eyes. "Mmm, he makes the best sugar cookies, though. Better'n sex . . ."

"Gladys!" Maeve said.

"What?" the old woman asked, feigning innocence. She looked to Addie for support. "Am I right or am I right?"

Addie shook her head. "I guess you never made love to my Theo," she said dreamily, still lost in the memory of her beloved belated husband.

Maeve sighed and continued to the gazebo-like space at the far end of the porch and offered Ivy Lee Byrd a cookie, but the tiny woman, crowned with snow-white hair, only eyed the tray suspiciously. "They're sugar," Maeve said, setting a glass of lemonade on the table next to her. Ivy took a cookie, but then just held it in her lap.

The screen door squeaked opened and a stout, bald, rosy-cheeked man wearing baggy black-and-white checked pants and a starched white chef's coat peered out.

"Sal!" Gladys cried. "When are you going to make us some catfish?"

"Catfish!" he exclaimed. "I guess when you catch us some, Miss Gladys."

"Pshaw! You can get some right down at Warren's Fish Market—my nephew Hollis runs the place and he always has the freshest fish."

Sal chuckled. "This is plow-to-plate, here," he teased, "not river-to-plate."

Gladys rolled her eyes. "This is B.S.," she said with a huff. "That's what it is!"

Sal raised his eyebrows, surprised by the old woman's inferred language. "We'll see what we can do, Miss Gladys." Then he looked to Maeve. "Do you know where Pammy is? She has a phone call."

"She left early to go to her kids' play. Is it her husband?"

"No, it's her son."

"I'll come talk to him," Maeve said, maneuvering between the walkers and canes again and setting her tray next to Gladys. "I'll be right back."

She went into the foyer, picked up the phone, and clicked the line to talk to Pam's ten-year-old son, Pete, who'd forgotten his costume. "Don't worry. I'll text your mom," she assured him, and after reaching Pam—who'd already been home and found the costume—stepped back onto the porch just in time to see Gladys unsteadily lifting the pitcher. Hearing the squeak of the door, though, the old woman looked up, sloshing lemonade all over the tray.

"I'm still thirsty," she said defensively, giving Maeve an accusing look, "and you startled me."

"No worries," Maeve said good-naturedly, soaking up the spill, "but if you drink too much," she added softly, trying to remind the old woman of the incontinence issues she'd been having lately, "you might end up having to hurry to the ladies' room."

"Don't be silly," Gladys whispered indignantly. "I know when I need to use the ladies' room."

"Okay," Maeve said with a sigh. "I didn't mean to offend you."

Gladys rolled her eyes and folded her hands in her lap. "Humph!"

Maeve knew, now, Gladys—who could be as stubborn and ornery as a mule in mud—wouldn't take another sip, even if she offered her money.

"Would anybody like another cookie?" she asked as she picked up empty glasses and napkins.

"You twisted my arm," Loren Olivetti said, setting his glass on the tray and taking another cookie. He looked up at her. "Did I ever tell you, you have the prettiest hair?"

Maeve laughed. "You *have* told me, but I don't mind hearing it again. It's probably going to start turning gray soon, and I'll be an old maid."

"It won't turn gray," Loren assured her. "Redheads always keep their color. My Frances," he added, "bless her soul, had beautiful red hair and it just got lighter as she aged. She looked like she had a golden halo—which she did, of course," he added with a wink.

"You're not going to be an old maid," Aristides chimed in, taking a cookie, too. "Especially with those captivating blue-green eyes of yours."

Maeve laughed. "Well, thank you. I hope you're right." She continued to the far end of the porch and noticed the seat where Ivy had been sitting was empty. She frowned. "Where'd Ivy go?" she asked, glancing back at the men.

Loren shook his head, and his twin brother, Landon, frowned.

"She was there just a minute ago," Aristides said, looking around.

Maeve felt her heart pound. In the time Ivy had been there, she'd already wandered off twice. The staff all knew she should have been placed in a home more suited to someone with Alzheimer's, but Ivy's son had begged the powers that be to let her stay at Willow Pond until a bed became available at the new memory care facility opening in Savannah, and everyone suspected that a little extra money had changed hands to make it happen.

Now, Maeve turned to see if the old woman had moved to a different seat, but all she saw were seventeen crooked backs straightening up as seventeen pairs of eyes peered over the railing, and then all she heard were seventeen voices starting to whisper.

Maeve hurried down the steps. "Ivy?" she called, scanning the wide front lawn and gardens. "Ivy!" she shouted, feeling the icy fingers of worry grip her heart.

"She's right there," a deep voice behind her called.

Maeve turned and saw Aristides Lincoln standing at his full height—six feet two instead of his hunched-over five feet ten—pointing. Maeve turned, and through the sun-dappled curtain of willow branches and wispy Spanish moss, she spied a tiny figure standing on the edge of the pond with two trumpeter swans and several ducks circling in front of her. Maeve hurried toward her, and Ivy looked up, revealing a gentle smile on her face, but as soon as she saw Maeve, her countenance became shadowed with fear and distrust.

"Ivy?" Maeve said softly. The woman gripped the last piece of her cookie and stared. Then she turned back to the pond, broke the cookie in half, and tossed it into the water. The swans glided along the golden surface, gracefully bending their long necks, and skimmed the placid water, scooping up the sinking pieces with their beaks.

"C'mon," Maeve said gently, holding out her hand. "It's almost time for supper."

Ivy pulled her sweater around her humped shoulders, pushed her bony hands into her pockets, and began walking toward the house, but as she crossed the lawn, she began to veer toward the driveway. "This way," Maeve corrected, putting her arm around her, but Ivy shrugged her off.

In the fading light of the golden afternoon, Maeve watched the tiny wisp of a woman make her way toward the house and thought of the photo her son had placed on her bureau. It was one of two; the first—which was more recent—was of Ivy with her son, Will. The second was a faded black-and-white photo of a slender girl in her late teens standing between two young men holding fiddles, and the year 1941 was scrawled in white waxed pencil in the bottom corner. Both men were wearing pressed white shirts with their sleeves rolled up and narrow suspenders, but the girl rested her hand on the arm of the boy who wore a fedora tipped jauntily forward on his head. The boys were laughing, their eyes sparkling with mischief, which raised the question: which—if either—had won the girl's heart? Maeve watched her climb the steps and wondered what heartaches and joys, passions and intimacies Ivy Lee had known. Who were those boys . . . and what had they meant to her? *Oh, Ivy*, she thought, *what stories are locked behind those frightened eyes?*

Just then, an old Chevy pickup pulled into the driveway, stirring a cloud of dust, and now, eighteen crooked backs straightened up again as eighteen sets of eyes peered over the railing. Maeve turned, too, and watched as a young man wearing a light blue T-shirt and a tattered John Deere hat climbed out.

Gladys raised her eyebrows in surprise and then put her hand on Maeve's arm. "That's him," she whispered conspiratorially. "That's the maid's beau!"

Maeve laughed. "Gladys, that's *not* the maid's beau. That's *my* beau."

"It *is*?"

"Yes, and you've met him before."

"I *have*? What's his name?"

"Gage."

"Gage what?"

"Gage Tennyson."

"That's a nice name!"

"That's what you said last time."

"I *did*?!"

The man held the door of the truck cab open and a happy-go-lucky yellow Lab rocketed out and raced up the path. "Easy, Gus," the man called, but the Lab, who was a regular visitor to the home, could barely contain his excitement.

"Hullo, Gussie," Maeve said, bracing herself so the lanky puppy wouldn't knock her over. "You have to take it easy up here," she admonished gently, and he seemed to understand because every part of him, except for his whip of a tail, slowed down as he wiggled down the porch, greeting all the seniors.

"Hey," Maeve said, smiling as Gage came up the steps. "I thought you had to help Ben?" she asked, knowing her brother-in-law often asked Gage for help with side projects.

"I did, and we're done . . . and since I was in the neighborhood, I thought I'd stop by so Gus could say hi."

"You mean so *you* could say hi," she teased.

"Maybe," he said with an impish grin. "You almost done?"

"No, I have to work late . . . remember?"

"Oh, right," he said, looking disappointed. "I forgot."

Just then, the screen door squeaked open and Sal peered out. "Hey, Gage," he said, smiling. Gage waved and Sal looked down the porch. "Dinner's ready!" he called, and immediately, Gus, who'd been watching Tallulah walk along the railing, turned and trotted toward the door.

"Not you, silly," Gage said, grabbing his collar as he tried to scoot by.

Maeve laughed. "I'll have to finish saying hi to you later," she said, kissing his cheek.

"All right," Gage replied. "We'll just go home and mope, won't we, buddy?" He held on to Gus and turned to look down the porch. "G'night, everyone."

The seniors looked up from gathering their walkers and canes and smiled at the blue-eyed country boy. "G'night," they replied, and Gladys smiled broadly. "*You* take care, sweetheart," she called, giving him a flirtatious wink.

"You, too, Miss Warren," Gage said with a chuckle.

Maeve watched Gus hop back in the truck and waved to Gage.

"You're not going to be an old maid," Aristides said. "That boy is smitten."

"That's because he doesn't really know me," Maeve said with a sad half smile, wondering if she'd ever find the courage to be completely honest with Gage about her past. She certainly hadn't found it in the two years they'd been dating, and the longer she waited, the harder it became.

Aristides frowned. "How could he not know you? You're a sweet girl, and he would love you no matter what—I can see it in his eyes."

Aristides continued toward the door, and Maeve watched Gage pull away. "I hope so," she said softly, feeling the familiar old ache in her heart.

# 2

The second oldest of six sons, Gage Tennyson grew up on a dairy farm in the foothills of the Great Smoky Mountains. His parents, John—who'd been named after his father but had always been called Jack—and Elisabeth, who'd always been called Libby by her family and friends, felt blessed to have six boys to help with all the endless chores around the farm. *Farming is a twenty-four-three-hundred-fifty-two job*, Jack liked to say, to which Libby would add, *Our boys knew how to feed chickens before they knew how to walk*. Suffice it to say, the blond-haired, blue-eyed Tennyson boys knew, from an early age, that hard work was expected. Seven days a week they were up before dawn, helping their father feed and milk the lumbering, bellowing, steamy-warm cows. Then they'd hurry back to the kitchen, wolf down the hearty breakfast their mom had waiting, grab one of the brown-bag lunches lined up on the counter, and race down the driveway to catch the bus.

When their legs grew longer—which was well before they were old enough to have licenses—they all knew how to drive their dad's old farm truck and John Deere tractors. *Many hands make light work*, Jack would say. He was a tall, quiet man, who prided himself on being fair but firm with his boys, and although he had a sense of humor, he didn't tolerate horsing around or laziness. *If you have a job, big or small, do it well or not at all* was another favorite saying his offspring had heard so often they murmured it in their sleep.

In the summer, the boys grew strong and tan in the Tennessee sun, their hands calloused from gripping coarse baling twine, their shoulders muscular and broad from tossing hay bales from the fields into the wagons and from the wagons into the haylofts, their short-cropped blond hair turning summer white. In September, they took their favorite cows, bathed and combed, to the Tennessee State Fair, and bathed and combed themselves—wearing the requisite pressed white shirts and pants of 4-H—and stood proudly next to them, hoping to win a coveted blue ribbon. They ate fried dough, crispy fried chicken, buttery fresh-picked corn on the cob, sticky cotton candy, and juicy strawberry shortcake, washing it all down with thick milkshakes before curling up—sleepy-eyed and satisfied—next to their warm blue-ribbon bovines in the sweet hay of the livestock barn. It was an idyllic childhood, filled with Sunday church and family gatherings that included grandparents, aunts and uncles, a hay wagon full of cousins, a picnic table laden with food, and whatever NASCAR race was on. Through the years, the tumbling, towheaded, wrestling Tennyson boys grew like the golden timothy in their parents' fields, and the farm thrived.

By the time Gage was seventeen, the Tennessee Tennyson Dairy Farm was legend. Home to five hundred head of Guernsey, Ayrshire, and Brown Swiss cattle, it was known across the South for its dairy products—from milk and butter to cheese and yogurt (as well as eggs from all those well-fed chickens)—but it was especially known for its ice cream and, at Christmastime, its famous creamy, glass-bottled eggnog. In fact, the newly opened Tennyson Dairy Bar had become a destination to which people from up and down the East Coast were making pilgrimages. Life was good, and Jack and Libby felt doubly blessed, knowing their hard work would pay off—the small farm they'd started when they first married would be a legacy they could pass on to their sons. Their oldest, Cale, was already at the University of Tennessee Institute of Agriculture, and the knowledge he gained there would keep the farm current and competitive. Jack and Libby could rest assured, knowing their boys would have secure futures, fulfilling lives, and someday, families of their own to carry on the farm's traditions.

That was why Jack was so dismayed when his second-oldest son came out to the barn one night, as he watched over a cow in labor, and told him he didn't think he wanted to be tied down to the farm all his life. Although the boy said he loved growing up on the farm and didn't mind hard work, he had no interest in learning about the latest farm equipment and technology, or how much silage and magnesium supplement was needed to keep the herd healthy, and he didn't want to get up before dawn every single day of his life. He had other dreams: he wanted to travel, see the country . . . and go to art school.

Jack raised his eyebrows but didn't look up. "I can't talk about this right now, Gage," he said dismissively, stroking the swollen belly of the reddish-brown Ayrshire.

"Mom already knows," the boy pressed. "She understands, but she said I had to talk to you."

"Well, right now isn't a good time—your cow, here, is having a hard time."

"I'm sorry if you're disappointed, Dad. I'm not like Cale."

"It's nothing to be disappointed about, Gage, and it has nothing to do with your brother." His father was starting to sound impatient. "I just don't know how you think you're going to make money by going to art school."

"You've seen my pencil drawings, Dad. I've won blue ribbons. I get caught up in it. It's what I want to do. My teacher says . . ."

"I don't care what your teacher says," Jack interrupted, standing to face his son. "Drawing is a hobby. It's not a way to make a living—a living that will support a family. Your mom and I have worked hard to provide for you and your brothers. We've worked hard so you will have a future you can count on, and with Cale away, I'm counting on *you*."

"I'm not going anywhere, Dad. You *can* count on me. I'm just telling you now because I know you're expecting me to apply to UT, and I think it would be a waste of money."

The cow beside them let out a deep, mournful groan and Jack turned his back to his son. "As I said before, this isn't a good time."

"Can I help?" Gage asked, stroking the cow's big head. She blinked at him with soulful brown eyes, and he recalled all the blue ribbons they'd won together. Chestnut was *his* cow, just as his brothers' favorite cows were *theirs*. "Do you want me to call Doc Jacobs?"

His father turned back and searched his son's eyes. "No, Gage . . . actually, I think if I'm going to learn to get along without you, I may as well get started."

"Dad, it's not like that. I want to help."

"It *is* like that, Gage. You just told me you don't want to be tied down. You don't want to have to get up early all your life . . . so you and I may as well get used to this new arrangement."

Gage bit his lip and felt tears sting his eyes. "Fine, Dad, if that's the way you want it."

"It's not the way I want it. It's the way *you* want it."

The boy shook his head and walked to the door, but before he left, he turned. "I told Mom you wouldn't understand." He slid open the door, pulled up his collar, and walked back to the house.

An hour later, from the bedroom he'd shared all his life with his older brother, who was now away in college, he heard the kitchen door slam and wheels spin on gravel. He got up from his desk and pulled back the curtain. All the lights were on in the yard and the barn doors were flung wide open. His mom was hurrying across the yard with an armful of towels, and Doc Jacobs was climbing out of his truck. Then he saw his sixteen-year-old brother Matt appear in the doorway, motioning for them to hurry. Gage's heart pounded—he wanted to help. He wanted to know Chestnut was okay, but the words his father had said were repeatedly playing through his mind, and his feet felt cemented to the floor. Finally, he let go of the curtain, turned up the lonesome country song on the radio, and picked up his drawing pencil.

# 3

"Sheesh, Aunt Maeve, if I were Mary, I'd tell Colin to go jump in a lake! He's such a pain in the as . . . butt!" Ten-year-old Harper Samuelson shook her head as she rearranged the fleece blanket draped over their legs. "Mary is trying to help him, but he's so damn . . . I mean *dang* ungrateful."

Maeve laughed at her niece's honest unadulterated interpretation of the characters in the book they were reading. Ever since Maeve's older sister, Macey—who'd endured more than her share of miscarriages over the last several years—and her sister's husband, Ben, had adopted the little girl, Maeve had felt as if she'd found a kindred spirit. She had offered to "niece-sit," because Harper found the term *babysit* insulting, anytime her sister and brother-in-law wanted to go out. Macey, seeing the growing alliance between her sister and new daughter—who had spent most of her young life being shuttled from one foster home to another and, due to a heart condition, ended up needing a new heart—and wanting Harper to have as many positive role models in her life as possible, had latched onto the idea. Date night had quickly become a weekly event that Maeve and Harper looked forward to as much as Macey and Ben. They'd even started their own book club, The Pepperoni Pizza and Root Beer Book Club, but instead of reading books and getting together to discuss them—as other book clubs did—they read their selection together, discussed it as they went along, and when they finished, watched the movie. The first two books they'd read were the classics *To Kill a Mockingbird* and *A Tree Grows in Brooklyn*, both of which featured young strong-willed female protagonists with whom Harper had fallen in love. And even though most people tend to like the books more than their movie adaptations, Harper and Maeve agreed that the movies made from these two books were perfect.

"What about Mary?" Maeve asked. "She wasn't much better. She acted like a spoiled brat when she first came to Misselthwaite Manor."

Harper nodded thoughtfully, gently stroking the furrowed dreaming brow of the golden retriever lying beside her. "She did, but she had an excuse. I mean she was an orphan, and no one loved her. She was just defending herself."

Maeve nodded, wondering if Harper could see how much the life of Frances Hodgson Burnett's spunky protagonist paralleled her own. Both ten years old. Both orphaned. Both had a sassy attitude. And both were making great strides toward becoming the amazing young women they were meant to be.

"I love Dickon," Harper added, taking a sip of root beer. "He reminds me of Sam."

"Does he now?" Maeve teased.

"Not like that," Harper said, rolling her eyes.

"Not like *what*?" Maeve asked, feigning innocence.

"*Not* like a boyfriend, duh. Sam is a lot like Dickon."

"How so?" Maeve asked, surprised that Harper drew a parallel between the young male character who loved animals and Sam Finch—the sweet boy and classmate with whom she'd become fast friends—before she saw herself in the audacious Mary Lennox.

"Well, you know how Soot and Captain and the little robin all love Dickon and trust him?" She looked up at Maeve. "Sam's like that. His mom, Sage, takes care of wild baby birds and animals that have lost their parents, so he is always around them. Last year, when we were in Mrs. Holland's class, and she had to clean out the guinea pigs' cage, Sam would hold Harold and Maude in his arms and they would fall asleep like it was the safest place on earth. He also has a pet raccoon named Ty Coon," she added with a smile, "and he follows him around like a shadow."

Maeve nodded thoughtfully. "But does he have eyes that 'look like pieces of moorland sky'?" she teased in her best British accent.

"They *are* very blue," Harper said with a laugh.

"And does he 'smell like heather and grass and leaves'?"

Harper rolled her eyes and pushed on Maeve's arm. "I said it's not like *that*."

Maeve raised her eyebrows and grinned. "Mm-hmm . . ."

Harper shook her head. "Keep reading!"

Maeve obediently turned back to the book, and as Harper listened, she watched Big Mac, their gray tiger cat, saunter in, hop on the couch, and curl up next to Keeper. She reached out to stroke his soft fur, too, and while she did, she pictured the ruddy-cheeked Dickon greeting the pale, self-absorbed Colin for the first time, and wished she had a secret garden to tend.

Twenty minutes later, Maeve realized there'd been no recent commentary from the peanut gallery and looked over to see Harper sound asleep, her breathing soft and easy. She reluctantly tucked the bookmark between the pages and reached over to stroke the heads of the big golden retriever and his feline sidekick. "Where'd we lose her?" she whispered, and Keeper opened one eye and swished his tail, but Big Mac just slumbered on peacefully. *Typical cat*, Maeve thought. She looked up at the clock on the mantle—it was after ten—and then she gazed at the embers in the fireplace, wondering what Gage was up to and deciding he was probably asleep, too. When they'd first started dating, she'd teased him about not being able to stay awake past ten o'clock, and he'd explained that his internal clock—from growing up on a farm—could not be reset. It was a curse from his father, he added—a comment that made her wonder. As she watched a piece of bark catch and flame up, she recalled the first time she'd heard Gage's name, and realized there'd been no way to know how much it would come to mean to her. She and Macey had been sitting on Macey's back porch eating ice cream from the Tennyson farm, when Ben had come home from work, seen the ice cream, and casually mentioned that he'd just hired a new guy named Gage Tennyson.

"No way!" Macey had said, as she licked her spoon.

"Way," Ben had said.

"Wait," Maeve had said as the progress of her own spoon stopped halfway to her mouth. "He's not from the same family that makes Sweet Irish Cream?" She had eyed her brother-in-law, unable to believe he had someone on his crew who might have something to do with her favorite ice-cream flavor.

"He might be," Ben had teased with a grin.

Macey had raised her eyebrows. "If you hired him, Ben, you *know* . . ."

Just then, there was a sound on the front porch and Keeper and Big Mac both perked up, pulling Maeve back to the present. "Are Mom and Dad home?" she whispered, and Keeper thumped his tail and hopped off the couch, landing deftly on three legs—one of his front legs, due to a bout with cancer, had been amputated—and he hurried to the door, his whole hind end wagging.

The doorknob turned, and Macey and Ben peeked in. "Hey," Macey said, kneeling down to greet their two rescue pets. Keeper pushed his bowed head into her chest—his usual hello—while Big Mac placed his front paws, light as a whisper, on her knee and sniffed her cheek.

"How was The Crab Shack?" Maeve asked, gingerly lifting the blanket off her legs while trying not to disturb her slumbering niece.

"Amazing, as always," Macey replied. "How was the weekly meeting of The Pepperoni Pizza and Root Beer Book Club?"

"Great!" Maeve answered, chuckling. "Except you-know-who fell asleep midchapter!" She nodded in Harper's direction and then looked back at her sister. "There's some leftover pizza in the fridge."

"Want to take it home?" Ben asked.

"No, thanks," Maeve said, shaking her head. "You guys can have it for lunch tomorrow."

"Are you sure?" Ben pressed, holding up a paper bag containing two takeout containers, "Because we have leftovers, too."

"Positive," Maeve answered. "I'm pretty sure Gage got a pizza tonight, too." She smiled. "He feels left out when Harper and I have book club."

"He can come over, too, you know," Macey said.

Maeve frowned. "Oh, no. This is girls' night, and besides, he's not a big reader."

"Okay," Macey said, laughing softly, "but, you know, Harper thinks he walks on water so I'm sure she wouldn't mind."

"I know," Maeve replied. "Maybe the three of us will do something together sometime."

"That reminds me—the Croo-Picnic is next weekend," Ben said.

"So I heard," Maeve replied, remembering the brief conversation she'd had with Gage about the annual summer barbecue Ben and Macey hosted for his employees and their families. "What can we bring?"

"Whatever you'd like," Macey said.

"Your world-famous deviled eggs and blackberry cobbler are always a hit," Ben suggested hopefully.

Maeve laughed. "Okay . . . maybe." She gave them each a hug. "Thanks for niece-sitting!"

"My pleasure," she replied and then leaned over to kiss Keeper's head. "Anytime."

# 4

Through a blur of angry tears, tall, slender Mason Callahan gazed up at the pink and coral clouds drifting across the Georgia sky. *How could a God who is supposed to be loving let someone so caring endure so much suffering?* He walked across the empty hospital parking lot—still steaming and puddled from a passing thunderstorm—unlocked his car, and opened the door, but instead of climbing in, he leaned against it, wiped his eyes with his palms, and waited for the trapped summer heat to drift out.

Mason had bought the old car the previous summer from a man whose family had decided he shouldn't drive anymore. At the time, Mason had been on the opposite end of the spectrum—he hadn't even had his license yet, but when he saw the For Sale sign propped on the windshield of the '67 Chevelle, he'd spun his bike around to take a closer look. He'd walked around the classic car, noting—but undeterred by—the rusty rocker panels and chrome bumpers. Not a minute later, an older gentleman emerged from the house and made his way slowly across the lawn with the assistance of a cane, and Mason moved toward him, held out his hand, and shyly introduced himself.

"Bud Hawkins," the man replied, shaking the offered hand. He was tall and slim, and under the brim of a US Navy hat, his eyes were dark blue. "I knew a Callahan—flew his Wildcat off the deck of our carrier."

Mason's eyes lit up. "My grandfather was a pilot during the war," he said. "His name was Winton Callahan."

"I never knew this fella's first name," Bud said, rubbing his chin, "but I'll never forget his call sign—Whiplash." He chuckled. "Probably got it from being catapulted off the deck!"

Mason smiled. "I don't know what his call sign was."

Bud nodded and gestured toward the old Chevelle. "She's a great car," he said. "N'er gave me a lick o' trouble. Just routine oil changes and tune-ups I done m'self."

"How come you're selling her?" Mason asked, adopting the inferred gender of the old car.

Bud sighed and leaned heavily on his cane. "My wife passed away last year, and she had sorta taken over all our driving. I've tried to get back into it, but my family thinks it's time for me to give it up." He nodded to the dented bumper. "Too many fender benders."

"Oh, man, that stinks. I'm sorry about your wife."

"Yeah, thanks. She was the love of my life—I miss her." He shook his head. "Now my family thinks I need to move to a nursing home, too. They say it's so I'll be closer to them, but I think they're just tired of driving all the way up here to see me."

Mason nodded, not knowing what to say.

"Anyway, that's why *I'm* sellin' her. I don't want *them* sellin' her after I'm gone. I want her to go to the right person—someone who'll appreciate her, and I honestly don't care what I get. They can't control everything I do."

Mason nodded. "What does she have for a motor?"

"Three ninety-six big block," Bud said, lifting the hood.

"Nice," Mason murmured, nodding his approval.

Bud watched the boy lean under the hood for a closer inspection and was reminded of himself at the same age.

"Does she run?"

"Oh, yeah, she runs," Bud said, beaming proudly and pulling the keys from his pocket.

Mason opened the car door, and the pine scent from a tree-shaped air freshener hanging from the cigarette lighter drifted out. He climbed in and looked around. The leather seats were cracked and faded, and the carpeting was worn in spots, especially under the pedals, but the interior was spotless. He slid the key into the ignition, turned it, and the car rumbled to life. "Oh, man," he whispered.

"Wanna take 'er for a spin?"

Mason hesitated. He knew how to drive, but he only had a learner's permit. "Sure," he said. "Just around the block."

Bud stepped back, and Mason put the car in gear and slowly pulled out of the driveway. The powerful engine was begging him for more gas, but on the quiet street—and without a license—he couldn't take any chances, so he drove slowly around the block and eased back into the driveway.

"You're awfully conservative on the gas pedal," Bud teased.

Mason laughed as he handed the keys back to him. "Wish I could buy her," he said wistfully. "Maybe someday."

Bud eyed him. "Why not now?"

"I don't have enough money—just what I've earned landscaping."

"I haven't even told you what I'm asking."

"Well, I'm sure it's a lot more than what I have."

"How much is that?"

"A little over three grand."

"That's a lot of landscaping."

"It is, but I'm sure it's still not enough."

"I'll take twenty-five hundred. That'll leave you enough to register her and fill the tank."

Mason looked astounded. "She's gotta be worth a lot more than that!"

"Not in this condition—she needs a ton o' work." Bud eyed Mason's tall, slender frame and short reddish-blond hair, searched his blue-green eyes, and sensed that he'd found a kindred spirit—a young man who was honest and sincere and who appreciated the car's value. "If you promise you'll take good care of her . . . and restore her someday, she's all yours. Besides, if you're related to Whiplash, I know you're a good man . . . not to mention it'll totally annoy my kids," he added with a mischievous grin, "so you'd be doing me a favor."

A slow smile crossed Mason's face and then he held out his hand. "Deal."

One month later, on the first day of his senior year, Mason had pulled into his newly assigned parking spot and climbed out, the envy of all his buddies.

A month after that, his mom had been diagnosed with stage four pancreatic cancer and their lives had been turned upside down.

# 5

As Maeve walked to her Jeep, she recalled the first time she ever attended Ben's Croo-Picnic, as he liked to call—and spell—it. He and Macey always invited the guys on his construction crew and their families over for a picnic during the Memorial Day weekend, but Maeve had never paid much attention to it because . . . well, she didn't work for Ben *and* she'd never been invited. But two summers ago, Macey—under the guise of needing her help—*had* invited her, and because she hadn't had anything else on her calendar (per usual), she'd made deviled eggs and a blackberry cobbler and arrived early to help set up. But if she'd spent more than two seconds thinking about the oddness of the invitation, she would have figured out that her sister was up to something.

That Saturday, after everyone had eaten their fill of hot dogs and hamburgers and summer salads of every variety—from potato to pasta to tossed—and the kids were trying to entice the adults into playing cornhole and volleyball, Maeve suggested they wrap up the salads and put them back in the fridge. Macey responded by looking at her phone and reluctantly agreeing, but when she stood up to help, she spied a man wearing faded jeans, a Kenny Chesney concert T-shirt, and a tattered John Deere hat walking up the driveway with a little yellow Lab puppy traipsing along after him. "OMG, what an icebreaker," she murmured, and Maeve, who was standing beside her, trying to find the elusive end of the Saran

Wrap, followed her gaze and exclaimed, "Oh, my goodness! How cute!"

The man stopped to shake hands with a couple of his coworkers, but the puppy, smelling food, trotted straight to the picnic table, plopped down at Maeve's feet, and looked up longingly.

"Well, you have that down pat, don't you?" she said, laughing. She leaned down to stroke his soft head. "*You* are a cutie!" she whispered. "Do you have a name?"

"It's not official, but I might call him Gus," a deep voice drawled.

Maeve stood up with the puppy in her arms, and met the gaze of its owner. "That's a great name," she replied, feeling instantly—and oddly—drawn to the man with the roguish scruff on his chin and whose eyes were the color of the pale blue Savannah sky.

"Hey, Gage! Glad you could come," Macey said, unwittingly interrupting the spark-charged moment her sister and the newcomer were sharing.

"Thanks for the invite," he replied, pulling his attention away from Maeve's strikingly Caribbean Sea–blue-green eyes. "Sorry I'm late." He held out a brown paper bag. "Ben said not to bring anything, but my mom wouldn't be happy if she knew I showed up to a picnic empty-handed."

Hearing his concern over what his mom might think, Maeve studied him more closely, trying to discern his age. *Late twenties or early thirties . . . maybe?*

Macey reached into the bag and pulled out a box of graham crackers, a package of chocolate bars, a bag of Jet-Puffed marshmallows, and a box of sparklers. "Thanks, Gage! This is perfect."

A slow smile crossed his face. "A picnic isn't complete without s'mores and sparklers."

"So true!" She paused and realized her sister was still staring at him. "Gage, this is my sister, Maeve Lindstrom . . . and Maeve, this is Gage *Tennyson*." As she said his last name, Macey channeled her sisterly telepathic power, hoping Maeve would make the connection, and then smiled when Maeve raised her eyebrows in recognition. She searched Gage's eyes, ruddy tan cheeks, short blond hair, and smiled the awestruck smile of someone meeting a celebrity. "Oh, wow! It's so nice to meet you!"

Gage nodded shyly. "It's nice to meet you, too."

"Well, well, it's about damn time," Ben interrupted, coming up behind them and slapping his newest employee on the back. "I see you met my pain in the ass . . . I mean my sister-in-law," he teased, winking at Maeve.

"I did," Gage confirmed with a grin.

"I hope you brought your appetite."

"I did that, too."

"Well, come fill a plate. I've got the grill all fired up—burger or dog?"

Gage looked at Maeve, still cuddling the puppy. "Want me to take him or are you good?"

"I'm good," Maeve replied, laughing. "You go ahead and eat."

Gage glanced at the table—still laden with everything from fried chicken, macaroni salad, potato salad, strawberry Jell-O salad with sour cream and bananas, and baked beans to cupcakes, brownies, and Macey's famous chocolate chip blondies—and grabbed one of Maeve's deviled eggs along with an ice-cold beer from the cooler and followed Ben.

Maeve watched him go and then turned to her sister and frowned. They'd only talked about Gage that one time when they'd been having ice cream on the porch, but Maeve had wondered, ever since, when she might meet him. "You didn't tell me he was going to be here . . ."

Macey shrugged. "I wasn't sure if he would be."

"You *also* didn't tell me how cute he is—he looks like he could be Brad Pitt's younger brother."

"I know, right?" Macey replied with a grin.

"When did you meet him?"

"A couple weeks ago . . . he stopped by right after Ben told us he hired him."

"Soo . . . is he a Tennessee Tennyson?" Maeve pressed.

"He *is* indeed and, not only is he a direct descendent, but he's also second in line to inherit the dairy dynasty."

"No way!" Maeve said, her eyes growing wide.

"Way," Macey replied, reaching out to take the puppy. "But Ben says he has no interest in the farm."

"How come?"

Macey shrugged. "I don't know. He didn't get into it."

Later that night, after they toasted s'mores and devoured Maeve's blackberry cobbler topped with Tennessee Tennyson's signature flavor—Plain Ole Vanilla—lit sparklers, and watched Ben's stash of bottle rockets scream into the night sky, everyone packed up their weary, marshmallow-sticky kids, thanked Ben and Macey for another wonderful time, and headed home. Everyone, that is, except Maeve and Gage, who were kid-free, and hung around to help clean up. Gage and Ben wiped down the tables and chairs, folded them and put them away, and then cleaned up the games, and Maeve helped Macey carry the food inside and rinse out the bottles and cans. When everything was shipshape, Gage picked up his tuckered-out little yellow Lab—who'd spent all day chasing kids and vacuuming up dropped tidbits, and could now barely hold his head up—took one last cold bottle of beer that Ben offered him, a "roadie," and said good night. Maeve—who was heading out, too—walked down the driveway with him. As they walked through the darkness toward her Jeep, a haunting sound filled the night air, and Maeve stopped in her tracks. "Is that a wolf?"

"You never heard that before?" Gage asked, undeterred, and continuing to walk.

Maeve hurried to catch up, still listening. "I don't think so."

"My brothers and I used to fall asleep to that sound all the time."

"It sounds so mournful and lonely."

"It does," he agreed, setting Gus—his name, after lots of approval, now official—on the seat of his truck. He closed the door, and as he'd twisted the cap off his beer, there'd been another sound.

"Now, I've heard *that* before."

"Those are loons," Gage replied. "They have four distinct calls. The first one—the one you thought sounded like a wolf—is the 'wail.' The male loon makes it when he's looking for his mate—he's saying, 'Yoo-hoo, where are you?'"

"Nice," Maeve said, laughing.

Gage took a sip of the beer and grinned. "And the one we just heard is the 'yodel'—he's telling everyone it's his territory."

"How do you know so much?"

Gage shrugged. "I dunno. Growing up on a farm, I guess, and listenin' to all the old folklore from my grandparents, especially Dutch—my mom's dad."

"You called your grandpa *Dutch*?"

Gage nodded. "Everyone does. His real name is Henrik Jansen, but when he was a kid, he loved baseball—he was a star pitcher—and all his buddies called him 'Dutch,' and it just stuck. He was a great guy—he'd do anything for you. One time, there was this huge barn fire on our neighbor's farm, and by the time everyone got there, the hayloft was fully engulfed, but Dutch ran straight into that barn and shooed out all the cows and chickens. The barn was a total loss, but not a single animal died."

"That's incredible!"

Gage smiled, lost in the memory of his grandad, and then offered her the beer.

She took a sip. "My grandmother was like that. I mean, she didn't run into a burning building or anything, but she was always willing to help. We called her Grandy."

Gage nodded. "Is she still alive?"

"No, she died when we were young. How about your grandfather?"

"He's still alive, but he's in a nursing home."

"Do you ever see him?"

"Not recently. My mom says he's getting pretty forgetful and sometimes he doesn't remember people."

"You should go see him. Elderly folks have unexpected moments of clarity—a voice or a song can trigger their memory, and seeing the light of recognition in their eyes—eyes that are usually far-off and lost—is like a gift from heaven."

"Yeah? How do you know so much?"

She grinned and handed the beer back to him. "Because I studied cognitive impairment in the elderly—dementia, senility, Alzheimer's. I'm drawn to old people, and I like to stay current on new studies."

"Where'd you go to college?"

"Emory."

"Did you grow up in Georgia?"

"I did, but I was born in Maine and lived there till I was in sixth grade, so I have roots in New England."

He took a sip of the beer. "Why'd you move down here?"

"My dad got a job offer from Gulfstream that he couldn't turn down."

He nodded, offering her the bottle again.

She took a sip. "Did you go to college?"

"Art school."

"Which one?"

"SCAD."

She raised her eyebrows. "Sooo, you're an artist-slash-construction guy?"

"More like a construction guy—slash-failed-artist."

"What was your major?" she asked, handing the bottle back.

"I didn't stay long enough to pick a major, but I was leaning toward illustration."

"How come you didn't finish?"

"I didn't have enough money."

Maeve frowned. "What about your par . . ."

But before she could finish, Gage shook his head. "It's a long story."

She nodded and watched him drain the last of the beer. The conversation was over, and she opened the door of her Jeep, but after she climbed in, she looked back at him. "You said loons have four calls. What are the other two?"

Gage smiled. "Well, there's the hoot," he said. "It's not very remarkable—just a little hoot like he's answering roll call, but the last call is the tremolo. It sounds like this . . ." He cupped his hand around his mouth and the sound that passed through his lips was so realistic that, a moment later, there was a response in the distance.

"Wow, that was really good," Maeve teased. "I think you've attracted a potential mate."

Gage laughed. "I hope so."

That had been two years ago, and as Maeve climbed into her Jeep tonight, she heard the haunting tremolo of a loon, and the coincidence made her smile, but the feeling that followed was bittersweet. Gage *had* attracted a potential mate; they'd started dating soon after and she couldn't believe how time had flown, but even though they'd grown close, there were still things she hadn't told him—things that had happened in her past that made her feel ashamed—and she sensed he had his own skeletons. Aside from his grandfather, he never talked about his family, and whenever she asked, he always found a way to change the subject. She stared up at the night sky. *Why does life have to be so complicated?*

# 6

The eggs were still warm when Gage cracked them on the edge of the cast-iron pan his mom had given him. He watched their translucent whites turn opaque, flipped the sizzling popping bacon, and then looked out the kitchen window. Eggith, Eggel, and Eggna, his Rhode Island Red hens, and their faithful protector, Pilgrim, a Plymouth Rock rooster, were all members of a tiny flock that had arrived in a peeping box two years earlier. They were now scratching and pecking the dusty earth along the fence, foraging for insects in the tall grass. He took a sip of coffee and thought about the day ahead. Between working all week and spending most of his free time with Maeve, he rarely had a day to himself, but when Maeve announced she was going shopping and out to lunch with Macey and Harper, he realized he'd finally have some time to catch up on projects around the cabin—and maybe even do a little drawing. He'd meant to get up early, but he'd lazed in bed, stroking the snoring blond head on the pillow next to him, and, feeling his light touch, the lanky yellow Lab had rolled onto his back, exposing the long curve of his belly, and waited expectantly, his front paws hanging in the air like a basketball player who'd just taken a jump shot. Gage had teasingly withdrawn his hand and waited, watching him with a half smile. Finally, Gus had opened one eye and looked over. *Well?* he seemed to say, and Gage had chuckled.

"You're silly, you know that?" he'd said softly, making the dog's tail thump the strewn-about sheets.

He turned the eggs and watched the lacey edges turn golden before sliding them onto a plate next to the bacon. He buttered a slice of toast, spread orange marmalade across it, and licked the knife. He rarely had time for breakfast—he was usually gulping coffee as he headed out the door, so today was a luxury. He refilled his mug, pushed aside the pile of mail on the old oak table, and took a bite of toast, savoring the sweet orange rind and sugar of his childhood.

When he was growing up, his mom had spent the long summer days canning and preserving every fruit and vegetable under the sun. Gage pictured her now, and knew—since it was late May—she'd be checking her strawberries for ripeness, and soon, she'd be picking string beans and peas. Then there'd be the endless parade of juicy red tomatoes, so fat they'd be splitting their skins, and the abundance would provide spaghetti sauce all winter. Next in line would be her candy cane and burgundy red beets. In between, she'd preserve *all* the berries—from the lush raspberries and blackberries that grew wild along the south pasture to the blueberries from the net-covered bushes in the side yard. He and his brothers, when tasked with the job of picking them, would pop more plump berries into their mouths than into their buckets; and then, of course, was the aforementioned—and *his* favorite—sweet orange marmalade.

Later in the summer, when the cicadas droned in the trees, the unmistakable aroma of apple cider vinegar, sugar, kosher salt, onions, and turmeric would waft from the kitchen windows, filling the boys' hearts with both expectation *and* melancholy. They would peer through the screen door and spy their mom's big white ceramic bowl filled with crushed ice and piled high with thinly sliced onions and cucumbers, and it would suddenly dawn on them that the lazy summer days were waning, and the school bus would soon be rumbling down the dusty road again. Libby Tennyson's last big day of canning always began in the coolness of an early morning in late August with the harvesting of her bumper crop of cucumbers hanging heavily on the vine, and it would culminate in the hazy heat of late afternoon with dozens of mason jars lined up on the kitchen counter, their metal caps popping like tiny suction cups, making the boys' mouths water at the thought of their mom's succulent bread-and-butter pickles—a memory of sunshine, warmth, and buzzing bees they would savor on winter nights when her pot roast had simmered all afternoon.

Libby gave away countless jars of her prize-winning pickles at Christmastime, and Gage always received two in the mail, along with two jars of marmalade, four jars of tomatoes, and a bottle of eggnog. Years ago, she'd enclosed a copy of her pot roast recipe, too, written out in her long, neat handwriting, but Gage had never been able to replicate the tender melt-in-your-mouth dish he'd savored as a boy. *You'll just have to take me to your parents' sometime so I can have hers*, Maeve had teased when he lamented about its lack of tenderness, but Gage had only responded with an unenthusiastic *mm-hmm*.

He sopped up the last of the egg yolk with the last of his toast, and eyed Gus, who was gazing at him longingly.

"What will it be, sir? Toast or bacon?"

Gus sat up and thumped his tail happily, thankful to be remembered.

"Can you gimme five?"

Immediately, the overgrown puppy slapped Gage's hand with his saucer-size paw.

"Good boy!" Gage said, tousling his ears and giving him the last of his toast topped with a small piece of bacon.

He wiped his hands and sifted through the mail, making two piles—junk and bills—and then glanced through the pages of the new Cabela's catalog, surprised to discover they were already promoting their fall line of products. *Everyone is always in a rush to start the next season!* He tossed the catalog on top of the junk pile—there was nothing he needed—and cleared his dishes.

As he filled the sink with hot, sudsy water, he looked out at the ribbon of river curling along his property and felt oddly thankful—there *really* was nothing he needed. Before he'd started working for Ben, Gage had been trying to survive as an artist, but the truth of the term *starving artist* had become a little too real. During the day, he'd spent long hours working at his big oak drawing table—a table that took up half of his tiny studio apartment. When he'd had enough drawings, he'd begun showing his portfolio to several galleries in downtown Savannah, and although the owners had all promised to keep him in mind, he'd never heard back from any of them. Finally, out of desperation, he'd taken a job as a bartender, but every night, he'd come home dead tired and dismayed that his only contribution to the world was helping people get drunk. He'd get back to his apartment well after midnight—which was way past his longtime bedtime of 10:00 P.M.—strip off his clothes, drop them in the hamper, and stand under the hot shower, trying to wash away the stale, sticky scent of alcohol. It had all seemed so pointless—a dead-end job with no future. His dad had been right—art was not a reliable way to make a living, but there was no way he'd ever let him know that. His father's dismissive words had stung him to his core, and he would never forgive him—especially after everything that happened later.

Before Gage knew it, twelve years had gone by and he had nothing to show for it. The only artwork he'd sold were commissioned pet portraits, a time-consuming endeavor that didn't pay well. In fact, when he'd started keeping track of the time he put into it, he'd realized he barely made minimum wage. Finally, one morning, after another long night of mixing craft cocktails and pouring craft beers, he'd poured a mug of black coffee, taken a sip, and with bleary eyes, scanned the Help Wanted section of the paper for the millionth time. As per usual, it was filled with ads for restaurant help, trolley and ghost tour drivers, groundskeepers, and hotel staff—the standard industry of a tourist destination, but none of the jobs had appealed to him. *God help me if I ever have to narrate a ghost tour!* He'd been about to close the paper when a small ad at the bottom of the page had caught his eye: "Small restoration and construction company looking for help. Willing to train the right person." He'd sipped his coffee, recalling all the fence posts and barn siding he'd repaired as a boy. *How hard could it be?* he'd thought. He knew how to measure twice, cut once, and swing a hammer, so he wouldn't need a lot of training. Plus—and this was a big *plus*—he'd be outdoors! Without giving it another thought, he'd thrown caution to the wind, tapped the number into his phone, cleared his throat, and clicked *call*. A second later, Ben Samuelson had answered, and the trajectory of his life had changed.

He'd met Ben at the jobsite on a quiet country road outside of Savannah—and they'd instantly hit it off. Ben—desperate for another set of hands—had hired him on the spot. On his way home, Gage had felt elated at the prospect of never having to bartend again (although he had given two weeks' notice), and it had been on the drive home across that quiet country road that he'd noticed a Rent to Own sign. He'd slowed, wondering if serendipity—his mom's favorite word—or her constant prayers for him had taken him down this road because suddenly everything had seemed to be falling into place. He'd been wanting to move out of his tiny apartment for years—he hated living in the city, and now that he'd secured a stable, well-paying job, maybe he could finally afford a place of his own. Curious to see what was hidden at the end of the long driveway, he'd turned in, but it had been so overgrown it was more like a tunnel. The low-hanging branches draped with Spanish moss scraped the sides of his old pickup, but at the very end, the driveway had opened into a bright, sunny meadow filled with daylilies and wildflowers—a slice of heaven—and in the middle of the meadow was what looked like an old hunting cabin.

Two years had passed since that day and so much had changed in his life. He'd moved out of his apartment in downtown Savannah and into the rustic cabin; he'd rescued a little yellow Lab puppy from the local shelter, met Maeve, and fallen in love . . . and although he was sure she was "the one," there were some things he hadn't shared with her—memories that haunted him, and memories he didn't want to talk about. He wished he could forget the past and forgive his father, but his pride stood stubbornly in the way, and the more time passed, the harder it became to tell her about it. He dried his hands on a dish towel and shook his head. *Why does life have to be so complicated?*

He reached for the pile of junk mail and was just about to throw it in the trash, when he noticed a light blue envelope sticking out of the last page of the Cabela's catalog. He pulled it out, recognized his mom's familiar handwriting, and frowned. *He'd almost missed a letter from home!*

# 7

"It only hurts for a second," Maeve said.

"Will it bleed?" Harper asked, frowning. "Because I'm not good with blood."

"I'm not good when it's my own blood, either, but if it bleeds at all, it will only be a little," Macey replied as they turned onto Abercorn Street.

"Thanks a lot," Harper said, her voice edged with sarcasm.

"Hey, you've been through a *lot* worse than this," Maeve consoled, putting her arm around her.

Harper rolled her eyes, knowing Maeve was referring to the heart transplant she'd had the previous winter. "That was different—I was asleep."

"Well they can't put you to sleep to pierce your ears," Macey said. "It's just a quick pinch."

"Should we have lunch first?" Maeve asked, hearing her stomach rumble and realizing they weren't far from her favorite lunch spot.

"Noo," Harper answered quickly. "I might throw up if I eat first."

"You're *not* going to throw up," Macey said, shaking her head.

"Sandy did," Harper countered.

"Sandy who?" Macey asked with a frown.

"Danny's Sandy—you know, the girl in the movie we watched

the other night. She puked in the bathroom when Frenchie tried to pierce her ears."

"You mean in *Grease*?" Macey asked, chuckling. "Well, she was drinking wine . . . and that *will* make you throw up."

Parenting—on all fronts—was a new adventure for Macey and Ben, and Macey often felt like she was wading into uncharted waters, especially since Harper—who was nine years old when they adopted her, was now ten—the age *Parenting Magazine* warned was very impressionable. Ever since she'd come to live with them, Macey had had so many questions *and* worries that she'd started reading every magazine and book she could about raising a well-balanced child. One of her biggest concerns was knowing when to talk to Harper about things like peer pressure *and* drinking. She also wondered when she should broach the subject of menstruation, *knowing she'd get no help from Ben on that one*! Macey wasn't sure what Harper already knew, but—because she worked in a pediatric office—she understood all too well that kids experimented with alcohol and sex at younger ages, and Harper, after spending her early childhood bouncing from one foster home to another, was more streetwise than the average ten-year-old.

"*You* drink wine and don't throw up," Harper pointed out.

"That's because I don't drink very much . . . *or* very often." Macey shook her head, suddenly wondering if she—since Harper was so perceptive and had obviously been observing her—should give up alcohol completely. She'd been reading about how parents' habits and behaviors affect children, and she'd realized she had to be more careful about everything she said . . . and *did*! She also remembered the crazy things she'd done as a teenager, and even though Harper wasn't a teenager yet, it wouldn't be long. Heaven help them if she even came close to tempting fate like she and her friends had!

"Whatever you say, *Mom*," Harper teased, and Macey smiled. They were both still getting used to Harper's new moniker for her, and Maeve, knowing how much her sister had been through—

wanting more than anything to be a mom and enduring five heart-breaking miscarriages—before becoming Harper's mom, looked over the little girl's head with raised eyebrows and smiled at her sister.

"Here we are," Maeve said, stopping in front of the business that advertised body piercings. Harper sighed. "Maybe we should wait."

"I thought you were looking forward to this," Macey said. "You've been bugging me for weeks."

"I know, but I'm not a fan of pain."

"Don't worry," Maeve said. "You'll be fine. I'll even go first."

"*You* are getting something pierced?" Harper asked.

"Yep. I'm getting a second earring."

"You are?!"

"Mm-hmm."

"She's having a midlife crisis," Macey teased, eyeing her sister. "Seriously, Maeve, if you want to surprise Gage, you should pierce your belly button."

"Or your tongue!" Harper chimed. "He'd really be surprised when he kisses you!"

"Why would he be surprised *then*?" Maeve said, feigning innocence. "I only kiss *on* the lips."

"Yeah, right!" Harper said, laughing.

"I don't know what you mean," Maeve said, trying not to smile even though Harper's laugh was contagious.

"Umm . . . remember . . . in the movie? How Frenchie got her name?" Harper asked, trying to regain her composure.

"Because she was good at French?" Maeve asked.

"At French *kissing*," Harper said, rolling her eyes and unable to believe her aunt was so naive.

Macey bit her lip, trying not to laugh, too, and eyed her sister. "I told you that movie was a bad idea."

"Hey, don't blame me!" Maeve said. "You're the one who started singing 'There Are Worse Things I Could Do.' . . ."

Harper finally regained her composure and straightened up. "I wasn't born yesterday, you know. I didn't learn anything new from that movie. I saw *Animal House* when I was eight."

"Good Lord!" Macey exclaimed, shaking her head in dismay, and then changed the subject and asked, "Are we going in, or not?"

"We are," Harper confirmed, pulling open the door.

Macey shook her head, and Maeve laughed, knowing her sister was going to have her hands full.

A half hour later, they were all sitting at a table by the window in Back in the Day Bakery. Maeve and Macey ordered Sunny Day Biscuits—one of the bakery's signature menu offerings—and Harper opted for a Cinnamon Swirl.

"See? That wasn't so bad," Maeve said, taking a sip of coffee.

Harper reached up and touched her new earrings. "It hurt, but it was worth it. How do they look?"

"Ahh-mazing!"

"I can't wait to wear the second pair we got—the silver and pink ones," Harper said, grinning.

Macey eyed her. "You have to wear the gold ones for at least a week *and* you have to wash your hands before touching them."

Harper rolled her eyes and looked at Maeve. "Don't touch your ear, Aunt Maeve!"

"You don't want to get an infection," Macey said, eyeing her sister, too. "Either of you!"

"Got it, Mom," Maeve said, laughing. "We have our instructions, right, Harp?"

"Yup! Wash your hands. Use rubbing alcohol and ointment twice a day, and gently turn your earrings . . . but *only* after you wash your hands."

Now it was Macey's turn to roll her eyes. "I'm glad you both understand—you really don't want an infection!"

Just then the waitress brought their orders and Macey took a bite of her biscuit. "So when's the next convening of The

Pepperoni Pizza and Root Beer Book Club?" she asked, brushing the crumbs from her lips.

Maeve raised her eyebrows. "I thought it was tonight . . ."

"I thought so, too," Harper said. "We have to find out what's happening in the garden!"

Macey pulled out her phone. "Didn't you get my text?" She opened her messages and realized she'd never finished sending her most recent text to her sister. "Dang. I forgot to hit *send*. Well, anyway, Ben's coming down with a cold—he probably caught one of the many germs I bring home from the office, so I thought we could do it next weekend."

Maeve nodded, knowing her sister's job as a physician assistant at Savannah Pediatrics put her in constant contact with sneezing, coughing kids. "Next weekend works for me . . . but won't you all be getting ready for the picnic?"

"Oh, shoot! Is that next Sunday?!" Macey asked. "Honestly, I'd forget my head if it wasn't attached!"

"It's not a big deal, right, Harp? We'll reconvene in a couple of weeks."

"It's fine . . ." Harper said, nodding and thinking about how much she wanted to find out what was happening in the world of Mary, Colin, and Dickon. "*Or* I could read on my own and we could watch the movie at our next meeting."

"What?!" Maeve teased. "Read without me?!"

Harper laughed. "You've already read it."

"I'm just teasing," Maeve assured her. "You can read it . . . although you're the one who fell asleep and put an abrupt end to our reading last time."

"You're right. I'll wait," Harper said, smiling. "What book are we reading next?"

Maeve raised her eyebrows mysteriously. "I have something in mind."

"What?" Harper asked eagerly.

"I'm not telling because you'll probably start reading it."

"No, I won't," Harper said, laughing. "I promise."

Maeve shook her head. "Nope. You have to wait and see."

"Dang," Harper said.

Macey laughed. "I'm sorry to mess up your plans."

"No worries," Maeve said. "We'll get through it, won't we, Harp?"

The little redhead nodded and popped the last of her Cinnamon Swirl into her mouth, and Macey smiled at her easygoing attitude. Harper had come such a long way in the year she'd been living with them—from an untrusting, withdrawn little girl with a barely penetrable wall around her to a funny, fun-loving spitfire with a shy smile who loved to tease Ben at every opportunity, and even called him Daddy-O (which Macey thought was quite fitting because she'd grown up calling him *kiddo*). She and Ben had also discovered that Harper was a talented artist, a good shot in basketball, and a stellar student with a love for science—especially marine life—and if she kept on the same trajectory, there would be no stopping her!

Harper licked the sugar and cinnamon from her lips. "Where're we going after this?"

"I thought we'd walk over to Woof Gang Bakery—you know, that specialty pet store in City Market that sells homemade dog biscuits," Macey said. "I want to pick up some treats and a bandanna for Keeper—something patriotic."

"Maybe I'll get a bandanna for Gus, too," Maeve said brightly.

Harper nodded her approval. "Then they can be twins at the picnic!"

# 8

Mason kicked off his running shoes, ran the water in the kitchen sink until it was cold, filled a glass, drained it, and filled it again. Ten minutes later, after showering, he stood in front of the stove, drying his hair with a towel. He tossed the towel onto a chair and opened a can of tomato soup. He scooped the contents into a small saucepan, added water, and stirred, and while it simmered, smoothed butter onto two slices of bread. He laid one slice, butter side down, into a frying pan, topped it with American cheese, and then dropped the second slice, butter side up, on top. It was the third time this week that he'd had grilled cheese and tomato soup for supper. Growing up, his mom called it comfort food. Her other favorite comfort food was mac and cheese. If she saw it on a menu—especially if it had lobster in it—she invariably ordered it. Laurie's own recipe for macaroni and cheese, however, was made with tomato soup and cheddar cheese, and in Mason's mind it was the *true* mac and cheese. Needless to say, he'd consumed a lot of tomato soup when he was growing up!

He stirred the soup, turned his sandwich, heard his phone hum, and glanced at the screen. It was a text from Ali asking him if he wanted to come over for dinner. He smiled—he and Ali Harrison had been friends since birth, but lately, their relationship, of its own accord, seemed to be evolving into something more. It had always been one of those easy friendships that had resulted from having moms who'd been lifelong friends and who'd loved to get together with their little ones in tow. Laurie and Sue had even ended up working together in the maternity ward at the hospital, so Sue had always felt as if Mason was one of her own and she'd immediately taken him under her wing when Laurie got sick, inviting him—and usually insisting he come—for dinner, and if he declined, she often sent over a plate heaping with food. Mason texted back that his dinner was already made, and Ali's next text showed how well she knew him:

Tomato soup and grilled cheese? (sigh)

My specialty!

So predictable

I know ☺

Have you studied for the AP Calc final?

No. Want to study together?

YES!!!

Come over when you're done

Okay

Mason slid his grilled cheese sandwich onto his plate and then glanced at the screen again.

My mom's sending over a blueberry pie

Tell her thnx! ☺

Will do!

Mason pushed aside the growing pile of mail on the table and sat down. He dipped his sandwich in his soup, took a bite, and blinked at the golden sunlight streaming through the window, illuminating the fine scratches on the rose-colored Formica table. The table was a relic from the 1950s and had belonged to his grandparents—in fact, the little house in which they lived was the same home in which his mom had grown up, so there were a lot of memories there. His mom often told him that she'd sat at that same table to do her homework. In keeping with tradition, Mason did his homework there, too, including, with his mom's help, every school project he'd ever been assigned between kindergarten and eleventh grade—from the three-dimensional map of the Appalachian Trail he'd made by dripping Sheetrock mud onto plywood to a model of the Hubble Space Telescope, which he'd made with a large V8 juice can, cardboard, balsa wood, aluminum foil, and suction cups. He'd also cut out, sanded, and painted—*without* his mom's help—all his Pinewood Derby cars. From the ranks of Wolf to Webelos, every car he'd made for the Pinewood Derby had had a NASCAR theme. His favorite—and by far, fastest—was inspired by Dale Earnhardt Jr.'s red number eight, and even though his scoutmaster had frowned at the Budweiser logo he'd painted on the side, the car had been a bullet! He'd never forget how proud his mom had been, making him hold his trophy and car while she took a dozen photos, and then she'd made an enlargement of her favorite, framed it, and hung it by the door where everyone would see it.

He smiled wistfully. He missed her being there, he missed her laugh and her unflappable disposition . . . and he didn't know *what* he would do without her. She always had such a positive attitude about everything—even when she'd received her devastating cancer diagnosis, she hadn't blinked, but told him not to worry and that she was going to beat it! The treatments had been brutal, though, and she'd lost all her chestnut-brown hair and a ton of weight—weight she couldn't afford to lose. Now, there was nothing to her—she was so frail and fragile you could push her over with a feather. But through it all, she'd never stopped smiling.

Two weeks earlier she hadn't been able to keep anything down, and she'd become so dehydrated he'd rushed her to the hospital. Although she'd hoped they would just give her fluids and send her home, they'd admitted her, and it didn't seem like they'd be ready to let her go home anytime soon. He thought she seemed weaker whenever he visited her, but she always managed to put up a good front, don her most colorful bandanna, and grip his hand with the fierceness of a lumberjack. She also seemed to be trying to think of—and share with him—every wise counsel a mom would say over a lifetime. "Everything's going to be fine, sweetheart. Your life is going to be rich with love and laughter . . . and lots of wonderful memories!"

She also told him she thought Ali, with her sweet smile and infectious laugh, would be a wonderful match, and this had made him blush. "Mom, I'm only seventeen."

"You're almost eighteen, Mase," she'd said, "and I want you to be happy. I want you to find a girl who'll love you with all her heart. You deserve it, and I know Ali loves you. . . . I've seen the way she looks at you."

He'd nodded, trying to fight back tears. If she wasn't going to cry, he wasn't going to, either, because he knew it would make her sad.

Finally, as her disease progressed, it became evident that her treatments weren't working, and she'd asked him to bring a notebook. "There's no mortgage," she'd said as she jotted things down. "There *is* a home equity line of credit, though—I took it out when we remodeled the kitchen, but my life insurance will more than cover it." She'd smiled. "You'll even be able to paint that old jalopy of yours."

"It's a muscle car," he'd said softly.

"I know," she'd said with a smile.

Then she turned back to the notebook and wrote down every account number and password she could think of, as well as the name of her attorney—Beau Bartholomew—who, she assured him, was getting her affairs in order. He knew she was trying to think of everything in case she wasn't around, but the whole process just made his heart ache.

"Did you send the deposit to Georgia Tech?" she'd asked, looking up.

He'd shaken his head.

"Why not?" she'd asked, frowning. "Mason, it's what you've always wanted and worked so hard for. All through high school, it's been your dream to go to Georgia Tech. . . . You can't let it go!"

"I can't go to college right now, Mom," he'd said.

"I know you've been putting your life on hold, Mase, but I really wish you'd sent in the deposit . . . just in case you change your mind. It would be good for you. . . . It would keep you busy *and* it would keep your mind off things."

"It wouldn't keep my mind off things."

"What will you do then?" she asked softly. "In the fall?"

"I don't know, Mom. Maybe I'll be taking care of you."

"Maybe you could call them and . . ."

"I'm not calling. It's too late—the deadline already passed."

She'd shaken her head. "I wish you'd sent it in." And like any good mom, she'd continued to press him. "You could call them and explain everything and maybe they would let you . . ."

"I'm not, Mom. Please understand—I can't think about that right now."

"Okay," she'd said finally. "I'm sorry for pushing you."

"It's okay."

"There's one other thing," she'd said, smiling and searching his eyes. "And I *won't* take no for an answer."

Mason had sighed, already knowing what it was.

"I want you to promise me you'll try to find her. . . . I know she would want you to."

He'd frowned. "How do you know?"

"Because all those years ago, I saw the look in her eyes."

Mason had looked away—he hadn't wanted to promise, but she'd reached for his hand. "Promise me, Mason . . ." she'd said, and it was almost a demand.

Mason had bitten his lip and fought back tears. "I promise."

There was a soft knock on the front door and Mason looked up. He started to push back his chair, but Ali was already coming down the hall with her backpack slung over her shoulder and a blueberry pie in her hands. "Hey," she called cheerfully, "when you didn't answer, I just came in. . . ." But when she reached the kitchen, she saw the look on his face and stopped. "You okay?"

Mason nodded. "Yeah, I'm fine."

"You don't look *fine*." She glanced at the table and saw the unfinished—and now cold—soup and sandwich. "I'm sorry . . . I thought you'd be done by now."

"I am," he said, picking up his plate and bowl and bringing them to the counter. "I guess I wasn't as hungry as I thought."

Ali frowned. "You still want to study? Cuz if you don't, you know . . . I can just . . . go."

Mason shook his head and looked out the window. "I want you to stay." The last thing he wanted was to be alone—not tonight . . . not *ever*.

"Okay," Ali said, placing the pie on the counter. She unzipped her backpack and pulled out a small glass Pyrex with a plastic lid. "My mom made whipped cream for the pie . . ." But when Mason didn't reply, she added, "I'll just stick it in the fridge." She opened the door of the refrigerator and was surprised by the emptiness of the shelves. "Mase, have you been eating *anything*?" she asked.

"Yeah, I've been eating."

"Well, you need to go food shopping because there isn't much in here." She paused. "I'll go with you if you want . . ." Ali walked over to him and put her hand on his shoulder. "You sure you're okay?" she asked softly.

Mason nodded, gazing out the window at the tire swing hanging from the ancient oak tree in the backyard. He still remembered the day his mom had hung it there. He'd held the ladder while she'd climbed, rope in hand, and secured it over a low-hanging branch. He could almost hear her voice reminding him not to let go of the ladder.

"Did you see your mom today?"

He nodded again.

"How is she?"

"The same," he said, tears springing to his eyes. He quickly wiped them away—he was so damn tired of crying. "She was sleeping—they have her on these really strong pain meds that make her sleep all the time." He shook his head. "She's going to sleep away what little time she has left. I honestly think she's just holding on till graduation."

"Do you think she'll be able to come?"

"She says she is, but I don't know . . ."

"Oh, Mase, I'm sorry." Ali rested her head on his shoulder.

Mason nodded and slipped his arm around her. "I'm sorry I'm not much fun anymore. I don't know why you even come over." He pulled her around to face him, and when she saw tears spilling down his cheeks, she reached up and gently brushed them away.

# 9

“Hold on, there, mister,” Maeve said as Gus moseyed over to her Jeep and tried to climb up onto her lap. “If you give me a sec, I’ll give you a proper hello.” She balanced the paper bag from Woof Gang Bakery on top of the pizza box and reached for the bottle of wine she’d tucked behind the seat. “I brought your favorite food . . . *and* I brought you a present!” she said as the big puppy wiggled around her. She knelt in front of him and he sniffed the pizza box, and then kissed her on the nose.

“Hey,” Gage said, holding open the screen door.

“Hey back,” she said with the same smile that had stolen his heart.

“How was your day? Did Harper muster the courage to get her ears pierced?”

“It was fun, and she *did*.” The question reminded her of her own new piercing, and she quickly turned her head, but it was too late—he’d already spied the tiny sparkle in the upper curve of her ear.

He gently turned her chin from one side to the other. “Just one?”

Maeve knew she didn’t need Gage’s approval to pierce her ear—it was *her* body after all—but she suddenly felt the odd need to defend her actions. “Do you know how many earrings I’ve lost over the years?”

He shook his head.

"A ton!" she said, putting the pizza and wine on the counter. "I bet I have a dozen earrings that have lost their mates and they just sit in my jewelry box, useless . . . but now I have a use for them."

"Sooo . . . it was a practical decision," he said, pulling her into his arms.

"Of course," she said, grinning. "Everything I do is practical."

"Mm-hmm," he murmured, kissing her lips.

"At least I didn't pierce my navel or my nose . . . *or* my tongue, as Harper suggested," she whispered into his kiss.

He pulled back and raised his eyebrows. "I wouldn't mind if you pierced your navel—you *do* have a cute belly button, but I don't know about your tongue . . . with food and everything?!" He made a funny face. "And how does a ten-year-old girl know about such things?"

Maeve shook her head. "That ten-year-old girl is wise beyond her years—she even said you'd be *really* surprised when you kissed me."

Gage laughed. "Oh, boy!"

"I know, right?" Just then, Gus pushed his head between them and Maeve looked down. "Do you need some attention, too, mister?"

"He just wants some pizza crust," Gage said.

Maeve laughed again. "I have to give you your present first," She reached into the paper bag, and Gus plopped promptly on his haunches and looked up expectantly. "First, we have all-natural homemade dog biscuits." She eyed him. "Which would you like to try—peanut butter or yogurt?"

"Duh, peanut butter," Gage answered, speaking for him with a knowing smile.

Maeve held out a treat and Gus took it politely. "Good boy," she said, ruffling his ears. "*And* I have something else for you." She reached into the bag and pulled out a red, white, and blue bandanna, which she folded into a triangle and tied around his neck. Gus sat patiently, and after she straightened it, she held his head in her hands and looked into his chocolate-brown eyes. "You look very handsome," she said softly, and he thumped his tail.

Gage watched. "Nice," he said, nodding his approval. Then he eyed the lanky puppy. "No pulling it off when we're not looking."

"He wouldn't do that," Maeve said. "Would you, ole pie?"

"Mm-hmm." Gage sounded skeptical as he riffled through his utensil drawer for a bottle opener. "So, no book club tonight?" he asked, pouring a glass of wine for her before opening the fridge for a beer.

"No, Ben's coming down with something so they're not going out," she said, wandering over to his drawing table and turning on the light.

"Yeah, he said he wasn't feeling well," Gage said, opening his beer.

When Maeve didn't answer, he looked up, and then walked over to stand beside her.

"This is amazing," she said, studying the detailed pencil drawing of his grandfather. She compared it to the photo next to it and decided Dutch, Gage's grandfather, must've been in his early seventies when it was taken, his skin suntanned and wrinkled, his light blue eyes kind and wise. The drawing was so realistic, it could have passed for the photo, but the cold-pressed texture of the paper gave it a softness no photo could ever replicate. "I can't believe you couldn't find a gallery to take your work—it's so beautiful."

Gage half smiled and took a sip of his beer. "If I'd gotten into a gallery, I probably wouldn't have met you."

"I don't know about that," Maeve said, taking a sip of her wine. "If something is meant to be, different paths can lead to it."

He raised his eyebrows. "Yeah? You think *this* is meant to be?"

"Sometimes," she teased, kissing his neck.

He leaned into her. "If you do that, our pizza is going to get cold."

"I'm not doing anything," she whispered innocently, pressing against him.

"Mm-hmm," he murmured, reaching for her wine glass and

setting it on the mantle next to his beer. He slid his hands along the sides of her snow-white tank top, and then, with an impish grin, pulled her down the hall.

"I guess we *will* be warming up the pizza," she said, laughing.

He smiled as he slowly pulled her shirt over her head.

Maeve shook out her hair and watched as he lightly traced his fingers along the smooth skin of her abdomen, then slowly circled her navel.

"I think a piercing would be nice," he said, half smiling. He slid his hands up her sides, caught her bra with his thumbs, unhooked it, and gently cupped his hands around her full breasts. "Damn, you're good-looking," he whispered. Maeve caught her breath, his touch sending a white-hot current of heat straight down.

"Damn, you're *good*," she whispered back, pressing against him and feeling how aroused he was. He unbuttoned her jeans and slid his hand inside, teasing her.

She pulled his T-shirt over his head and unzipped his jeans, but before she could do anything more, he was pulling her onto the bed on top of him.

"Damn, Maeve," he whispered, his hands on her hips, their bodies intimately entwined as the rocking rhythm grew increasingly urgent.

Finally, she collapsed on the sheets next to him. "Whew!" she said, laughing, and then—hearing a swishing sound—peered over his shoulder and saw Gus standing next to the bed with his chin on the sheets, wagging his tail. "How long have you been there?" she asked in surprise.

Gage turned to look, too, and smiled. "He must've *just* come in," he assured her, "because he wasn't there a minute ago."

"Like you would've noticed," she teased.

He laughed, knowing it was true. Then he scratched the dog's ears. "Are you finally ready for pizza, mister?" Gus thumped his tail faster and Gage laughed. "Okay, okay," he said, "I'm getting up." He kissed Maeve and reluctantly slid from the bed, and as he pulled on his jeans, he looked back at her lying naked on his bed with the sheets strewn about. "Want me to bring your pizza in here?"

"Oh, that would be nice," she said, stretching, "but, no, I'm getting up, too."

"You don't have to get dressed," he said, grinning.

She rolled her eyes. "But I am," she said, and as she sat up, he leaned down, picked up her shorts and tank top, and tossed them to her.

"Thanks," she said, swinging her tan legs over the side of the bed. She watched him disappear down the hall, with Gus at his heels, and then pulled on her clothes. She glanced in the mirror to see how disheveled she looked, ran her hand through her hair, and shuffled to the kitchen.

"Want to sit on the porch?" she asked, reaching for her wine and taking a sip.

"Sure," he replied, handing her a plate with a slice of reheated pizza on it. He grabbed his beer, held open the screen door, and followed her out into the evening sunlight. "This is such a pretty spot," she mused as the sun sank below the horizon, casting a golden hue across the gardens.

"You say that every time we sit out here," Gage said, sitting in the old, wooden Adirondack chair across from her, and she chuckled, knowing it was true.

The cabin had been in rough shape when Gage first drove into the overgrown driveway to look at it. It was so run-down that he'd dismissed the idea of living there, but after passing the Rent to Own sign every day for two weeks, he'd finally called the number and arranged to meet the owner for a walk-through. They'd stood in the middle of the neglected gardens and looked around, and because of its condition, he'd been able to negotiate a deal that made repairs part of the rent. Six months later, the owner—a divorce attorney who happened to be going *through* a divorce—had contacted him to say he was looking to free himself from all of his assets, and the little hunting cabin on the river, which had been left to him by his grandfather, was the first thing he wanted to unload. He had to get rid of it, and Gage, who'd been scraping and saving since he'd started working for Ben, had bought it for a song. In the two years since, he'd made the most of the construction skills he'd been acquiring, and with Ben's guidance, they'd begun restoring it. He'd started with the exterior, repairing and replacing rotting windows and scraping and painting everything that needed it—which was *everything*! But the real blessing had come when the owner of a house they'd been working on decided to gut his kitchen and scrap all the cabinets, countertops, and appliances—which were practically new! Ben had asked the owner if he could have them, and the owner had agreed, happy to save on disposal fees. After work, Gage and Ben had hauled everything out to the cabin and spent the next two weekends installing the new kitchen.

"Did you get everything done that you wanted to get done today?" Maeve asked, hungrily taking a bite of her pizza.

"I don't think I'll ever *get everything done*."

"That's one of the drawbacks of owning a house," Maeve teased, "endless maintenance! Which is why I rent," she added with a grin.

"I rented for a long time and I always felt like I was throwing money away. In the end, you spend a ton and you don't own anything."

"But you also save," Maeve countered, "because you don't have to pay property tax."

"The taxes out here are next to nothing. I don't think this place has been assessed in years. It's a hidden treasure."

Maeve chuckled. "I'm surprised they didn't assess it when you bought it, and you better hope they never come out to *reassess* it because when they see your view, your taxes will skyrocket—being on the river is like being on the ocean."

"It *is* nice . . ." Gage agreed, looking out over the field of wildflowers at the sunlight reflecting on the winding river.

"I love it here," she said with a sigh. "You're so lucky."

"I *am* lucky," Gage agreed, taking another long sip of beer, "but my favorite view is sitting right next to me."

Maeve rolled her eyes. "*You* are almost as silly as your dog," she said, giving Gus a morsel of her pizza crust.

Gage smiled; he loved how Maeve adored Gus, and he knew the feeling was mutual—his big yellow puppy absolutely adored her, too. He distractedly wiped the condensation on the side of his bottle. "When I was young, we had a little barn cat named Mike. She was smoke gray with white paws . . ."

"Wait," Maeve said, raising her eyebrows. "You had a female cat named *Mike*?!"

Gage nodded and took a sip of his beer, trying not to laugh at his own memory. "We did. My brother named her after Mike Mulligan—you know . . . from the book?"

Maeve laughed. "I know the book, but how come he didn't name her after Mary Anne? She was the real hero of the story."

Gage chuckled at her observation. "I guess because we boys always considered Mike to be the hero—growing up around tractors, we wanted to *be* Mike Mulligan."

"Gotcha," Maeve teased.

"Anyway, do you want to hear the story?" he asked, feigning dismay at being interrupted.

"I *do*," she assured him, eager to hear any tidbit from his childhood.

"So, when Mike showed up on our doorstep, she was pregnant. Cale and I were little . . . probably no older than five—if he was four, I would've been three—we were very close in age, and our mom decided it would be neat for us to see Mike give birth to her kittens so she put a towel-lined box on the porch, hoping, when her time came, she would use it and we would get to watch. Sure enough, early one summer morning, our mom woke us up, and we hurried downstairs in our pajamas, knelt down on the porch near the box, and watched Mike squeeze out five little squirmy, wet babies . . . well, actually, only four were squirming . . . one was completely still, and no matter how much nudging and cleaning Mike gave it, it wouldn't move. Finally, my mom scooped it out and started to carry it toward the barn to give to our dad, but Mike would have none of it. She hopped out of the box and trotted after my mom to see where she was going."

"That's so sad," Maeve said, her heart aching for the little cat.

Gage nodded. "It was sad, but it doesn't end there. My mom was, of course, able to get Mike back to the box, and even though she looked sad, she was a good mama and continued to care for her other kittens. Later that evening, when my dad came in from haying, we were still out on the porch, entranced by the kittens. We noticed our dad talking to our mom. He had something in his hands, and a few moments later, he walked over and set a baby bunny in the box."

"No way!" Maeve said in surprise. "What did Mike do?"

"She sniffed it, pulled it in close, and started to clean it."

"Did she let it nurse?"

"She did, and that little bunny grew up right alongside those kittens—we think the bunny thought she was a cat. Cale named her Moon because there's a bunny in *Goodnight Moon* . . . and we had her for five or six years."

"That's amazing," Maeve said, shaking her head. "Where did your dad find her?"

"He never told us, but as we got older, we knew—because we learned that bunnies sometimes made their dens in the fields—that something probably happened to the mama and other babies."

"That is such a great—albeit sad—story," Maeve said softly. "Mike must've been a wonderful cat."

Gage nodded. "Mike was the sweetest cat. She lived to be around seventeen—which is pretty old for a barn cat. My mom had a soft spot in her heart for her and she used to let her in the house. The rest of our cats were all true barn cats—they stayed outside."

Maeve nodded. "*You* should get a cat."

"I've thought about it—I could use a good mouser, but I'm not sure what Gus would do."

Maeve gently nudged the lanky Lab at her feet with her toe, and Gus looked up. "You'd love a little kitten, wouldn't you, you big moose?" Gus thumped his tail happily, and they laughed.

Gage took a sip of his beer and looked over. "Gus would love it if *you* lived here, too."

Maeve smiled—it was a conversation they'd had before, and even though there was nothing she'd love more than waking up next to Gage every morning, she felt as if they still had some things to work out before they made such a big commitment.

"If you think about it," he pressed, "either you're staying here, or I'm staying at your place, so it's almost like we're living together."

"Almost," she agreed. She wanted to say more—she wanted to finally tell him about the foolish mistake she'd made in college and the heartbreaking decision she'd had to make afterward—it was all right there on the tip of her tongue, but she was afraid he would think less of her; she was afraid she might lose him.

Gage—who'd gotten up to look at the setting sun—didn't see the sadness in her eyes, so when he turned back and leaned against the railing, he only smiled. "I love you, Maeve . . . and I'd love to come home to you every night."

Now it was Maeve's turn to look away. She looked at the river, tears stinging her eyes. "I love you, too, Gage. I love you more than life itself." She paused, searching for the right words, "but I feel like there're still things we haven't talked about—things standing between us. I mean why don't you ever talk about your fam . . ." But before she could finish, he was pulling her up and gently putting his finger over her lips.

"There's just you and me, Maeve," he said. "Nothing else matters. There's nothing standing between us." As he said this, Gus pushed his head between them and Gage laughed. "Except this silly dog."

Maeve couldn't help but laugh, too. Gus had been the icebreaker when they first met and it seemed like his silly antics would always take the seriousness out of serious moments.

"I've never loved anyone as much as I love you," Gage said solemnly. "Come live with me," he whispered.

Maeve closed her eyes, trying to shut down the storm of thoughts swirling in her head. The words she wanted to say were right there—the words she'd rehearsed a million times. Her explanation, her excuses, her heartache . . . if she could only let them spill out, and then, come hell or high water, pray it wouldn't matter—if she only knew that he would say, *Maeve, your past is your past, and mine is mine. It doesn't matter. It's all behind us. The only thing that matters is us. Us, now . . .* If she could just be assured of this, she would tell him everything . . . but she wasn't sure what her sweet country boy would think, and the more time passed, the heavier it weighed on her heart. And it wasn't just Gage she hadn't told. . . . She'd never told *anyone*—not her parents . . . not even Macey.

"A penny for your thoughts," he whispered.

She mustered a smile and thought how crazy it was that she couldn't just say what was on her mind. If she'd only realized, back then, what a profound effect her actions would have on the rest of her life—*but how do you know when you're eighteen . . . and scared?* "Nothing," she whispered back, kissing him. "Just thinking about how nice it would be to wake up next to you every day."

His face brightened. "So . . . you'll move in?"

She laughed. He sounded so hopeful. "Okay, I'll move in!"

"Yes!" Gage said, and then he looked down at the Lab squeezing between them again. "Gus is happy, too."

She laughed. "I think he just wants more pizza!"

# 10

Even though Willow Pond Senior Care did include *care* in its name, the elderly folks who lived there weren't considered patients and they didn't require a tremendous amount of *care*. Dinner was provided every night and there were daily activities, including crafts and an enthusiastic book club; there was an ecumenical church service every Sunday, and a happy hour (instead of cookies and lemonade) on the last Friday of each month, but the staff didn't administer medicine or become involved in personal care. Most of the residents had pill trays, which they—or their families—filled . . . and then they tried to remember to take them, too. They each had their own kitchenette, private bathroom, bedroom—all of which were equipped with emergency pull strings—and a living room furnished with their own furniture, TV, and sometimes a computer. Some folks even had Facebook pages to keep up with their families' activities and photos—although Addie insisted that Instagram was more hip, or so she'd been told by her grandchildren!

The staff included Maeve, Pam, and Kate—who staggered their start times to cover the 7:00 a.m. to 7:00 p.m. days, with Maeve usually taking the early shift because she didn't have kids. Janey, a part-timer, came in on weekends. They also used the Willow Pond van to drive the residents, who no longer drove, to the grocery store or Walmart once a week, and there was a Willow Pond car, too, if someone had a doctor's appointment—of which there were many! Jim, the handyman, lived in one of the apartments and was available for overnight emergencies; Maryellen, the housekeeper, kept all the kitchenettes and bathrooms sparkling and often helped the residents change their sheets, if needed; and there was chef extraordinaire, Sal. Finally, there was LeeAnn, who worked magic from her upstairs office and took care of an endless myriad of tasks—from billing and scheduling activities to coordinating rides and resident turnover. Together, this formidable group looked after their elderly charges and made sure everyone was safe and accounted for, so when Pam asked Maeve to cover for her again—as she often did when one of her kids needed something—Maeve was happy to help.

"Maeve, I'm so sorry to ask . . ." Pam said as she hurried into the kitchen of Willow Pond Senior Care. "I have to take Pete to the doctor—he came home with a sore throat, and I have a feeling he might have strep."

"Oh, no!" Maeve said, looking up from putting cheese and crackers on a plate for the last Friday of the month happy hour. "Poor Pete! I can absolutely cover for you. My sister said the school is a giant petri dish right now."

Pam nodded as she dumped a can of defrosted frozen lemonade into a pitcher for anyone who didn't partake (the residents were responsible for their own wine or beer). "He just got over a cold, and he's so busy with end of the year activities—he has two field trips coming up and the school picnic, not to mention sixth-grade graduation, so he'll be disappointed if he has to miss any of it."

"Is Pete in sixth grade already?!" Maeve asked, offering her a cracker.

"He *is*," Pam said, taking one. "Thanks . . . and I can come back after his appointment."

"No, no," Maeve said. "If he doesn't feel well, he's going to want his mom."

"Thanks, Maeve, I owe you one . . . I actually owe you *more* than one." She added water to the lemonade, stirred, and set the pitcher on the tray.

"You don't owe me anything," Maeve said. "I don't have kids, so I don't have all the worries and responsibilities you have."

"Someday you will," Pam teased, laughing. "And then, *I* will be there for you."

"Maybe," Maeve said.

"What do you mean? *Maybe?* You and Gage make a wonderful couple, and I think it's great you're moving in with him. You just have to put everything in the Lord's hands."

Maeve laughed. "You sound like my grandma."

"Your grandma must've been a very smart lady, and I know from experience—things with Big Pete"—as she always referred to her husband—"weren't always smooth sailing," she said with a smile. "Every couple has issues they have to contend with . . . obstacles they have to overcome. . . . Relationships take work—and lots of patience! You just have to listen to your heart, Maeve."

Pam looked up at the clock above their heads. "Sheesh, how'd it get so late?"

"Time flies when you're havin' fun," Maeve said, laughing.

"It does," Pam said. "Are you sure about staying?"

"Absolutely! I hope Pete feels better!" Maeve said as she set the crackers on the tray. "And say hi to Macey if you see her."

Pam reached for her sweater. "I will." She pushed open the side door and then looked over her shoulder. "Make sure Mr. Hawkins remembers we have happy hour today."

"Oh, right! Thanks for reminding *me*."

When the architects drew up the plans for Willow Pond Senior Care, the town's strict historic regulations had limited the changes that could be made to the old farmhouse, so the company had hired a highly respected local craftsman with extensive knowledge of Southern homes to restore it to its original charm and glory. Ben Samuelson and his crew had gone to great lengths to protect the floor-to-ceiling windows, wide hardwood flooring, and massive stone fireplace before gutting the interior, removing the cracked plaster walls, and turning the entire front of the house into a welcoming common room—complete with built-in shelves for a library and furnished with tables for games and puzzles, a large flat-screen HDTV for movie nights, and enough comfortable seating for all the residents. The back of the house was transformed into a bright, airy dining room with a screened-in breakfast porch on one side, and a beautiful state-of-the-art kitchen on the other. The upstairs—once bedrooms—had been turned into a bright, sunny office space and storage rooms.

While Ben and his crew worked on the restoration of the farmhouse, a different company was brought in to build the addition—a one-level square structure with a garden courtyard, the design of which had also been approved by the historic commission. It was accessible by a glass-enclosed crosswalk and had white clapboard siding and tall windows to match the farmhouse. Each cozy apartment had French doors that opened either into the garden courtyard or onto the expansive lawn.

Maeve hurried down the long corridor, which was often used by the residents for their daily constitutionals, and turned left. She continued to walk briskly, thinking about the residents on the porch—waiting for their snack—and finally stopped in front of the last door on the right and knocked.

"C'mon in," a voice drawled.

Maeve pushed open the door. "Mr. Hawkins?" she called softly.

"Yes, ma'am," the old man said, sitting up in his leather recliner.

Maeve looked around the room at the piles of boxes and frowned. "Do you need help unpacking?"

"Oh, no," he replied, waving dismissively at the boxes and leaning back in his chair. "There's no hurry. It's not like I'm going anywhere."

Maeve nodded. "Okay. Well, I came down to remind you that we have happy hour tonight—it's always on the last Friday of the . . ."

"Thank you for the reminder, but I'm not interested."

Maeve frowned. "Are you sure? Everyone's out there, and I think you'd enjoy . . ."

"I'm sure. Thank you."

"Okay, well, don't forget we have dinner at five."

"I won't forget."

"And let me know if you need anything. I'm happy to help."

The old man nodded and mustered a reassuring smile.

Maeve smiled back, but she still worried as she closed the door. She paused in the hallway to let Gage know she'd be working late again and then hurried back to the kitchen, still picturing the old man in his recliner, silently gazing out the window. She had witnessed similar scenes before: elderly folks who'd been moved—sometimes against their will—into senior living. Some came willingly, it was true—and even looked forward to the opportunity to socialize with folks their age—but others resented it. It made them feel as if it was the end of the line—as if they'd lost their home, their freedom, control of their lives, and their independence. Life no longer had purpose or meaning, and they often became withdrawn and depressed. Maeve had studied the psychological effects such changes had on the elderly, especially when the move wasn't voluntary. And she knew, from experience, that a successful adjustment depended on a person's attitude. If they didn't have a positive outlook, it was difficult to lift their spirits *or* get them to engage. Mr. Hawkins was obviously not happy about his new arrangement, but if anyone could cheer him up, she could . . . and she loved a challenge!

She pushed open the door of the kitchen and Sal looked up from spreading cornmeal, flour, and spices on his work counter. "I wondered where you disappeared to," he said. "Kate was looking for you. She already took the tray out."

"Okay. I was reminding our newest resident about happy hour."

"Mr. Hawkins? Is he coming?" Sal asked as he dipped a long translucent white filet into a bowl.

"No," she replied with a frown. "I think he's having a hard time. . . . I hope he comes to dinner."

Sal nodded as he laid the filet, dripping in egg, onto the cornmeal and flipped it to coat both sides. "If he doesn't, we can bring a plate down to him."

Maeve nodded and then raised her eyebrows. "What *is* for dinner, Sal?"

He smiled. "What does it look like?"

"Catfish?"

He grinned mischievously. "Don't tell Miss Gladys!"

Maeve laughed. "I won't. We'll see if she complains about having fish again."

Sal laughed. "She better not!"

Maeve was about to go out and help Kate when her phone hummed. She looked at the screen and saw a photo of Gus lying in the sunshine with his head between his paws, looking forlorn. She shook her head and typed: Tell him not to look so sad—I'll see him soon! Then she slid her phone back in her pocket and stepped out onto the porch where she was greeted by a chorus of "Here's Maeve!" and "We knew you didn't get lost!"

"I didn't get lost," Maeve said, smiling as she picked up empty paper plates and napkins.

"Would you like a little vino?" Gladys asked with a wink as she held up her glass and gestured to the bottle of Chardonnay she and Addie were sharing.

"No, no," Maeve said, laughing. "Someone has to behave around here."

"We never behave, do we?" Gladys said, eyeing Addie with a mischievous grin.

"*I* behave," Addie replied, feigning indignation and eyeing her friend. "You're the mischievous one. I heard you stopped by Mr. Hawkins's apartment and tried to give him a kiss."

"Pshaw," Gladys said, her eyes sparkling. "He was happy to see me. Everyone enjoys a warm welcome when they're the new kid."

"Oh, dear," said Maeve, looking alarmed. "Did you really?"

"Absolutely!" Gladys said. "He said, 'Don't ever do that again!' but I know he was just foolin'. Playing hard to get, that one!" She refilled her glass, and Maeve frowned. She wasn't a big fan of happy hour, but she knew that just because the residents were older, it didn't mean they couldn't enjoy a cocktail now and again. They were adults with fond memories and human desires like anyone else. They couldn't help it if they were trapped in old bodies. They were alive and kicking and had the capacity to enjoy life just as much as the next person.

"Maybe you should give him a little time to adjust," Addie suggested.

Gladys took a sip of her wine. "Oh, I'm giving him time," she said with a seductive come-hither smile, her cheeks rosy from the wine . . . *or was it the lusty conversation?*

Maeve shook her head. The staff were well aware of the shenanigans, clandestine encounters, middle-of-the-night visits, and walks of shame (or fame) that went on, mostly because Willow Pond, like any other residential community, was a hotbed of gossip, and some of the ladies—Gladys included—were notoriously flirtatious and chatty. Even with the addition of Mr. Hawkins, the ratio of men to women, however, was four to fourteen, and this only made the men more attractive to the ladies. Three of the men—the Olivetti twins and Aristides—were used to the attention, but Mr. Hawkins was not, so the staff needed to make sure he wasn't made to feel uncomfortable. At the same time, Maeve had to constantly remind herself that, despite their age, the residents still felt natural human desire.

"Gladys," Maeve said quietly. "I think he lost his wife recently, so please make sure you give him room and time to adjust."

"Humph!" Gladys grunted. "I'll give him all the room in Texas and all the time in heaven." And Maeve knew, because she'd said something to her the old woman probably wouldn't even *talk* to him again—never mind just give him a little space.

Just then, Sal pushed open the screen door. "Ten minutes till dinner!"

"We'll be right in," Maeve called back, picking up glasses and napkins.

She reached the end of the porch where the men were sipping cans of Budweiser, and Kate, who'd overheard the tail end of Maeve's conversation with Gladys, was shaking her head. "Still up to her old tricks."

"She is," Maeve agreed with a smile. "I hope I have her sex drive when I'm her age!"

"I don't even have it now," Kate said, laughing. "I can barely stay awake when I get home!"

"I know what you mean," Maeve said, laughing. She picked up the untouched glass of lemonade on the table next to Ivy and then spied Tallulah, the cat, curled up in the old woman's lap. "Ready for dinner, Miss Ivy?" she asked, but the tiny lady didn't answer. She was gazing solemnly at the swans gliding across the pond.

# 11

"Hey," Maeve said, coming into the kitchen and unloading the contents of her arms onto the counter. She hugged her sister and knelt in front of Keeper, who wiggled all around her and pushed his bowed head into her chest.

"*You* are such a good boy," she whispered into his fur, making him wiggle even more.

"Thank goodness you're here," Macey said. "I don't know how I used to get everything ready before you started coming."

"I don't know, either," Maeve teased, grinning. "It's not my fault you didn't invite me."

"Did you make blackberry cobbler?" Macey asked hopefully.

"I did," Maeve said, "which reminds me! The ice cream—" She reached into one of the bags and pulled out several pints of ice cream to put in the freezer.

"What kind did you get?" Macey asked, opening the freezer.

"Tennyson's Plain Ole Vanilla, of course," Maeve replied. "Is there any other kind for blackberry cobbler?" she teased.

"There's Sweet Irish Cream," Macey said, putting the containers on the shelf.

"Oh, I brought that, too!" Maeve said, smiling and handing it to her. "But that's not for the cobbler. *That* is just to have!" She looked around. "Where's Harper?"

"Still in bed!" Macey said.

"No!"

"Yep," Macey said, nodding. "She stayed up late reading the book you gave her."

"*Harriet the Spy*?" Maeve asked, smiling.

"Mm-hmm. She devours every book you give her—I even caught her with a flashlight under the covers."

Maeve chuckled. "Good for her!"

"You can wake her, though—she needs to get up and take her medicine."

"Okay," Maeve said. She tiptoed up the stairs and peeked into Harper's room.

The little girl was flopped across her sheets, reading, but when she heard a sound in the hall, she looked up. "Aunt Maeve!"

"You stayin' in bed all day?" Maeve teased, giving her a hug.

"I might," Harper said, laughing. "What are you doing here?"

"Did you forget today is the picnic?"

Harper frowned, and then her eyes lit up. "I *did* forget!" She eyed her aunt's shirt, hopped out of bed, pulled open her dresser drawer, and riffled through it, looking for her version of the same shirt. "Found it!" she said triumphantly, holding it up with a grin. They'd gotten the same shirts when they'd been shopping together, and although Macey had declined to get one, they knew she really wanted one because it said in big letters: I HAVE RED HAIR BECAUSE GOD KNEW I NEEDED A WARNING LABEL!

"Wearing it?" Maeve asked.

"Of course!" Harper said, pulling her pajama top over her head, but before she pulled on the T-shirt, she stopped to look in the mirror. "Thanks, Kari," she whispered solemnly. "We're a team now."

Maeve smiled wistfully—she knew, because Macey had told her, that Harper made sure to thank her friend every time she got dressed. She'd also shared that Harper said she would never forget the promise she'd made to Lana. Kari's heartbroken mom had found the courage, after her little girl's tragic accident, to make the difficult decision to donate her organs, and Harper had received Kari's heart. Afterward, Harper had promised Lana—who she'd known before the accident—that she would always carry her spirit with her, too, and she would visit Lana so she could listen to her daughter's heart.

Maeve watched as Harper ran her finger lightly down the scar and then solemnly crossed her heart, before pulling her shirt over her head and brushing her hair out of her eyes. Next, she pulled on her shorts and socks and grinned at her aunt. "Ready!"

"It's about time," Maeve teased, getting up from the bed. She watched in amazement as Harper slid along the hardwood floor to the top of the stairs. In the year and a half since her surgery, Harper hadn't had any noticeable side effects or setbacks. She had more energy than she'd ever had before, and her doctor said she could even play sports. The most important thing she needed to do was remember to take her medicine, but that was the one thing she always seemed to forget.

Harper slid into the kitchen. "I'm here!" she announced to her mom.

"It's about time!" Macey teased as she—with Keeper at her feet, watching intently—chopped the celery for her potato salad. "Have some breakfast and take your medicine."

"Okay!" Harper said brightly. "What can I have?" she asked, looking around the kitchen.

"You can have an apple cider doughnut," Maeve said, coming into the kitchen behind her and reaching for the box she'd brought.

"Are Gage and Gus coming?" Harper asked hopefully, as she reached for a doughnut, suddenly realizing Maeve's two usual sidekicks weren't with her.

"They are," Maeve confirmed. "A little later."

Harper nodded, and then Macey noticed their matching outfits. "Nice shirts!"

Harper grinned. "I know. We gingers have to stick together!"

Maeve laughed. "We do!" She looked at Macey. "Mace, you still have to get one."

"I know," Macey replied. "We forgot to look last Saturday when we were shopping."

"We will next time," Harper said.

"Okay, Harp, take your medicine before you forget—it's right there on the counter."

Harper put her doughnut on a plate. "Anyone else want one?" she asked, holding the box open.

"Me," Maeve, said, reaching for a second plate. "I was breathing in their wonderful scent all the way over here. Mace, you want one?"

"No, thanks," Macey said, "but Ben might . . ."

"Ben might *what*?" her husband asked, coming into the kitchen and wondering what his wife was volunteering him for now.

Macey nodded to the box. "Want a doughnut?"

"Ooh, you twisted my arm," he said, smiling at Maeve. "I knew there was a reason we continue to invite you."

Maeve rolled her eyes, and he chuckled. "Are all women born knowing how to do that?" He loved teasing his sister-in-law, whom he'd known since she was in sixth grade.

"Do what?"

"Roll their eyes."

"We are," Maeve said. "It's because we have to put up with you men."

He laughed. "Want some coffee?" he asked as he refilled his mug.

Maeve nodded with her mouth full. "Mmm, yes, please."

Ben poured a second mug and spied Keeper gazing longingly at Maeve. "You are such a beggar!"

"He's fine," Maeve said, giving him a small piece. "How can you say *no* to this guy? He's so darn cute."

"That's the problem," Macey said, as she scooped the celery into the bowl.

Maeve smiled and licked the sugar from her lips. "Okay, now I'm ready," Maeve said. "What can I do?"

"Want to chop onions?" Macey asked.

"You want me to cry?"

"You won't cry if you do it right."

Ben popped the last bite of his doughnut in his mouth and eyed Harper. "You helping me?"

"Yep!" Harper said, giving Keeper her last bite, too, and hopping off her stool. "You comin', Keep?"

Macey looked over. "I doubt he's going to leave the kitchen when there's food prep going on."

"Yes, he will," Harper said, reaching for his collar. "Oh! Where's his new bandanna?"

"Over there," Macey said, nodding to a bag on the counter.

Harper pulled out the red, white, and blue bandanna, and while he stood patiently, wagging his tail, she tied it around his neck. "There!" she said, stepping back to admire him. "You look so handsome!"

"That reminds me," Maeve said, pulling her phone out of her pocket. "I bet Gage will forget."

"Yeah, they're supposed to be twins today," Harper said. Then she turned toward the door. "C'mon, Keep."

"Don't forget your medicine!" Macey reminded again.

"Oh, right!" Harper said. "I'd forget my head if it wasn't attached," she said, repeating the phrase she'd often heard Macey say, and Macey shook her head—mentally noting the truth in the theory that kids noticed what their parents did *and said*.

A moment later, Harper was out the door with Keeper in tow, and Macey was opening the fridge to retrieve two green peppers and a bag of carrots.

Maeve picked up the container of deviled eggs she'd made with eggs from Gage's hens. "While you're in there, Mace, can you find room for these?"

Macey eyed the large, flat container while Maeve peered over her shoulder at the overflowing contents of her sister's fridge. "Sheesh, Mace, I don't think you have enough food!"

"I can make room," Macey assured her sister, moving the hamburgers and hot dogs to the bottom shelf and then rearranging several bowls of salad. "See?" she said proudly. "Plenty of room!"

Maeve shook her head. "Are you letting anyone else bring stuff, or are you like Mom and have to make everything yourself?"

"I let people bring stuff," Macey said innocently, biting her lip and trying to suppress a smile. She knew all too well what her sister meant—their mom, Ruth Lindstrom, was famous for making too much food . . . and doing it all herself! Her daughters considered themselves lucky if she ever assigned a dish for them to bring.

Maeve eyed her sister. "You're turning into Mom."

"I am not."

"Yes, you are."

"Mom is much more set in her ways . . . and I let *you* bring stuff."

"You did, but when I asked you if you needed anything else, you turned me down."

"Oh, stop! I'm letting you help now," Macey countered, "and I'm *not* like Mom."

"Mm-hmm," Maeve replied.

"Anyway," Macey said, putting an onion on the cutting board and changing the subject, "if you don't want to cry, it helps to leave the root attached." She showed her sister how to quickly and systematically slice an onion without having to chop it.

"How'd you learn how to do that? Because that's definitely not how Mom does it—she just chops and cries."

"From Gordon Ramsay," Macey said, handing her sister the knife and then watching her wield it toward the second onion *and* her fingers. "Don't cut yourself," she warned. "I don't have time to take you to the ER!"

"I won't, *Mom*," Maeve said, rolling her eyes.

Finally, confident her sister had Onion Chopping 101 under control, Macey started on the peppers. "Sooo . . . when are you moving?"

"Well, my lease is up at the end of the month—which is this week, so this week."

"You don't sound very excited," Macey said, looking up.

"I'm excited."

"Really? It's a little hard to tell," Macey said, eyeing her. She hesitated, uncertain if she should ask what she was thinking. "Do you wish he'd proposed instead of asking you to move in?"

"I don't know," Maeve said with a sigh. "I *wish* he'd open up a little more about his family. The other day he told me this great story about a cat he had when he was little, and the cat—who already had kittens—adopted a baby bunny."

"No way!" Macey said in surprise.

"I know, crazy, right?" Maeve replied, smiling, "I love hearing stories like that—from when he was younger. It makes me feel closer to him, but he so rarely opens up. He never talks about why he doesn't go home—even around the holidays—and, Mace, even if he did ask me to marry him, I don't know what I'd say. I love him like crazy, but I want to know what happened. I have a feeling it has something to do with his dad because I'm pretty sure he talks to his mom. At the same time, there're some things that I—" But before she could finish her sentence, there was a commotion on the back porch. Macey looked out, and saw Keeper and Gus—sporting his new bandanna—greeting each other, nose to nose, tails wagging, and then Gus bounded off the porch and raced across the yard with Keeper hopping after him.

"Hey, Gage!" Macey said, holding open the screen door.

"Hey, Mace. Hope you don't mind me bringing Gus."

"Are you kidding?! We love Gus—he's the reason we invite *you*," she teased, giving him a kiss on the cheek.

"Ha ha. I figured." He smiled and held out a paper bag

containing his usual contribution—sparklers and the ingredients for s'mores.

"Thank you, my dear! Your sweetheart is over there trying not to cry as she chops onions."

He smiled at Maeve and then turned back to Macey. "I brought beer and ice, too," he said, gesturing over his shoulder. "Is Ben around?"

"He was just outside with Harper, setting up," Macey said, looking past him into the yard. "Maybe they went down to the river."

Gage nodded. "Well, if the cooler's around, I'll just fill it."

"Hmm . . . it might be in the basement."

"I can go down and get it."

"No, no, you don't want to go down there," Macey said, laughing. "We might never hear from you again."

"Oh, it can't be any worse than my parents' basement," he said.

"Oh, it can!" Macey said, heading for the basement door, and as she passed her sister, she raised her eyebrows—Gage had, without provocation, mentioned his parents!

"Hey," he said, walking over to give Maeve a kiss.

"Hey back," she said, smiling.

He eyed the onion. "No tears?"

"Nope," she said. "Turns out, it's all in the way you cut it. Who knew?" She nodded to the box of doughnuts on the counter. "Help yourself."

"Ooh," he said. "Thanks!"

Just then, Harper charged into the kitchen. "Uncle Gage!" she shouted, almost bowling him over.

"Hey, Harp," he said, hugging her back.

Maeve looked over and smiled. When Macey and Ben had first adopted Harper, she'd looked around the dinner table, trying out all the monikers for her new family members, including calling Gage *uncle*. When Maeve had tried to explain—without going into great detail—that Gage wouldn't *really* be her uncle, he had interrupted her and said that Harper could absolutely call him Uncle Gage if she wanted to, and the name had stuck. It had turned out to be fitting because Gage—who loved to play games and never turned Harper down when she challenged him to checkers—was the perfect uncle. Anytime they had a family gathering or summer picnic, he was the biggest kid there and always rounded up all the other kids to play Wiffle ball, or volleyball, or badminton, or cornhole. There was no *trying* to entice Gage into a game—he was their ringleader!

"I'll beat ya in cornhole, Uncle Gage," Harper said.

"Cornhole?!" Gage said. "Don't you know I'm the cornhole champion?"

"You are not!" Harper said, laughing.

"I am!" He looked to Maeve for confirmation. "Maeve, tell her."

Harper looked at her aunt, and even when Maeve raised her eyebrows and nodded, she wasn't convinced. "I don't believe her, either!"

"Game on!" Gage teased, grinning.

"All right!" Harper said, heading for the door, but just as she reached it, they heard a *clunk*, and Macey pushed open the basement door carrying a big cooler with a metal tub on top.

"I would've brought that up, you know," Gage said, taking them from her, and then looking at Harper. "We have to finish setting up first."

"Okay," Harper said.

They disappeared outside to put the drinks on ice, and Macey turned to her sister. "Gage is such a great guy, Maeve. I'm sure you two will eventually work through this."

Maeve nodded, but Macey was still eyeing her. "Is there something else?" she asked, but Maeve just shook her head and kept slicing the onion. If the tears stinging her eyes accidently spilled down her cheeks, at least she had an excuse.

# 12

Perspiration trickled down Mason's back as he stood in line, waiting for rehearsal to begin. Graduation was still two days away, but the excitement in the gym was palpable. Finals were over, grades were posted, summer vacations and college orientations loomed for many of the students, and all the yearbooks—which had been handed out that morning—were, at that very moment, being inscribed with well-wishes, reminiscences, and the bittersweet sentiments of reaching the long-sought milestone *and* the end of an era. All the yearbooks, that is, except Mason's. Mason had decided to spare his friends the awkward task of trying to write something that was both upbeat and sympathetic. After all, he thought, *How do you wish good luck to someone whose mom is dying?*

He brushed the perspiration from his cheek and wished it was over. If it wasn't for his mom's tenacious determination to see him walk across the stage, he would've happily spent the day working; even spreading mulch would be better than watching her struggle. He'd tried to tell her it wasn't a big deal—he could arrange to have his diploma mailed or presented to him in her hospital room, and he'd even wear his cap and gown—but she wouldn't hear of it. *My son is class salutatorian*, she'd said, and although he knew how much she wanted to be there . . . and be a normal, happy, proud, cheering mom, he also knew how much watching her expend every ounce of energy she had to be there was going to shatter him.

"Hey, Mase," a voice called.

He turned and saw Ali walking toward him. "Hey," he replied, mustering a half smile.

"Where's your yearbook?" she asked, eyeing his empty hands.

"In my locker."

"How are people going to sign it there?"

"They don't need to sign it."

"Umm, yes, they *do* . . . *I* do."

"*You* can sign it anytime. It doesn't have to be here."

She sighed and looked around the gym. "When are they gonna get this show on the road?"

"I don't know, but if it isn't soon, I'm leaving."

"You can't *walk* if you miss rehearsal."

"Fine with me," he said, knowing the rules for *walking* across stage included attending rehearsal. "I'd rather be working."

"Are you goin' to the party at the lake after graduation?"

"I guess so," he said. "I was gonna skip it, but I made the mistake of telling my mom about it."

Ali grinned. "I love the way your mom is still in charge."

Mason smiled. "*She* will always be in charge."

Just then the high school band began to play the traditional entrance music and Ali raised her eyebrows. "I guess I better get back to my spot. Meet me after?"

He nodded and watched her go, and as he did, he thought about her comment. Being in charge was definitely in his mom's DNA, and it paired well with her indomitable can-do spirit. Laurie Callahan had grown up in the heart of the Blue Ridge Mountains. Slender and petite *and* every bit a tomboy with short brown hair and kind hazel eyes, Laurie was the only child of Winton, an air force pilot, and Lena, a schoolteacher who filled their home with books. When Laurie hadn't been reading—one of the much-loved pastimes she'd passed on to her son—she and her mom had baked pies—half of which they gave away. She'd also spent most Sunday afternoons hiking with her dad in the sun-dappled Chattahoochee Forest or fishing in the crystal-clear Ellijay or Coosawattee Rivers. She was a nature lover and a book lover and, living in the "Apple Capital of Georgia," she could also bake a mean apple pie. When it came time for college, Laurie had applied to one school—nearby Chattahoochee Technical College—to which she could commute from home, and from where she earned her degree in nursing. She had been a devoted daughter who put her life on hold when her parents could no longer care for themselves, and she was by their sides when, in their nineties, they passed away within days of each other. Soon after, however, she'd been back working in the maternity ward at the hospital—a job she loved so much she'd often gone in on her day off to "cuddle" the preemies in the NICU.

Mason closed his eyes, remembering her enthusiasm for the program. She would pick him up at school after volunteering—something she did in addition to working at the hospital—and tell him all about it. "The baby was so little, Mase, you wouldn't believe it, but he was perfect in every way—just like you. His whole little hand barely wrapped around the tip of my finger."

Six years old at the time, Mason had listened in wonder, trying to imagine a baby's ten tiny fingers and ten tiny toes. "Did you sing that song to him that you always sing to me?"

"'Someone to Watch over Me'?" she'd asked, and he'd nodded.

"I did," she'd said, laughing and tousling his hair.

"I'm going to be a cuddler someday," he'd announced proudly, looking out the window. Then he'd looked back at her. "How old do I have to be?"

"You have to be eighteen, and you should definitely do it because it's so amazing. *You* would make a wonderful cuddler!"

"Okay," he'd said, beaming. "I'm gonna do it, Mom . . . just like you!"

Suddenly, Mason felt a nudge. "Mase, you going?" Joe Cameron asked, and Mason opened his eyes and realized his line had begun moving. He nodded and took a step forward, still lost in the memory of the conversation he'd had with his mom when he was little, amazed that he'd forgotten it, but even more amazed that he'd remembered it today, the day before he turned eighteen.

# 13

Maeve swept up the dirt that had spilled when she was putting her plants into the last box. She'd already cleaned the bathroom and kitchen, and Gage had just left with the last load in his pickup. She couldn't believe how much stuff she had accumulated while living in the apartment! So much, in fact, they'd had to rent a storage unit. It seemed like they had two of everything—two beds, two couches, two kitchen tables, and two—*or three!*—of everything else. From TVs and toasters to pots and pans and coffee makers, they took the best of each and put the second—or third—item in storage.

Now the apartment she'd lived in—*and loved living in*—for the last ten years was empty. She looked around at the bare walls and hardwood floors and remembered how excited she'd been when she first moved in. Finding such a lovely apartment in the upstairs of a downtown Savannah home had been a stroke of good luck, and the price had been a steal. Her parents had tried to convince her to move back home after college, but she'd been determined to spread her wings, and she'd loved making the apartment her own. She'd loved the dark mahogany trim and the ancient tile fireplace—over which she'd hung a long bayberry garland every Christmas—and she'd loved the big windows.

She sighed and shook her head, and then finished sweeping the dirt into a dustpan. She dumped it into the trash bag, set the dustpan and broom next to it, and went into the kitchen to rinse her hands. As she dried them on her jeans—because Gage had thrown the last roll of paper towels in a box—she realized he'd forgotten to take the plants. She carried them into the living room and set them on the floor next to the trash, and then walked through the rooms one more time. She had to admit she was excited about moving in with Gage, but she was also a bit nervous. It was a big step, and even though she loved his cozy cabin, she was going to miss her sunny old-fashioned kitchen, *and* her independence. *Life goes on*, she thought with a sigh and a wistful smile, *and maybe this is the next step toward making a lifetime commitment to each other!*

The late-day sun filtered through the tall windows, splashing light and shadows in all the familiar places, and filling her heart with melancholy. She gazed at the corner where she'd sat in her "prayer chair" every morning, saying countless prayers for loved ones and friends, and then she turned to the opposite corner—the spot where she'd always set up her Christmas tree. *Oh, how she'd loved looking up from the street and seeing the tiny lights sparkling in the window.* Next, she walked into her bedroom and smiled. *If these four walls could talk!* she thought. *Although they wouldn't have much to say about the first eight years, they certainly would have something to say about the last two with that country boy in her bed!*

"Time to move on," she whispered softly, "come what may."

AN HOUR LATER, AFTER HER LANDLORD HAD WALKED THROUGH THE apartment, told her he was sorry to see her go, and given her back her security deposit, she turned into Gage's driveway—*and my driveway now, too*, she thought. As she parked next to his truck, Gus gave a welcoming bark and then rocketed across the lawn. "Hey, there, Gussie," she said, laughing. "You ready for another roomie?"

He wiggled all around her, thumping her head with his tail until she finally stood up. She hoisted her big leather bag—which contained her entire life—onto her shoulder, and the still-wiggling

Lab escorted her to the cabin. Balancing the box of plants, she pulled open the screen door. "Anybody home?"

"In the kitchen," Gage called.

She made her way through the maze of boxes. "It smells so good in here!"

Gage looked up from sliding garlic bread into the oven. "Thanks," he said, smiling. "I thought you might be hungry after all this moving."

"I'm starving!" she said, and then she noticed the table by the window was beautifully set with candles, a glass milk bottle with a bouquet of lilacs in it, and cloth napkins. "Oh, my goodness!" she exclaimed. "It looks so . . . romantic." She eyed him suspiciously and teased, "Who are *you* and what did you do with my boyfriend?"

He laughed and held up two bottles of wine. "Red or white?"

"What are we having?"

"Spaghetti."

"Red," she said and then looked down at Gus. "I don't know why I didn't move in sooner."

"We don't know, either," Gage said, handing her a glass.

"You even have my favorite music playing," she said, hearing Van Morrison's "Crazy Love" drifting from the speaker on the counter. "Such a great song."

"It is a great song," he said, pulling her into his arms.

"Don't start something you can't finish," she murmured as he pressed against her, already aroused, "or our dinner will get cold again."

"The sauce is simmering and the pasta's not in yet," he whispered back, unbuttoning the top of her blouse.

"What about the bread?" she whispered back.

He frowned. "Damn," he said, considering his dilemma. "I could take it out," he suggested hopefully.

"I really *am* starving," she countered.

"All right," he conceded, stepping back, but as he reached for his wineglass, he pretended it was a microphone. *"Yeah, it makes me mellow, down into my soul . . ."*

"Do I know you?" she teased, laughing.

"I hope so," he said, turning the flame under the water back to high. "You just moved in with me."

"I did indeed," Maeve mused, carrying her glass over to admire the table and realizing the napkins had been folded into pockets that held silver flatware. "This is pretty fancy, Gage. I didn't know you had cloth napkins . . . *or* knew how to fold them."

"Ah . . . from me ole bartending days," he said, tossing the salad. "When it was slow, we folded."

"You're a man of many talents."

He laughed. "Folding napkins is just one of many," he teased as he dropped the pasta into the boiling water.

Maeve lifted the cover off the smaller pot and peered through the savory steam. "Mmm . . . did you make the sauce, too?

"Sort of. I added sausage and ground beef, but the base is from my mom's tomato preserves."

"Well, it all smells amazing," she said, taking a sip of her wine. "Is there anything I can do?"

He shook his head as he stirred the pasta. "I think I have everything under control." But just as he said this, smoke began to drift from the oven and he realized he'd forgotten the bread. "Damn!" he said, opening the door and pulling it out bare-handed.

Maeve peered around him. "It's fine. Want me to slice it?"

"Sure," he said. "The cutting board is right there." He pointed to it and a nearby knife, and she nodded, happy to have a job. As she sliced the bread and rewrapped it in the same foil to keep it warm, he poured the pasta into a waiting colander, slid it into a pretty blue bowl, and dropped butter on top of it. "Want to grab the plates?" he asked, hoping she didn't mind having her dinner served buffet-style.

"Absolutely," she said, handing one to him.

"Ladies first," he said, motioning. "After all, I don't want you to pass out from hunger."

She took his teasing in stride and heaped her plate with salad and pasta, ladled sauce on top, sprinkled it with fresh parmesan, and then took her wine and the foil-wrapped bread to the table. Gage always insisted she go first—it didn't matter if they were in line for a movie or passing out plates for a buffet dinner at her parents' house. He was always courteous and polite. She would never forget the first time she'd brought him home to meet her parents. He'd politely shaken her mom's hand first, and then turned to firmly clasp her dad's. When her mom had said dinner was ready, her dad—who considered himself an authority on gentleman's etiquette—had waited, watching, and then smiled approvingly when Gage, without prompting, waited for the ladies to be seated before sitting himself. Gage was an old soul and a true Southern gentleman, and it hadn't taken long for her to fall head over heels in love with him. "I can't believe you did all this after spending all day helping me move," she said, eyeing him as he sat down.

"It wasn't hard—just pasta," he said. "My mainstay," he added with a smile as he opened the bread. "Plus, I'm really glad you're here."

"I'm really glad I'm here, too."

They heard a thunk on the floor and looked under the table to see Gus sprawled at their feet. Gage laughed and shook his head. "So, did you get your security deposit back?"

"I did," she said, and then eyed him. "Do I need to give it to you?"

"Hmm," he said thoughtfully. "I don't know . . . do you?"

She laughed. "I don't plan on doing any damage." But as she said these words, the irony wasn't lost on her—the potential *emotional* damage she could exact was profound.

"Then I'm good," he said, squeezing her hand.

# 14

"Happy Birthday, honey," Laurie said as Mason leaned over to give her a hug. "Can you believe it's June?!"

Mason shook his head. "I cannot."

"And look at you! From a three-pound, six-ounce preemie to a strapping six-foot-two handsome, smart, amazing young man. Who would've thought it?"

Mason felt his cheeks flame and shook his head. "You wouldn't be biased at all?"

"Me? Heck, no!" She tried to sit up, but moving—even the slightest bit—sent a shooting pain through her body and she winced.

"You okay?" he asked, standing to help her adjust her pillow.

"I'm fine," she assured him, but he knew she'd asked the nurses not to give her any pain medicine so she wouldn't be drowsy, and now she was paying the price.

"So, are you excited about tomorrow? Do you have your speech prepared?"

"Yep," he lied.

"Good! And you don't need to worry about me. I'll be fine. Sue is bringing me, and she'll make sure I don't embarrass you."

"Mom," he said, tears springing to his eyes. "I'm *not* worried about you embarrassing me. That's not it. I *want* you to be there, I just don't want you to wear yourself out. It's not worth it."

"It *is* worth it to me, Mason," she said softly. "I've been looking forward to seeing you graduate for as long as I can remember. That's what moms do—their hearts fill with hopes and dreams for their kids—they imagine them doing amazing things, and they pray that they will never be disappointed or hurt. Mason, it means everything to me to be there tomorrow."

Mason bit his lip. "Okay," he said, his voice choked with emotion. "I'm sorry I've been trying to make it sound like it isn't a big deal. I didn't see it that way. I want you to be there, Mom. It's just going to be . . ." But before he could finish his sentence there was a knock on the door.

He wiped his eyes and turned to see Ali and her mom coming into the room, carrying a birthday cake, and singing "Happy Birthday to You."

"Happy birthday, Mason!" they both said, giving him a hug.

"Thanks," he replied. "You didn't have to do this."

"Are you kidding?" Sue teased. "Not have cake on your eighteenth birthday?"

Ali nudged him. "I know there are no candles, Mase, but you can still make a wish."

"Absolutely," prompted Sue.

Mason nodded, closed his eyes, and thought of a wish.

When he opened them again, his mom smiled, her eyes sparkling. "I hope you wished for something good!"

"I did," he said, his own eyes glistening, knowing it would probably never come true.

Sue cut the cake and put the slices on festive paper plates, which Ali handed out, but Laurie only took one small bite of her requested sliver before setting it on her tray table. "I'm gonna have to eat mine a little later," she said, smiling. "I'm still full from supper."

Mason nodded, even though he could see her untouched dinner on the table in the corner. "This is really good, Mrs. Harrison," he said. "Thank you."

"I know how much you like chocolate, Mase," she said with a

smile. “We were going to bring ice cream, but we thought it might melt.”

“This is great,” he said. “We don’t need ice cream.”

“Sooo . . . graduation is at eleven tomorrow,” Sue said, eyeing her friend. “Shall I pick you up at ten?”

“That would be perfect,” Laurie said, smiling to hide the pain she was in.

“Your doctor okayed it?” Mason asked, sensing that all was not well.

“Absolutely,” Laurie said.

“Okay, well, we better let you get some rest then,” he said, hoping that once they left, she would let the nurse give her something for pain.

“Oh, my goodness!” she said suddenly. “I almost forgot to give you your present!”

Mason frowned. “You didn’t have to get me anything.”

“I didn’t *get* you anything,” she said, smiling. “I *had* it . . . I’ve had it for a long time, and I’ve been waiting to give it to you.” She looked to Ali, who pulled a small wrapped gift from her bag and handed it to her. “Of course, I had to have Ali find it and sneak it out of the house,” she said, laughing. “Thank you, Ali. Was it where I said?”

Ali nodded and smiled, and Mason eyed his friend suspiciously.

“You were in the bathroom,” she said innocently.

Laurie looked back at her son. “This is for your birthday *and* for graduation.”

Mason pulled the paper off a small gray box, opened it, and blinking back tears, lifted out a wristwatch.

“It was my dad’s . . . your grandfather’s,” Laurie explained. “When he gave it to me, he told me that most of the pilots in WWII wore Elgins . . . and now, it’s yours.”

“Wow,” he whispered in disbelief, no longer able to fight back his tears. “Thanks, Mom,” he said as they spilled down his cheeks.

"You're welcome," she said, smiling. "I had it refurbished last year. It keeps perfect time."

Mason nodded, lightly tracing his finger over the worn engraving on the back—it read: *Winton Callahan, "Whiplash," 1943*. "Was Whiplash his call sign?"

"It was."

He smiled, realizing his grandfather was indeed the same aviator Bud Hawkins had remembered being catapulted off the deck of his aircraft carrier. He put it around his wrist, hooked the buckle, and showed it to Ali and her mom.

"It's beautiful," Sue said admiringly.

"Very special," Ali said.

Mason nodded. "It is," he said softly. He leaned down to give his mom a gentle hug. "Thank you so much. I will treasure it always."

She smiled and squeezed his hand. "I know you will, hon. Now, you guys better get going—you and Ali have a big day tomorrow."

Mason nodded and watched his mom's best friend give her a hug. "I'll see you in the morning," Sue said, wrapping up the cake and handing it to Mason.

Laurie nodded and hugged Ali, too. "Thanks, sweetie," she said.

"You're welcome," Ali replied. "Have a good night."

Mason smiled sadly. "Night, Mom. Love you."

"Love you, too, Mason," she said. "See you tomorrow."

# 15

Hearing a loud *er-er-er-er-errr*, Maeve opened her eyes, uncertain for a moment of her surroundings, and realized Gage's rooster, Pilgrim, was letting her know it was time to rise and shine. She rolled to her side and smoothed the soft cotton sheet on which she and Gage had made love the night before. She felt the summer breeze drift through the window, rustling the white curtain and cooling her bare skin, and then looked up at the pale blue sky outside, wondering what time it was. She sat up, swung her legs over the side of the bed, pulled one of Gage's shirts around her, and shuffled to the bathroom. She stopped to look at her reflection, and frowned—the light must not have been as bright in her old bathroom because the mirror in this bathroom was definitely less forgiving! She looked around for her toothbrush, which she usually balanced on her travel case, but it wasn't there, and then she saw it in the ceramic toothbrush holder—making it official that she was no longer a guest. *She lived here!*

She went back to the bedroom, pulled on shorts and a T-shirt, and noticed how quiet it was—*Where is Gus?* She went into the kitchen to make coffee, and as she waited for it to brew, she saw a sticky note tacked to the mug she always used when she stayed over:

*Good morning! Thought I'd let you sleep in.*
*Gus is with me so he's not pestering you all day.*

*We'll try to be home early.*
*Have fun unpacking!* ☺

*xo Gage*

Maeve had never spent time in the cabin alone—without even Gus for company, and it was oddly peaceful. She poured a mug of coffee and began looking for her Bible and the daily devotional she always tucked between its pages, but after opening several boxes and having no success, she gave up, and began scanning Gage's bookshelf instead. She paused in front of a calendar to admire the painting of an old yellow Lab resting his chin on the knee of an old man. You could absolutely see the devotion and love in their eyes, and she smiled, and then it dawned on her that the calendar needed to be changed. She pulled out the pushpin, flipped the page, and gazed at the next painting of two black Labs standing in a field of grass—the image was stunning, and she wondered who painted it. She was just about to look for the artist's name, when her eyes fell on the date—June 1—and she caught her breath. Her mind immediately counted the years, and then she shook her head as if trying to shake the memory from her mind.

She turned away and refocused her attention on the shelf until she found what she was looking for—a Bible. She slid it out, took it outside, settled into one of the Adirondack chairs, and set her coffee on the wide, flat arm. She gave herself a moment to regroup, and while she did, she watched Eggith, Eggel, and Eggna scratching and pecking the ground in front of the porch while Pilgrim strutted around protectively. Finally, she took a sip of her coffee, looked down at the worn leather book in her lap, and lightly traced the name engraved on the cover—*Gage Henrik Tennyson*.

Without her devotional to guide her, Maeve opened to her favorite old standby—the book of Psalms—but as she turned the thin, fragile pages to her favorite psalm, two faded newspaper clippings fluttered out and fell to the floor. She picked them up and studied the picture of a young man wearing a John Deere hat. At first, she thought it was Gage, but then she saw the headline and the name printed beneath the picture, and her heart stopped. She began to read the words and her eyes filled with tears. "Oh, no," she whispered. "I had no idea . . ."

**TRAGEDY STRIKES LOCAL FARM**

> Cale Tennyson, 19, was killed in a farming accident Sunday evening. He was the oldest son of Jack and Libby Tennyson, owners of the Tennessee Tennyson Dairy Farm. Cale had just finished his sophomore year at the University of Tennessee Institute of Agriculture where he was studying the latest innovations in dairy farming. He dreamed of one day modernizing the operations of the family farm. The accident is still under investigation.

Maeve stared at the faded yellow paper in disbelief and then slowly unfolded the second clipping and realized it was the obituary, and from it, she learned more about Gage than she'd ever known. At the top, there was a picture that looked like it might've come from Cale's yearbook. He was wearing a jacket and tie, and his blond hair was cropped short and neatly combed. He was handsome and had the same crooked smile she knew all too well, and even though he was all cleaned up, there was no hiding the mischievous country boy behind those sparkling eyes. Cale was born on August 13, 1983—making him Gage's Irish twin—and he died on August 8, 2003, five days before his twentieth birthday. It went on to say he was survived by his parents, three grandparents—including Dutch—and five younger brothers: Gage, Matthew, Eli, Grayson, and Chase. The service was held at the First Congregational Church and a reception in Fellowship Hall had followed. Underneath was a second picture, showing all six Tennyson brothers standing together. *Damn! Those Tennyson genes ran strong!*

Maeve looked up from the clipping and watched the hens still scratching the sun-dappled earth. *This explains a lot . . . but it doesn't explain everything.* She looked down at his Bible, expecting more clues to fall from its pages, and as if on cue, she noticed a blue envelope tucked inside the back cover. She slid it out and looked at the return address—it was from Tennessee. She turned it over to see if Gage had opened it. He had, which meant she could easily read it and put it back . . . *but*—and this was a very big *but—was this a line she wanted to cross?* It was one thing to innocently read clippings that had accidentally fallen out of his Bible, but it was quite another to open and read someone's mail. Still, she wanted to understand what had happened in his life. She swallowed the lump in her throat, slowly lifted the flap of the envelope, and slid out the letter, but just as she was about to unfold it, Gage's rooster screamed like he was possessed, and the hens started to squawk nervously and flap their wings. Maeve looked up and saw a bushy red tail flicking above the tall grass. "Oh, no you don't! Don't even think of it!" she shouted. "Go on!" She rose from her chair and a fox—ready to pounce—looked up in surprise. Maeve began waving her arms and then flew off the porch, causing the fox to hightail it through the fields.

"Oh, my goodness!" Maeve said, her heart pounding. "That was close!" She looked around for any more predators lurking in the grass, picked up the Bible, tucked everything back where it belonged, and smiled at the rooster still strutting around and clucking indignantly. "Good job, Pilgrim!" she said. "You saved us . . . *all*!" And then she took the Bible inside, slid it back into its spot on the shelf, refilled her coffee mug, and started to unpack.

# 16

Mason slid his arms into the sleeves of his graduation gown and hitched it up onto his shoulders. He attached the tassel to his mortarboard and balanced it on his head—thank goodness he didn't have to wear this thing for very long! He paused to admire his new—old—watch and check the time.

"Ready?" Ali asked, coming up behind him, already dressed and wearing her National Honor Society stole and several honor cords around her neck.

Mason looked up from zipping his gown. "Ready as I'll ever be."

"Such enthusiasm," she teased, as she adjusted his tassel. "This, my friend, stays on your right side till we all have our diplomas and are instructed to move it over to the left. . . . Weren't you paying attention during rehearsal?"

"No," he said, smiling.

"Where're your stole and honor cords?" she asked, straightening his tie.

"In my locker."

She rolled her eyes. "You're going to need them," she said, reaching for his hand and pulling him through the throng of graduates toward his locker. "Besides," she said, standing beside him as he spun the combination lock back and forth for probably the last time, "our lockers are supposed to be empty."

"Well, it's going to be empty once I take these out."

"Is your yearbook in there?"

"Maybe," he said impishly.

"Mason!" she said, feigning disbelief—even though she wasn't surprised. "Have you let anyone sign it?"

"Maybe," he said, giving her a funny face.

"You haven't! I can tell by the look on your face!" she said, raising her eyebrows. "And since your locker is supposed to be empty, what are you going to do with it during graduation?"

He shrugged. "Carry it?"

Ali shook her head and held out her hand. "I'll give it to my mom."

"Are *they* here?" Mason asked in surprise, his stomach suddenly twisting into a knot.

She nodded. "I peeked out a little while ago and saw them right up front."

"How'd my mom look?"

"She was smiling."

Mason looked relieved and handed his yearbook to her. "Okay. Tell her thanks."

She nodded. "I'll be right back."

He reached into his locker, and trying to expel the kaleidoscope of butterflies now fluttering around in his stomach, lifted out his stole and the rainbow of colorful cords. As he draped them around his neck, several of his friends—fellow distance runners from the cross-country and track teams—stopped to congratulate him on his recently revealed status as salutatorian, and their usual banter and teasing helped him relax.

"All right, Mase, you da man," Jackson Temple said, pointing at him.

"Keep it short, sweetheart," Randy Stephens teased, slapping him on the shoulder. Mason laughed, shaking hands as they all headed off in different directions to find their places in line.

Mason reached into his pocket and pulled out a single folded sheet of paper—his speech *would* be short . . . because he had no idea what he was going to say.

Just then, Ali returned. "Is that your speech?" she asked brightly.

He nodded and she tipped the paper to see it.

"Oh, dear," she said, raising her eyebrows at the blank page, but then quickly added, "no worries. I'm sure you'll think of something!" She kissed his cheek. "I'll see you after. You got this, Mase!"

Mason watched her go. Then he looked down at the piece of paper in his hand. He'd gotten up early that morning, hoping to jot down some thoughts—thoughts his classmates might find poignant or profound and maybe even funny . . . he'd wanted to keep it light but he'd just stared at the page. Finally, he'd scanned his mom's bookshelf—the one on which she kept her most favorite books—and there between Anne Lamott and Mary Oliver was her Bible. He'd reached for Anne Lamott's *Help, Thanks, Wow*, but his hand had, instead, settled on her Bible—which he knew was stuffed with scribbled quotes and thoughts, and not just Bible verses, but with all the little things she'd jotted down over the years. He'd sat down in her favorite chair, and when he'd opened the cover, an old photo of him taking his first steps had fallen out. He'd seen the photo before but never really studied it, and he had realized he must've been walking into her arms because he was laughing and his arms were reaching out. Mason had smiled, absentmindedly flicking the corner of the old photo, but then he'd noticed there was another photo stuck to it. He'd frowned, and as he pried them apart, they made a sticky, scratching sound. He'd stared at the second photo—it was not one he'd seen before—of a girl in a hospital bed with a tiny baby in her arms. Her hair was a golden halo of copper, just like the baby's. He'd stared at her uncertainly—his mom had taken care of so many babies over the years that it could've been anyone, *but why had she saved this photo and why was it in her Bible?* He had turned it over to see if there was anything written on the back, but it was blank—*just like the piece of paper on which he was supposed to be writing down his thoughts!* Mason had tucked both photos back between the pages, and turned to the task at hand, leafing through the quotes written in his mom's careful handwriting.

"Hey, Mason! You comin'?" Joe Cameron called. Mason looked up, realized everyone was in line, quickly folded the paper, tucked it in his pocket, and took his place. "Congrats, man!" Joe said, patting him on the shoulder. "Better you than me!"

Mason smiled. "We'll see 'bout that."

The regal sound of *Pomp and Circumstance* drifted from the gym, and the line began to move. When he walked into the gym, he scanned the front row and spotted his mom sitting in a wheelchair next to Mrs. Harrison. She was wearing her favorite white blouse with a pretty cobalt blue bandanna on her head, and when she saw him, she smiled and gave him a thumbs-up, which he promptly returned.

Mason sat in his seat and only half listened to the speeches before his—those of his principal and their guest speaker (a local author)—because he was still trying to formulate his own thoughts. Finally, he heard his name announced, and he felt Joe elbow him. "Good luck, man!"

Mason stood, and feeling his heart pound like a jackhammer, made his way to the front. He crossed the stage slowly, shaking the hands of the administrators, and then stood resolutely in front of the podium. He pressed his lips together pensively and took in his audience, but when his gaze rested on his mom—and she smiled at him—he felt an odd peace wash over him. He smiled back, his heart swelling with pride because this amazing woman was *his* mom . . . and he was *her* son.

"Thank you for your kind welcome," he began, adjusting the mic and smiling. "As many of you know, this has been a turbulent year for my mom and me, but as difficult as it has been, it is her unending support and encouragement that has me standing up here. She is the fiercest warrior I know." He looked over and smiled. "Mom, this is for you."

Laurie Callahan nodded, her eyes glistening as Sue put her arm around her frail shoulders and pulled her close.

"This morning, I got up early with the goal of trying to write down some thoughts so I wouldn't get myself thoroughly lost up here." As he said this, he pulled the paper out of his pocket and unfolded it. "But this is as far as I got," he said, holding up the blank page—which made everyone chuckle. "For some reason, not a single thought would come to me—it was kind of like all the blank pages I've faced before when I've had to write a paper." He smiled, pausing for more chuckles. "So I began to think about all the times I've felt this way—you know, lost and uncertain about what is going to happen . . . about the future—as I'm sure many of you feel today . . . full of trepidation and, in some cases, absolute terror about what the future holds . . . about making the right decisions . . . about getting along with the total stranger some computer algorithm has chosen to be your roommate, or . . . if you're like me, and not going to college right away, trying to decide which path feels right." As he said this, he looked at Ali, and she nodded. "So, as I sat in my mom's chair this morning, thinking about all the times I've felt this way over the years, I tried to recall how I'd gotten through them, and I realized that it was my mom who helped me—all the little quips she used to say to give me encouragement, simple things that would focus my mind. . . . And these are the things that helped me push through, so I thought I'd just share some of them with you."

He looked up at his mom, saw that she had a tissue clutched in her hand, and then took a deep breath and swallowed before pressing on. "As I made my way up here, I could almost hear my mom whisper one of her most famous phrases in my ear: *Be bold and mighty forces will come to your aid!*" He looked at her and she laughed. "This quote is one of her favorites—she has said it to me so often that it rattles through my head on a daily basis, often on repeat, like the lyrics of a song that gets stuck in your head." He looked around. "For the longest time—in fact, right up until this morning—I thought it was from the Bible, but I googled it and discovered it's actually paraphrased from a longer quote: 'Go at it boldly, and you'll find unexpected forces closing round you and coming to your aid.' It's attributed to the Canadian clergyman and author Basil King and it is included in his book *Conquest of Fear*—a book that was written a hundred years ago, but is still as profound today . . . and all this time, I thought it was from the Bible." He paused. "I'm sure I thought this because I know the Bible—another of my mom's favorite books—is filled with assurances to not fear. So, in my head, I heard my mom whisper it because it has given me courage throughout my life when I've faced other daunting tasks—like public speaking," he added and then waited for the laughter that ensued to die down.

"You see, my mom has always loved to read—a passion she has passed on to me. Our house is full of books—we have so many books, in fact, we could probably open a library! From poetry to prose; from history to science; and from mystery to romance, it's from the pages of all those books that my mom has gleaned an endless wealth of wisdom . . . and trivial knowledge," he added with a grin.

"One of her favorite authors is the esteemed Maya Angelou, and another timeless quote she often shared was Maya's: 'I've learned that people will forget what you said, people will forget what you did, but people will never forget how you made them feel.' It's such a simple quote, but we would all do well to take it with us when we leave this place—these halls, classrooms, playing fields, and cross-country trails—where we've grown up and learned about life . . . as we leave the teachers and coaches who have taught and inspired us . . . and as we leave the friends with whom we've done all this learning. It doesn't take a high school diploma or a college degree to keep this in your heart, because when it comes right down to it . . . how did *you*, by your actions and your words, make other people feel?" He smiled. "It's probably one of the most important things we can learn in life."

He paused, looking around at his classmates. "We have come so far, but I'd like to leave you with one final quote." With a smile, he continued. "When the poet Mary Oliver died, my mom mourned her passing as she would a dear friend. That winter night—I remember it well because it was dark at five o'clock when I got home, and my mom was so sad as she told me about her passing and her poems, and then she went to the shelf where her most cherished books are kept, and pulled out a dog-eared volume of *House of Light*. She flipped through the pages until she came to her favorite poem: 'The Summer Day' . . . but my mom didn't need the book to share the poem because she knew it by heart. . . . And when she reached the last line, she looked right at me and made it her own. *Tell me, dear one, what is it you plan to do with your one wild and precious life?*"

Mason pressed his lips together. "These are just some of the things my mom has taught me, but I believe they are more important than any diploma or honor or degree, and I think we would all do well to keep them in our hearts. I know I will." He turned, and with glistening eyes, looked solemnly at his mom. "With my one wild and precious life, Mom, I plan to be bold . . . and to be kind . . . *and* to make you proud."

Tears streamed down Laurie Callahan's cheeks as her son made his way toward her. The crowd around them rose, weeping and clapping thunderously, and when Mason reached his mom, Laurie pulled herself up and wrapped him in a hug. She held her son as if she would never let him go. She would never feel more proud—the young man she'd raised was so poised and well-spoken, respectful and honest, handsome and strong. He had given a poignant message straight from his heart . . . and she knew he would do well, no matter what path he chose. "Thank you, dear one," she whispered, and he smiled and kissed the top of her head. Then he gently helped her sit down, hugged Mr. and Mrs. Harrison, too, and went back to his seat—the audience still standing and clapping.

# 17

Maeve heard her phone hum, felt her back pocket, and frowned. She picked up large clumps of crumpled packing paper and pushed them into an empty box, but she still couldn't find her phone so she stood in the middle of the room, waiting for it to hum again. Finally, it did, and she looked up and saw it on top of the mantle—right where she'd left it. She looked at the screen and saw a text from Gage:

How's the unpacking going?

It's going.

Do you have anything planned for dinner?

She raised her eyebrows—she hadn't even thought about dinner. Leftover spaghetti? She watched the bouncing dots that told her he was typing, but when they disappeared, she frowned. She went into the kitchen to see what other options there were, but when she opened the fridge, her phone hummed again, and she stared at the screen in surprise.

My little brother's in town and wants to get together. Would u b up for that?

*Wow! Was this a gift from heaven because I found the wherewithal and willpower to not read his letter?* She swallowed and typed back: That would be awesome! but before she hit *send*, she reread her words, decided they sounded a little too enthusiastic, and backspaced. Carefully considering, she typed Sounds fun, left off the exclamation mark, and added a smiling emoji. Reviewing again, though, she decided to delete the emoji, and finally hit *send*.

Great! Can you meet us at The Distillery at seven?

Maeve looked at the time—it was 4:30 P.M. She started to write back, but before she could finish, another message popped up. I forgot I have Gus with me :-/ Will be home

Okay, she wrote back, and then she glanced around the room with fresh eyes and realized it looked like it had been hit by a tornado! With renewed vigor, she set to work, disposing of packing paper, breaking down empty boxes, and putting still-full boxes into new, more organized piles—at least you could walk from the front door to the kitchen without taking your life in your hands.

She headed to the bedroom to get ready . . . and groaned—the bed was covered with clothes *and* more boxes. Gage had made room for her clothes in his closet, but she'd filled the space in no time. There hadn't been room for her bureau in the small bedroom, so he'd emptied two dresser drawers, which she'd also filled, all the while wondering what she was going to do with everything. Obviously, it was time for a major purge and a trip—*or ten*—to the thrift store!

She pulled her shorts and tank top off, threw them in the hamper, and stood in front of the closet, trying to figure out what she could wear to dinner. A minute into deliberating, she heard a sound on the front porch, and a second later, Gus charged into the room, wiggling around with his tail thumping. "Hello, Gussie!" she said, laughing. "I'm happy to see you, too!"

The puppy—living in a full-grown Lab body—raced around

the small room, sliding on the throw rugs and nearly taking out the bedside table. "Hey!" a voice commanded, and Maeve looked up to see Gage standing in the doorway with a beer in his hand. Gus screeched to a halt, looked up at Gage with eyes wild and haunches in the air, and then, as Maeve tried to suppress a smile, he started to race again. "Enough!" Gage commanded and like a helium balloon that had run out of gas, the puppy stopped, panting, and flopped onto one of the crumpled rugs that had been pushed against the wall. "Sheesh! Someone's a little excited!"

Maeve smiled. "A girl loves it when someone is excited to see her," she said, laughing.

Gage eyed her with raised eyebrows and took a sip of the beer. "I'm excited to see you," he said, smiling and walking over, slowly backing her against the wall.

"Hmm, I can tell," she whispered, as he kissed the curve of her neck and pressed against her, "but there isn't time for this."

"Maybe you should've considered that before you chose your attire."

"I've been trying to straighten up," she said, "*and* get ready."

He glanced around the room. "I can tell," he teased, sliding his hand around her back and unclasping her bra.

"And I need to shower," she murmured into his shoulder as his other hand slid toward her waistband.

"I can help with that."

"I don't know if *that* will help," she said, laughing. "You'll make us late."

"Not if you're quick," he teased.

"I think you should feed Gus," she whispered, nodding over his shoulder.

Gage glanced back at the dog—who was still lying on a clumped-up rug, watching them. "Good idea," he said, taking a step back. He turned to the big yellow Lab. "Ready for supper?" he asked, and Gus scrambled to his feet and raced, slipping and sliding, toward the kitchen.

Maeve was rinsing her hair when Gage returned. He pulled his T-shirt over his head and dropped his jeans and boxers to the floor. Then he peered around the shower curtain. "I knew there'd be perks to having you move in," he said with a grin.

She rolled her eyes, but when he offered her his beer, she smiled. "Ooh, okay! I love cocktails in the shower!"

She took a sip while cool water splashed over his head and down his broad brown shoulders. Finally, he opened his eyes and gently pulled her against him. "Soo . . . do you want a cocktail . . . or the whole rooster?" he teased with an up-to-no-good smile.

"I want the whole rooster," she said, setting the beer on the shower shelf and reaching for him. "And that reminds me," she said, looking serious. "There was a fox in the yard this morning."

He pulled back. "Really?"

She nodded. "It was stalking the hens, and if Pilgrim didn't start raising holy hell, I think it would've gotten one."

"Wow! I wonder if I should keep them penned in for a while."

"It might be a good idea—now that it knows they're here, it'll probably come back."

Gage nodded thoughtfully. He hated to keep the hens cooped up, especially with summer coming, but he didn't know how else to keep them safe. "Hmm, I'll have to think about that . . . but, in the meantime," he said, gently backing her against the shower wall, "this rooster's raising holy hell, too."

"I can tell," she murmured into his kiss, as he lifted her off the shower floor and slowly lowered her down. "Damn," she whispered, closing her eyes and feeling him push deep inside her, the water cascading all around them.

Fifteen minutes later, they were laughing and hurrying toward the truck with Gus watching from his perch on the couch in front of the window, and the hens and rooster clucking safely in the henhouse.

"So which brother am I meeting?" Maeve asked.

"Chase," Gage answered, as he put the truck in gear.

"And where does he fall in the order of royalty succession?"

"Last," Gage said. "He's the youngest." He paused thoughtfully. "Let's see, he is ten years younger than me, so he must be twenty-six."

"What's he doing in Savannah?"

"He didn't say—just that he was gonna be in town if I . . . *we* . . . wanted to get together."

Maeve nodded, her stomach suddenly twisting into a knot as she thought about the obituary she'd found that morning. She looked out the window, wanting to ask Gage about Cale, aching to know what had happened.

Gage looked over again. "There's something I should tell you, though . . ."

Maeve's heart pounded—*did Gage know, somehow, that she'd found the obituary? Had she not put his Bible back in the right spot? Had something else fallen out that she hadn't noticed?*

"Chase is bringing a friend," he began. "I've never met him before—in fact, I haven't seen Chase in a couple of years."

"Okay," Maeve said. "Honestly, I'm just looking forward to meeting someone from your family."

"Good," Gage said. "I just didn't want you to be surprised . . . or wonder."

"Hey! You know me—I'm easy," she said.

"Mm-hmm," Gage replied, eyeing her skeptically as they passed through the campus of the Savannah College of Art and Design.

"Your old stomping grounds," Maeve observed, looking out the window.

"Yep," Gage said, glancing up at the darkened window of an apartment overlooking Liberty Street. "Anyway, Chase has had a hard time because our dad . . . well . . . he hasn't really been . . ."—he paused, trying to think of the right word—"receptive."

Maeve nodded uncertainly. Suddenly, she wasn't sure what Gage was trying to say. *His brother was bringing a friend to dinner. . . .*

*What did that have to do with their dad?* She gazed out at famous Forsyth Park. At least she was getting to meet one of his brothers, and maybe she would learn more about Gage. It was like watching an onion being peeled back, layer by layer.

Gage pulled into a parking garage on Liberty Street, and as they hurried toward his former place of employment, the Savannah Distillery Ale House—a hip craft beer and cocktail bar—he reached for her hand. "The Distillery," as it was better known, was in an old brick building in Elbert Square—one of the original wards of historic downtown Savannah. Even though it hadn't always been a bar—it had once been a pharmacy, and then, a furniture store—it did have roots in alcohol production. From 1904 to 1907 the building had been home to the Louisville and Kentucky Distilling Companies, and during the Temperance movement—when *all* the spirits in Savannah were being dumped in the streets—bathtub gin and beer were still being distilled and brewed upstairs.

They came around the corner and Maeve saw two young men sitting at an outdoor table under a red café umbrella. There was no mistaking Gage's younger brother. Slender and tan with short blond hair, Chase Tennyson looked like a younger version of Gage, and when he saw them coming, he stood to greet them. He was wearing faded jeans, a slim-fitting button-down oxford with sleeves rolled to his forearms, and stylish Ray-Ban sunglasses.

"Hey, big bro," Chase said, grinning as he gave Gage a hug.

"Hey, yourself," Gage said. "When the hell did you get so tall?"

Chase laughed and then propped his sunglasses on top of his head. Eye contact, Maeve noted, and then realized he had the same pale blue eyes as his brother. "So, is this the famous Maeve—the girl who's finally stolen my big brother's heart?" he teased.

"This is," Maeve said, laughing and shaking his extended hand, surprised that he knew her name. "It's really nice to meet you, Chase."

"It's really nice to meet you, too," he said, and then he turned and gestured to his friend. "This is Liam . . . Liam Evans."

Liam smiled, revealing perfectly straight white teeth, and shook their hands, too. Like Chase, he was stylishly dressed but had short dark hair and wasn't quite as tall, and instead of Ray-Bans, he wore expensive Maui Jims, making Maeve wonder what in the world they did for a living.

"It's great to meet you, Liam," Gage said, smiling. Then he looked over his brother's shoulder at their table.

"We were a little early," Chase said, "so we thought we'd try a couple of their beers."

"Which ones?" Gage asked, all too familiar with The Distillery's offerings.

"I'm having Wild Heaven and . . ." Chase looked at Liam and frowned. "Which one did you get?"

Liam smiled. "Let There Be Light."

Gage nodded approvingly.

"So, do you want to sit out here?" Chase asked. "Or we can see if there's a table inside . . ."

Gage looked questioningly at Maeve, and she smiled. "It's a beautiful night," she said. "Outside would be nice."

"Perfect," Chase said, pulling out a chair for her. "Dinner is on us, by the way," he added with a smile that immediately tugged on her heartstrings.

# 18

Mason watched his classmates pump the keg, fill their cups with foamy beer, and then wander off unsteadily. He wasn't a drinker. Occasionally, he sipped a beer, but it was only when one was thrust into his hand by a teammate—like tonight. He didn't care for the taste, and he didn't like the feeling it gave him. *What was the point of numbing your senses? Of not being completely present?*

Growing up, he'd never seen his mom drink. She'd rarely even gone out, and when she did, she was famous for having a cup of black coffee. One time he'd asked her why she never dated anyone, and she made a goofy face that told him it was a ridiculous question, and said, "Because my favorite date is right in my living room!" Mason had rolled his eyes, but he knew it was true—his mom enjoyed his company, and he enjoyed hers. They could almost always be found at home together—she in her favorite chair, the one that had been his grandmother's, and he, stretched out on the couch—both with their noses in books, perfectly content just knowing the other was nearby. And if they weren't reading, they were watching the History channel or a program on PBS. Recently, Laurie had subscribed to a video-on-demand service that streamed British TV shows, and they'd become instantly hooked on *Midsomer Murders* and *As Time Goes By*. They also binge-watched all the episodes of their perennial favorite, *Keeping Up Appearances*, laughing, over root beer floats, as snooty Hyacinth Bucket tried to prove her social superiority. For musical entertainment, there was an old upright piano in the corner that was regularly tuned. Laurie had started teaching Mason how to play it when he was eight, but by the time he was ten, he had far surpassed her skill level and usually played the more complex parts of the duets for Gershwin's "I Got Rhythm" and "Someone to Watch Over Me." It was also their tradition to take turns playing every Christmas carol they could think of while drinking eggnog . . . and laughing all the way!

Mason sat in one of the beach chairs that a classmate had vacated, leaned back, and watched the orange sparks from the bonfire shoot up into the night sky. Sue had taken his mom back to the hospital right after graduation, and when he'd stopped by to see her later that afternoon, she'd been sleeping. Now, as he listened to the celebration going on all around him—the laughter of classmates who had decided to go for a swim mixed with the country music drifting from a nearby radio—he watched everyone dancing on the sand with drinks in their hands . . . and felt completely out of place. *What was he doing here when his mom was in the hospital?* Suddenly, he felt hands gently cover his eyes, and he heard a whisper in his ear that said, "Guess who?" He smiled, put his hands over Ali's, and pulled her in front of him, spilling the beer in the cupholder of the chair.

"Look out!" she said, laughing as she pulled him away from the deluge. "Come dance with me!" she pressed, but Mason just stood there, shaking his head.

Ali frowned. "C'mon," she said, pulling him. "You only live once . . . and you have a reason to celebrate—you're the salutatorian!" As she said this, Kenny Chesney's "Summertime" started to play, and someone turned the radio up, and everyone started to sing. Mason smiled sadly—even though his heart wasn't in it, he let Ali pull him into the circle of their friends. He looked around at all the kids he'd grown up with and felt overwhelmed with bittersweet emotions—this was it. They would never be together like this again, united in their accomplishments, but all preparing to take different paths.

As the song ended, he felt his phone vibrate and he pulled it out and looked at the screen. He had just missed a call from Mrs. Harrison. He frowned. *Why was she calling him*? A second later, it pinged, alerting him to a message. Mason walked away from the noise and into the darkness so he could listen to her message, but her words made his heart pound: *Mason, come to the hospital as soon as you can!*

# 19

Gage woke with a start and listened, certain he'd heard a sound outside, but all he heard was a summer breeze rustling the curtains. He found Maeve's hand under the sheets and gently squeezed it. She murmured and stirred, but didn't wake. He lay still, trying to fall back asleep, but the events of the evening before began to swirl in his mind. Finally, he got up, almost tripping over Gus as he made his way to the kitchen. He filled a glass with water, and as he drank it, his eyes fell on the bottle of whiskey Chase had given him. He picked it up and studied the label—it was an expensive, commemorative bottle celebrating Jack Daniel's 150th anniversary, and instead of the usual 80 proof, this bottle of the Lynchburg-crafted amber liquid was 100 proof. Gage hadn't had a glass of Old Number 7 in years, but Chase—when he'd handed it to him—had said, "This is for when you have something special to celebrate, or when times get tough . . . as they often do . . . or if you just can't sleep." With a smile, he had added, "No ice. Just neat."

"Son," Gage had said, eyeing him, "I tended bar for ten years. You don't need to tell me how to drink my whiskey."

His little brother had laughed. "Just making sure."

Gage broke the seal as he twisted the top off and sniffed—yep, it would definitely help him sleep. He leaned against the counter and thought about the number of drinks Chase and Liam had had during dinner. They'd started off with one of The Distillery's craft beers, and while they had waited for dinner to arrive, they each tried the craft cocktail he'd suggested—Sweet Georgia Peach, a peach vodka, iced tea, and lemon concoction. Maeve had loved the drink, but per usual, she only had one—she never had more than one, and he had never even seen her slightly tipsy. But the boys—as he and Maeve had started calling them—had switched back to beer during dinner, and declining dessert, followed up with tumblers of whiskey. *If I drank that much,* he thought, *I wouldn't be able to function!*

Gage—who'd left home when Chase was only eight—wondered what experiences his brother had endured to make him reach for a glass of whiskey. Gage had heard from their mom that he'd had a hard time in high school, but she'd never gone into detail—even when pressed. It was only recently that he'd learned from their brother, Matt, that Chase was gay—a revelation, Matt said, that had nearly sent their father into orbit. Gage wasn't surprised by this news, or by their father's reaction. Chase had always been a quiet, sensitive kid, and although Gage had no problem with it—believing that *everyone* was created in God's image and that the message of the New Testament was entirely about love and acceptance—he knew their father's interpretation of the Bible was absolute and literal. He'd often heard his dad tell jokes that weren't kind, and he knew he'd stopped going to church when the congregation decided to be open and affirming. There was no gray area in Jack Tennyson's interpretation of the Bible . . . *and* there was no arguing about it. Gage was certain that, when Chase had finally found the courage to be open about the person God created him to be, their father had been more concerned about what people thought of *him* than about how his youngest son *felt*.

*It must have been hard for Chase*, Gage thought, but he could certainly relate. After he'd told their father he didn't want to be tied down to the farm, his father had barely looked at him. And after their sweet Ayrshire cow Chestnut—with whom Gage had won so many blue ribbons—had died giving birth to a little stillborn calf, his dad hadn't spoken to him for weeks. Later that fall, his mom had finally been able to convince him to let Gage apply to art school, but the tension between father and son had continued to grow.

The following summer, their fragile relationship was shattered when tragedy struck. After a heavy rain, Cale had been out in the field, helping their dad free a tractor that was stuck in the mud. He'd hooked one end of a rusty chain to the immobile tractor while Jack had hooked the other to the hitch of a second tractor, but just as Jack had begun to put tension on the old chain, it had snapped, sliced through the air like a whip, and struck Cale in the chest. Jack had looked back in horror as his son crumpled to the ground, and then scrambled to his side, shouting for help. He'd frantically administered CPR, but when he couldn't revive him, he just cradled him in his arms and sobbed. Later, the doctor said there was only one tiny pink mark in the middle of Cale's chest—the chain hadn't even broken his skin, but it had instantly stopped his heart.

Jack had been despondent, blaming himself, but Gage, who was enduring his own staggering grief, fully believed—because his father wouldn't even look at him—that he wished *he'd* been the son who had been helping him in the field . . . and *he'd* been the son who'd died. At least, then, the son his father loved most . . . the son who loved the farm most, would still be alive.

And then there was Chase. *Damn!* Gage thought. *The manure must've really hit the fan! Yep, things definitely hadn't turned out the way Jack Tennyson planned . . . and it served him right!*

Gage reached into the back of the cabinet for a tumbler—one of two he'd taken as parting gifts from The Distillery. He poured two fingers, and then, because life was complicated, drizzled in a third. "Neat," he said, smiling at Gus when he appeared at his side, hoping that his master would be having a cookie with his whiskey. Gage chuckled. "You're silly," he said softly, tousling the dog's velvet ears. Then he reached into the ceramic canister full of dog treats and added, "Let's go out on the porch where it's cooler."

Gage settled into one of the Adirondack chairs, and while Gus clumped to the floor at his feet—happily chomping on his midnight snack—he swirled the amber liquid, took a sip, and felt the heat trickle down his throat. He looked up at the stars, and the memory of the first time he'd had Jack Daniel's—triggered by the warm sensation in his belly—suddenly came back to him, a memory he thought he'd pushed away for good. It was the summer he'd turned eighteen—the summer before Cale died.

It hadn't taken long for heads to turn the summer River Jordan Raines had moved into the parsonage next to the church. She had corn-silk blond hair and eyes the color of jade—or the color of a John Deere tractor, as all the farm boys joked. Her long, tan legs were barely covered by her tattered denim cutoffs—so short Libby Tennyson wondered out loud, "Why bother?" Her full, perky breasts made all the country boys' hearts skip a beat, but River had eyes for only one country boy—at least, in the beginning.

The youngest daughter of Pastor Tommy Raines—the new minister—and his wife Leigh, River was a preacher's kid, and like every other "PK," she got away with murder. Mischievous as a youngster, and seductive as a teen, River knew instinctively how to set the proverbial tender teenage trap, so when she first spied Gage, dripping with sweat as he tossed hay bales into wagons, the cogs in her mind started turning. Soon after, River saw him picking up supplies at the feedstore in town, and as she walked past him, she cast an alluring spell: "My, those feed bags look heavy," she called, and poor Gage, a red-blooded teenage boy with raging hormones, took the bait—hook, line, and sinker. "She may be the daughter of a minister," Libby warned her brooding artistic son, "but she is trouble!" Unfortunately, Gage barely heard his mom's cautionary words—he was already head over heels.

"That boy is being led around by his testicles," Jack observed one night when he saw the young couple walking through the dairy barn at the fair, hand in hand. And it was true: Gage's testicles were *fully* involved—especially when River led *him* to a secluded spot overlooking the fair. River had pointed to the dark hillside from the top of the Ferris wheel. "Let's go up there."

Gage had nodded—they'd been seeing each other all summer, and he would have climbed Mount Everest if she'd asked him to. They got off the Ferris wheel, ditched their friends, and wandered through the food booths, the scent reminding him they hadn't eaten, but oddly, he wasn't hungry. "Want anything?" he asked.

"Just you," she teased, pulling him away.

They walked up an old bridle path to the top of the hill and looked back at the lights of the fair. They could hear the escalating and sliding music of the games, the screams and laughter of people on rides, the announcer at the tractor pull—calling the names of the contestants and measurements of their draws—and they could hear the country band on stage covering an old Patsy Cline song. The sky above them sparkled with stars, while the fair below sparkled with dazzling colors, shooting and spiraling everywhere.

"It's so beautiful," River murmured. "I wish summer would never end," she added, and then slid a half pint of Jack Daniel's out of the back pocket of her tight shorts, took a sip, and ran her tongue seductively around the top of the bottle.

"What are you trying to do to me, girl?" Gage asked, laughing as he pulled her close.

"What do you think I'm trying to do to you?" she murmured, handing him the bottle.

Gage took a long swig, felt the surge of heat burn his throat, and then searched her eyes intently as she reached down, unzipped his jeans, and slid her hands inside. He closed his eyes, feeling the blood surging to his groin. "What do you want?" he whispered.

"You," she said softly, pushing his jeans down and freeing his rock-hard erection.

He barely breathed as she knelt in front of him. "Damn," he whispered, running his fingers through her hair, and then just when he didn't think he could last another second, she slid her lips away.

"Watch," she commanded, and he'd opened his eyes and watched her slide down her shorts.

"Are you sure about this?" he asked, trying to think clearly, "because I don't have any protec—"

She put her finger on his lips. "Shhh . . ."

Gage swallowed, unable to form a coherent thought as he lay on the grass beside her, kissing her lips hungrily, exploring her body, and feeling her fingers stroking him where her lips had just been, and then in one easy motion, she slid on top of him.

One week later, on a Sunday night after youth group, Gage had been looking for her behind the parsonage when he'd heard whispering and giggling. He'd quickly stepped into the shadows, and in the fading light, saw her leaning against the barn, her blouse unbuttoned, kissing Jimmy Thompson. He'd stared in disbelief, and then backed away, clenching his jaw *and* his fists.

Now, as he swirled his whiskey, he realized he still hadn't put it completely behind him. Even though it was a long time ago, he'd never forgotten the way it had made him feel. He'd been just a kid, and she'd broken his heart. Forever after, he'd been wary of relationships . . . of falling in love. And when he did go out with other women, the memory of that night always seemed to cast a shadow over any possibility of a future. It was because of this, that none of his relationships had lasted. Finally, he'd resigned himself to a lifetime of being single . . . that is, until he met Maeve. Maeve's kind smile and stunning blue-green eyes had stopped him in his tracks. She had never pressured him about anything—even when he was admittedly evasive about his family—and she always gave him space when he needed it. She laughed at his dumb jokes and she loved to tease him, but always in a friendly way. She was kind to everyone she met, especially her newly adopted niece and the old coots at the senior home where she worked. She was genuine and honest and had a strong faith in God. And aside from snoring occasionally, he thought with a smile, she was pretty perfect. He was even thinking about asking her to marry him. If there was any woman on earth he'd love to spend his life with, it was Maeve. *Of course, I'll have to talk to her parents first!*

He took another sip, and his thoughts turned to his own family. Over the years, he'd managed to stop by and see them a few times—always when he knew his dad would be away—but he still missed them . . . especially his grandfather, Dutch. He so badly wanted them to meet Maeve, and he knew she wanted to meet them. He'd loved introducing her to Chase, and he especially wanted his mom to meet her . . . but he didn't care if he ever saw his father again. He could just see the *I-told-you-so* look on his face, and he knew he would make a comment about working construction, pointing out that it was manual labor just like working on a farm. *Yeah, there was no way he was ever going to give him the satisfaction.*

He lifted the tumbler to his lips and realized it was almost empty. *Damn, that went down easy. . . . No wonder buried emotions are resurfacing and old stream-of-conscious memories are running rampant through my mind.* He thought of the letter his mom had sent . . . the one in the blue envelope . . . the one he'd almost thrown away . . . and then the words his brother had said earlier that night echoed in his head: *Dad's not doing well, Gage. You should go see him.*

Gage threw back the last of his drink and shook his head. "Yeah . . . tha's not happenin'," he slurred bitterly.

# 20

"Want me to go with you?" Ali asked, as Mason hurried to his car.

"No, you should stay here and have fun. Celebrate with everyone else."

"Mason," she said, "there's no way I'm going to have fun if you're not here. Especially if . . ." She didn't know how to finish her sentence, so she stopped. "I'm going with you," she said with conviction, following him to his car and opening the passenger door.

Mason blinked back tears as he pulled out of the parking lot.

"Slow down," Ali implored, as she texted her mom. She stared at the screen, waiting for her to reply, but there was no sign that her mom was writing back. "What exactly did she say?"

"To come as soon as I can."

Ali swallowed. *Why would her mom leave such a cryptic message?*

The hospital was fifteen minutes away, but they made it in ten, and as they hurried toward the entrance, Ali's phone chimed and she looked at the screen. "Your mom is in a different room—it's on the third floor . . . she's been moved into the . . ." Ali stopped reading because the next words her mom had written were *hospice unit.*

"She's been moved into *where*?" Mason asked, looking over.

Ali swallowed. "A room on the third floor."

Mason didn't even stop at the security desk, and because the guards had seen him so often and knew his mom wasn't well, they didn't stop him. He pushed the button, and they waited, watching the light indicate the elevator's slow descent, seeming to stop at every floor. "I'm taking the stairs," Mason said finally, turning away in frustration. He and Ali—because their moms both worked there—were very familiar with all the different halls and doorways, and he pulled open the heavy metal door and took the steps two at a time with Ali at his heels. They reached the nurses' station, and Mason immediately recognized one of his mom's friends.

"Hi, Mrs. Carroll, do you know which room my mom is in?"

The older woman looked up and saw Mason. "Oh, Mason, dear," she said, getting up to give him a hug, but Mason was already backing down the hall. "Your sweet mom is in room 310," she said, gesturing behind him. "It's the last one on the right."

"Thank you," Mason said, sprinting down the hall.

Ali watched him go, and then searched the woman's kind eyes. "How is she?" she asked quietly, but Sally Carroll just pressed her lips together and shook her head.

Ali nodded, tears springing to her eyes.

"*Your* mom is with her."

Ali brushed back her tears as she walked down the hall. Mason had been right—his mom had been hanging on until he graduated. She peered around the door and saw him standing next to the bed holding her hand while her own mom looked on. Sue looked up, saw Ali in the doorway, and got up. "I'll be right outside, Mason," she said. Mason nodded and sat on the edge of the bed.

"Hey, hon," Laurie said weakly, and even though her breathing was labored, she mustered a smile. "You did such an awesome job today."

Mason bit his lip, tears welling up in his eyes. "You shouldn't have come," he said. "It was too much . . . it took too much out of you."

Laurie shook her head. "I wouldn't have missed it for the world," she whispered. "I loved it. I loved everything you said."

Mason shook his head and tears spilled down his cheeks. "I need you, Mom," he whispered, his voice choked with emotion.

Laurie squeezed his hand. "Mason, I love you more than you'll ever know, and I will always be with you." As she said this, she reached up and touched the middle of his chest. "Right here. I'll be watching over you—just like in that old song you love so much."

Mason swallowed and shook his head. "Please don't leave," he whispered.

Laurie reached up and gently brushed away his tears. "You are an amazing young man, and you're going to be an amazing pilot . . . and I'm going to be with you on every flight, making sure you're doing it right," she teased with a grin.

Mason bit his lip, feeling his heart break. "Oh, God, I can't do this," he cried in anguish.

"I know it hurts, sweetie, but it won't always feel like this. When your grandpa and grandma died, I thought I was gonna die, too . . . but I didn't. . . . And then *you* came along and filled my heart with more love than I ever thought I could feel. That's how life is. . . ."

She winced in pain, and Mason squeezed her hand. "I love you so much, Mom," he whispered, his voice barely audible.

"I love you, too, Mason." Her eyes brightened. "Don't forget your promise . . ."

Mason shook his head. "*You* are my mom," he said defiantly. "Nothing is ever going to change that."

"I know, sweetheart. I would never want that to change. I just want you to try."

He shook his head slowly, trying to understand.

"Promise me?" she said, eyeing him.

He nodded solemnly, and she touched his cheek. "You're the best son a mom could ever ask for, Mason. You've blessed my life with so much joy and light and love."

"You're the best mom," he whispered, his vision blurred by tears. "You've blessed my life more than you'll ever know."

She smiled and squeezed his hand, and then her breathing slowed.

"Oh, God," Mason cried out.

Hearing him, Sue hurried into the room and put her arms around him while Ali stood by, watching.

"Oh, Mason, hon," she whispered, realizing her friend's life was slipping away. "I'm so sorry." But Mason just sobbed inconsolably, his shoulders sagging with grief.

# 21

"MAYBE YOU'RE DEHYDRATED," MAEVE OFFERED WHEN GAGE CAME INTO the kitchen the next morning, rubbing his temples.

"Maybe," he said, reaching for the Tylenol. He shook a couple of capsules into his hand, popped them in his mouth, and downed them with the rest of his coffee. Then he kissed the top of her head. "Thanks for making my lunch," he said, picking up his cooler. "Love you."

"Love you, too. Feel better."

"Thanks." He stepped out into the summer heat with Gus happily trotting beside him, and as he glanced at the Adirondack chair in which he'd been sitting just six hours ago, he shook his aching head.

Maeve poured a cup of coffee and watched him pull away. Gage had mentioned not being able to sleep, but she hadn't even noticed him missing from their bed. She had slept like a rock, risen early, caught up on her morning devotionals, showered, and made lunch for both of them, and she still had a half hour before she had to leave for work. She toasted an English muffin, spread it with some homemade marmalade she found in the fridge, sat down at the kitchen table, and opened her laptop. With everything going on the last few days—the picnic at Macey's, packing up her apartment, moving in with Gage, unpacking, and going out to dinner with Gage's brother—she hadn't even had time to check her email.

She clicked on her Facebook page and slowly scrolled through her newsfeed—smiling and "liking" posts. She wasn't a huge fan of social media. She enjoyed seeing what her friends were up to, but it sometimes made her feel a little jealous. They all seemed to be living lives that were much more exciting—and perfect—than hers. They posted photos of themselves in all kinds of amazing places—from long sandy Caribbean beaches to the breathtaking sights and summits of national parks. They posted photos of artistically plated food and frosty craft cocktails with comments like *It's all in the presentation!* . . . and they posted photos of their families. When she did find time to go on Facebook or Instagram, she usually found herself scrolling past photos of cute kids doing amazing things—winning games, holding up trophies, going to proms, *and* hugging their moms. All the fun and love in their lives made her feel oddly sad, and sometimes, for her own mental health, she just had to avoid it. She wanted these things, too, and she often had to remind herself how lucky and blessed she was to have the wonderful family she *did* have, including sweet Harper—who'd brought light and love and laughter to all their lives—but Maeve would love to have a child (or three) of her own someday. The one time she and Gage had talked about children, she'd teasingly said, "A whole tribe!" but he'd only smiled and said, "*Maybe* one or two." She'd found it ironic that he—who'd come from a family with six kids—only wanted two, and she—who'd come from a family with *only* two—wanted more. Now, here they were, both almost thirty-six and they weren't even engaged. A family was beginning to seem less and less likely.

She was just about to close her laptop when the notification of a new friend request popped up. She clicked on it and discovered it was from Chase. Without hesitation, she confirmed him, and then curiously clicked to his page. There he was, the handsome young man she'd met the previous night, and although he absolutely *looked* like Gage, their personalities were very different. Chase was much more easygoing, and his style of dress was definitely trendier than Gage's casual, faded Levi's and T-shirts . . . *and* with those classy sunglasses, he looked like he should be a model. In the large background picture behind his profile picture, he and Liam were standing shirtless and tan—Chase's hair so blond it looked white—on the deck of a gorgeous wooden sailboat floating on clear blue-green water. It was a stunning photo, and she clicked on it to see if he'd added a location. There in the sidebar were the words: *Finally . . . Mykonos!* Inclusion of the word *finally* made her think it had been a destination they'd wanted to visit for a long time, but she had never even heard of it. She googled "Mykonos," and when images of a lovely Mediterranean island appeared, she found herself nodding approvingly. "Nice," she murmured. "I would *love* to go to Greece someday."

She scrolled through Chase's timeline and saw photos of all kinds of exotic places, and it suddenly dawned on her that they'd never talked, last night, about what Chase and Liam did for a living—just that they lived in DC and owned their own business. "Sheesh, Chase, what the heck *do* you do?" she murmured. She clicked on his bio and discovered that he and Liam owned their own travel agency, and when she clicked on the link to their website, she realized their agency specialized in LGBTQ-friendly destinations. She'd never even considered there might be places that wouldn't be friendly, but he and Liam had obviously found a need and filled it—that's what you do when you have an entrepreneurial spirit. She scrolled through the pictures, looking at all the lovely destinations. Yep, Chase was definitely a millennial—sophisticated, tech savvy, *and* worldly!

Gage, on the other hand, had very little interest in technology. He had an iPhone, but that was it, and he only used it for texting, calls, and listening to music. She'd tried to tell him that having a website might help him get into a gallery, but he was leery of putting his personal info online. He was only ten years older than Chase, but he seemed to be from a previous generation when it came to technology.

She took a bite of her English muffin and licked her lips,

savoring the sweetness of the marmalade. "Oh, my goodness, this is really good," she murmured, and then, feeling like an unrepentant snoop, clicked on the left side of Chase's page to see *all* of his photos. As she scrolled through them, she told herself she wasn't trolling or stalking. She was just *interested*. She scrolled past an old photo of all six brothers standing in front of a sign that had TENNESSEE TENNYSON DAIRY FARM painted on it. She clicked on the picture and studied the larger version that popped up. It looked just like the photo that she'd seen in the newspaper clipping about Cale's accident. In it, Gage looked to be about seventeen, which meant the little towhead on the far end must've been around seven. She looked at the description to the right of the picture and realized that all the brothers except Cale and Gage had been tagged—which meant they all had Facebook pages, too—and the name of the farm was also highlighted in blue, which meant it also had a page. *What a gold mine!* she thought. She clicked on the farm's Facebook page, and found herself looking into the soulful brown eyes of several cows. Behind them was a big white barn. As she scanned the page, she realized the farm also had a website *and* an online store! *Why hadn't she thought of looking the farm up before?* Of course, they'd have an online presence—they were a brand with a following. She was just about to click on the website when she heard a loud ruckus outside and looked out the window. Pilgrim was squawking and flapping his wings frantically inside the fenced-in area around the coop. Maeve pushed back her chair, knocking it over, and flew outside just in time to see the fox pulling itself through a hole under the fence with one of the hens in its mouth.

"Nooo!" she screamed, running toward it, but the fox just stared at her and then raced off with the hen still clutched in its jaws.

"Dammit!" Maeve shouted, tears springing to her eyes. She stared up at the blue summer sky. "Why?" she asked angrily. "Why did you let that happen? It was just a sweet little hen."

She clenched her fists, not knowing what to do, and then pulled out her phone to call Gage. She tapped his number and waited, but he was either driving or didn't hear his phone because he didn't answer. She left a message and reluctantly hung up, and then opened the gate into the pen and tried to console the rooster and two remaining hens. Pilgrim was still strutting around, squawking anxiously while the poor hens were in the back corner of the coop, clucking nervously. "It's okay," she said softly. "It's gone." Maeve felt terrible—*but how did she know the fox wouldn't come back?* The defenseless chickens were easy prey and the fox knew it. She stepped back out, closed the gate, found several big stones, and piled them in and around the hole, and then walked back to the cabin. She finished her coffee, closed her laptop, grabbed her lunch, and glancing one last time at the henhouse, prayed they'd be okay.

# 22

HOLDING A FOIL-COVERED PLATE, MAEVE KNOCKED ON THE LAST DOOR AT the end of the hall. Even though Bud Hawkins had been with them for more than two weeks, he still preferred having dinner in his apartment.

"It's open," he called.

She turned the knob, pushed open the door, and peered in. "I brought your dinner," she announced cheerily.

"Thank you," he replied from his recliner. "You can leave it on the table."

Maeve walked over and set the plate on the table. "It's roast beef and gravy with mashed potatoes," she said, "so don't let it get cold."

"I can warm it up."

Even though he was gazing out his sliding glass doors and not looking at her, Maeve nodded. But then she spoke: "Sal knows you like it rare, so don't warm it up too much."

Bud didn't answer, and Maeve saw something flutter past his sliding door. She stepped forward for a closer look and realized he'd hung a small bird feeder from the branch of the dogwood tree next to his patio. "You put up a bird feeder?" she asked in surprise.

He nodded. "It didn't take 'em long to find it, either."

She stood next to him, watching the little flock, chirping and swooping in from the branches to the feeder. There were finches, titmice, chickadees, nuthatches, and woodpeckers. There was even a female cardinal. "You know what they say about cardinals, don't you?" she asked.

He shook his head, watching the female hop around on the patio picking up seeds the finches had dropped.

"They say a cardinal represents a loved one who's passed, and they appear when you miss them the most and need reassurance that they're near and always with you."

"I didn't know that," he said, smiling. "Thank you for telling me." He looked back at the little female cardinal, and she stopped what she was doing and cocked her head. "Look at that," he said. "Ethel used to give me a look like that when she was teasing me."

"There you go," Maeve said, smiling. "She's keeping an eye on you."

He laughed. "That would be just like her."

Maeve marveled at the cardinal's appearance on his patio—she had heard this lore many times over the years but had never actually witnessed it. "I have a few minutes," she said. Even though she knew dinner would be getting under way in the dining room soon, she also felt like this—a possible breakthrough with their newest resident—was more important. "Would it be all right if I stayed for a bit?"

"Of course," he said, gesturing to the couch.

They sat together, watching the birds, and then Maeve looked around the room and noticed what looked like a violin case leaning in the corner. She gestured toward it. "Do you play the violin?"

The old man followed her gaze. "That's a *fiddle* case," he corrected, "and I haven't played it since Ethel got sick. I don't know why I even brought it. I should have given the damn thing away."

Maeve nodded. She wanted him to open up, but she didn't want to pry or upset him. "What's the difference between a violin and a fiddle?"

"The difference is the type of music—you don't play any of that classical stuff on a fiddle."

Maeve smiled. "How long were you and Ethel married?" she ventured softly.

"Sixty-four years," he said, smiling wistfully. "Best damn years of my life. I think there's a picture of her in that box there," he said, pointing to a box at the end of the couch with the word *Pictures* printed on it in black magic marker.

Maeve smiled. "May I look?"

"Oh, sure," he said, waving at it as if it was no big deal, but when she opened the box and lifted out the packing paper, he immediately sat up, his face brightening.

Maeve pulled out a framed picture and carefully unwrapped it. It was a black-and-white photograph of a young Bud wearing his dress uniform and, on his arm, was his lovely bride wearing a beautiful satin wedding dress. "Wow!" she said. "Look at you! And your wife—she's stunning!"

Bud nodded, smiling, and when she handed him the picture, he gazed at it, his eyes glistening. "She was the most beautiful bride . . . and she was so good to me." He looked up. "There're more," he said, motioning to the box.

Maeve nodded and, one by one, she unwrapped and admired all of Bud's photos, handing them to him, asking him questions, and then, at his direction, placing them on empty shelves and tables around the room. Finally, she sat down again. "I just moved, too," she said, "so I know how hard it is."

Bud nodded. "Ethel and I bought our house when we were first married. It was brand-new. After she died, I continued to live there by m'self, but my kids wanted me to move closer, so here I am." He shook his head. "I've been here two weeks and they've only stopped by twice."

"They must be busy. I'm sure they'll stop by when they can."

He shrugged. "They have kids o' their own and they're always goin' somewhere."

Maeve nodded. "Well, the folks upstairs are a lot like a family," she said softly. "Not real family, but they're all very nice and many are widows or widowers, so they know how hard it is. I think you'd like them. Aristides Lincoln was in the navy, too, and I think Landon and Loren Olivetti were in the army."

Bud looked up in surprise. "I didn't know there were other vets here." But then a shadow crossed his face. "I don't need that woman comin' 'round." He shook his head. "She's a piece o' work!"

"You mean Gladys?" Maeve asked.

"I don't know her name, but I am *not* interested!"

Maeve nodded. "You don't need to worry about her. I told her you weren't interested."

"You *did*?"

Maeve nodded. "She understands."

"Some women come on too strong."

"They do," Maeve agreed, and then, hearing a sound, she turned and saw Tallulah peering in and realized she'd left the door open. "Have you met our Tallulah?" she asked.

Bud frowned. "No, who's Tallu . . . ?" he started to ask, but before he could finish, the little orange tiger cat padded across the floor and swished between his legs. "Oh!" he said in surprise. "Is this Tallulah?"

"It is," Maeve replied. "She's our resident hall monitor."

"What a cutie," he said, as Tallulah hopped on his lap and sniffed his chin. He laughed, and she seemed to approve of him, too, because she immediately curled up on his lap. Tallulah then spied the activity going on outside his door and gazed intently at the little flock of birds. "Hmm, I hope she's not a hunter," he said worriedly.

Maeve raised her eyebrows, recalling the scene she'd witnessed two weeks earlier when the fox had taken one of the hens. Gage had been heartbroken, and although he'd reinforced the fence around the coop as soon as he'd gotten home, he continued to worry that it wouldn't keep the fox out, and he felt sorry for the hens because they couldn't roam freely around the yard anymore. She'd also seen rifle ammunition on the counter and asked him about it. "What if the fox has kits it's trying to feed?" she'd asked. "If you kill her—or him—they'll go hungry."

"What do you want me to do?" he'd asked. "Let it eat all the chickens?"

Maeve had sighed. It seemed like there was no easy solution.

Now, she watched Tallulah—who had hopped down and was sitting in front of the door with her tail twitching. Maeve knew she was very adept at catching mice and chipmunks, but she didn't know if she would pose a threat to Bud's little flock of birds. She hoped not—especially the female cardinal! "There's no hunting down here, missy," she warned.

"Well, I should head back," she said, standing. "Are you sure you won't come to dinner? It's not too late—they're probably just starting their salads."

"What about the plate you brought down?"

"I can bring it back up or we can put it in your fridge, and you can have it for lunch tomorrow."

Bud hesitated, considering. He didn't want to have dinner by himself again, but he also didn't want that woman bothering him. "Are you sure that woman won't try to kiss me?"

Maeve suppressed a smile and nodded. "I'm sure."

Bud nodded. "Okay," he agreed. "I'll come up."

"Good!" Maeve said. "I'll walk with you." She picked up the plate. "Shall I put this in your fridge?"

He nodded and reached for his cane and his navy hat. "Lead the way, ma'am," he said with a smile, and they walked side by side with Tallulah darting up the hall ahead of them.

# 23

Mason pulled into the hospital parking lot and looked up at the last window of the room on the third floor. It had been two weeks since his mom had died, and a week since they'd celebrated her life at a memorial service. In that time, Mason had avoided the hospital, taking a longer route home from his summer job on a landscaping crew—a job he'd jumped right back into—but today, he'd arranged to meet Mrs. Harrison at the hospital, so he had no choice. He sat in his car, and looked up at the window of the room in which his mom had died, and the memory of that night—and its aftermath—came rushing back.

It had started raining after he and Ali arrived at the hospital, and it had continued to rain all the next day—it was as if the heavens were joining Mason in his grief. In the early hours of the next day, he'd stood in the lobby with Ali and her mom, sipping the coffee she'd bought for him, and watching it rain. Mrs. Harrison had insisted he come stay with them, but he told her he'd be more comfortable at home and assured her he'd be fine. After all, he'd been living alone for the last two months. Mrs. Harrison hadn't been easily convinced. He knew his mom had probably asked her to look after him, and she was now determined to keep her promise. "Do you want Ali to stay over?" she'd asked, but he'd smiled at Ali and shaken his head. They'd both given him hugs, and when Mrs. Harrison finally, reluctantly, let him go, she made him promise to call if he needed anything, and if he *didn't* need anything, he had to call anyway, just to check in—which he'd done several times, but only when he was sure he didn't sound stuffy from crying.

That first night had been the longest of his life—he hadn't been able to sleep and he'd wandered through the empty house, wondering if he should've taken Mrs. Harrison up on her offer. Being at the house alone had felt completely different because, even though his mom had been in the hospital for the last two months, she'd been alive—and he'd clung to the hope that she'd be coming home eventually—but now, there was nothing to cling to. There was no hope. She was *never* coming home.

When the rain had finally stopped, he'd gone outside and looked up at the stars sparkling in the vast canopy of darkness and wondered if she was watching over him. When he was little, they'd lain together on a blanket in the yard, gazing up at the night sky, and she'd pointed to all the constellations. But the night after she died, he'd looked up at the Big Dipper and felt just as small and insignificant as he had when he was little. He'd also felt torn—he'd wanted her to be there, but he'd been thankful she wasn't suffering anymore. He'd wanted her spirit to be free, but he hadn't wanted to let her go, *and* he'd felt guilty because he'd wanted it to be over because *he* couldn't bear it anymore . . . and then, suddenly, it had ended. "Oh, God. Help me," he'd whispered, looking up at the stars as tears filled his eyes.

The following morning, Mrs. Harrison had picked him up and they'd gone together to take care of the arrangements. Laurie had given her friend ideas for her service, *if they decided to have one . . . because they didn't have to*, but Sue had tearfully said they would absolutely be having one! Laurie had shared some of her favorite hymns, and Sue had dutifully jotted them down, and then Laurie had eyed her friend and said, "Keep it simple and small!"—and that *had* been the plan. But when word got out that Laurie Callahan, just forty-six and a lifelong resident of the little town, daughter of

Lena and Winton "Whiplash" Callahan—not to mention one of the most caring nurses any of them knew—had died, the outpouring of love and support for her son had been overwhelming.

The service had been set for the following Saturday, and the entire town, along with as much hospital staff as could get away without leaving the hospital utterly unmanned, had come out. The church had filled to capacity, and then overflowed. Among the many mourners were all the preemie babies Laurie had cuddled over the years, along with their grateful parents. Mason had looked around in tearful wonder—it was evident that his mom had touched countless lives.

When the service began, a young soloist sang "On Eagle's Wings" and "I Can Only Imagine"—which had left no eyes dry—and then together, they'd sung her favorite hymns, "Here I Am, Lord" and "Lord of the Dance," because, as Mrs. Harrison had said in her eulogy, Laurie had wanted it to be a celebration. She'd gone on to talk about her gentle, kind friend who was a veritable fountain of wisdom, who was authentic to her core . . . and who would be dearly missed. Others were invited to recall fond memories, too, and Mason learned things he'd never known about his mom—like the time she had changed Mr. Franklin's flat tire in the pouring rain, or the time she had rescued a little girl that almost drowned in Blue Ridge Lake. It truly was a celebration of a life well lived, and it left Mason feeling inspired—more than ever—to be just like her. As people left the sanctuary, they'd reached into baskets to take one of the small smooth river stones inscribed with the word *Celebrate*, and everyone had agreed that there wasn't a more appropriate keepsake—Laurie Callahan, lover of nature and books, had, indeed, embraced and celebrated life.

After the reception—which had been held in Fellowship Hall, and for which the women of the church had baked all week—Mrs. Harrison had tried again to get Mason to stay with them, but he'd declined. He'd gone home, pulled off his jacket and tie, closed his weary eyes, and replayed all the kind words and funny stories he'd heard, and then he recalled all the things she'd said to him in the days before she died. Finally, he'd reached for her Bible, opened the cover, and looked at the picture of him as a toddler, laughing as he took his first steps toward her . . . and then he'd studied the second photo of the girl with copper hair holding the tiny baby. He'd stared at it, wondering . . . and then he'd suddenly known what he wanted to do.

Now, as he sat in his car in the hospital parking lot, looking up at the third-floor window, he decided he wasn't going to wallow in grief and anguish. He knew his mom wouldn't want that. It was time to start honoring her life. He climbed out and walked through the main door into the lobby. He didn't stop at the elevator, but took the stairs, two at a time, and found Mrs. Harrison waiting for him outside the conference room where they were having an orientation class for the new NICU volunteers. She gave him a hug and tousled his red hair. "Your mom would love this."

# 24

MAEVE CLOSED THE BOOK IN HER LAP AND LOOKED OVER AT HARPER. "So, what did you think?"

Harper sighed contentedly and stroked Keeper's soft fur. "It was awesome. I love how they didn't tell anyone that Colin was getting better so he could surprise his father."

"It's amazing what a little positive energy and positive thinking will do," Maeve said.

Harper nodded.

"Mary was quite a character. She started off being ornery and grouchy, but she really turned around."

"She did," Harper agreed. "Colin did, too. I loved all the animals, especially that little robin who showed Mary where the key was."

"That robin loved having them working on the garden and keeping her company."

"She did," Harper agreed. "She liked when they turned over the soil because it helped her find bugs and worms." She smiled. "But I still like Dickon the best."

"Still remind you of Sam?" Maeve teased, raising her eyebrows.

"Yeah," she nodded. "I miss him . . . *and* Rudy." It had been nearly a month since she'd seen Rudy. Rudy was the daughter of her caseworker at DFCS, Cora Grant—the wonderful lady who'd jumped through hoops to find a home for her. Harper had spent so much time at their house—because she'd been kicked out of so many other homes—that she and Rudy had grown as close as sisters, and when Harper had finally been adopted by Ben and Macey, the two friends had vowed to stay close.

"I'm sure you can have them over sometime," Maeve said. "And before you know it, you'll be back in school and you'll see Sam every day."

"When does school start?" Harper asked.

"Middle of August, I think."

"Sheesh, summer just started."

"I know," Maeve said. "Summer always flies by."

Harper nodded and then frowned. "That reminds me—I'm supposed to sleep over at Rudy's next weekend, sooo . . . no book club."

"What?!" Maeve teased. "I already picked up our next book at the library."

"You *did*? What is it?"

"It's a surprise."

"Tell me! I won't read it!" Harper said. "That would ruin everything."

"Okay, so long as you promise."

Harper rolled her eyes, waiting, but Maeve didn't say anything. "Well?"

"It's called '*Because of Winn-Dixie*.'"

Harper frowned, thinking. "What's it about?"

"It's about a girl and a dog."

"Is there a movie?"

"There is," Maeve confirmed, "which reminds me! If we're gonna watch *this* movie, we better get started."

Harper nodded. "I'm gonna have another slice of pizza. You want one?"

"Sure," Maeve said, opening her laptop to find the movie online. "Do you want me to heat them up?"

"No," Harper said, gently lifting Keeper's head off her lap, and getting up and stretching. "I can do it."

Two minutes later, she came back with two warmed-up slices of pizza and handed one to Maeve. "I wish I had a secret garden, Aunt Maeve."

"Gardens . . . *and* gardening can definitely be therapeutic," Maeve said, thinking about all the weeding she'd been doing since she'd moved in with Gage. It had become her new pastime. Weeding made her feel honest, and it kept her out of trouble. Mainly, it kept her from snooping around the internet for more information about the Tennyson family because she'd decided she wanted to wait for Gage to share *when* he was ready. He'd introduced her to Chase and that was a step in the right direction. Besides, she didn't want to be dishonest—she already had enough skeletons. "Gage has some lovely gardens," she said with a smile, "but he hates to weed."

"I'll help you weed," Harper offered hopefully.

"You don't think you'd get bored?"

She shook her head. "I'd love it," she said, taking a bite of her pizza. "Is Gage gonna get more chickens?"

"Funny you should ask," Maeve said, clicking on the movie, "because he's picking up two new chicks tomorrow."

"He is?!" Harper asked. "Can I go?"

"If you want to," Maeve answered, thinking about their plans for the next day. "And then you can come over and help weed."

"Can we plant something, too?"

"Sure! We can pick up some plants when we're at Agway."

"Yes!" Harper said, pumping her fist.

Maeve chuckled. "I don't think I've ever seen a kid so excited about weeding."

As Harper reached for her root beer, Big Mac sauntered in, hopped on the couch, and curled up next to them. "I'm just excited about working in a garden."

* * *

Early the next morning, Gage and Maeve picked up Harper. "You should've taken her home with you," Macey said when Maeve came into the kitchen and reached for a coffee mug.

"I thought about that," Maeve replied as she poured the steaming coffee, "but she was sound asleep and I knew she'd have to have her medicine. It was late and it just seemed complicated, but maybe we can plan an overnight soon."

Coming into the kitchen and overhearing her aunt's words, Harper grinned. "I could stay over tonight," she said hopefully, looking from her aunt to her mom.

"Fine with me," Macey said with a shrug, but then she raised her eyebrows and eyed her sister questioningly. "You just had girls' night last night."

Maeve nodded. "That's okay. We can do tonight. We've been talking about it long enough, right? We should do it!"

"Yes!" Harper said, pumping her fist. "I'll go pack!" And before anyone could change their mind, she was racing up the stairs.

"Make sure you pack clothes for church!" Macey called. Then she turned to Maeve and asked, "Are you going to church?"

"I can," Maeve said. "It would probably make Mom happy because she thinks I've fallen off God's list of potential candidates for heaven."

"It probably would," Macey said. "Should you ask Gage first?"

"He'll be fine. We don't have anything goin' on. Just picking up the baby chicks and working around the house."

"Okay," Macey said, sounding unconvinced. "By the way, have you seen the fox again?"

"Not since it took Eggna. I think I scared the bejesus out of it with all my yelling . . . and it's a good thing because Gage is planning to shoot it if it comes back."

Macey looked alarmed. "He keeps his gun locked up, right?"

"Of course! Don't worry."

"Mm-hmm," Macey said skeptically.

"Tell me Ben doesn't have a gun," Maeve said defensively.

"He does, but I know it's locked up and the key is tucked away."

Just then, Gage peeked in the screen door. "You and Harper comin'?"

"Good morning to you, too," Macey said.

"Mornin', Mace," Gage replied with an impish grin, as he came in with Ben behind him. "Forgive me for forgetting my manners."

"You're forgiven," she said, giving him a hug. "Now, tell me, do you keep your gun—or guns—locked up?"

"Yes, ma'am," he replied. "Why?"

"Just checking," Macey said.

"Harper's gonna sleep over tonight," Maeve said, "and her worried mom wants to make sure our house is safe."

"No need to worry," Gage said. "I'm a very responsible gun owner."

Ben frowned. "How'd you get on this topic anyway?"

"Mace asked if we'd seen the fox lately, and I told her we hadn't but it better not come back because it would meet a sorry end."

"It would indeed," Gage confirmed.

"Hey, Uncle Gage," Harper said, coming into the kitchen with her backpack over her shoulder and giving him a hug.

"Hey, Harp," he said. "I hear we're stuck with you."

"Yep," Harper said, beaming happily.

"Don't forget to take these," Macey said, as she handed Harper a Ziploc bag with her medicine in it.

"I won't," Harper said, stuffing the bag into her backpack.

Macey eyed her sister and warned, "Sometimes she needs reminding."

"Don't we all," Maeve said, suddenly realizing she'd forgotten to take her birth control that morning. She finished her coffee and set the mug in the sink. "Thanks for the coffee," she said, giving Macey a hug.

"You're welcome. Hope you guys have fun." Macey gave Harper a hug, too. "Be good."

"I will," Harper assured her. Then she hugged Keeper, whispering, "I'll be back tomorrow, Keep."

"You *do* know we have weeds around here, too," Ben said as he hugged her, too.

"I know, but we're going to pick up Amelia Egghart and Mother Clucker this morning," Harper explained.

Macey raised her eyebrows. "*Who?*"

Harper looked to Gage for confirmation, but he feigned innocence. "I didn't pick those names."

"Yes, you did," Harper countered, grinning. "Aunt Maeve told me you said a fox would never mess with a chicken named Mother Clucker."

Maeve and Gage and Ben bit their lips, trying not to laugh, and Macey eyed her sister.

"Don't worry, Mace," Maeve said, putting her arm around her young niece. "She'll be fine with us . . . and you can have her back tomorrow after church."

# 25

"You got your car back!" Ali said, coming out of the house when she heard Mason pull into the driveway. She knew he'd been riding his bike everywhere for the last several days, and because balancing a gallon of milk on his bike was tricky, he'd even taken her up on her offer to drive him to the store to do some food shopping.

"Temporarily," he said, nodding.

She frowned. "What happened to it?"

"Nothing," he said.

"Um, it used to be rusty blue . . . and now, it's ugly gray . . ."

"It used to be *Marina* Blue," he corrected, "and now, it's *primer* gray."

"So, that's not the new color?"

"Um, no," he said, as if it was a silly question. "Wanna see under the hood?"

"Of course, I'd love to see under the hood," she teased.

He raised his eyebrows, trying to decide if she was flirting with him. As he walked around to open the hood, a tall man wearing a dress shirt with sleeves rolled up and a tie, loosened at the neck, came out of the house. He had thinning salt-and-pepper hair. "Hey, Mason," he said.

"Hey, Mr. Harrison," Mason said.

"I'm glad we were finally able to talk you into joining us for dinner." He eyed him. "It's been too long, and you need to put some meat on those bones."

"Thanks for the invite. I guess I am getting a little tired of grilled cheese and tomato soup."

David Harrison smiled. "Ali tells us that's a staple in your house."

"It is. My mom called it comfort food."

David squeezed his shoulder. "You must miss her."

Mason nodded. "I do, but I know she wouldn't want me moping around, so I'm trying to keep busy. I've been working for Black Lab Landscaping every day and, in my free time, Jeff Bresson's been helping me restore my Chevelle."

"Jeff's a great mechanic," David said. "He knows his cars—especially these old muscle cars." He looked under the hood at the pristine engine. "Wow, you've done a lot—it looks awesome!"

"Thanks! We *just* put the engine back in. It was a lot of work—thank goodness he was willing to help me. We cleaned off the grime and removed the transmission, bell housing, flywheel, clutch . . . drained all the fluids, got a bunch of new parts—the valve covers, intake manifold—adjusted the rockers . . . cleaned and painted the block . . ."

Ali laughed. "Sheesh, it's a good thing you came out here, Dad, because I wouldn't have a clue what he's talking about."

Mason smiled. "It's really pretty simple when you come right down to it," he said. "I mean, I knew how engines worked before, but I've never had much hands-on experience . . . besides changing oil. I've never taken an engine completely apart and put it back together, so I've definitely learned a lot."

"Well, it looks great—very clean." David eyed the outside. "Looks like you've had some bodywork done, too."

Mason nodded. "We had to find new rear quarter panels—the originals were pretty rusty, and I have new bumpers ordered."

"What color is she gonna be?"

"Same color—Marina Blue."

"How's the interior?" David asked, looking in the window.

"It's clean but some of the seat covers are cracking. Jeff knows where I can get new ones."

"Well, it looks super," he said, clapping Mason on the shoulder. "And it's a good way to stay busy. Keeps you out of trouble."

"It does. I've been running, too, but I have to get up early or run late because it's been so hot."

"You must be dead tired . . . I mean *really* tired by the end of the day," he said, catching himself.

Mason nodded. "Yes, I definitely sleep better when I've been busy." He looked at Ali. "Do we have time to go for a ride?"

Ali eyed her dad questioningly, but he shrugged. "You're asking the wrong person—I'm just an underling."

Ali rolled her eyes. "I'll go ask."

Mason closed the hood, and Mr. Harrison took advantage of their minute alone. "Sue told me you asked her to go with you to your appointment with your mom's attorney."

"Yes, sir. My mom said everything would be taken care of, but I'd feel better if Mrs. Harrison was there, too—a second set of ears, you know? There are a lot of medical bills coming in, and I'm not sure about paying things until other expenses are settled."

David nodded. "Sue is very good with money . . . *and* living on a budget, and even though I work in finance *and* I hate to admit it, she has more common sense than me." He paused thoughtfully. "She also said you're not going to college—at least not right away."

Mason nodded. "My mom wanted me to go this fall, but I never sent in the deposit, so . . ."

David nodded thoughtfully. "You know," he began, "if you feel like you're ready, they might make an exception . . . considering everything you've been through."

Just then, Ali came back out. "Mom says dinner is in half an hour, but she also has appetizers, so if we do go, we have to be quick."

Mason nodded and opened the door for her, and then saw

Mr. Harrison standing there. "Do you want to come, too, sir?" he asked.

David shook his head. "No, no, you two go. I'll get a ride when it's all done—maybe we can go to one of those car cruises at the Blue Mountain Diner."

"That would be fun," Mason said, his face brightening.

He climbed in and turned the key, and the Chevelle rumbled to life.

David smiled. There was nothing like the sound of an old classic big block. He waved and watched as Mason backed out of the driveway onto the street. Then he stood and listened as they pulled away.

"Very cool," Ali said, as she admired the graduation tassel hanging from his rearview mirror.

Mason looked over and smiled. "Thanks."

He turned onto a road Ali had never been down before. "Where are we going?"

"Just up here a bit," Mason said. "This is where the man I bought the car from lives. I want to see if he's home."

Ali nodded and looked out the window at the row of small, neatly kept homes. Finally, Mason slowed down and pulled up to the curb in front of a small ranch with two shutters hanging askew.

"Is this it?" Ali asked, looking at the For Sale sign posted in the long grass.

Mason nodded. "It is," he said, frowning and turning off the car.

Ali nodded, and watched him walk across the lawn and knock on the door, but then he just stood there. He knocked again, waited, and then tried to look in the windows. Finally, he started walking back to the car, but a man in the next yard called out, and he stopped to talk. Ali watched Mason nodding and then, finally, he waved to the man, walked back to the car, and got in.

"Where is he?" she asked.

"His neighbor isn't sure. He said his family moved him to a nursing home about a month ago, but he hadn't wanted to go."

"Oh, no," Ali said. "That's sad."

"Yeah. Back when I bought the car, he said his family was talking about it and, even back then—last summer—he hadn't wanted to go."

"It's so hard," Ali said. "My grandma is getting to a point where my mom doesn't know if she'll be able to live alone, and they're going to have to make a decision. My mom thinks she might have to come live with us."

"Mr. Hawkins seemed perfectly capable of living on his own. He said his family was tired of driving up here to see him, and they said *he* shouldn't be driving. That's why he sold his car."

Ali nodded. "Does his neighbor know where the nursing home is?"

"He doesn't, but I remember Mr. Hawkins saying that his family lived down near Savannah."

Ali raised her eyebrows. "There're probably a hundred nursing homes—or more—down there."

Mason shook his head. "I meant to come see him sooner, but with everything going on, I never had the chance. He wanted me to restore it—that was part of the deal—and I wanted to show him I was making progress."

"Well, you tried, Mase," Ali consoled. "Don't be hard on yourself. You came as soon as you could."

"I know. I just feel bad," he said, looking over. "I guess we better head back," he added, remembering Mrs. Harrison had dinner waiting.

# 26

Gage clicked on the light over his table and studied the drawing he'd been working on—it wasn't finished, but it was coming along. In fact, when Harper had walked by it the night before, she'd stopped in her tracks and stared at the intricate details. "Wow, Uncle Gage, how did you make those tiny white lines and highlights . . . and those little wrinkles around his eyes?"

Gage had looked over her shoulder at the image of his grandfather and pulled out a kneaded eraser. He showed her how to twist it into a point that was as sharp as a pencil, and then how to use it to make the highlights in the old man's eyes and the wisps of wild white hair.

"Here," he'd said, handing it to her. "I have a whole drawer of 'em. You just knead it—kind of like Silly Putty—to keep it clean. It's good for stress relief, too," he'd added with a smile.

"Thanks!" she'd said. "I can't wait to try it."

Later that morning, when she'd been packing up her things before heading to church with Maeve, he'd also given her a roll of his favorite drawing paper and two pencils. "You can have these, too." She'd been wide-eyed, and given him a big hug. "Thanks, Uncle Gage!"

He smiled, now, thinking about it—*Harper is so smart . . . and curious about everything*. Yesterday, in the heat of the day, she and Maeve—both fair-skinned and freckled—had coated themselves with sunscreen, donned big straw hats, and weeded the gardens. They'd also planted the two new blueberry bushes they'd picked up at Agway, along with the chicks—which were in a box on the front porch, peeping . . . *and* they'd talked him into getting a bag of sunflower hearts and a bird feeder, which the birds had already found.

The previous night, they'd sat on the porch while Maeve began the newest selection of The Pepperoni Pizza and Root Beer Book Club, and he'd questioned the legitimacy of their meeting because they'd had burgers, not pizza, but they'd said they would agree to make an exception this one time. He'd also warned that if he was allowed to listen to the beginning of the book, it would only be fair that he keep attending the meetings so he could find out what happens to Opal and Winn-Dixie. And although they'd initially frowned at his proposal, feigning uncertainty because it was a *girls-only* group, they'd eventually agreed to allow it—but just this one time.

Gage absentmindedly kneaded the eraser in his hand, thinking about how lucky Ben and Macey were to have a little girl like Harper come into their lives, and he hoped that, if he and Maeve were blessed with children, their kids would have at least some of the wonderful traits Harper had. As he thought about this, he pulled open the little oak drawer under his table in which he kept his Palomino Blackwing pencils, erasers, and all kinds of odds and ends, including the key to the oak box his grandfather had made for his rifle, several old photos, and an envelope full of tickets to movies, races, and concerts he'd attended when he was younger. He looked through the envelope, fondly recalling each event, and then paused when he came to a faded ticket for a NASCAR race. It was dated August 28, 1999—his fifteenth birthday, a night he'd never forget. Dutch and his father had taken Cale, Matt, and him to Bristol Motor Speedway. Prior to that night, he and his brothers had only watched NASCAR on TV, but that night at the track, the deafening roar of the cars and the excitement of the crowd had been like nothing they'd ever experienced before. He still remembered how the race had ended . . . Terry Labonte had had the advantage over the other drivers because, with just five laps to go, he'd stopped for fresh tires and then easily motored past everyone into the lead . . . that is, until Dale Earnhardt Sr. had come up behind him—as he loved to do—and bumped his car, spinning him around, and then powering past him for the win. The crowd had gone wild, but the most surprising part for Jack Tennyson's boys was seeing their ever-composed father pumping his fist and shouting, "Woo-hoo! Bump and run, baby! Bump and run!"

He tucked the ticket back into the pile and studied the next one, dated May 9, 1998—a year earlier. He and Cale had been thirteen and fourteen, and Dutch had taken them to Nashville to see Garth Brooks in concert. He'd never forget that night, either. They'd gone to the Loveless Café first, ordered chargrilled cheeseburgers and iced tea, and then had slices of the most amazing chocolate chess pie he'd ever tasted. Afterward, along with the throngs of other concertgoers, they'd headed to the arena. He and Cale had been familiar with many of the country singer's famous songs from hearing them on the radio, but they'd been mesmerized by the live performance, especially when Garth had sung their grandfather's favorite song, "The River," and they'd looked over to see tears glistening in his eyes. Gage smiled wistfully at the memory and then tucked all the tickets back in the envelope, pulled the narrow drawer out all the way, and reached in back for a small black box. He hadn't had a chance to open the box since he'd brought it home a week earlier because Maeve was always around now. In fact, she'd been sitting in the living room when he'd come home with it in his pocket, but he'd pretended to be looking for something in the drawer, and then tucked it all the way in back. He had no idea when he would give it to her . . . or what he would say when he did, but at least he had it for when the time felt right. He lifted the lid, and the perfectly cut diamond sparkled in the sunlight, casting tiny rainbows on his table.

A moment later, he heard Gus—who'd been sleeping on the porch—scramble to his feet, barking. At the same time, Pilgrim started squawking frantically, and Gage got up to look out the window. "How did you get in there?" he shouted angrily. He reached into the drawer for the key to his gun case, opened it, lifted out the rifle, loaded it, and went outside. The fox was on the inside of the reinforced fence of the coop, staring down Gus—who was going nuts. "Back off, Gus," Gage growled, and the big yellow Lab—to his surprise—listened.

Gage lifted his rifle and looked down the sight. The fox was staring right back at him, its dark eyes defiant. Feeling his heart pound, Gage slowly pulled back the trigger until it clicked, and then clenched his jaw determinedly—he had never killed anything before. His dad and Cale had loved to go hunting, but whenever he'd gone, he'd never been able to pull the trigger. It didn't matter if it was a buck or a grouse, he could only see the beauty of the creature. Afterward, his dad always teased him about not being able to pull the trigger, and finally, he'd just stopped going. The only reason he had a gun at all was because his grandfather had given him one of his old refurbished Winchesters and made a fine oak case to keep it in. Now, the fox with its copper-red fur and white twitching tail was daring him to take its life, and he knew, if he didn't, it would continue to torment his chickens and they would always have to be cooped up in their pen.

"Damn you," he whispered, blinking back tears, and then he closed his eyes, and squeezed the trigger. The powerful rifle slammed his shoulder and he fully expected to see the fox running off, but when he opened his eyes, it was lying in the grass. A moment later, a little copper head peered out of the grass and playfully hopped over to sniff the lifeless body and then lie down next to it.

# 27

"Thanks for coming, Mrs. Harrison," Mason said, as he held open the door of the attorney's office.

"Oh, Mason, you don't have to thank me. I'm happy to help. If you ever need anything—anything at all—please don't hesitate to ask." She stopped and put her hand on his cheek. "You are part of our family and you always will be."

"Thanks," he said, smiling. "That means a lot."

"And we fully expect you to spend the holidays with us. We've always loved having you and your mom come over, and we expect you to continue the tradition."

Mason laughed. "Okay. I wouldn't want to be anywhere else anyway."

"Good," she said, as they approached the receptionist's desk.

"Good morning," the silver-haired receptionist said without looking up. "How may I help you?"

Sue looked at Mason, and he cleared his throat. "Umm, we—I have an appointment with Mr. Bartholomew."

"Your name?"

"Mason Callahan."

The receptionist looked up and her stoic face crumpled as she removed her glasses and came around from behind her desk. "Oh, Mason, I'm so sorry about your dear mom," she said, reaching for his hand. "She was the kindest person I've ever had the privilege of knowing . . . *and* she baked the most delicious apple pies. Did you know she would bring us a pie every time she came into the office?"

Mason smiled. "Thank you. I'm not surprised. She was always baking pies and giving them away."

The receptionist smiled. "I hope she baked some for you, too."

"She did."

"You must miss her."

He nodded and then gestured to Sue. "This is my mom's friend, Sue Harrison."

The receptionist let go of Mason's hand and extended hers to Sue. "How do you do? I'm Carol Carson."

"It's nice to meet you, Mrs. Carson," Sue said, shaking the older woman's hand.

Mrs. Carson nodded. "Well, you may sit right over there," she said, motioning to two stiff Queen Anne chairs in the corner, "and I'll let Mr. B know you're here."

She returned to her post and resumed her all-business demeanor, as she called into the office to let her boss know his client had arrived. Then she looked up again. "May I offer you some coffee or water?"

Mason pressed his lips together—he hadn't had breakfast or coffee that morning. He looked questioningly at Sue and she nodded that it was okay, but he declined. "No, thank you. We're all set."

He leaned back in his chair and looked around at the dark paneling, wishing he could be anywhere else—anywhere, even mulching.

He was just about to reach for a magazine when a tall, stately gentleman with a mane of white hair filled the doorway. He was wearing a light blue seersucker suit, crisp white shirt, and red bow tie. "Mason?" he boomed.

And because the man's demeanor demanded respect, Mason lurched to his feet. "Yes, sir."

The older gentleman smiled and extended his hand. "Beau Bartholomew."

Mason shook it politely. "It's nice to meet you, sir."

"I'm very sorry about your mom. She was a sweet lady . . . and her apple pies, oh my!" he said in a slow Southern drawl.

"I already told him," Mrs. Carson chimed in, smiling.

"Thank you," Mason replied, and then turned to Sue. "This is my mom's friend, Sue Harrison."

"Good. I'm glad you brought a friend—it's always good to have an extra set of ears." He turned to Sue. "It's a pleasure to meet you, I'm sure. Please, call me Beau." He eyed Mason. "You, too, young man. Bartholomew is a bigger mouthful than a mouse in a tomcat's jaws."

Mason smiled, already feeling at ease.

"C'mon back," he said, motioning for them to follow him, "and let's take care of this." He looked at Mason. "I'm sure you'd rather be anywhere else on this beautiful summer day than in a stuffy lawyer's office. Maybe up at the lake with your girlfriend?"

"I don't have a girlfriend, sir."

"What?!" the old man teased. "A handsome fella like you? Why, I'm sure all the girls love that hair o' yours!"

Mason smiled. "I—I don't know," he stammered, feeling his cheeks flame.

"My own dear mother—rest her soul—had hair the color of a copper penny, but none of us kids got it. I would've loved it."

Mason nodded as they followed him down the hall.

"Carol," he called over his shoulder. "Could you bring us some coffee and maybe a cookie or two?"

"Yes, Mr. B," she called back.

"Right in here," he said, pushing open the door to a large conference room with tall windows overlooking a lovely rose garden. He gestured to two chairs and then sat across from them with a large folder. "Your mom has been a client of mine for a very long time. She cared for her own parents—your grandparents—and they were among my first clients, so we go way back." As he said this, he opened the file and perched his reading glasses on the tip of his aristocratic nose. "Let's see," he began, humming to himself.

A moment later, Mrs. Carson brought in a tray with three coffee mugs, a silver creamer and sugar bowl set, and a plate of chocolate chip cookies. Beau peered over his glasses at the cookies. "Are those Mrs. Stoeffler's?"

"They are," Mrs. Carson confirmed.

"You are in for a treat, my boy," he said. "We consider ourselves blessed when Mrs. Stoeffler bakes us some of her chocolate chip cookies, just like your mom's apple pie—which we never shared with anyone," he added with a wink.

Mason offered the tray to Sue and then helped himself, and they munched and sipped while the distinguished old attorney his mom had left in charge of her affairs proceeded to explain everything.

By the end of the meeting, Mason realized he should not have spent so much time worrying. His mom had assured him that all would be well, and it was. Beau Bartholomew would pay off the home equity line of credit and any other outstanding bills, including her medical bills . . . after, of course, the insurance company had renegotiated down the allowed expenses and paid their part. The remainder of his mom's savings and her sizable life insurance benefit would be added to the trust, and a set sum would be deposited in Mason's new checking account every month.

"Can you get by on that?" Beau asked, jotting a figure on a scrap of paper and peering at Mason over his glasses.

Mason swallowed. "I'm sure I can—I actually think it's too much. The only real expenses I have are food and gas and utilities."

Beau chuckled. "I'm sure there will be other things that come up . . . especially when you find yourself a pretty girl who wants to spend all your money . . . and then, you better look out!"

Mason smiled, thinking about Ali—he didn't think she would

ever want to spend all his money, and he would've loved to tell the kind gentleman all about her . . . except that her mother was sitting right next to him!

"How will it work if I decide to go to college?" Mason asked.

Beau looked up and frowned. "I thought you *were* going to college," he said, sifting through his papers. "Your mom had me send a deposit to Georgia Tech for the fall semester, along with a letter explaining why it was late, and they confirmed receipt and are holding a place for you." He looked up. "Am I wrong about this?"

Mason sat up in his chair. "Well, no, you're not wro . . . She did *that*?" he asked, sounding stunned.

"She did. She called me . . . let's see, it was . . ." He looked at the paperwork again. "It was toward the end of May, and she asked me to contact the school because, with everything going on, she said you had forgotten." He looked up again. "She was so proud of you, and she said you were planning to major in aeronautical engineering and had already applied for—and been accepted into—the Air Force ROTC program, including a scholarship." He looked down again. "She sent me copies of everything."

Mason shook his head. He couldn't believe—no, actually, he *could* believe it! Sue reached over and squeezed his hand. "Mason, if you don't feel ready, I'm sure you can get a deferment."

Mason swallowed and nodded. "I just thought it wasn't an option because I missed the deadline." He took a deep breath and let it out. His mom had been right—he didn't have anything holding him back, except himself . . . and what was he going to do for the next year except continue to work for a landscaper and wander around an empty house? Even Ali was going to Emory and wouldn't be around. "I don't know," he said uncertainly, and then he looked up. "I'll have to think about it."

"That's fine," Beau said, "but don't think too long. Freshmen—or I guess they're called 'first-years' now—are expected to arrive at the end of August . . . and athletes even sooner. Your mom mentioned you're a runner."

"Okay," Mason said, nodding. "I'll decide soon."

"Okay, good." He shuffled his papers and then spied a light blue envelope sticking out of the folder. "Oh, there's one more thing . . . and it's probably *the* most important thing," he said, smiling. "At least to your mom."

# 28

When Maeve pulled into the driveway, she saw Gage down near the river behind the cabin, and as she walked through the grass and wildflowers toward him, she realized he was digging a hole. "I guess you didn't like where we planted the blueberry bushes," she teased, but when he looked up, she realized his eyes were rimmed with tears. "What's wrong?" she asked, her face suddenly shadowed with worry.

He motioned to Gus lying solemnly on the grass next to the lifeless body of the fox. "Oh, no!" she said softly. "What happened?"

"I heard a commotion, looked out, and the fox was inside the fence again—she'd dug a hole behind the coop." He shook his head. "I had to, Maeve," he blurted, "or she'd keep coming back," he said, trying to justify his actions. "What's the point of having chickens if . . ."

"I know," she consoled. "You did the right thing. What else could you do?"

He nodded. "And that's not the worst part," he said. "You were right—she did have a kit. It peeked out of the grass right afterward and then it just lay down next to her."

Maeve took a deep breath and let it out slowly. "Just one?"

"That's all I saw."

"Did it run off?"

"No. It's a *he* . . . and he was inside the fence, too, and he couldn't find his way out, so I was able to catch him, but what the hell am I going to do with a baby fox?"

"Where is he now?"

"In Gus's old dog crate."

Maeve nodded thoughtfully, wondering if a wild baby fox could be domesticated.

Gage eyed her. "I know what you're thinking, but I am *not* keeping him or trying to turn him into a pet. I have enough going on . . . besides, his instinct is to hunt, so the hens would never be safe, and I would've killed his mother for nothing."

"I know," Maeve said. "You're right, but maybe we can find a wildlife rehabilitator who takes in injured and orphaned animals."

Gage nodded. "Maybe."

"I'll see if I can find someone online." She started to walk back to the cabin, but stopped and turned around. "Are the hens okay?"

"Yeah. Just traumatized."

She nodded, turned back, and Gus—who was watching her—gave the lifeless body of the enemy one last sniff and trotted after her . . . just in case she was planning to have a snack. She smiled and tousled his soft ears as they crossed the lawn. When they reached the porch, though, the fur between Gus's shoulders stood up on end and he stopped in his tracks. Maeve followed his gaze and realized the dog crate was on the porch and the baby fox was trying to dig his way out. She knelt down next to the crate and the fox quickly scampered to the back corner, almost taking an unplanned swim in the water bowl Gage had put in the crate. "It's okay," she said softly. "I'm sorry this happened, but we're gonna find a new home for you. Everything is going to be okay."

Then she stood up and looked back at Gus, whose fur was still standing on end. "C'mon, silly, he's not going to hurt you." The very tip of Gus's tail wagged tentatively, and with his ears back, he tiptoed across the porch as far from the crate as possible.

Maeve dropped her bag on a chair and walked across the room to get her laptop, but as she passed Gage's drawing table, she realized the lamp was on and the little narrow drawer beneath it was open. When she started to push the drawer closed, she noticed a small black box from a jewelry store in Savannah on the table and froze, staring at it.

With a pounding heart, she glanced out the window. Gage was still digging, and she knew he would be occupied for a while. She looked back at the box, and then slowly reached over to pick it up. *Would it hurt to look? Honestly, wouldn't any girl—given the opportunity—peek inside a little black jewelry box . . . just to see what was inside?* It was probably earrings—after all, she'd recently complained about how many earrings she'd lost—but as she held the box in her hand, the temptation tore at her heart. On one hand, she could hear her friends and her sister absolutely encouraging her to peek, but on the other hand, something was stopping her. She knew Gage had left this room in a hurry, abandoning whatever he'd been doing . . . and if he were to come in right now, what he would think? What would he expect of the woman he loved and trusted? Would he be disappointed if he saw her opening the box? She knew, deep down, he would. She looked out the window again and suddenly felt as if she were seeing him for the first time . . . and it didn't have anything to do with the box *or* its contents. It was because he was sweating and struggling to dig a hole that would be deep enough to protect the body of the fox he'd had to kill. This good, honest, kind, gentle man was trying to make things right the only way he knew how, and his eyes were glistening with tears because killing the fox had been against every fiber of his being . . . and *how incredibly lucky was* she *that this tenderhearted man loved her?* She bit her lip, put the box in the drawer, closed it, and reached up to turn off the light, but before she did, she noticed Dutch's eyes gazing up at her. "I didn't open it," she whispered with a half smile, and then she clicked off the light and picked up her laptop.

She sat down at the kitchen table, opened her laptop, and googled "wildlife rehabilitators in Savannah, Georgia." Several names and websites popped up, but one name sounded oddly familiar: Sage Finch, licensed wildlife rehabilitator, Tybee Island. Maeve frowned. *Where had she heard that name before?* She clicked on the link, and in the banner of the website there was a picture of a boy with a little raccoon trailing behind him. The caption read: "Sam and Ty Coon." *Of course*, she thought. *Harper is always talking about her friend Sam and his gentle affinity for animals. Harper even mentioned that his mom takes care of orphaned animals. That is how Sam came to have a pet raccoon.*

She scrolled through the page, looking for information, and after jotting down the address, she called the phone number and Sage picked up after the first ring.

When Gage came in a few minutes later, carrying his rifle, she told him about the call.

He nodded. "Would you mind taking him?"

"Sure," she said haltingly. "Don't you want to go?"

"No," he said, shaking his head. "I don't think I want to meet someone who rescues wild animals when I'm the one who orphaned him."

"Sage actually said it happens pretty often—wild animals become too bold around humans and their dwellings and it creates problems. She was surprised, though, that there was only one kit because there're usually several in a litter."

Gage shrugged. "I only saw one, but I'll keep my eye out . . . not that I'd be able to catch any. The only reason I caught this one was because he was inside the fence."

Maeve nodded. "Maybe, if there are others, they're old enough to get by on their own."

"Maybe," Gage said, "but I hope they don't settle around here." He wiped his brow with the shoulder of his shirt. "When are you taking him?"

"I told her I'd be right over."

"I think the crate will fit in the back of your Jeep . . . unless you want to take the truck."

"It doesn't matter—whichever you think is better."

"Okay, I'll go see." He went outside, gingerly picked up the crate, and carried it to her Jeep, trying not to spill the water, but he ended up putting it in the back of his truck, and when she came out, he handed her his keys.

"I'll be back," she said with a sad half smile. "Don't be so hard on yourself. I still love you."

He smiled, too. "Well, that's good to know." He pulled her toward him. "Even though I'm all sweaty?"

"Especially because you're all sweaty," she said, glad he was smiling. She kissed him and then turned to go, but stopped and looked back. "Try to be showered when I get back, though."

"I don't have time for hanky-panky," he teased.

"Your loss," she said, waving as she pulled away.

"My loss, indeed," he said, laughing. He went back inside with Gus at his heels, the big Lab trotting happily across the porch, thankful that the infiltrator had been removed from the premises, but he did peer into the box holding the new little chicks and gave them a quick sniff—no danger posed there!

Gage cleaned his rifle, and as he locked it back in its case, he ran his hand over the smooth, glowing wood and smiled. Unlike his dad, Dutch had understood when he told him he didn't like hunting, but he'd said, "You just keep it for when you need it, Gage."

"I guess I needed it today, Dutch," he whispered. He looked at the picture of his grandfather on the drawing table and then remembered the jewelry box. *Had he really had the presence of mind to put it away?* Everything had happened so quickly, so he couldn't be sure . . . but he must've, thank goodness. He really wanted to surprise Maeve!

# 29

"ARE YOU HUNGRY?" SUE ASKED AS THEY LEFT BEAU BARTHOLOMEW'S office.

"Starving," Mason replied. "Those cookies were really good—I could've eaten the whole plate, but I thought better of it because they seemed a little possessive of their baked goods."

"Especially your mom's apple pie," Sue said, laughing, as she unlocked her car.

Mason nodded. "I have her recipe, and she showed me several times how to make her crust . . . maybe I'll try to bake one and bring it over. They were so nice."

"They were," Sue agreed. "So, where should we go for lunch?"

Mason shook his head and shrugged. "You pick."

"Cantaberry?"

"That sounds good. I haven't been there in a long time."

"Want to see if Ali wants to meet us?"

"She's not working?" he asked, knowing Ali's job as a lifeguard kept her very busy in the summer.

"Nope, she has the day off."

"That would be great. I'll text her," he said, pulling his phone from his pocket.

Ten minutes later, they were sitting at a table by the front window, waiting for Ali and scanning their menus. "Know what you're gonna have?" Sue asked, taking a sip of her iced tea.

Mason frowned thoughtfully. "I'm definitely having a bowl of tomato basil soup, so maybe I'll do the half sandwich and soup combo."

"I'm sure you can eat a whole sandwich."

He smiled. "Probably." Then he looked up. "By the way, lunch is on me."

"Oh, no it isn't!"

"Mm-hmm," he said. "You came with me . . . and you've done so much, and besides, I just came into a small fortune."

"You did *that*," Sue said, laughing. "But I still want to treat."

"Nope. It's on me," he said firmly.

"Okay, okay," she said, relenting. "*You're* just like your mom—stubborn!"

Mason laughed and sipped his iced tea.

"It's nice to hear you laughing, Mason," she said, her kind eyes seeking his.

Mason nodded. "It's good *to* laugh," he said. "Before Mom died, I didn't think I would ever laugh again, but she said I would, and I should've known she'd be right."

"She usually was right," Sue said, smiling. "She was a very wise lady."

Mason nodded.

"How do you really feel about her asking Mr. Bartholomew to send in your deposit?"

Mason shook his head. "It's just like her to do something like that, and, honestly, I *was* kind of upset at first, but how can I be mad? I was such a mess back when it was due, and I didn't think I'd ever be ready to go to college, but now, I'm faced with fall and winter alone in an empty house, working a dead-end job, and I guess I might go a little crazy. I also know how much she wanted me to go, so now, at least it's an option."

Sue nodded, and then paused, studying him. "Mason, I know it's not my business . . ."

Mason looked up. "The envelope," he said with a half smile, finishing her thought.

She nodded, but she didn't want to press him, so she waited.

He took a deep breath and let it out slowly. "I know she wants me to find her—I mean, she made me promise, but I've never understood why it's so important. After all these years, what's the point? She didn't want me. She didn't want to be part of my life, so how do I know she'd want me to reach out now, and why should I let *her* be part of my life?"

Sue bit her lip. "I completely understand why you feel that way, hon. It's natural to think she didn't want you . . . or want to be part of your life. She gave you up, right?"

Mason nodded.

"But it wasn't that simple. Your mom and I were both there that day. I wasn't in the delivery room like your mom, but I saw her being brought in, and she was so young—late teens at most—and she looked terrified."

"That's no excuse," Mason said. "Lots of teenage women—*and men*—raise children."

"They do," Sue agreed, "but not every one of them is ready."

"Maybe she should have thought about that before she got pregnant."

Sue nodded. "Maybe she should have, Mason, but people aren't perfect, and you don't know what was going on in her life."

Mason leaned back in his seat and folded his arms, obviously unmoved.

"When you came into the world, Mase, you didn't even weigh four pounds, but you were perfect in every way, and your mom—who was such a pro with preemies—had you cleaned up in no time, and after she had you all settled, she went back to the young woman's room and found her crying. She told your mom she had a summer job at her college and couldn't possibly keep you—she hadn't told anyone she was pregnant, not even her parents, and she wasn't ready to be a mom. She said she was planning to look into adoption but she hadn't had the chance. She'd been hiking when she started to have labor pains and realized you'd decided to come early. Your mom—knowing she was giving you up for adoption—whisked you out of the delivery room before she saw you or even knew if you were a boy or girl. That evening, she was absolutely beside herself and begged your mom to let her hold you, but your mom told her it was better if there was no contact and, in fact, it wasn't allowed. But later, your mom gave in, and with me keeping watch, she smuggled you into her room.

"You were this tiny little bundle with a copper halo, and we could tell you were going to have red hair, just like her. And when your mom gently laid you in her arms, she looked at you for such a long time with tears streaming down her cheeks, and then she looked up at your mom and said, 'Can you take my picture with him so he can have it someday?' And your mom agreed and quickly took a picture with the camera we kept in the nursery.

"By then, your mom was misty, too, and the young woman tearfully thanked her, and seeing how tenderhearted your mom was, she asked her if there was any way *she* could be the one to adopt you. Your mom didn't know what to say. It was such an unexpected request. Your mom loved babies, but she wasn't married and didn't think she'd ever have children. She had devoted her life to taking care of her parents, and she'd just lost both of them within days of each other. She was so brokenhearted, and then out of the blue, this happened—and to her, it felt too timely to be a coincidence. It was as if it was all happening for a reason . . . and she wondered if you were a gift from God to fill the empty void her parents had left. So, without knowing how in the world she would do it, she said *yes*."

Mason bit his lip, his eyes glistening. "How come she never told me this?"

"I don't know why she never told you, but I do know, as you grew up and started asking questions—some of which she didn't have answers to—she sensed you were struggling to understand why your real mom gave you up, and because you stopped wanting to talk about it, she prayed that, one day, you'd find it in your heart to forgive her. She believed if you met her, your questions would be answered and you might understand what happened—what was going on in her life back then. Your mom thought it would heal the sadness in your heart, and she was very thankful, several years ago, when the young woman sent a note, thanking her for taking care of you, and including her address—just in case you ever wanted to find her."

Mason shook his head. "So much time has passed . . ." He looked out the window and saw Ali hurrying across the parking lot, her blond hair streaked with highlights from lifeguarding, and her golden suntanned skin looking even darker against her new snow-white Emory University T-shirt.

He looked back at Sue. "You know I'm going to keep my promise," he said with a half smile.

Sue smiled back and nodded. "I know you will, and I hope you end up being glad you did. And before I forget, are you coming to the NICU tomorrow?"

"I am," he said, wiping his eyes with his palms and mustering a smile for Ali.

Ali gave them each a hug and sat down next to Mason. "Well? How'd it go?" she asked, picking up her menu.

"It went," Mason said.

"Yeah?"

He nodded.

She glanced at the three iced teas on the table. "Is one of these for me?"

"It is," Mason confirmed.

"Thank you," she said, taking a sip. "I'm parched! So, do you guys already know what you're having?" she asked, glancing at the menu and seeing two of Mason's favorites.

Sue nodded. "I'm having chicken salad."

"And *I'm* having . . ." Mason began, dramatically closing his menu.

Ali eyed him suspiciously. "Please tell me you're *not* . . ."

"Yep . . . but in my defense, the tomato soup has basil and the grilled cheese is made with American, cheddar, *and* Swiss—not just American."

# 30

As Maeve drove back home after dropping off the baby fox, she turned on the radio in Gage's truck and heard George Strait's familiar voice drift from the speakers, singing the much-loved song "I Cross my Heart," and as she listened to the tender lyrics, her thoughts drifted back to Gage working in the hot sun, digging a grave for the mama fox. And then she remembered the jewelry box she'd seen on his table—the box she'd somehow managed to resist opening. It *had* to be earrings, she surmised now, because she couldn't imagine Gage going into a jewelry store and picking out an engagement ring all on his own! She tried to picture him standing in front of the glass case in his jeans and T-shirt . . . or maybe he'd dressed up . . . which, to him, meant putting on a button-down. She smiled, her heart swelling with love for his casual, down-to-earth ways, and then she pictured him in his blue button-down—the one that matched his eyes—talking to a jeweler and choosing a diamond, a setting, and a band. *Did he even know what the four Cs—carrot, clarity, cut, and color—were?* Because if he was seriously thinking about proposing, and if he'd already purchased a ring, then she needed to seriously think about telling him what had happened in her past. It wasn't fair to let him venture down this road when she was holding back something that had always cast such a long shadow over her life.

As she turned onto their road, she started to rehearse the

words she'd rehearsed so many times before—describing how . . . and explaining why—but that she'd never let spill from her lips because she worried what he would think . . . and how he would react. *Damn*, she thought miserably, tears stinging her eyes. *I may as well just move out. How could I have not told him before now?*

She pulled into the driveway and looked in the rearview mirror to make sure she didn't look like Sam's pet raccoon. Then she bit her lip and gathered her courage—if she didn't put this behind them once and for all . . . she wouldn't be able to live with herself.

"Mmm, you smell good," she said when she walked into the kitchen.

"You told me to shower before you got back . . . and I *always* listen."

"Mm-hmm," she said, sounding skeptical. "I don't know about *always*."

"Did you have lunch?" he asked. "I just had a sandwich, and I can make one for you."

She shook her head. "I'm not hungry. We had snacks at coffee hour after church."

He nodded, putting away the mayo and mustard. "How was church? I never got to ask you."

"It was fine."

"Were your parents there?"

"Yep," she said, trying to sound cheerful.

"*And* . . . how are *they*?" he asked, exaggerating the word *they*, and eyeing her curiously because her answers were so brief.

"Fine," she said, studying the drawing on his table. "You know, this really is amazing."

"Thanks," he said, coming up behind her.

"You should enter it in a contest."

"Maybe," he replied.

"You have his eyes," she said, smiling. "And now I know where you and Chase got your good looks."

"Dutch was better looking," he said, smiling. "Anyway, how'd it go? You know, dropping off the fox. What did she say?"

"She said she was going to release it into the wild as soon as it was old enough."

"Not around here, I hope."

"Probably up in the Blue Ridge Mountains somewhere."

"The farther away, the better," he said, putting his arms around her.

Maeve reached up and put her hands on his arms as he softly kissed her neck.

"Mmm, you smell pretty good, too."

She closed her eyes and felt him press against her, already aroused. "It doesn't take much, does it?" she teased.

"Nope," he murmured.

"Gage," she began haltingly, "there's something I need to tell you."

"Mmm, what is it?" he asked, sliding his hands over her hips.

Maeve swallowed, trying to remember the words she'd rehearsed as she'd driven home, and then she felt him slide his hands under her blouse and bra, lightly touching her breasts.

"Hmm, doesn't take much, does it?" he teased.

"Nope," she murmured, laughing and still trying to think of how to begin.

"I thought you had something to tell me," he whispered, as he unzipped the front of her jeans.

"You're making it hard," she said.

"No, *you're* making it hard," he whispered in her ear.

"I mean hard to concentrate."

"I can stop," he offered, as he slid his hand inside her underwear.

"No, you can't," she teased.

And then, to prove he could, he started to withdraw his hand, but she put her hand on his and guided it back down.

"So you *don't* want me to stop? Okay . . ." He pushed her jeans down and then unzipped his own and pressed against her bare skin.

She opened her eyes and noticed the picture looking up at them. "I don't know if Dutch would approve of this," she whispered.

Gage chuckled. "Yes, he would," he said, turning the picture over. "He would absolutely approve," he said softly. He pulled her toward the bedroom, and leaving his jeans and boxers in a heap on the floor, lay on the bed beside her. She turned to him and he brushed his lips across hers before kissing her deep and full, all the while teasing her body. Unable to hold on any longer, she pulled him on top of her and felt him press deeper, rhythmic and solemn and intimate and true, and she pulled him in as deep as she could.

Finally, breathless, he slipped to her side. "Now, wasn't there something you wanted to tell me?" he whispered, lightly brushing wisps of copper hair out of her turquoise-blue eyes.

"There was," she said, realizing she'd lost all her resolve. "My parents invited us for dinner on Friday."

"Oh, okay. I thought it was something more serious—you sounded kind of funny."

"Nope," she lied. "Just that. Ben and Macey and Harper are going, too."

"Sounds fun," Gage said. "We haven't been over there in a while."

"That's what my mom said . . . and she said to be sure to bring Gus."

"That reminds me . . . where is Gus?" But just as he said the words, they heard thumping and looked over to see the big yellow Lab with his chin on the quilt, wagging his whole hind end. "There you are," Gage said, laughing. "Did you hear the news? You get to go, too!"

# 31

Sue handed a cloth gown to Mason and waited while he slipped it on. "Did you check in?" she asked.

"Yes, ma'am," he replied.

"Disinfect?"

He nodded.

"No cold or sore throat?"

"Fit as a fiddle."

She laughed. "Okay, so normally, if I'm not here, you just log in," she said, and then waited as he signed the logbook. "Disinfect your hands again because the immune systems of these little guys are not up to snuff yet, so there's no such thing as too clean." Mason nodded, and she led him into the NICU where there were six cribs. "Some babies are more fragile than others, and as you learned in orientation, the more fragile, the more precautions you have to take, but these little guys—and one little gal—are pretty sturdy."

She walked to the first crib, gently picked up a tiny bundle, and eyed Mason. "Have you ever held a baby before?"

"No," he said, grinning impishly.

"Okay. Well, why don't you sit in the rocking chair?"

Mason did as he was told, and Sue brought the blanket-wrapped bundle over to him. "The most important thing to remember when you're holding a newborn is to support its head." As she said this, she showed him how to cradle the baby's tiny head in his palm, and then she gingerly placed the baby in his arms. "This is Logan."

"Hey, there, Logan," Mason whispered, and then he looked up at Sue. "He hardly weighs anything."

Sue nodded. "You were that tiny once."

Mason shook his head in disbelief and then pulled the blanket back to see Logan's fingers. Immediately, the baby boy reached up and wrapped his tiny fingers around one of Mason's. "Wow, Logan," he whispered softly, "you have a strong grip for a little guy."

Sue smiled, and then took out her phone, and Mason looked up as she tapped the screen. "You've come full circle, Mase," she said, showing him the picture.

"Can you send it to me?'

"Absolutely." She tapped her phone, sending the picture to him, and then slipped it back in her pocket. "You okay for a few minutes?"

He smiled and nodded.

"Okay, just hit this button if you need help. I'll be right down the hall."

"Okay," he said, completely swept away by the amazing little person in his arms. As tiny as he was, he had all the working parts—miniature organs, ten fingers and toes, and a tiny beating heart. He was a miracle—it was almost too amazing to believe, and the idea that *he* had once been this small was even more unbelievable. He looked into the baby's dark blue eyes. "You know any songs, little man?" he whispered, and then he started to softly sing the Gershwin song his mom had always sung to him when he was little. Mason smiled as he softy sang, and the baby's eyes grew wide as he made a small "O" with his mouth and then smiled a little, crooked half smile that lit up his eyes. "Wow," Mason whispered. "Singing really does make a difference."

"It really does," Sue said, and Mason looked up to see her

leaning against the doorway. "I didn't know you were such a good singer, Mason."

He laughed at being caught. "Not really."

"Your mom had a beautiful voice, too."

He nodded and looked down at Logan. "I can't believe how perfect he is—to think he has all these little parts, all working together just the way they're supposed to. He's so tiny, but he has emotions, sensations, thoughts, talents . . . and a whole big life ahead of him. I wonder what he'll do with it."

Sue smiled. "That's why your mom and I loved working in maternity and in the NICU—it gives you pause, and makes you realize just how miraculous life is . . . not to mention how calming holding a baby can be . . . when he's not fussing," she added with a chuckle.

Mason nodded and then looked up. "Soo . . . I've made my decision."

Sue eyed him questioningly. "Decision about what?"

"College."

"*And?*"

"I'm gonna go this fall."

"Oh, that's awesome, Mason. I think it's the right decision."

He nodded. "I'm also going to try to find her soon."

Sue's face lit up with a smile. "Your mom would be so happy. I'm sure she's looking down and beaming right now. She's still watching over *you*, you know."

"I know," he said with a wistful smile. "So, do you have another little miracle for me to sing to?"

"You bet," she said.

Mason got up and gently laid Logan back in his crib. "Don't worry, little man," he said softly. "We'll do this again."

Sue lifted out another baby and handed it to him. "You're not gonna believe this, but this little guy is named Mason."

Mason looked down at the baby. "Nice!" he said with a grin.

# 32

"GUESS WHO *I* MET THE OTHER DAY," MAEVE SAID, EYEING HARPER AS she sat with her sister and niece in one of their favorite downtown restaurants, Goose Feathers Café, having breakfast.

"Who?" Harper said, taking a bite of her chocolate croissant.

Maeve casually dipped her spoon into the café's signature dish, the Bird's Nest, a yummy bowl of grits with homemade salsa, poached eggs, cilantro, and a ring of cheddar cheese, making it look very much like its name. "None other than Master Sam Finch."

"No way!" Harper exclaimed. "Where?"

"Way," she said nonchalantly. "At his house . . . and I can definitely see why you're enamored of him."

Harper's cheeks flamed. "I'm *not* enamored of him."

Maeve raised her eyebrows. "How can you *not* be? He's very cute . . . and he definitely has eyes that 'look like pieces of moorland sky,'" she teased in her best British accent. "Oh, and I also met the infamous Ty Coon."

"What were you doing over at the Finches'?" Macey asked, sipping her coffee. "And how come you didn't stop by?"

"I was making a delivery . . . and I didn't stop by because I'd just seen you at church."

Harper frowned. "What kind of delivery?"

"We had another incident with the chickens, and we ended up with an orphaned baby fox, so I brought it to Mrs. Finch."

"Oh, no," Macey said, eyeing her sister. "What happened?"

"Did Gage kill its mother?" Harper asked, looking horrified.

Maeve nodded. "He had to, Harp," she explained. "She was attacking his chickens, and she was going to keep coming back."

"That's so sad," Harper said, shaking her head.

"It is," Maeve agreed, "and I wasn't going to tell you, but I thought you might hear it from Sam, and then I'd be in trouble. Fortunately, Gage was able to catch her baby, and Mrs. Finch said she would release it when it gets a little older." She blew on a spoonful of her grits, and commented, "She has quite a menagerie over there—two baby possums, a baby owl, a baby robin, and a whole host of other little critters."

"Yeah, everyone says she has a very gentle way with them," Macey said, sipping her coffee. "They say she's an animal whisperer."

"Sam's an animal whisperer, too," Harper said, and then looked at her mom. "Can we stop by and see the baby fox on the way home from Sea Camp today?"

"Maybe," Macey said. "I'll have to call her and ask. If she's planning to release it back into the wild, she probably doesn't want it to have too much interaction with humans."

"I know," Harper said hopefully. "I don't want to hold it. I just want to see it."

"I'll ask her," Macey assured her daughter, who she knew loved animals. She turned to Maeve. "So, are you guys going to Mom and Dad's tomorrow?"

"We are," Maeve said. "You?"

"Yep. Hopefully, we'll both get out of work on time."

"How are things at the germ center?" Maeve teased.

"Germy as ever . . . and busy! Lots of back-to-school physicals and inoculations. I can't believe school starts again in less than a month. Seems like they just got out."

Maeve nodded. "Summer's flying by, per usual." She eyed Harper. "And how is Sea Camp?"

"It's awesome! Monday, we studied sea turtles; Tuesday, we studied dolphins; Wednesday, we studied plankton . . . and today, we're studying sharks!"

"Nice!" Maeve said. "And how are afternoons with Grandma and Grandpa?"

"Great!" she said. "I've beaten Grandpa at checkers every day this week."

Macey laughed, remembering how merciless their father had been when they'd played board games. "Are you sure he's not letting you win?"

Harper frowned. "No way. He said I'm the best checker player he's ever played."

Maeve laughed and eyed her sister. "Either that or he's turned into an old softie."

Macey nodded. "It's possible, although Ben loses to Harper *all* the time."

Maeve swallowed. "Is Mom letting you bring anything?"

Macey laughed. "She's letting me bring an appetizer, so I think we're gonna bring buffalo chicken dip."

"Mmm," Maeve said. "That sounds yummy."

"It's Ben's favorite."

"Mine, too," Harper chimed in, grinning.

"How 'bout you?"

"She's letting me bring dessert, so I'm thinking of making a chocolate chess pie."

"Ooh, that sounds yummy, too."

"I have a new recipe, so we'll see," she said, laughing. "No promises, but Gage was recently talking about a chocolate chess pie he had years ago, and how good it was, so I thought I'd give it a whirl."

"How is that boy?" Macey teased. "How's shacking up together going?"

"Good," Maeve said. "I love living out there, and it's nice having him around all the time and not having to schlep back and forth to my apartment." She suddenly remembered the jewelry box and eyed her sister. "Remind me to tell you what I saw on his drawing table."

Macey nodded, and Harper looked up. "Did he finish his drawing?"

"He did," she confirmed.

"I can't wait to see it," Harper said, and then mused, "I always thought he only drew animals."

"That's what I thought, too, but I guess when you can draw, you can draw anything. Unlike me," she added. "I can't draw a stick figure." She looked at her phone to see what time it was and then scraped the bottom of her bowl. "I hate to run, but I better get to work."

Macey nodded, popping the last bite of her poached-egg breakfast sandwich in her mouth. "We have to go, too. I have to get this one to camp."

"How was your sandwich?" Maeve asked, gathering her things. "I don't know how many times I've almost ordered the Eggetarian."

"It was really good, but *you* will never order it," Macey teased. "You love your Bird's Nest!"

"I do!"

"That's cuz you're such a bird, Aunt Maeve," Harper teased, giggling.

Maeve tousled her niece's hair and pulled her into a hug. "That's enough outta you, missy," she said. Then she hugged her sister. "See you guys tomorrow!"

# 33

Mason rose early, showered, shaved, pulled on a clean pair of Levi's and a light blue oxford, and wolfed down a bowl of cereal. He threw some extra clothes and his toothbrush and deodorant into a duffle bag, and then stood inside the door, trying to decide if he had everything. He tapped his left and right back pockets, respectively, for his phone and wallet, and then remembered the envelope on the table. He retrieved it, folded it in half, and tucked it into his shirt pocket. He turned the button lock on the door, and stood there, trying to decide when he'd be back. He switched the porch light on and off twice, and then left it on—just in case. He had filled up his car and checked the fluids the night before, so this morning he had only two stops to make, and the first one was the Ellijay Coffeehouse for two coffees—one black, and one regular.

Ten minutes later, he came out of the coffee shop and set the cardboard cup tray on the passenger floor. Then he climbed in, pulled the envelope out of his shirt pocket, and opened the maps app on his phone. He slipped the stationery out of the envelope, typed in the address his mom had carefully printed, studied the route that popped up, realized there was a traffic delay, and prayed it would clear by the time he got there.

He put his phone on the passenger seat, and as he pulled out of the parking lot, everyone who happened to be walking by stopped and watched the rumbling old car, and when several boys gave him a thumbs-up, he smiled. Five minutes later, before he'd even had a chance to park in front of J.B.'s Garage, Jeff was walking out with a big smile on his face. "I heard you a mile away."

Mason grinned, climbed out, and watched Jeff walk around the car, nodding his approval. "Looks great, Mason," he said. "You know, my grandfather had a '67 Chevelle . . . same color, too—Marina Blue."

"No, I didn't know. What happened to it?"

"He sold it before anyone realized muscle cars would be in such high demand."

"It's too bad you can't find it—you should look around the internet."

"Yeah, maybe," Jeff said. "That's why it was so much fun to work on this one." He spied the duffel bag on the back seat and eyed him curiously. "You goin' somewhere?"

"Savannah."

Jeff frowned. "That's a long drive."

"Five hours."

"By yourself?"

"Yep, but I wanted to stop by to show you the paint job and thank you for all your help." Then he suddenly remembered the coffee. "I brought you a coffee, too," he said, and then eyed him uncertainly. "Cream and sugar, right?"

Jeff nodded. "Yeah. Thanks," he said. "I can always use a cup of coffee, but you didn't have to . . . I loved working on this car. I wish I had more work like it, and less like *that*," he said, gesturing to a Ford Taurus on the lift behind him.

Mason nodded. "You should get a website and spread the word. I'm sure muscle car enthusiasts would come out of the woodwork if they knew about you."

"Yeah, maybe," Jeff said, wiping his hands on a rag. "When are you going?"

"Now."

Jeff nodded. "Visiting a friend?"

Mason shook his head. "Keeping a promise," he said, closing the hood.

"Well, safe travels . . . and don't forget, before you head off to college, we need to go to a cruise night at the diner."

Mason nodded. "We will," he said, a smile lighting his face. "Mr. Harrison wants to go, too. Maybe this Sunday, if they have one."

Jeff nodded. "Sounds good."

"All right, I better get going," he said, reaching out to shake hands. "Thank you again."

Jeff nodded. "You know how you're going?" he asked as Mason turned the key.

"My phone knows," Mason said, holding it up.

Jeff nodded and stepped back and waved as Mason pulled away.

Mason waved back, glanced down at the open app, and tapped *start*.

As he drove, his mind checked off all the things he still needed to do this week. A large blue-and-white envelope had come in the mail, and when he opened it, he realized it was a welcome packet from Georgia Tech. It had been full of information for incoming first-years—from everything he'd need for his dorm room, like extra-long bedding, which he still needed to find, to the schedule for the looming move-in date for athletes. There was also a note from the cross-country coach to give him a call. And as he'd looked through it, he'd been surprised by how excited he felt about going. For the first time in a long time, he had something to look forward to.

The drive was uneventful and traffic was light—the slowdown his phone had highlighted before he left had cleared by the time he got there—and five hours later, just as the map app predicted, he pulled up in front of a historic old house in downtown Savannah. "This is for you, Mom," he whispered.

He climbed out, eyed the upstairs windows warily, walked up the steps, and stood on the porch, his heart pounding like a drum.

He stepped forward and looked at the name scribbled on the strip of white paper that had been slipped into the brass slot next to the bottom doorbell—it wasn't the name his mom had given him, and the slot next to the upper doorbell was empty. He held his finger over it anyway, closed his eyes, and whispered, "Here goes nothing." He heard a bell upstairs ring, but it was followed by silence, and he looked around the porch. There were two wicker chairs and a small table between them with a lush geranium loaded with red blossoms, and then he noticed a sign in the window: APARTMENT FOR RENT. He frowned, pushed the doorbell again, but for a second time, the only sound he heard was a faintly ringing bell. "I guess I'm off the hook," he said, smiling, his heart feeling lighter. "I kept my promise—I tried, and she is not here."

He'd turned to go down the steps, but then heard a door open. "May I help you?"

Mason turned back and saw a man peering through the screen. "Hi . . . I . . . uh . . . I'm looking for the woman who lives in the apartment upstairs," he said, gesturing upward.

The man nodded. "She moved out two months ago."

"Oh," Mason said. "Uh . . . you wouldn't happen to know where she moved?"

The man shook his head. "No, I'm sorry. I don't."

"Okay, thanks," Mason said, turning to leave. "Sorry to bother you."

"I know where she works, though," the man offered.

Mason turned back.

"Last I knew, she worked at the new nursing home outside of town." He paused, frowning uncertainly. "It's called Willow something . . . Willow Lake or Willow River. I'm not sure, but I know it's out near Bonaventure. Do you know where the old cemetery is?"

And even though Mason had no idea where Bonaventure Cemetery was, he nodded because he was certain the app on his phone did. "Okay. Thank you."

The man studied the tall, slender boy standing on his porch and noticed the startling resemblance he had to the petite redhead who used to rent from him, so he couldn't help but wonder what the boy wanted with his former tenant.

Mason sat in front of the house, considering his options. He'd kept his promise, and he could easily justify heading home, but he felt oddly nudged to keep trying . . . and he knew who was nudging him. He could almost hear her voice. . . . *Oh, Mase, you've driven all this way, go on . . . go find her!*

He groaned, feeling frustrated. He was never going to be able to put this behind him if he didn't find closure. He tapped the search engine on his phone, and began to type "Willow," but before he'd even finished, Willow Pond Senior Care popped up, and he tapped the link. Immediately, a beautiful photo of an old Southern home appeared—it looked nothing like a nursing home. He tapped the address, studied the map, and realized it was only three miles away. "All right, Mom," he muttered, "but if she's not there, I'm going home."

# 34

Maeve was standing in the spacious Willow Pond kitchen, slicing cheddar cheese and placing it on crackers for the last-Friday-of-the-month happy hour snack while Sal stood nearby, drizzling a maple glaze over the salmon filets that were on the menu for dinner that night. "There're bread and butter pickles in the fridge," he offered.

"Okay," Maeve said, knowing the combination of cracker toppings was a favorite with the residents.

Sal opened the fridge. "Do you know whose pie this is?"

"It's mine . . . my lame attempt at a chocolate chess pie. Gage and I are going to my parents' for dinner tonight after work, so I stuck it in there. Is it in your way?"

"No, I just need to move it to a different shelf. Is that okay?"

"Sure," Maeve said.

He took out the jar of pickles and set it on the counter next to Maeve, and then slid the pie out, too. "What do you mean, 'lame'? It looks *delizioso*!"

Maeve laughed, as she scooped pickles and set them on top of the cheddar slices. "That's truly a compliment coming from you, Sal," she said, "but looks aren't everything. I'll have to let you know how it *tastes*."

"If it's good, you better save me a piece," he teased. "Maybe you can make it for dessert sometime."

"Okay," Maeve agreed. "I can do that."

Sal rearranged the contents of the commercial-size fridge and slid the pie onto the bottom shelf. Then he covered the salmon trays with Saran Wrap and slid them onto the top shelves. "I hope your pie doesn't end up smelling like fish."

"I hope not," Maeve said, raising her eyebrows at the possibility, as she put the lid back on the jar of pickles. "Maybe I'll put Saran Wrap over it, too." She slid the pie back out, tore off a piece of Saran Wrap, laid it over the top, and then put it back in the fridge. "I'm sure it'll be fine."

"I'm sure it will be, too," Sal reassured her. "So is Gage coming here first?"

"He is," she confirmed, looking up at the clock. "He should be here soon."

Sal nodded as he measured rice.

Maeve picked up the tray and turned to take it out to the porch, but just as she did, they both heard an odd sound, and eyed each other. "What in heaven's name was that?" Sal asked.

Maeve smiled. "*That* must be Mr. Hawkins's fiddle. I told him he should bring it to happy hour, and he must've taken me up on it!"

Sal chuckled. "Never a dull moment around here with these old coots!"

"True," Maeve agreed. She walked through the foyer and pushed open the screen door.

"Here she is!" Addie said cheerfully, turning to Gladys. "I told you she'd be right along."

Gladys took a sip of her Chardonnay. "Well, it's about time!" she exclaimed. "We thought you got lost."

"I didn't get lost," Maeve said, offering them the appetizers.

Addie—ever prim and proper—took one, her pinky finger daintily up in the air, and placed it on the napkin Maeve offered, but Gladys stacked one on top of another and put them on the table next to her, and then reached for a third and popped the whole thing into her mouth. "What's for dinner?" Gladys asked with her mouth full of crumbs. "Please don't tell me it's fish!"

"Sal is making maple-glazed salmon," Maeve said, bracing for a stormy reaction, but Gladys just nodded and smiled.

"I like salmon," she said, reaching for the wine she and Addie were sharing, and shakily refilling their glasses, giving herself the lion's share. Maeve watched with raised eyebrows, waiting for her to spill, and then realized the bottle was half-empty—which was probably why she was being so agreeable.

Maeve continued down the porch, maneuvering between the walkers and canes, and stopping to offer the tray to each of the residents. Per usual, the men were at the far end, but now, Bud was among them, laughing jovially and enjoying a beer while he adjusted the strings of his fiddle. Aristides, who was sitting beside him, gently stroked sleeping Tallulah's soft orange fur. Maeve offered Landon and Loren Olivetti the crackers, and after all the men had been served, she put one on a napkin and set it next to Ivy Lee, along with a glass of lemonade. As she turned to make her way back, she saw Gage parking his truck, and heard Gladys whisper to Addie. "The maid's beau is here again!"

She watched Gage let Gus out, and she quickly made her way to the top step to slow the pup's rocket-ship trajectory. "Hey, there, mister," she said, laughing as he vaulted over the steps and nearly bowled her over. "Don't forget, you need to take it easy up here."

She knelt down, and he wiggled all around her, thumping her head with his tail, and then he continued wiggling down the porch, happily scoffing up dropped cracker crumbs and the one whole pickle chip Gladys had dropped. Finally, he looked up, sniffing the air, spotted Tallulah curled up on Aristides's lap, and slowly—almost catlike—tiptoed toward her, but Tallulah, sensing a game was afoot, opened one eye and rose, arching her back. Feeling her move, Aristides looked up and saw the confrontation unfolding. "It's okay, Miss Tally," he whispered, stroking her arched back, but his touch triggered her fight-or-flight mechanism, and she leapt from his lap and streaked down the porch, under and between all the walkers and canes with Gus in gleeful pursuit.

"Whoa!" Bud exclaimed as the two animals flew by.

And Gage—who'd just reached the top step—shouted the dog's name, and much to everyone's surprise, especially Gage's, the yellow Lab almost tumbled over himself as he came to a halt and looked back. "Come back here, mister!" Gage commanded, and with his ears back and tail hanging, the big puppy plodded back to him. "Good boy for listening," Gage said softly, "but you know you're not supposed to chase poor Tallulah," he added sternly.

Gus sat down and put his paw on Gage's knee, looking for forgiveness, and Gage tousled his ears. "It's okay."

Addie smiled. "You're such a good boy, Gussie," she cooed. "That darn cat likes to tease you," she added softly, "and you're only doing what your instincts tell you." She offered him a cracker, and as his tail began to wag again, Addie looked up at Gage. "How are you, young man?"

"I'm fine, Miss Addie. How are you?"

"Able to sit up and take nourishment," she said, chuckling.

Gage smiled, remembering how Dutch used to say the very same thing. He looked down the porch. "Good afternoon, everyone."

"Good afternoon!" a chorus of cheerful voices replied.

"Would you like a glass of wine?" Gladys asked, giving him a flirtatious wink.

"Why, no thank you, Miss Gladys," Gage replied politely. He turned to Maeve. "Almost finished?"

"In a bit," she replied. "Why don't you chat with the men for a few minutes?"

Gage greeted each of the ladies by name as he made his way to the end of the porch, and sat down next to the men. "Here's himself!" declared Landon, as Loren pulled a frosty beer out of their cooler and handed it to him—all of them happy to have his company.

"Gage, this is Bud Hawkins," Aristides drawled, as Gus curled up at their feet.

Gage nodded and reached across the porch to shake his hand. "Pleasure, sir."

"Pleasure's mine," Bud replied.

"You play?" Gage asked, nodding to the lustrous maple-wood fiddle in his lap.

"I'm a little rusty, but I still play—I used to compete," he added with a shy smile.

"You did?"

"Yes, sir."

"You know 'Orange Blossom Special'?" Aristides asked hopefully.

"Oh, sure," Bud said.

"Will ya play it for us?"

Bud took in a deep breath and let it out slowly. "Oh, I dunno. Like I said, it's been a while."

Gage watched the old man's face and could tell he really *did* want to play—he just needed a little encouragement. "Tell you what," he offered. "You play somethin' and, if you'll let me, I'll play somethin', too."

Maeve, who was standing in the middle of the porch with her tray, looked up in surprise. "Wait. What?!" she said, eyeing him. "You know how to play the fiddle?! After two years of knowin' you, how could I not know *this*?"

"I don't know," Gage teased. "It's not like I've been hidin' it." He turned back to Bud and winked. "So whad'ya say?"

Bud nodded and stood up. "I jus' need a little room."

"There's room right there," Gage said, nodding toward the open space across from Ivy Lee, but when Bud walked over, the tiny woman frowned fretfully.

Bud's gnarled, old fingers curled around the fingerboard as he touched the bow to the strings and played a few tentative notes. "All right," he said with an impish grin, "here goes nothin'." He slowly bowed a few more notes before launching straight into the old fiddle favorite, "Orange Blossom Special."

Within moments, everyone on the porch was clapping and tapping their feet, and Maeve—who'd sat in Bud's seat to listen—watched in amazement as Ivy Lee's frown faded and she began to move her hands as if clapping. She nudged Gage and whispered, "See? I told you music can have an effect on the memory of an old soul."

Gage nodded and smiled.

Bud kept playing while Aristides stomped his foot and finally got up and danced around, his whole face smiling, and when Bud finished with a flourish, everyone cheered. "Not bad for an ole coot," Bud said amiably before eyeing Gage. "Now, let's see what this youngster can do!"

Gage laughed. "It's been a while for me, too," he said, "so no promises."

"Aww, it's jus' like riding a bike," Bud teased, "or making love," he whispered as he handed Gage his beautiful old fiddle.

"I don't do those very well, either," Gage said, laughing. He stood, and walking over to where Bud had been standing, nodded to Ivy Lee, and ran the bow slowly across the strings—getting a feel for the beautiful instrument—and then he began playing the familiar beginning notes of "Tennessee Waltz."

Maeve watched in wonder as the handsome man she loved pulled the bow slowly back and forth across the strings with a solemn intimacy she'd never seen before, and then she looked over and saw Ivy Lee close her eyes and begin swaying back and forth with a gentle smile on her face. A moment later, Gage transitioned smoothly from the slow, dreamy waltz into the upbeat rhythmic tempo of "Callin' Baton Rouge," and Ivy Lee opened her eyes and—beaming—started stomping her foot in time.

# 35

When Mason pulled into the driveway of Willow Pond Senior Care, the thundering horses under the hood of the old Chevelle drowned out the fiddle and drew the attention of everyone on the porch, but it especially turned the head of the silver-haired veteran leaning against the railing. Bud Hawkins turned and raised his eyebrows in surprise as a tall, slender boy climbed out.

"Who is *that*?" Gladys quipped.

"I don't know," Addie said, trying to see over the railing.

"I bet it's the maid's *son*," Gladys whispered, sipping her wine.

"Or maybe it's Bud's grandson," Addie offered, watching Bud walk down the steps and cross the lawn.

Everyone, including Maeve and Gage, watched curiously as the two shook hands. The boy gestured to the house and Bud nodded, and then they made their way back to the car. Bud walked around it slowly—smiling broadly—and when the boy lifted the hood, the old man raised his hands in what appeared to be genuine amazement. He pointed to different motor parts, asking questions, and the boy nodded, replying and gesturing, too. Finally, Bud clapped him on the shoulder, and just when it looked like they might be considering taking the car for a spin, Sal came out and announced that dinner was ready. He held the door, and everyone gathered their walkers and canes and started to move slowly toward it. Meanwhile, Maeve began cleaning up glasses, cups, and napkins and

Gage looked around for Bud's fiddle case. Finally, he spied it behind a chair, but just as he leaned down to pick it up, Bud and the boy reached the bottom step and he heard Bud say, "So what brings you here anyway? You surely weren't looking for me." He glanced over and saw the boy smile.

"I saw your house was for sale," he answered, "and I've been wondering where you went, but you're right—I'm actually here looking for someone else. I never expected to find *you* here."

"The Lord works in mysterious ways," Bud said, chuckling. "Who are you looking for?"

"Her name is Maeve Lindstrom. I was told she works here. Do you know her?"

"I sure do—she's that lovely lady right there," Bud said, smiling, and Maeve, who was hurrying so she and Gage could head to her parents' house, overheard their conversation and glanced up in surprise.

"Maeve," Bud said, "this handsome fella is looking for you."

Hearing this, Gage looked up again and watched curiously.

"I thought that handsome young man was your grandson," Maeve teased.

"I wish he *was* my grandson," Bud quipped. "Did you see the fine job he did restoring my old Chevelle?"

"Is that your car? Wow! He *did* do a fine job," she said, setting down the tray of glasses and napkins. She gave Gus the last cheese and cracker, and came down the steps, but when she saw the boy's face . . . and his eyes, she felt her heart start to pound.

Mason stood there, and Bud looked from one to the other, frowning uncertainly. "Maeve, this is Mason Callahan—he's from up in the Blue Ridge area."

As he said this, Sal peered out. "Comin' in for dinner, Bud?"

Bud looked up and nodded. "Maybe we can take her for a spin after," he suggested hopefully, and Mason smiled at him and nodded. Bud turned and slowly climbed the steps, and when he reached the screen door, he saw his fiddle case leaning against it, but Gage was at the far end of the porch now, so Bud just picked it up and went inside.

Maeve searched the boy's blue-green eyes—so like her own—and shook her head in disbelief, as the years of pent-up tears filled her eyes. "I've dreamed of this day," she said softly. "Oh, my, oh my, oh my . . ."

Mason bit his lip, feeling tears welling up in his own eyes. Maeve reached up tentatively and rested her hand gently on his cheek and smiled. "You are so tall and handsome."

Mason nodded, but still didn't say anything, and Maeve could see the aching pain and sadness in his questioning eyes. "I'm so sorry," she said softly. "Giving you up was the hardest thing I ever did. I have regretted it every day of my life."

"Why did you?" he asked.

Maeve took a deep breath and let it out slowly. "Because I was young and scared . . . and I know that sounds like a terrible, lame excuse, but I wasn't ready to be a mom, and I was terrified. I hadn't told anyone I was pregnant—not even my parents . . . and I was so afraid of what they'd say . . . what they'd think of me . . . but at the same time, I worried about what would happen to you . . . who would adopt you . . . who would take care of you. After you were born, I begged the nurse—your mom," she said with a smile, "to let me hold you and she told me if I was giving you up for adoption, I couldn't. . . . Well, that just about put me over the edge. I was beside myself. But then later—probably because I wouldn't stop crying—she brought you in."

Maeve shook her head and smiled. "It was so amazing to hold this sweet little bundle—*my son!* My heart overflowed with love . . . so much love I almost changed my mind, but your mom was like this angel that appeared at just the right time. She had the kindest eyes I'd ever seen, and I asked her—begged her—to take care of you . . . and not just while you were in the hospital . . . but *forever* . . . and when she said yes, I was so thankful and amazed. I felt at peace in that moment because it seemed as if it was meant to be. It was as if we all needed something—I needed someone to take care of you, you needed a mom, and she needed someone to love, and I felt as if God had planned it all." She smiled wistfully. "At least, that's what I've told myself all these years."

Mason frowned. "What about my dad?"

Maeve took another deep breath and slowly shook her head. "I know this is going to sound absolutely awful, and it's a big part of why I never told anyone. . . ." She pressed her lips together pensively. "I'm ashamed to say I don't know who your father is, Mason."

Mason raised his eyebrows and waited for her to continue.

"Mine is the classic walk-of-shame tale of a naive freshman who attended a college party, drank more than she could handle, and ended up in an upstairs room with a tall, athletic boy from another school. Things got out of hand, and when I woke up, he was gone. When I asked my friends if they knew him, no one did. Two months later, I realized I was pregnant." Maeve paused, searching his eyes. "You may or may not believe me, Mason, but I wasn't a drinker, and before that night, I had never even kissed a boy."

Mason looked away, trying to absorb these revelations—these answers to the questions he'd struggled with all his life. Maeve reached for his hand. "I've always prayed you'd find me. I didn't want to pressure you, but I sent my address to your mom at the hospital, and she wrote back and even sent some pictures of you. I've treasured them."

She paused again, searching for the right words. "Mason, it broke my heart to not be there to watch you grow up, to not be your mom, but I took comfort in knowing you were in good hands . . . that you were well cared for." As she said this, she heard a motor start, and she looked over to see Gage pulling away. Suddenly, she remembered that they were supposed to be heading to her parents' house, and then, with a sinking feeling, she wondered how much Gage had heard.

She turned back to Mason and smiled, still finding it hard to believe that this tall young man was her son. "I'm so glad you came," she said softly. "How is your sweet mom? Does she know you're here?"

Fresh tears filled Mason's eyes and he shook his head, unable to utter the words. Maeve frowned. "Oh, no," she said softly. "What happened?"

He shook his head again and the tears, like water breaching a dam, spilled down his cheeks. Maeve stepped forward and, for the first time since his birth, held her son, his slender frame wracked with sobs.

"I'm so sorry," she whispered.

Mason nodded, wiping his eyes with his palms until he was finally able to speak and tell her about his mom's diagnosis, her indomitable spirit, her warrior faith, and her undaunted determination . . . right up until the day he graduated from high school. "She made me promise to find you."

"I'm glad she did," Maeve said with a gentle smile.

"Yeah, because I probably wouldn't have," he said, half smiling back.

"How are you managing?" she asked.

"I'm heading to college soon—next week if I try out for the cross-country team. Their practice starts on Tuesday."

Maeve's face brightened. "You are?! Where are you going?"

"Georgia Tech on an Air Force ROTC scholarship."

"Wow! That's very impressive! Do you want to be a pilot?"

He nodded shyly, but then added, "We'll see if I have what it takes."

"I'm sure you do," Maeve assured him. "My dad—your grandfather—was an aeronautical engineer for Gulfstream, so airplanes run in the family." As she said this, they both realized there was a whole family who didn't know about him, but who, Maeve now believed, would welcome him with open arms—something she hadn't been certain of eighteen years earlier. "I'm supposed to go to my parents' for dinner tonight." She eyed him hopefully. "Would you like to come?"

Mason frowned, considering her invitation, but then shook his head. "No, I think I'll take a rain check. Maybe after you have a chance to tell them about me."

"*You* have given me the courage, Mason," she said, and then she searched his eyes. "Is there any way you could stay a little longer? I mean . . . you drove all this way and I just got to meet you . . . *again*." She smiled as she said this, remembering the tiny baby she'd held in her arms the first time.

"I can stay," he said. "I'm waiting for Mr. Hawkins to have dinner . . . but aren't you supposed to be going to your parents' for dinner?"

"I am, but they'll understand. Are you hungry? I'm sure Sal made more than enough food. He was making salmon tonight . . ."

Mason smiled. "No thanks, but I *do* want to hear about your life. I want to get to know you."

Maeve shook her head. "Oh, my life is pretty boring. I'm sure yours is much more exciting."

"I don't know about that," he said, laughing.

As they walked toward the pond, Maeve turned to him. "So, how'd you meet Mr. Hawkins?"

"I was riding my bike home from work last summer and his car was parked in front of his house, for sale, and when I stopped to look at it, he came out. He sold it to me for a song—I didn't even have my license yet, but part of the deal was he wanted me to restore it someday."

Maeve nodded. "He's such a great guy—he didn't want to be here at first, but I think he's finally adjusting." They stood near the pond, watching the swans glide gracefully across the water. "You said you were riding your bike home from work—what do you do for work?"

"I work for a landscaper."

"Do you like it?"

"It's okay, but I wouldn't want to make it my livelihood."

Maeve nodded and then looked over. "Sooo . . . do you have a girlfriend?" she ventured, raising her eyebrows, and then she bit her lip. "You don't have to answer that! Tell me if I'm being too nosy or crossing the line—I can do that sometimes, just ask my sister," she added, laughing. "I can't wait for her to meet you."

Mason smiled, feeling his heart already reaching out to this woman—his biological mom. *What was it about her? She was sweet and funny and she seemed to have such a warm heart.* "I have a friend who is a girl," he offered with a grin.

"Yeah?" Maeve said. "Does she have potential to be more?"

"Yeah . . . maybe," he answered, smiling. "At least, I hope so . . ."

Maeve smiled. "I hope so, too, then." She searched his eyes. "I'm so glad you came, Mason."

He nodded solemnly. "I'm glad I came, too." And then he looked at her as if he was seeing her for the first time—this beautiful woman with the same color eyes and hair as him—this woman who many would call his *real* mom. *But what made someone real? Was it having the same DNA . . . or was it being the one who'd always been there . . . who'd loved you all your life without condition . . . who'd picked you up when you fell, and who'd comforted you when you were sick or sad . . . who'd been there to celebrate your triumphs and console you when you failed? Which woman was his real mom?*

"Are you married?" he asked, suddenly realizing they were still talking about *him*.

Maeve shook her head. "No. I'm living with someone though . . . the guy with the dog who was just here . . . but left, and who, I hope, went to my parents'." She eyed him. "Are you sure you don't want to come? My mom—your grandma," she added with a smile, "is a wonderful cook, and she always makes too much food."

Mason shook his head again. "I would, but I think I've caused enough surprise for one day, and besides, I have to take Mr. Hawkins for a ride, and then I'm heading home."

"Okay," Maeve said, "but I'm going to hold you to that rain check. I know I haven't been part of your life up to now, but I would really like to be . . . if you'll let me."

"I'd like that," Mason said. "Do you have a cell phone?"

"I do," Maeve said, pulling her phone out of her pocket. They exchanged numbers and Maeve gave him her new address. "I'm glad you didn't give up when you didn't find me at my old apartment."

Mason smiled. "Me, too."

As he said this, Mr. Hawkins came out on the porch. "You're still here," he said cheerfully. "I thought you'd be long gone."

"Nope," Mason replied, grinning. "I've been waiting for you."

"Okay! Let me grab my hat."

He headed back inside, and Maeve turned back to Mason. "Please let me know if you need anything. Anything at all."

Mason nodded. "I will."

Maeve eyed him. "Promise?"

Mason laughed. "Now I have someone new to make me promise stuff."

"Absolutely," Maeve said, laughing, too.

"Okay, I promise."

"Good," she said, and he leaned down and gave her a warm hug.

"Ready," Bud said, coming out wearing his faded navy veteran hat.

"Do you want to drive?" Mason asked, grinning.

Bud furrowed his brow. "Oh, I don't know. . . . Are you sure?"

"Absolutely," Mason said, handing him the keys as they walked to the old Chevelle.

Maeve stood in the driveway and watched in amazement as Bud—with a youthful spring in his step—walked beside *her* beautiful son. It was almost too much to take in, and as they pulled away in the old car, she turned to see the house awash with a warm golden light—as if an artist had brushed pink and orange watercolor paint across the Savannah sky.

Maeve looked up. "I know it's you," she whispered. "Thank you."

# 36

As soon as the rumbling motor of the Chevelle faded into the distance, Maeve hurried inside to retrieve her pie. Flying through the kitchen and shrugging off queries about the boy she'd been having "an intense conversation with," she said, "It's a long story, and I have to go." She bid them good night and was out the door again. Reaching her car, she set the pie on the passenger floor, pulled her phone out of her pocket, and called Macey.

"Where the heck are you?" her sister asked. "Mom is fretting about everything getting cold."

"On my way," Maeve assured. "Something came up."

"Okay . . . is Gage with you?"

There was silence on the other end, and then Maeve spoke. "He's not *there*?"

"Uh, *no*."

"Are you sure?"

"Yes, I'm sure, Maeve. Don't you think I'd know if he was here?"

Maeve bit her lip. "Where can he be?" she murmured.

"What?" Macey asked.

"Nothing," Maeve replied. "I just thought he'd be there. He left before me."

"Nope."

"Okay, tell Mom I'm sorry and I'll be there soon."

She hung up and tried Gage's cell phone, but it went straight to his voice mail.

Ten minutes later, she pulled into the driveway of her parents' New England–style home, scooped up the pie, and hurried inside.

"Here you are!" Ruth Lindstrom exclaimed, giving her a hug and admiring her pie. "Looks like a picture, my dear!"

"Well, looks aren't everything. We'll have to see how it *tastes*."

Ruth glanced behind her. "Where's Gage?"

"I don't know," she said, setting the pie on the counter. "I thought he'd be here."

"Maybe he didn't feel well," Hal Lindstrom offered, coming into the kitchen.

"Maybe, but it's kind of odd that he didn't mention it," she replied, giving him a hug.

"He didn't seem sick at work," Ben said, who was leaning against the counter with a beer in his hand. "In fact, he seemed unusually cheerful."

Maeve nodded. "He wasn't sick when he came by Willow Pond, either. In fact, he even challenged one of the residents to a fiddling contest."

"Wait! Uncle Gage plays the fiddle?!" Harper asked. "Sheesh, I only thought he could draw."

"Gage is a man of many talents," Macey said, laughing and taking a sip of her wine.

"I know, right?" Maeve said. "I didn't know it, either." Just then, Keeper, hearing her voice, wagged his way in, and when Maeve knelt to say hello, he bowed his head and pressed it into her chest. "Hullo, ole pie," she said softly, kissing the top of his head.

"Well, let's eat—everything's ready," Ruth said, "and I don't want it to get cold. If he doesn't show up, you can bring a plate home."

Maeve nodded, although she couldn't shake the feeling that Gage's absence—and his lack of an explanation for it—was more serious than not feeling well. She didn't know how much he'd overheard, and she wished she'd just told him everything a long time ago. She'd texted him twice and called him again, but he still hadn't replied . . . or answered.

"Something to drink?" Hal asked, gesturing to the array of options on the counter.

"I'd love a glass of whatever wine is open," Maeve said.

"White or red?" Hal pressed.

"White," Maeve said, scooping some of her sister's spicy buffalo chicken dip onto a hunk of French bread and taking a bite. "Mmm, this is yummy!"

"I told you."

"You did."

Hal handed her a glass of wine, and she took a long sip. "Thanks, Dad."

"Do you mind buffet style?" Ruth asked, donning her oven mitts and pulling a crock of baked beans from the oven and setting it on one of the trivets on the counter.

"We usually serve dinner that way when the gang's all here," Hal said, "so why would they mind?" Ruth ignored her husband's teasing quip and reached back into the oven for her famous mac and cheese.

Maeve frowned. "Mom, do you need help?"

"No . . . just a couple more things," she said, pulling a spiral-sliced baked ham out and setting it next to the other dishes. Then she slipped off her oven mitts, opened the fridge, and pulled out a tray of deviled eggs and a bowl of potato salad.

"Gee, Mom," Macey teased, "I don't think you made enough."

Ruth smiled and slid a tray of rolls into the oven. "Hon, can you slice the ham?"

"It's already sliced," Hal said.

"Well, put some on a platter, please."

Hal chuckled, but did as he was asked, and then Ruth gestured to the plates. "Help yourself," she said cheerily. "The rolls just have to heat up for a minute."

Ben handed plates to his daughter, wife, and sister-in-law, and hung back, waiting for Ruth to serve her plate. "Dad, you want another beer?" he asked, opening the fridge.

"Sure," Hal said, setting the platter of ham next to the brown-sugar-and-pineapple-glaze Ruth had just set out.

Ben handed him a beer and smiled. "I think you're going to be eating leftovers for a while, Dad."

"Oh, no," Hal said, laughing. "You kids will be taking some of this home. I like ham, but after a couple nights, it's time for a change."

Ben laughed. He knew his father-in-law wasn't a big fan of leftovers. The two men filled their plates and waited for the women to sit before seating themselves. And then, finally, they bowed their heads and Hal said grace.

When he finished, Maeve took a sip of her wine, gathered her courage, and cleared her throat. "So, I have some news. . . ."

Harper's face lit up. "Are you and Uncle Gage engaged?!"

Maeve shook her head. "No, but it's something *just* as good. . . ."

# 37

The cabin was dark when Maeve pulled in, and she frowned, wondering where Gage could be, but then she heard an excited bark, and a moment later, Gus emerged from the shadows, wagging his tail. "Hey there, Gussie," she said, opening her door. The big Lab put his front paws on her lap and sniffed the air. "Yes, I have food," she said, laughing. She reached over for the plate her mom had piled high with food and covered with foil, all the while—like everyone else in her family—asking questions about, and expressing dismay over, Maeve's long-kept secret.

She climbed out of her car, balancing the plate and the last piece of pie—which had turned out to be *amazing*—and made her way up the dark path. When she reached the porch steps, though, she was startled to see Gage sitting in one of the old Adirondack chairs with a whiskey tumbler in his hand and a bottle of Jack Daniel's on the table.

"Hey," she said.

He reached up and pulled an earbud out of his ear, but didn't say anything.

"What happened? Why didn't you come to my parents' house?"

He swirled his glass and took a sip.

"Why haven't you been answering your phone? I've been worried."

"Yeah?" he said, his voice edged with sarcasm.

Maeve felt her heart pound. "Gage, what's wrong?"

He clenched his jaw and shook his head. "You should *know* what's wrong."

"Well, I *don't*," she replied, hoping his odd behavior wasn't because of Mason. "So just say it."

"How come *you* didn't tell me, Maeve?" he asked. "We've been together for two years and you never thought that you should mention that you have a son?"

"I wanted to mention it, Gage, but I worried about how you might take it."

"And how's that?"

"Like *this*," she said, setting the plate on the table and sitting in the chair opposite him, eyeing the level of whiskey in the bottle.

Gage shook his head, drained his glass, and refilled it.

"It happened a long time ago," she said. "It has nothing to do with us."

"It has everything to do with us."

Maeve shook her head. "I don't know why," she said defensively. "Giving up my son was a decision I made when I was eighteen—I was young and scared. I didn't know what to do. All I knew was my whole future lay ahead of me and I wasn't ready to have a child, but on one foolish night, I drank too much . . . and I . . . I didn't even know the guy's last name. . . ."

Gage raised his eyebrows. "Oh, wow, that makes me feel *so* much better."

"I suppose you were a virgin when we met."

"That's not it, Maeve," he said, shaking his head in disbelief. "It has nothing to do with *who* came before. Don't you get it?"

"No, I guess I don't," she replied.

Gage swirled his glass and didn't say anything, but when the haunting call of a loon broke the silence, he shook his head. "How ironic."

Maeve pressed her lips together. "Gage, I'm really sorry I didn't tell you. It happened such a long time ago—long before I knew you. I would never do anything to hurt you . . . and I don't understand why you can't forgive me."

Gage pressed his lips together, carefully considering his words. "The summer before I went away to college, I fell head over heels in love with a girl who I would've done anything for, and even though we were young, I honestly thought we would spend the rest of our lives together. I had it all planned—I even started saving for an engagement ring . . . and then, one summer night, I happened to be looking for her . . . and I found her . . . behind a barn, half-undressed with another boy." He paused and took another sip. "I was devastated, and I vowed I'd never let myself get hurt again. And that's how I moved forward—I never let anyone get too close. I never let anyone in. . . ." He searched her eyes. "Until I met you. You were different, Maeve. You were down-to-earth, funny, sweet and—most of all—I came to trust you completely. I felt blessed to have you in my life." He looked up. "Maeve, I honestly felt like I could spend the rest of my life with you, but now, I can't seem to wrap my mind around why you didn't tell me about this. You have to admit, it's kind of a big deal—what you went through . . . you know, having a child and giving it up for adoption. In my book, that's a pretty major life experience, and yet—for whatever reason—you failed to mention it, and now, I sort of feel like I don't really know who you are . . . or what other secrets you might be keeping."

"There are no other secrets," Maeve whispered, her eyes filling with tears. "I'm sorry. I should've told you. I guess I was more afraid of what you'd think of me for giving him up."

Gage shook his head. "I feel like not being forthcoming and completely honest isn't a good foundation to build a relationship on."

"In my defense," Maeve said softly, "you haven't been completely forthcoming, either."

Gage raised his eyebrows. "I haven't kept any secrets. What you see is what you get."

"That's not true," Maeve countered, shaking her head. "I know very little about your family . . . or why they aren't part of your life, and every time I ask you, you change the subject."

Gage swirled his drink, took a sip, and looked away, and Maeve could see tears glistening in his eyes. *Had she just said the wrong thing* again? *Had she just hammered the last nail in the coffin?*

Gage bit his lip, as buried memories from his youth swirled to the surface. He swallowed. "Do you want to know what happened?" he asked in a voice that sounded bitter.

"Only if you want to tell me," she said.

"Okay," he said, refilling his glass. He swirled the golden liquid, and then began to haltingly share the memory of the night in the barn that always played in his mind when he thought about his father.

When he finished, he shook his head. "I know my dad was worried about our cow—I was, too. She was this beautiful reddish-brown Ayrshire and I'd shown her many times. We'd won countless blue ribbons together, but that night, she was having a really hard time. I asked my dad if he wanted me to call our vet, but he said if he needed to get by without my help, he may as well get started, so I went back in the house. A little while later, I heard a commotion and I looked out to see my brother Matt silhouetted in the barn doorway motioning for Doc Jacobs and my mom to hurry."

Gage took a sip and pressed his lips together. "I didn't go down to see what was happening because my dad had been so dismissive, and I didn't find out till the next morning that Chestnut had died and her calf was stillborn."

"Oh, no," Maeve whispered.

"For a long time, my dad hardly looked at me, but things finally started to get better between us the following summer," he continued. "I'd been accepted to SCAD and Cale was home—which always put him in a good mood. But then, later that summer, Cale was helping my dad pull a tractor out of the mud, and the chain they were using snapped, ricocheted around like a whip, and hit

Cale in the chest." Gage put down his glass and rubbed his eyes with his palms. "He died instantly."

Maeve blinked back tears. Even though she knew this from the news clipping, she didn't know everything that had transpired between Gage and his father. "I'm really sorry," she said softly.

"After the accident, my dad was despondent, and it seemed like he and I were back at square one. We were both grieving, but I also began to think he wished it was me helping him that day instead of Cale. Cale loved the farm—he was the one who really wanted to take it over one day. But after the accident, that would never happen. I don't know if my dad wished it had been me instead of Cale, but it sure felt that way." Gage closed his eyes and fell silent, the whiskey making his thoughts swirl around in his head like a summer storm.

"I'm so sorry all that happened," Maeve said. "I'm sorry for everything."

"Me, too," Gage said softly. "I'm sorry because . . . honestly, Maeve, I don't think this is going to work out."

Maeve frowned, uncertain if she'd heard him right. "Wait. What?" she said. She shook her head as fresh tears filled her eyes. "You mean *us*?"

Gage nodded. "I mean *us*. I love you more than you'll ever know, Maeve, but after all we've been through, and done together . . . through all the times we've been intimate . . . wrapped up in each other . . . you never said *anything*. I trusted you more than I've ever trusted anyone . . . and . . ." He shook his head. "It's just different now."

Maeve stared into the darkness, her vision blurred by her tears.

# 38

"No one's ever slept in here," Macey said, fluffing the pillows on the guest room bed, "except, maybe, Big Mac or Keeper. . . . Keep's old bed is in here."

"I probably won't sleep, either," Maeve said, sitting on the edge of the bed, her eyes puffy and red-rimmed from crying. She still couldn't believe everything that had happened—from finding Mason to losing Gage. It was all so unreal . . . so unfathomable, and as new tears filled her eyes for the umpteenth time, her sister sat down and pulled her close. "My heart is just a big ache," she whispered, using the phrase they both used when they felt sad, beginning way back when their grandmother, Grandy, had died.

"He'll come around," Macey whispered softly. "Every relationship has ups and downs, and this is just a down. If it's meant to be, you'll get through it. Just remember, you didn't tell *me*, either—which I can't believe, but *I* still love you."

"I know. . . . I'm sorry, Mace," Maeve said, shaking her head, "but I don't know if he'll come around. He was so adamant, and said *he* would leave if I didn't, but he'd had so much to drink, I couldn't let him be the one to leave. Not to mention, it's *his* cabin."

"Well, that there is probably a big part of the problem. He might not have been so irrational if he wasn't drinking. You know," she teased gently, handing her sister a tissue, "drinking and poor decision making are very often partners in crime."

"You're not kidding," Maeve said, wiping her eyes.

"So tell me more about Mason. . . . And by the way, did his adoptive mom give him that name?"

"She did."

"Do you realize it might be a tribute to you? *Mae's son?*"

Maeve smiled through her tears. "I didn't think of that." She shook her head. "But it would be just like her. I only met her that one time, but she was such a sweet woman—and she did such a good job raising him. I can't believe she died. He must be so heartbroken."

"How old was she?"

"Midforties."

"That's really sad. How did he seem to be handling it?"

"He seemed okay. It's been a few weeks, so he's had some time to adjust, but I'm sure he must get overwhelmed at times—how could he not? It was just the two of them."

Macey nodded, listening and letting her little sister process all her emotions out loud. She knew talking was often the best way to deal with trauma, and Maeve had definitely had her share of trauma—*and* drama—that day.

"Mace, you should see him—he's so tall and handsome and polite. I can't wait for you to meet him. I can hardly believe he's part of me."

"I can't wait *to* meet him," Macey said. "When do you think that might happen?"

"I tried to get him to come to dinner, but he's definitely wiser than me because he suggested I tell you first . . . and he was right. Dad seemed to have a hard time absorbing everything, but Mom—she was too funny—the way she wanted to help him shop for college supplies." Maeve shook her head. "Dad will love his car, though . . . when he gets to see it." Maeve suddenly felt tears filling her eyes again. "Mace, what's wrong with me? Why can't I stop crying?"

"Oh, Maeve," Macey said, pulling her close again and resting her chin on top of her sister's head. "You're tired and you've been through a lot—you've had two huge monkey wrenches thrown into your life today, not to mention, you've been thrown out of your home."

"At least Gage opened up, finally," Maeve said with a wry smile. "You know what they say—there's truth in wine . . . or, in his case, whiskey."

Macey shook her head. "Yeah, well, you were right to point out that he wasn't forthcoming. Just because his story is tragic, doesn't mean he couldn't share it with you. He's just as guilty."

Maeve bit her lip. "I'm going by tomorrow to pack up some things."

"Want me to go with you?"

"Would you?" Maeve asked hopefully.

"Absolutely," Macey said. "And you can stay here as long as you need to. Even when he *does* come around, which I'm sure he will, I wouldn't go running back. He needs to realize all he's losing."

"I know," Maeve said, nodding. "He's gonna miss Harper the most," she said, laughing.

Macey laughed, too. "That's for sure . . . and at least you're smiling." She yawned. "Well, I need to get back to bed. You gonna be okay?"

Maeve nodded. "Yeah. Thanks for being there. I never thought I'd need a place to stay."

"Hey, that's what sisters are for," she said, kissing the top of Maeve's head.

Just then, a black nose pushed open the door and Keeper peered in, wagging his tail.

"Well, look who's here," Macey said softly. "Are you checking on our guest?" she asked, and the big golden retriever wagged his tail as he wiggled in. A moment later, Big Mac sauntered in, too, and hopped up on the bed. "They're not used to someone staying in this room."

"They're welcome to stay," Maeve said hopefully. And, as if on cue, Keeper curled up on his old bed, while Big Mac curled into the fleecy cover at the end of the bed.

"There you go," Macey said, watching her two rescues get comfortable. She gave her little sister a hug. "Can't believe you're a mom, Maeve! Now, I know why you pushed so hard on us adopting."

"There are a lot of good kids out in the world who need homes. Just look at Harper . . . *and* Mason," Maeve said, smiling.

# 39

Gage slid his hand over to Maeve's side of the bed, felt the coolness of the sheets, and opened his eyes, as the events of the previous night washed over him like a crushing wave and filled his aching head.

"Damn," he whispered, rubbing his temples. He heard a thumping sound, looked over, and saw Gus resting his chin on the edge of the bed, his tail hitting the bureau, happy to find evidence of life. "I'm getting up, buddy," he assured him. "Just give me a minute."

Ten minutes later, Gage pulled on his jeans, shuffled to the bathroom, and purposely avoided looking in the mirror. Meanwhile, Gus waited patiently, and when Gage finally let him out, the big Lab lifted his leg for a full minute. "Sorry to make you wait so long," Gage said. "I didn't know it was urgent." He filled Gus's bowl with kibble, freshened his water bowl, and while the adult-size puppy wolfed down his breakfast, made a pot of coffee. He swallowed Tylenol with a full glass of water, poured a mug of steaming coffee, and went out on the porch. Thunder rumbled in the distance, and he looked up at the slate-gray Savannah sky and realized he hadn't seen a forecast in days, but in the humid South—especially along the coast—summer storms were common. Gage set his mug on the table between the chairs and walked across the yard to the fenced-in area around the henhouse in which—for safety reasons—the chickens were still spending their nights. He opened the gate. "Mornin', ladies and gent," he said, tossing feed on the ground. "How's it goin', missy?" he asked, kneeling down next to one of his new hens. Both Amelia Egghart and Mother Clucker had grown out of their fluffy chick stage and moved into the coop, and the two remaining hens, Eggith and Eggel, along with their fearless protector, Pilgrim, had welcomed them into the flock with open wings.

Gage left the gate open so they could free-range and walked back to the porch. He folded himself into the same chair he'd sat in the night before and took a sip of his coffee.

"Obviously, coffee should be the only thing I drink," he muttered, and Gus—hearing him—looked up and thumped his tail in seeming agreement, making Gage wonder if animals sensed a difference in their owners' demeanor when they were drinking. "Sorry if I behaved badly last night and made you worry." The dog thumped his tail again and Gage was certain his faithful companion—whose love was notoriously unconditional—had already forgiven him.

Unfortunately, the same wasn't true for humans. Gage looked out over the lilies, bee balm, and black-eyed Susans, and rubbed his temples, but his head wasn't the only part of him that ached. He replayed everything that had happened. He pictured the tall, slender boy talking to Maeve, and although he realized she must've been shocked to be confronted—out of the blue—by the child she'd given birth to eighteen years earlier, he still couldn't for the life of him understand why she'd never told him.

"Why, Maeve?" he whispered. He'd been stunned when he'd witnessed from the porch the scene playing out before him . . . but *had he overreacted when he'd left without explanation? Had it been an overreaction to not answer his phone because he was hurt, angry, disappointed?* It had definitely been an overreaction to drink as much as he had—because not only was he paying the price today, but also the alcohol had allowed his emotions to get the best of him. Then again, maybe his reaction had been triggered by all the loss and pain he'd felt when he was younger—the intense grief of losing his brother, the heartbreaking betrayal by the one girl with whom he'd fallen in love . . . and his estranged relationship with his dad. He'd needed time to think . . . time to wrap his mind around the realization that the person he'd grown to love and trust most in the world had purposely not shared an experience that must have played a huge role in shaping her life . . . in shaping who she'd become as an adult.

"What the heck, Maeve?" he whispered, wiping his eyes with his palms, and then, suddenly he remembered the engagement ring. "Damn!" He just wanted to see her . . . to look in her eyes and try to understand.

As if on cue, his phone rang, and hoping it was Maeve, he hurried inside to retrieve it from the kitchen counter, but when he looked at the screen, he frowned.

"Hey, Chase," he said, trying to sound cheerful, but a moment later, his voice grew solemn. "Wait! What?" he asked uncertainly, trying to understand his little brother, whose voice was choked with emotion. He listened, nodding. "Okay. I'll come." He rubbed his head, about to hang up, but then asked, "How's Mom?" He nodded, still listening. "Okay," he said softly. "Thanks. I'll come as soon as I can."

He slid his phone in his pocket and frowned, trying to remember where he'd tucked the letter from his mom—he could picture the envelope and he knew he'd put it in a safe spot. That was the trouble with safe spots, though—they were so safe, you couldn't even find them yourself. He looked through the pile of papers on the kitchen table, and then stood in front of his bookcase and pulled his tattered Bible off the shelf, slipped out the blue envelope, sat down at his drawing table, and turned on the light.

# 40

Mason glanced around the coffeehouse. Just twenty-four hours earlier, he'd stopped in the same shop to get coffee before driving five hours to Savannah . . . and then home again. And after Mr. Hawkins had thanked him profusely, given him a hug, and made him promise to keep in touch, Mason had turned back onto the highway. Almost immediately, his mind had started replaying everything that had happened, but instead of finding a hotel—as he'd planned to do—he'd continued to drive . . . and think, and before he'd known it, he'd pulled into his own driveway, and been thankful he'd left the porch light on.

That morning, he'd texted Ali to see if she wanted to go hiking, or maybe shopping, and she—of course—had chosen the latter. But coffee first! she'd added with a sleepy emoji, and they'd agreed to meet at Ellijay Coffeehouse.

"So?" she asked when Mason slid into the seat across from her with his breakfast of choice—an Appalachian Sunrise breakfast panini and a black coffee. "How'd it go?"

"It went well," he replied, smiling. Then he realized she didn't have any food in front of her. "Don't you want something to eat?"

She shook her head. "I'm good with coffee."

"You want half of this?" he asked, gesturing to his sandwich.

"No, thanks," she said. "I'm cutting back."

"Cutting back?" he said with a frown. "What for? There's nothing to you."

"There will be. Have you ever heard of the freshman fifteen?"

"That won't happen," he said dismissively, as he took a bite. "You're way too active."

"Anyway, back to my original question . . ."

Mason looked up, feigning puzzlement.

She rolled her eyes in exasperation. "How. Did. It. Go?"

"It went well," he answered, smiling innocently.

"Oh, my goodness!" Ali said. "You have to tell me more than that. Was she what you expected? Was she surprised? Did she cry? Did *you* cry?"

Mason laughed and eyed her suspiciously. "Are you writing a book?"

"Maybe," she teased. "You never know. . . . It's certainly book material!"

Mason shook his head and sipped his coffee. "Guess who else I saw," he said, changing the subject.

Ali rolled her eyes again and shook her head. "I don't know. Who?"

"Mr. Hawkins—the man I bought my Chevelle from."

"Where did you see *him*?" she asked in surprise.

"You're not gonna believe this, but he's a resident at the senior place where Maeve works."

"No way!"

"Way. I got to take him for a ride . . . actually, he took *me* for a ride."

"That's crazy."

"What . . . him taking me for a ride?"

"No, that you found him there."

"Well, when I bought the car, he told me his family wanted him to move to Savannah, but what are the chances . . . right?"

Ali nodded. "My mom always says 'God works in mysterious ways.'"

Mason smiled. "My mom used to say that, too."

"So . . . is that what you're gonna call her . . . Maeve?"

Mason took a sip of his coffee. "I guess so. I don't really know what to call her—calling her *Mom* doesn't feel right. At least, not yet . . . maybe not ever."

Ali nodded. "Well, you still haven't told me much."

"What did you ask again?" he teased.

"Was she what you expected? Was she surprised? Did she cry? Did you cry?"

"Oh, yeah! She was great. Very surprised. And yes, we both cried."

"Do you look like her?"

"Maybe a little," he said with a shrug. "She has red hair."

"You should've taken a picture," Ali said, looking disappointed, and then her face lit up. "Maybe she's on Facebook!" She pulled out her phone, tapped her Facebook app, and when it opened—like any good detective—she tapped the magnifying glass icon. "How do you spell her name?"

Mason groaned and reluctantly spelled Maeve's name, and as Ali typed, several possible profiles popped up. She tapped the first one and looked at the photo. "A little?!" she said in disbelief. "Mason, she looks just like you—she could be your sister, never mind your mother! She's beautiful." She enlarged the picture and continued to study it. "You definitely have her eyes—they're the same color and everything . . . and your hair is the exact same color!"

Mason raised his eyebrows and held out his hand, and Ali handed her phone to him. He gazed at Maeve's photo and a crooked smile spread across his face. Yep, that was the kind lady he'd met. And Ali was right—she *did* look like him . . . or he like her—whichever it was. He quickly scrolled through her timeline and realized that either she didn't post very often or her page was set on private. He handed the phone back to Ali, and she eyed him. "Am I right or am I right?"

Mason smiled and shrugged.

"You should friend her," Ali said. "I'm sure she'd confirm you."

"Maybe," Mason said.

Ali rolled her eyes and put her phone away. She knew Mason well enough to know he wouldn't be coerced into anything—if he wanted to friend his biological mom, he would do it when he was ready and not a second sooner.

"So, where should we go shopping?" she asked.

Mason pulled a piece of paper out of his pocket and unfolded it. "I have a list."

"Perfect," she said, holding out her hand.

He handed it to her and while she perused it, he took another bite of his sandwich. "Where do I find extra-long sheets? I didn't even know they made extra-long beds . . . because if I had, I would've asked my mom to buy one for me a long time ago."

"My mom says all the stores have them, especially this time of year because all the dorm rooms have extra-long beds."

"Nice," Mason said, smiling. "I'll look forward to not being cramped or having my feet hang off the end of the bed."

Ali looked up. "I wouldn't know—I've never had that problem." She looked back at his list. "I need a lot of this stuff, too. I guess our best bet is Walmart."

"Figures," Mason said, frowning—he hated shopping. "Are you sure you don't want to go hiking?"

Ali laughed. "We both need to get this done. When are you leaving?"

"Monday. I'm thinking of trying out for the cross-country team, and preseason starts on Tuesday with a meeting Monday afternoon."

"Wait! What? I didn't know you were leaving so soon," she said, her smile fading.

Mason nodded. "I know. I wasn't sure if I was going to—I just decided . . ."

"Can you do that—just show up and try out?"

"I talked to the coach and told him some of my race times in high school, and he said I was welcome to try out, but I've been pretty lax this summer so it's going to be a challenge."

"Do they have a room for you?"

"Yep, athletes move in early."

"Then I think we should definitely go shopping because when else will you do it?"

Mason shrugged. "I don't know. I guess I thought I'd do it after I got there."

Ali frowned. "No, we should go today . . . and maybe we can go hiking tomorrow . . . *if* you're all packed."

"I'm planning to pack tonight," he said, and then he smiled sadly. "I'm gonna miss you, Al. Who's gonna get me through the hard times?"

She looked in his eyes. "I'm gonna miss you, too, Mase. But we're only twenty minutes apart."

"Yeah, *if* you're driving," he said, "and first-years can't have cars."

She smiled. "I heard there's a shuttle between Emory and Georgia Tech."

Mason's face brightened. "There *is*?"

She nodded, and Mason grinned. "Game changer!"

Ali eyed him with a frown. "If you can't have a car, how are you planning to get there?"

"I don't know," he said, and then his face lit up. "Want to drive me?"

"I guess I'll have to," Ali said, shaking her head and laughing. "I love the way you go through life, Mason, without a set plan, just hoping things will work out."

"And they usually do," Mason said, grinning. "My mom called it 'a wing and a prayer.'"

"And she was right," Ali said, laughing.

# 41

"Where the heck is he now?" Maeve asked, as she and Macey pulled into the driveway of the cabin on Saturday afternoon and found Gage's truck missing. "I was hoping he'd be here so, you know, he could tell me he how much he regretted everything he said last night."

Macey eyed her. "What did *we* talk about?"

"I know, I know. Don't go running back," Maeve said as she climbed out, "but I was still hoping it was just the whiskey talking."

Macey followed her sister up the path, admiring the flowers. "Your gardens are gorgeous, Maeve."

"Thanks. I've spent a lot of time out here, but they're not gonna be mine to tend anymore."

"They'll be *your* gardens again," Macey said dismissively. "You should've let Harper come with us—she still talks about the day she came over and helped you in the garden."

"I would've let her come if I knew Gage wasn't going to be home."

"Did you try to call him?"

"I texted, but he hasn't written back."

Macey shook her head. She liked Gage. He was a sweet, funny, and fun-loving person. He was a perfect match for her sister, not to mention he fit in perfectly with their family—Ben, their parents, *and* Harper, who adored him—so she didn't understand why the news of a long-ago transgression had made him react so strongly. Maeve said he'd had his heart broken when he was younger, but that, too, had been a long time ago. In fact, it must've happened around the same time, and what an odd twist that would be. *Was it possible that they'd both gone through something traumatic and heartbreaking around the same time . . . when they were around the same age?*

"Remember when we were having breakfast at Goose Feathers the other day, and I asked you to remind me to show you something?" Maeve asked, as she pulled open the screen door.

"I do," Macey replied.

Maeve tried to turn the knob of the main door, but it was locked. "That's odd. He *never* locks the door." She reached under the mat for the key, unlocked it, and put the key back.

They went inside and Macey watched as her sister looked through the contents of the drawer under Gage's drawing table. "What was it?" she asked.

"It was a little black jewelry box. I don't know what was in it . . . because I didn't look—even though I had the chance—but I thought it might be an engagement ring."

"No way!" Macey said in surprise.

Maeve nodded and closed the drawer. "It's not here now, though," she said glumly. She clicked on the lamp and realized Gage had framed the small photo of Dutch and stood it on the shelf above his table. "Here's that drawing he just finished of his grandfather, though—the one Harper was talking about."

Macey looked over her shoulder. "Wow! That's amazing!" she said, admiring his work. "He's very talented." She studied the image. "Do you think there's a little family resemblance?"

"I know, right?" Maeve said. "You should see his brothers."

Macey frowned. "Where have you seen his brothers?"

"On Facebook," Maeve said. She knew her sister wasn't a fan of the social media site, so when Macey raised her eyebrows, Maeve admitted, "Yeah, I was snooping." She reached up to turn off the lamp and noticed a sheet of blue stationery on top of the pile of papers—*was it the same letter she'd seen in his Bible?*

Macey had disappeared into the kitchen. "Want some coffee?"

Maeve looked up. "Sure, it's in the cabinet next to the sink." She picked up the letter and studied the long, elegant handwriting.

*Dear Gage,*

*It was so good to hear your voice a couple of weeks ago! You don't know how much I miss it! Anyway, I don't know if you will remember when we spoke that I mentioned Dad hasn't been feeling well—headaches and nausea—and on the day of your call, because somehow you know when he's not around, he'd been to the doctor for some tests. Well, today, we both went back to find out the results . . . and as I sit here, tonight, I can barely believe the news I have to share. Gage, I know your relationship with Dad has been difficult, but he has just been diagnosed with a very aggressive form of inoperable brain cancer and the doctor has given him only a couple of months to live. As I write these words, I can barely see the page because of the tears that are welling up in my eyes.*

*For years, I've prayed that you two would find a way to reconcile your differences. We miss having you here—even having you visit, especially on the holidays. I know you come by when he's not around, but that isn't enough for your poor mother's heart—a heart that aches to see and hug her strong, handsome son—the one with the sensitive old soul. It aches for all the time we've lost not being together while on this earth. Life is much too short.*

*Gage, I know you believe your dad blames you for some of the things that have happened, but I also know, with all my heart, that it isn't true! He only blames himself. He blames himself for not letting you call Doc Jacobs when Chestnut was struggling; he blames himself for not being more understanding when you wanted to pursue your own dreams; and most of all, he blames himself for Cale's accident. No matter how many times I've tried to tell him it wasn't his fault—just like I try to tell you he doesn't blame you (you two are more alike than you know!)—he doesn't believe me. It's something he will never get over. I know he seems distant and difficult and stubborn to you boys, but he loves you with all his heart . . . and he misses you. He doesn't tell you these things, though, because, as you know, it's just the way he is.*

*As I write these words to you on this summer night, the loons are calling—it's such a haunting sound, but it reminds me of when you and Cale were little, when it was just the two of you, before your younger brothers all came along—and how you, especially, loved lying in bed, listening to them . . . and how you knew what each of their calls meant, thanks to Dutch, of course—someone else you should visit!*

*Oh, Gage, I know how hard it will be for you to come home and see your dad, but I truly believe if you don't make amends and find it in your heart to forgive him, you will carry this unresolved sorrow and regret all your life, and I don't want that for you. Dad loves you so much, and I know he would love to see you. His diagnosis has devastated all of us. Please think about coming home. God wants us to forgive, Gage, because when we hang on to the pain someone has caused us, we only end up hurting ourselves. Dad and I love you so much! Please come home and see him!*

*Love,*
*Mom*

Maeve was still staring at the page when Macey came into the room, carrying two steaming mugs of coffee. "You still take it black, ri—?" she started to ask, but then saw her sister's face and stopped. "What's the matter?"

Maeve exchanged the letter for one of the mugs and waited while Macey read it. Finally, her sister looked up. "Wow, this is so sad. I know you said he's had a lot goin' on, but sheesh . . ."

Maeve nodded. "Now I really I wonder where he is," she said softly.

Just then, Macey's phone hummed, and she pulled it out of her pocket and read a text from Ben.

Are you still at the cabin?

Yes

Gage just texted—he's gonna be away for a few days and he needs someone to look after the chickens.

Macey frowned.

Where'd he go?

Home to Tennessee, Ben wrote back. Family emergency

Macey took in a deep breath and slowly let it out.

"What?" Maeve asked.

"Gage is on his way to Tennessee—something must've happened."

"Oh, no," Maeve whispered.

# 42

Cars and trucks were parked every which way when Gage pulled into his parents' driveway. Gus sniffed the air excitedly, wagging his tail, ready to leap out and explore, but Gage just sat there, looking at the old white farmhouse. He needed to gather his thoughts . . . *and* his courage. *What* do *you say to someone who is dying, especially after so many years of silence?* Suddenly, he heard a commotion, and then the screen door swung open and a man emerged with his hands over his face. Gage frowned. Two of his brothers, Matt and Eli, looked so much alike they were often mistaken for twins, but Matt was taller, so when a second figure strode out behind him, Gage knew the one in front had been Matt. He wondered if Grayson and Chase were there, too. Of all his brothers, Matt had grown closest to their dad after Cale died, doing his best to fill their oldest brother's shoes.

Gage opened his door, and Gus—finally free—leapt over his lap and raced across the yard, taking in all the wonderful barnyard scents, but when two coon hounds charged around the house, bellowing, the happy-go-lucky Lab came to a stiff halt. The three dogs greeted each other with obligatory sniffs, and finally—deciding all was well—trotted off, wagging their tails and marking one another's scents.

Gage climbed the steps of the wraparound porch and immediately saw his brothers' tears. "Dad's gone," Eli said, giving him a hug.

"He is?!" Gage looked stunned. He turned to go inside and found his mom surrounded by their family and friends in the big country kitchen, drying her eyes, but when she saw him standing in the doorway, tears immediately filled them again.

"Oh, Gage, you just missed him," she cried.

Gage closed his eyes and held her. His mom's tears were almost harder to bear than losing his dad. He let her pull him into the room where his father lay, and with a clenched jaw, gazed at the frail frame of the man who had, at one time, towered over him in stature *and* authority. Libby put her hand on his arm. "It was peaceful," she consoled softly. "He's had so much pain, but the morphine helped, and he just . . ." She paused. "I'm so sorry you didn't get here in time." She looked up at her son. "I'll let you have some time alone—you can still talk to him. . . . His spirit will hear you."

Gage raised his eyebrows, wondering if this was true, and after she quietly closed the door, he walked over to the window and looked out across the fields of golden timothy swaying in the summer breeze. *Time for third cutting*, he thought. He glanced around the room, trying not to look at the bed and trying to remember the last time he'd stood in his parents' bedroom. He gazed at their wedding picture hanging above his dad's bureau—*how young they'd been—much younger than he was now—and their eyes were so bright with dreams*. A second framed photo on the bureau was of his dad surrounded by all his sons . . . except for Chase—who was on his shoulders. Tucked in the corner was a smaller photo of Cale standing in the opening of the hayloft with his hands on his hips. He was smiling. It was one of those rare photos that truly captured his brother's spirit. Cale had been tough and hardworking, but also kind to a fault, and he had a streak of mischief, too. In the photo, he looked every bit the part. Gage turned on the small lamp next to the photo and saw the wooden bowl of loose change he and his brothers would "borrow" from when they were little—pulling up a nearby chair so they could reach it. Next to the bowl was his dad's old Timex watch, which absolutely lived up to its name and taken a licking but kept on ticking—even out-ticking its owner.

Gage closed his eyes. Behind him lay the great Jack Tennyson: the man who had not only confounded him, and wittingly—or unwittingly—crushed his dreams, but who also had, his mom insisted, loved him. And now, this giant of a man had fallen, conceding—as every mortal must—to death. *How,* he wondered, *did the loss of his father make him feel? Did he feel less angry? Did he regret lost time and opportunity? Did he regret the pride that had kept him away?* He shoved his hands into his pockets and turned to look at his dad's lifeless body, waiting for some emotion—*any* emotion—to hit, but all he felt was . . . numb. For years, resentment, anger, and pride had built up inside him—enough to keep him away . . . and now, he just felt empty.

*Where had the fiery spirit of the tall, strong man who'd ruled his household with a firm, even hand gone? Was he in heaven? Had he already been reunited with loved ones who had passed before him? Was he, at that very moment, embracing Cale?* Gage swallowed, trying to wrap his mind around the concept of eternity, the concept of time, and, picturing the joyous reunion his brother and father might be sharing, decided his father certainly wouldn't want to be interrupted by words from his prodigal son—that would be an unwelcome, ironic repeat of the past. So, Gage just stood there, stoic and silent.

Finally, feeling the sudden need to breathe fresh air, he opened the bedroom door, and—purposely avoiding the kitchen—walked toward the front porch. Before he could make it outside, he encountered his brothers Grayson and Chase, along with Liam, talking to their uncle Mike—their mom's younger brother, who was the spitting image of a young Dutch—in the living room. Gage shook hands with all of them.

"Mom make you go in and talk to him?" Chase teased with a half smile.

Gage eyed his youngest brother, wondering if the same request had been made of him. "I don't have much to say."

"Do you know if any of the arrangements have been made?" Mike asked, eyeing Grayson, who still worked the farm with Matt and Eli.

Grayson nodded. "She wants to have the wake Monday night and the service Tuesday morning."

"That's pretty quick," Mike said, raising his eyebrows.

"That's how we do things around here," Chase said wryly. "We don't mess around—it's all business, *all* the time."

Gage listened as the conversation turned to their mom and her capacity to carry on, and they all wondered if she would be just as strong after losing the love of her life. Grayson and Chase thought she would, but Mike—who'd known her all her life—wasn't so sure. "She'll put up a good front," he said, "but her sorrow will be lasting and deep, just as it was with Cale."

Gage nodded, and then excused himself, saying he needed to check on the whereabouts of his dog. He walked out into the steamy August heat, expecting to find Matt and Eli, but the porch was empty. He continued across the yard, and when he didn't see Gus, he frowned. He called him and peered into the open doors of the barn, the heady sweet scent of hay enveloping him and taking him back in time. He looked up at the rays of dusty sunlight streaming through the old glass windows and wondered how many hay bales he and his brothers had tossed up into the hot, airless space. Even now, he could feel the prickly twine on his hands. Except for the buzz of flies trapped in the windows, the barn was quiet.

He went back outside and walked past the line of John Deere tractors and implements, noting that their old red New Holland baler—with several parts on the ground—must be broken, which was probably why the grass was so high. He whistled for Gus and called his name, but there was no sign of him, and he began to wonder if his brothers' hounds had mischievously led his unsuspecting pup off somewhere and left him.

"Gus!" he shouted, starting to worry. He walked over to the pasture fence, and looked across the field, dotted with cattle grazing lazily in the hot summer sun. Some of the wiser ones had congregated under a stand of trees and were lying on the grass, chewing their cud and swishing their tails at the flies. Just then, Gage saw the two hounds nosing around the water trough, and he waited hopefully to see Gus appear, too, but when he didn't, he walked toward them. "What did you two rascals do with my dog?" he asked, but they just wagged their tails innocently and lay down in the cool shade. "This is crazy," Gage muttered. "Where the hell is he?" He walked in the opposite direction, past the house again, and Chase came out on the porch with a beer in his hand.

"Haven't found him?" he asked.

Gage shook his head. "No. I have no idea where he is."

"I'll be right out," his brother said.

Gage walked on, feeling stupid. His family was all here, mourning the loss of his father, and he was out looking for—and worried about—*his dog*. "C'mon, Gus," he muttered. "Show yourself . . ." As he rounded the corner of the house, he heard a commotion and looked up to see a flock of panicked loons rising above the trees, their wings whistling as they beat the air, and he suddenly knew where his dog had gone. He looked across the field at the big, muddy cow pond and saw Gus splashing happily in the water. A wave of relief swept over him—even as he shook his head in dismay.

"Found him!" he called to his brother, who'd just come out again.

"Good!" Chase called, waving and going back inside to retrieve his beer.

"Gus!" Gage commanded, and the wayward Lab looked up, splashed out of the pond—the bottom of which he'd stirred into a muddy froth—and raced toward him, loping like a porpoise through the swaying grass, and then, before Gage could stop him, he shook his entire body from head to tail, sending mud and water everywhere!

"Nice," Gage grumbled, looking down at his clothes, but when he looked up at the beaming face of his carefree dog, all he could do was laugh. "I can't take you back to the house like that, so it's the hose or the river . . ." And since Gage wasn't eager to go back to the house yet, he said, "I guess it's the river for you."

Gus trotted happily alongside Gage as he followed the once-worn path to the river that ran along the south pasture. He passed the place where his dad had, so long ago, gotten his tractor stuck, and continued over the rolling landscape to the spot in the river where the rushing water fell into a deep swimming hole. "Okay," he said, and Gus plunged into the cold, clear water, all the mud on his legs and paws and fur swirling away. Under Gage's watchful eye, he splashed around for several minutes until Gage was sure he was clean—albeit still wet—and then they turned and walked together in the direction of the gnarled, old oak tree he and his brothers had long ago dubbed the "Tennyson Tree." The majestic tree stood on a grassy knoll overlooking the entire farm. It had endured years of sun, wind, and rain . . . and even two tornadoes. It was under this tree that Cale was buried.

# 43

When Ruth Lindstrom looked up and saw Maeve standing at the end of their pew, her whole face brightened into a smile and she poked her husband to make room. It had been several weeks since Maeve had made it to church, but for some odd reason, the stars had aligned that morning—she hadn't had to work and she hadn't been lazing in bed beside Gage—so when she'd felt the nudge to attend, along with additional pressure from Harper the night before (who loved going to church because she usually saw her friend Rudy there), she couldn't say *no.* Her dad stood up, kissed her cheek, let her into the pew, and sat down beside her. Sitting between her parents, Maeve felt like a little kid again, and when she turned to see Harper in the same position—between *her* parents—right behind them, she winked. Harper grinned and winked back.

Maeve scanned the bulletin to see what was planned for that morning and was delighted to see the sermon would be delivered by the younger of their church's two ministers, Jennifer Whipple. Even though Maeve didn't go to church very often, when she did go, she always loved Jen's insightful sermons and this one, titled *A Gentle Whisper*, immediately piqued her curiosity. She'd heard—and ignored—plenty of gentle whispers in her lifetime. Maybe it was time she listened. She gazed out the window, watching a robin hop along the branches of a dogwood tree, looking for berries, and thought about everything that had happened in the last twenty-four hours.

She and Macey had packed up a few of her necessities, but because they didn't know who would be looking after the chickens—and there was a chance *she'd* be the one—they'd kept their packing to a minimum, at least for now. Saturday evening, while Ben and Macey went out to dinner, The Pepperoni Pizza and Root Beer Book Club had their long-overdue meeting, and Ben heard from Gage again. This time, he called and he told Ben his dad had passed away, and since the service was planned for Tuesday, he wouldn't be back to work until at least Wednesday. Ben had told him to take all the time he needed, and then asked if it would be okay for Maeve to stay at the cabin to look after the chickens. Gage had agreed, but when Ben hung up, he admitted to Macey that he'd sounded a little reluctant—all of which, Macey had, under duress, shared with her sister.

Maeve continued to watch the robin, her thoughts drifting now to the evening before with Harper, which had turned out to be just the distraction she needed. Her niece had been reluctant to finish their book, *Because of Winn-Dixie*, without Gage—who'd listened to the beginning with them, but Maeve said she didn't know when Gage would be able to listen again, and Harper, because she was eager to find out what happened to India Opal Buloni and her beloved—albeit wayward—dog Winn-Dixie, agreed. In the end, they not only finished the book, they also stayed up late to watch the movie—both of which were, in Harper's words, *awesome!*

"Aunt Maeve, how do you find so many books about orphaned girls who all end up finding what they need?" she'd asked when Maeve tucked her in next to Keeper, after Macey and Ben had already gone to bed.

Maeve had smiled at the simple—yet profound—question. "Maybe, because it's also what a thirty-six-year-old girl needs to hear once in a while," she'd said laughing.

"Are you comin' to church tomorrow?" Harper had asked hopefully.

"If I wake up in time after this late night," she'd replied, kissing her niece's forehead.

"Night, Aunt Maeve," Harper had said, smiling sleepily. "Thanks for our book club."

"Night, kiddo," she'd replied. "You're welcome."

Later, when she'd gotten back to the cabin and checked on the quiet chicken coop, she had—even though it was late—texted Gage to express her condolences, and she'd been surprised when she saw the little dots that meant he was writing back, but his reply was simply Thanks.

She'd stared at it. *It was better than nothing*, she thought, but then, the tears she'd been holding back all day spilled down her cheeks. So much had happened, all at the same time—it was as if the endless years of her own hesitation and lack of conviction had spiraled into a perfect storm. Grandy, her beloved grandmother, had always told her that God's timing was perfect, but Maeve couldn't see how his timing was perfect in this unbelievable mess. If Mason had come into her life just one day later, she'd be with Gage in Tennessee right now—she'd be there to support him and finally meet his family. . . . But, then again, if she'd been in Tennessee when Mason came *one day later*, he wouldn't have found her . . . and what an incredible loss that would be, so maybe God's timing *was* perfect. "Oh, jeez," she'd muttered. "Who knows what's right?" She'd shaken her head in dismay and then buried her face in Gage's pillow, breathing in the scent of him and whispering, "Oh, God, please don't let me lose him."

That morning, she'd woken up to the predawn raucous sound of Pilgrim crowing, shuffled to the kitchen to make coffee, and gone out in her slippers to feed them—her singular reason for being there. "Good morning, ladies and gent," she'd said softly, just like Gage always greeted his tiny flock. She'd reached into the nests and found three warm eggs. "Good girls!" she'd praised, just as he would say, but then she'd deliberately closed the gate behind her—blocking their freedom. *There was no way she was going to let anything happen to them while they were in her care!*

Sitting in church now, she felt a gentle tug on her hair that also tugged *her* back to the present. She realized everyone was standing to sing the first hymn, and when she stood, she looked back at Harper, the culprit, and teasingly raised her eyebrows—but Harper feigned innocence and pointed to Ben. Maeve eyed her suspiciously, and then joined in singing "Amazing Grace," feeling oddly as if it was meant for her.

After the hymn, one of the deacons made his way up to the pulpit to read from the Old Testament a passage from 1 Kings, familiar to Maeve from her Sunday school years. It was about God appearing to a very reluctant Elijah, and what made it memorable from her childhood was that he hadn't spoken to his wayward servant in any of the dramatic ways one might expect—a powerful wind, an earthquake, or a fire. He had spoken to Elijah in a gentle whisper.

Maeve settled in to listen to the sermon, hoping—somehow—it would speak to her, and from it she might discern what God wanted her to do. *Was it crazy to think this?* Perhaps, but there had to be a reason she'd felt nudged to come to church that morning.

The young minister stepped up to the pulpit, leafed through the tremendous Bible that rested there, and read the lectionary passage from the New Testament—Psalm 85. When she finished, she looked up and smiled. "Sooo, my friends, do any of you see similarities in our two readings this morning?" She paused and looked around the congregation. "Yep," she continued, chuckling, "I can absolutely see . . . from the looks on your faces," she teased, "that you noticed that both the Old Testament and the New Testament readings are examples of God *trying* to communicate with us! In Psalm 85, he is *speaking* . . . and in 1 Kings, he is *whispering*! This is important to remember because, in this very church, we are *all about* God trying to communicate with us—in fact, we even have a banner that says, 'God is still speaking!' Unfortunately, however—for us—even though God is always trying to communicate with *us*, quite often, *we* aren't listening. While he's trying to tell us there's more good news to hear, we are more concerned about other things. Even as we sit here, I bet more than a few people have been wondering what they will have for dinner tonight . . . or if the Braves will win their game this afternoon . . . or maybe their minds are on a myriad of other legitimate concerns and worries."

Maeve smiled as she listened; Jen's words were spot-on and she could definitely relate to being distracted when she was supposed to be paying attention—just look at how her mind had wandered when the service was beginning. With renewed resolve, she tried to stay focused on the sermon, and Jen continued to share stories and funny anecdotes about what happened to God's servants—both biblical *and* in her own family—when they didn't pay attention. She expounded on the belief that although "the faith of the church is more than two thousand years old, its *thinking* is not. Each generation is called to make faith their own." And in the end, her simple but profound lesson cast light on the benefits of finding time to "be still . . . to listen . . . to let God reveal himself . . . and to know he often speaks in unexpected ways. He may speak to you through the voice of a friend or mentor . . . or if you're paying attention when you're out in nature—replenishing and nurturing your tired soul—he may speak to you in the swaying dance of the willows . . . or in a gentle whisper in the wind. You just have to be listening," she said softly, and then smiled. "Amen."

Maeve smiled, too, and murmured, "Amen."

After the service ended, they walked down to fellowship hour, and Harper, immediately spying Rudy, towed her mom and aunt over to say hello to Cora. They all exchanged big hugs, and Harper bumped fists with Cora's two boys, Frank, who was a six-foot-four rising sophomore and already a star basketball player on his high school's varsity team, and Joe, who was younger than Rudy, and loved video games almost as much as his brother loved basketball.

While Macey, Maeve, and Cora chatted, the two girls went over to the kids' table for snacks and, while sipping lemonade and munching on cookies, hatched a plan and returned to test it on their moms.

"Cora, can Rudy sleep over tonight?" Harper asked, as her friend looked on hopefully.

Cora frowned. "Child, haven't you learned you're supposed to check with your mom *first*? And don't you have school this week? Because my tribe all goes back on Tuesday . . . thank goodness!" she said, winking at Macey.

With raised eyebrows, Macey waited to hear Harper's reply.

Harper turned to Macey. "Mom, through my *friend* Rudy, I heard God speaking . . . *and* he said Rudy should sleep over tonight."

Macey and Cora both chuckled, impressed that Harper had been paying attention to the sermon. "Did he now?" Macey asked.

"Mm-hmm," Harper replied solemnly.

"I guess we better listen then," Macey said, smiling. "Rudy is more than welcome to stay over, so long as it's okay with Miss Cora."

Harper turned back to Cora. "Is it okay?"

Cora smiled. "Far be it from me to not listen when God is speaking," she replied.

"Woohoo!" Harper said, embracing Rudy.

Just then, Maeve—who'd stepped away for a cup of coffee—rejoined them. "Somebody's excited," she said, smiling at Cora and Macey.

"Indeed," Cora said, laughing. "Oh, to be young and sleeping over your best friend's house."

"Amen to that," Maeve said, laughing.

# 44

"I WISH YOU HAD COME TO CHURCH WITH US THIS MORNING," LIBBY SAID, climbing the porch steps. "Everyone would've loved seeing you."

Gage was sitting in one of the chairs on the front porch with Gus at his feet. "They'll see me tomorrow," he replied, taking a sip of coffee while Gus thumped his tail in greeting.

Libby knelt down to stroke Gus's soft fur, and in the bright sunlight, Gage noticed the smile creases around her eyes, and realized, suddenly, she was getting older. *How had he not noticed before?*

"Well, my dear boy, will you please do *one* thing for me?" she asked.

"Depends," he teased, knowing from experience to never commit to an unknown.

"I would appreciate it if you would go see Dutch."

Gage frowned. "Aren't you bringing him to the service?"

"I'm not sure. It depends on how he is that morning. He has good days and bad days, so we'll have to wait and see."

Gage nodded. "Does he recognize anyone?"

"Sometimes."

"Okay," Gage agreed. "I'll go see him."

"Do you want me to go with you?"

"You can if you'd like," he said with a gentle smile.

"Thank you," she said, squeezing his hand. "We'll go after lunch."

Gage nodded. "Do you need help with lunch?"

Libby shook her head. "I'm just going to set out the meat and cheese platter and some rolls. You kids can all make your own sandwiches . . . and there're three different kinds of pie, too, including Mrs. Fergusson's chocolate chess pie—have you ever had it?"

Gage looked up in surprise—he hadn't heard the words *chocolate chess pie* in years, and then after he'd mentioned it to Maeve, she had decided to make one . . . but then all hell had broken loose in their lives and he'd never had a chance to try it. "I've only had chocolate chess pie one other time—the time Dutch took Cale and me to Nashville to see Garth Brooks."

"Well, her pie is delicious."

"I'll be sure to try it," Gage replied, and, as if on cue, three more cars pulled into the yard and Gage watched his brothers' families clamber out—a scene that reminded him of clowns spilling out of a Volkswagen Bug. Between Matt, Eli, and Grayson, there were a total of ten Tennyson grandkids—eight boys (of course) and two girls (who could definitely hold their own); they ranged in age from ten years to ten months, *and* there were two more on the way (genders unknown, but they all knew the odds!). So, even though his mom would miss his dad dearly and would undoubtedly be lonely, she would never be *alone* . . . and that, Gage knew, was a very good thing.

The kids all clambered up the steps and shyly gave their elusive uncle Gage a fist bump as they traipsed by wearing their Sunday best. Gage smiled at each of them; even though they were unsure of him now, they would eventually learn that he was a cool uncle—a master of all board games and unbeatable at horseshoes or cornhole, whichever form of defeat they preferred!

His brothers and their wives greeted him, too, and a moment later, he followed them inside to make a sandwich and to try Mrs. Fergusson's chocolate chess pie.

Two hours later, Gage was holding the door of the nursing home open, but when he followed his mom in, he was overwhelmed by the stagnant air in the lobby. He raised his eyebrows, wondering how long he'd be able to endure it. He recalled the refreshing breeze that always carried the scent of lilacs through the airy windows of Willow Pond Senior Care or the delicious aroma of Sal's cooking wafting from the kitchen, and he wished his grandfather could be in a place like that.

"His room is on the courtyard," his mom said, seeming to read his mind, "so we can sit outside . . . although it's probably cooler in his room."

Gage nodded. "I'll take the heat over this stale air any day."

They walked down the hall, and Libby smiled and waved to all the staff members and greeted each of the patients by name.

"Do you know everyone here, Mom?" Gage teased.

"Well, I come every day," she said, "so I've gotten to know people."

Gage shook his head. "I didn't know you came every day."

"Dutch is my dad, Gage. I'm not just going to forget about him . . . even if he doesn't always recognize me."

Gage nodded, wondering if her words were a guised rebuke because he hadn't been to visit his grandfather, but he quickly decided there was no way his mom would ever say something hurtful—intentionally *or* unintentionally. "Have you thought about trying to take care of him at home?"

"We *did* try for a while. Uncle Mike and I were taking turns, but when it reached a point where he needed help with almost everything"—she looked up at him—"and I was taking care of your dad, too, we had to find a different solution. Mike and Jess both have jobs and a busy family, and I have plenty to do around the farm. Plus, there was no way I could take care of him *and* your dad, so when it got to be too much, we decided, very reluctantly, that this was the best option. He could linger like this for years, and caregiving is a full-time job."

"Have you ever considered having someone come in . . . a live-in caregiver? There's plenty of room in that house."

"To be honest, Gage, I haven't had a chance to consider that—

life has been so hectic, and after your dad got sick, it became even more hectic. I've been so busy taking care of him, I haven't had a minute to myself."

Gage nodded thoughtfully. "Maybe you'll have time now—I'm sure Dutch would be much happier at home."

"He probably would be," she said, smiling sadly. "We'll see . . ." She paused. "Well, here he is," she said, gesturing to the last door in the long corridor. "Hi, Dad," she said cheerfully, bustling into the room. "I brought someone to see you."

Gage walked in behind her and saw a frail man sitting next to the window in a wheelchair. "Hey, Dutch," he said, and the man looked up. Gage searched his face, hoping his grandfather would recognize him, but his eyes were far away and listless. Gage swallowed and bit his lip. He'd been trying to prepare himself for the very real possibility that his beloved grandfather *wouldn't* recognize him, but the empty stare that greeted him was not at all what he had expected.

"Would you like to sit outside, Dad?" Libby asked, releasing the brakes on his wheelchair, but when the old man didn't respond, Gage took his cue from his mom and walked around to open the door. Libby wheeled him out into the courtyard and pushed him to a shady area under a small dogwood tree and sat down next to him. "How've you been today?" she asked softly, but Dutch still didn't answer.

Gage watched and listened as his mom gently talked to her dad, telling him about her day and news she'd heard at church that morning, and he was amazed by her utter devotion to him. "Does he ever respond?" he asked.

"Sometimes, but the times are becoming fewer and farther between."

Gage nodded. The faraway look in his grandfather's eyes reminded him of the little lady Maeve took care of at Willow Pond—Ivy Lee Byrd—and then he remembered how Ivy's face had lit up when he and Bud had played the fiddle, and she'd even started clapping and tapping her feet. Maeve had talked about the profound effect music had on people with dementia or Alzheimer's. "Have you ever tried playing music for him?" he asked.

"There's a radio in his room, but I can't say I've ever turned it on."

Gage nodded, thinking about the music he knew Dutch loved—hymns, for sure, and country music, but what song might he remember? He pulled his phone out of his pocket and scrolled through his playlist, and then it hit him—he knew exactly what song to play. He looked at his mom. "Is it okay if I play a song for him?"

"Absolutely," Libby said, and even though she doubted it would make a difference, she was glad her son was trying. "I'm sure he'd love it," she added encouragingly.

Gage nodded and scrolled to a song he'd been listening to lately, turned up the volume, and tapped the start arrow. He waited, knowing the song had a quiet intro, and then held the phone near his grandfather's ear. A moment later, the unmistakable voice of Garth Brooks drifted through the air, and the moving lyrics of "The River" began to stir his grandfather's memory.

Gage watched Dutch lift his head, his eyes brightening, and then—almost imperceptibly—he began to nod his head to the steady rhythm. Gage looked over at his mom and she smiled, her eyes filling with tears. They both watched the old man listen intently, his eyes glistening, and then as the lyrics swelled, his lips began to move—he was singing!

Gage stared in amazement—Maeve was right! Hearing an old favorite song had awakened his grandfather's sweet spirit, and as Gage searched his grandfather's blue eyes in wonder, he was given the priceless gift of a smile. Then Dutch reached out and squeezed his grandson's hand. "Thank you, Gage," he whispered.

"Want to hear it again?" Gage asked, smiling, and Dutch nodded.

# 45

When Maeve turned in to the Willow Pond parking lot on Monday morning, she was half-asleep, but when she was almost sideswiped by an ambulance coming around the corner, her eyes grew wide. She jerked to the side just as the lights started to flash and the siren began to scream. She waited for it to pass, and when she finally pulled in to the parking area, she saw a fire truck and two police cars parked on the lawn. "What the heck?" she whispered, looking up to see if the house was on fire, but all she saw was a crowd of residents standing on the porch—many still in their bathrobes. She climbed out of her car and hurried over to where Sal and LeeAnn were standing. "What happened?!"

LeeAnn shook her head and explained. "When Jim came outside this morning to put out the garbage, he found Ivy lying in the grass near the pond—we don't know how long she'd been there . . . or why."

"Is she okay?"

Sal shook his head. "Her clothes were wet and she was freezing, but they were able to find a faint pulse. She was hypothermic, and they think she may have had a heart attack or a stroke—it could be just about anything. She's so tiny and frail to begin with."

"That's awful," Maeve said. "Did you call her son?"

LeeAnn nodded. "Yes, he's headed to the hospital." She glanced over to where Jim was talking to the policemen. "But you can bet there's going to be an investigation."

Maeve raised her eyebrows, suddenly grasping the potential legal ramifications of having a resident suffer a catastrophic injury, or worse . . . die! "Oh, no," she murmured.

LeeAnn nodded. "And with a parent company like ours, the payout would be significant. Either way, we're going to have the state looking over our shoulder all the time now. They could even shut us down."

"That won't happen," Maeve said, frowning. "It wasn't our fault. You documented all the times she's wandered off, and you told the higher-ups—*and* her son—that she needed more care than we offer."

"I know," LeeAnn said, "but anything can happen."

Maeve bit her lip. "Well, I hope she's okay, and at least now, they'll move her to a more suitable facility."

"True," LeeAnn agreed. She nodded toward the residents still lingering on the porch. "Well, the excitement is over. Do you guys want to see if we can get everyone back inside?"

Maeve nodded, and while LeeAnn went over to talk to the policemen with Jim, she and Sal climbed the porch steps. "I guess we've had a little excitement this morning," she said to the residents.

"I guess we have!" Gladys exclaimed. "What in the world was that woman doing outside?"

"We don't know," Maeve said.

"I'll tell you what," Gladys continued, "she shouldn't even be living here. She never talks . . . and she's always wandering off or feeding those damn ducks. She's loony, I tell ya, and I'm surprised something hasn't happened to her before now."

Maeve nodded. Everything Gladys said was true, but she thought she could be saying it with a little more humility. "Why don't we all go back to our rooms and get dressed?" Maeve suggested. She looked at Sal and smiled. "Meanwhile, Sal will make some coffee and I'll set it out in the sunroom, and anyone who'd like to come sit in there—because it's been such a crazy morning—is welcome to."

"*Crazy* doesn't even come close!" Gladys blustered, shaking her head.

"I hope she's okay," Addie said softly. "She loved those swans."

"And she loved my fiddle," Bud added.

"She did," Maeve said, smiling. "Maybe we can all say a prayer for her. She can't help that she is confused or quiet. It happens to the best of us."

"She belongs in the loony bin!" Gladys said, which prompted an unexpectedly stern look from Maeve.

"Gladys, we should always try to be kind," she scolded, suddenly having enough of her lack of compassion, and the old woman looked stunned.

"I'm kind!" she retorted. "*And* I will absolutely pray for her."

"Good," Maeve replied, as she held open the door. "Enough said."

Everyone maneuvered their walkers and canes through the door with the men bringing up the rear, all of them smiling. "Good for you!" Bud said with a wink. "It's about time someone spoke up."

LATER THAT AFTERNOON, THE STAFF AT WILLOW POND RECEIVED NEWS that Ivy's condition, although critical, had been stabilized and everyone breathed a sigh of relief. Her son also asked if someone might be able to locate his mom's hearing aids. He knew she never wore them because she never remembered to, but he wanted to be able to talk to her. So, shortly before the afternoon snack, Maeve went down to Ivy's room to look for them. It was dark in her apartment—the only light coming from the window that looked out over the courtyard—and even though she'd been asked to look around, she still felt like an intruder. She propped open the door, switched on a light. The apartment was as neat as a pin—which was odd for someone with dementia. She knew housekeeping came in twice a week, but Ivy's apartment almost looked like no one lived there. She went into the bathroom and looked in the cabinets, and then went into the bedroom to search some drawers, but she didn't see them anywhere. She stopped in front of her bureau, and the old black-and-white photo she'd noticed when Ivy first moved in caught her eye again. She picked it up to look at it, and in doing so, disturbed a little box that had been slipped between the frame and its cardboard easel. Maeve picked it up, opened the lid, and inside—neatly put away—were the hearing aids! She tucked the box in her pocket and walked back into Ivy's living room with the photo in her hand—just as Tallulah peeked in the door. "Well, hello there, Miss Tally," she said, and the friendly cat meowed and sauntered in to swish between her legs. Maeve knelt down to pet her, and then heard a knock on the open door and looked up.

"Is this a private meeting?" Bud asked with a smile.

"Not at all," Maeve said, standing and smiling. "Ivy's son wanted us to try to find her hearing aids . . . and Tallulah came in to check on me."

"Does that mean she's okay?" Bud asked hopefully.

"She's critical, but stable."

"That's good," Bud said, "but it might be the beginning of the end. Sometimes something like that can be . . ."

Maeve nodded—he didn't need to finish—and then she remembered the picture she was holding and looked at it. "I love this old photo of her . . . and thank goodness I picked it up to look at it again, because her hearing aids were behind it."

"I didn't know she wore hearing aids."

"That's because she never puts them in."

"Maybe that's why she seems lost all the time—she can't hear anything."

"It's possible," Maeve agreed, "but she was able to hear your fiddle."

Bud nodded. "Well, we *were* standing right next to her." He paused thoughtfully. "She really did respond to it, though—it was wonderful to see her smiling and tapping her feet."

Maeve smiled. "It was great! She must have some fiddling friends because the young men in this photo are both holding fiddles."

She held the photo out and Bud took it from her, held it in the light, and frowned. "That's Ivy?" he said, sounding incredulous.

"Yep," Maeve said. "Why?"

Bud shook his head. "The fellow on the right is . . . *me*."

"No way!" Maeve exclaimed in astonishment.

Bud nodded, still frowning. "I didn't know her name was Ivy . . . everyone called her 'Birdie.'"

Maeve shook her head. "That's odd . . . so Byrd must be her maiden name."

"It's possible—that would explain why people called her that."

Now it was Maeve's turn to frown. "But she has a son . . . do you know if she ever married?"

"I don't. I only met her that one time—it was at a Pickin' 'n Fiddlin' contest up in Nashville."

"Do you know who the other boy is?"

"I'm pretty sure his first name was Will—he was one heck of a fiddler!"

Maeve raised her eyebrows. "Ivy's son's name is Will."

"Sounds like you could write a book with this story."

Maeve laughed. "You could except, sadly, the main character doesn't seem to remember it."

"At least we don't think she does," Bud said with a laugh.

"It's such a great old photo," Maeve mused, "but what's odd is that *you*, who only met her that one time, are in a photo she has kept all her life—no offense intended."

"No offense taken," Bud said with a smile, "but I can't explain it, either."

"Were you interested in her?"

"She was very pretty, but in 1941, I was already taken."

Maeve nodded, and then she suddenly remembered that she needed to get back to the kitchen. "Oh, my goodness! Sal is going to think I got lost! And you're going to miss out on his famous snickerdoodles!"

Bud laughed. "Well, I wouldn't want that to happen."

Maeve returned the photo to Ivy's bureau, and then picked up Tallulah—who'd made herself comfortable on the bed. "C'mon, missy, you don't want to get left in here." She turned off the lights, closed the door, and set the cat down out in the hall. "I still can't believe that's *you* in that photo," she said, as she walked beside Bud toward the kitchen. "You were pretty cute!"

"I still am," Bud said, laughing.

"You are indeed," Maeve assured him, putting her hand on his arm.

# 46

Gage had slept on the couch the first two nights he was at the farm. Prior to falling asleep there, he'd spent the evenings with his mom, brothers, and Liam sitting out on the porch, while Chase—who'd agreed to give a eulogy—jotted down some of the memories they talked about. Afterward, he'd promptly fallen asleep in the living room, and he hadn't moved until morning, but on Monday night, his mom suggested he sleep in his old room. So, after they got home from the wake, he gathered Gus—who was worn-out from all the sniffing he had to do on the farm every day—climbed the stairs, washed up, switched on the light in his bedroom, and felt as if he'd stepped back in time—the room he had shared with his brother growing up was virtually untouched. There was a twin bed against each wall, each covered with the same—now faded—matching quilt, and with the same small table between them; on the table was the same John Deere tractor lamp from his childhood and the Big Ben alarm clock that had roused them every morning to help with chores—it even had the correct time on it! There were two oak desks—one under each window—and two oak bureaus against the walls. There was also a cork bulletin board hanging on the wall, and on it, the countless blue ribbons they'd won, along with photos of them dressed in white and standing next to their big bovine counterparts. There was even a photo of him curled up next to Chestnut in the dairy barn at the fair. Gage shook his head in amazement . . . *and* with a little bit of alarm. The room was like a time capsule from his childhood, and it seemed a little crazy that his parents had kept it that way for almost twenty years!

He sat down at his desk and thought about all the homework and drawings he'd done while sitting there, and then he reached over and clicked on the radio, and Kenny Chesney's voice drifted out, singing "Back Where I Come From." He pulled open the top drawer of the desk, lifted out an old drawing pad, and slowly leafed through it, smiling at all the animal portraits—they were still his favorite subject.

There was a quiet knock on the open door, and he looked up. "I brought you some fresh towels," Libby said, putting them on his bed.

"Thanks," he replied, smiling. "I can't believe how many people came tonight—the line was all the way down the street. I think the whole county turned out."

She nodded. "Your dad knew a lot of people and touched a lot of lives. Also, some folks have to work tomorrow, so they came tonight." She turned and eyed Gus sprawled out across Cale's bed, "I hope you're comfy there, mister!" Gus opened one eye and thumped his tail, and she turned back to Gage. "Does it feel funny to be in your old room?"

"It *does* feel funny," he admitted, loosening his tie. "It's almost as if we never . . . I mean as if *I* . . ." And then he stopped because he didn't know how to continue without making her think of Cale.

"I know," she said, sitting on his bed. "I don't think we meant to keep it the same, but I guess we just didn't know what to do with all this good, solid furniture, and it's not like we need the room for anything. I don't come in here very often except . . ."

"To dust," he teased, "because it's not even dusty." His eyes fell on the closet door, and she followed his gaze. "I don't know if I even want to open *that*," he said, laughing. "There's probably old clothes of mine from high school in there."

"There probably is," she said, laughing. "I guess I better start going through some of these things and taking them to Goodwill."

"I guess," Gage mused, "except you've held on to it this long, and now you have ten growing grandkids . . . and two more on the way. They'll grow into the clothes before you know it . . . and maybe they can use some of the furniture, too."

"True," she said, nodding. "The style of clothes is probably outdated, though, and the girls won't be interested."

"They're all farm kids—they'll be fine. Besides, jeans and T-shirts never go out of style."

Libby nodded and then eyed her son. "I know I probably won't get any grandkids from Chase," she ventured, "but what about you? Are you still thinking of marrying Maeve? I thought you might bring her so we could meet her, although I know a funeral isn't a very happy reason to bring a girl home . . ."

Gage nodded, but avoided his mom's question by changing the subject. "You don't know Chase won't have kids," he countered. "Lots of LGBTQ couples are wonderful parents—they adopt, use a sperm donor, or find a surrogate mom . . ."

Libby nodded. "I know, but I don't think it's an ideal situation. Don't you think it's a little confusing for a child to have two dads or two moms? Don't you think other kids will make fun of him . . . or her?"

Gage smiled gently. "Not if the child is truly loved, Mom. There are a lot of heterosexual couples who shouldn't be parents, but they are. Besides, I think Chase would make a great dad—he's funny and caring and gentle. He's also happy . . . and healthy. That's all that matters. I'm sure it took a lot of courage for him to come out . . . especially to Dad."

"That's the understatement of the century!" she said, shaking her head. "Your father had a very hard time."

"I heard."

Libby smiled. "But he came around. He loved Chase . . . just like he loved you."

Gage nodded, but didn't say anything.

"You're right about Chase, too . . . I'm glad he's happy. I just worry about him . . . and Liam. The world can be so cruel—even in this day and age, and with all the traveling they do . . . I just don't want them to run into any trouble."

"Chase is very aware of which places are safe—that's what his travel agency specializes in."

Libby nodded. "Well, my dear, somehow, you've managed to change the subject. I was asking about *you* . . . and Maeve."

Gage smiled sadly. "We broke up," he said simply.

Libby frowned. "Oh, no! How come? I thought you were going to propose to her."

"I was, but something happened."

"You *know* you're not going to get away with being evasive, so you may as well just tell me."

Gage rolled his eyes. "I don't know if you noticed, Mom, but I'm not sixteen anymore."

"And I don't know if you noticed, but I'm still your mom—who cares . . . and who has been through a lot lately . . . and who is still rolling with the punches, I might add."

Gage nodded. "I'm sorry—you're right." He took a deep breath and slowly let it out. "Maeve has a son, and somehow, she never managed to tell me about him."

Libby frowned. "I'm confused. How in the world, for two years, did she hide having a son?"

"He wasn't part of her life. She had him when she was eighteen and gave him up for adoption."

"Why didn't she didn't tell you?"

"She said she was ashamed of what happened and she didn't know how I'd react."

Libby nodded. "If you broke up, it doesn't seem like you took it very well."

Gage shook his head and frowned. "Mom, I'm not upset that she has a son, or how it happened. I'm upset that she didn't tell me. I feel like she was keeping it from me. . . . And how do you build a trusting relationship on that?"

"Did he just show up without warning?"

Gage nodded.

"That must've been quite a surprise for her," she mused, trying to imagine—as a mom—how she'd feel if a child she hadn't seen since birth suddenly reappeared in her life eighteen years later. "It must've been amazing, too."

"I wouldn't know."

"Gage, from what you've told me about Maeve, she sounds like a lovely girl, and even though I've never met her, I don't think she meant to hurt you."

"Maybe not," Gage replied, looking away.

"Well, I'm sorry to hear this," Libby said, standing.

Gage nodded, but didn't reply.

"Let me know if you need anything," she added, smiling gently.

"Thanks, Mom," he said, half smiling, too.

She started to close the door, but then turned back. "It was such a gift to have Dutch smile yesterday . . . *and* recognize you!"

"It was," Gage agreed. He paused, carefully considering his words. "I know it's easy for me to just say this and leave it in your lap—especially after I didn't do anything to help with Dad—but I wish you could move Dutch home . . . and find someone to help take care of him. It would be so much better for him to be *here* than to just sit by himself all day in a place that isn't home. I know you visit him every day, but when he's just sitting there, he doesn't get any kind of mental or physical stimulation, and if he was here, there's always so much activity—kids and dogs . . ."

Libby smiled. "I *am* going to think about it, Gage," she said. "I can't thank you enough for showing me what a difference music can make."

Gage smiled. "I really can't take the credit—Maeve's the one who told me about that."

Libby nodded. "I wish I *could* thank her, then," she said with a sad smile.

Gage nodded but didn't say anything.

"Would you be willing to go with me tomorrow morning and see if Dutch is up to going to the service?"

"Absolutely," Gage said, sitting up. "What time do you want to go?"

"Well, the service is at eleven, but we should get there early, so I was thinking nine?"

"Okay," Gage said.

She smiled. "Thanks, hon. That would be a tremendous help."

"No problem," Gage said, smiling, too.

"Good night, then. Love you . . . and love having you home, even if it is for a sad reason."

"Night, Mom," he said, standing to give her a hug. "Love you, too . . . and I love being here."

Libby closed the door, and Gage undressed, hung his clothes over the chair—just as he'd done when he was a boy—turned off the lamp, stretched out on his old bed, and listened to the sweet summer breeze whispering through the curtains. A moment later, he heard Chase and Liam come up the stairs, talking quietly as they washed up and got ready for bed. He listened as the door to Chase and Grayson's old room clicked closed, and even though it was set up the same way as his room was with two twin beds, he was surprised his mom let them stay in the same room—and he wondered if she'd let Maeve sleep in the same room as him. He smiled, realizing how much she had mellowed.

In the quietness, he heard the sound of the train whistle in the distance, and then he heard Chase—ever the clown—calling, "Good night, Mama! Good night, Liam! Good night, Gage!"

When his mom replied, he could hear the smile in her voice. "Good night, Chase . . . good night, Gage . . . good night, Liam!"

Next, Liam replied, and in the darkness, Gage smiled, wondering if he should pretend to be asleep, but then he chimed in, and in the spirit of the Walton family, called out, "Night, Mama . . . night, Liam . . . night, *John-Boy*!"

He heard Chase snicker, and then the old house grew quiet, and except for the ticking of the alarm clock and Gus snoring, the only sound he heard was the haunting call of the loons.

# 47

"THANKS FOR THE RIDE *and* FOR HELPING ME MOVE IN," MASON SAID, AS he came in with the last box.

"You're welcome," Ali said, looking around his dorm room. "You didn't bring very much, though. It's pretty sparse in here."

"I have my extra-long sheets," he said with a grin. "That's all I need."

She shook her head. "I think you should've gotten more than one set."

"There'd be no point. I hate folding sheets. Especially fitted ones—they always ends up being a balled-up mess. So I'll just wash 'em and put 'em back on."

Ali shook her head. "When's your roommate coming? Is he a runner, too?"

"He is . . . and I don't know. I thought he'd be here before me."

"What time is your meeting?"

Mason pulled out his phone and looked at the time. "In an hour."

Ali nodded. "You're here first, so you get to pick which side you want." She eyed the bed on the left. "I think you should take that one."

Mason frowned. "Why?"

"It's closer to the window."

"Works for me," he said, setting the box on the desk.

"Want help making the bed?"

"Sure, if we can find the sheets."

"I think they're in that bag over there," she said, pointing to a bag in the corner.

"I think you're right," he said, pulling out the package of gray, stretchy cotton sheets.

"I thought you got the blue ones," she said, frowning.

"Nope, I liked these better." He eyed her. "Don't you like them?"

She raised her eyebrows. "Um, gray?"

"Luckily, you don't have to sleep on 'em," he said, as he unzipped the package.

"Thank goodness," she said, shaking her head. "Where's the mattress pad?"

"Oh, right," he said, looking in the bag again. "Good thing I brought you."

"I know! I don't know how you've managed on your own all these months."

"I don't know, either," he said, laughing.

She reached for a corner of the new snow-white extra-long mattress pad and stretched it around the corner of the flimsy mattress. "Ideally, all of this would've gotten washed first."

"What the heck for? It's clean. Why make more work for yourself? It'll be lucky if it gets washed once a month!" he teased.

"Good grief," she said. "I hope you wash your bedding more often than that!"

She finished helping him make the bed, and then as she was slipping on his pillowcase, he reached into his backpack and pulled out a tattered, floppy teddy bear. "You brought Travelin' Bear?" she asked in surprise, touched by the unexpected appearance of Mason's longtime stuffed animal—a gift she'd given him for his birthday one year when they were little.

"Of course," he said, propping the old bear on the bureau.

"Nice," Ali said, nodding her approval.

Just then, there was a light knock on the door and a good-looking young man with short chestnut-brown hair peered in the room. "Mason?" he asked.

Mason smiled. "You must be Pat."

"I am," Pat said, coming into the room and shaking Mason's hand. "I guess that roommate algorithm colleges use decided we might be compatible, so we're bunking together."

"Guess so," Mason said, laughing, and then turned to introduce Ali.

"Nice to meet you," Pat said, smiling. "Do you go to Georgia Tech, too?"

Ali shook her head, but before she could say a word about Emory, Pat's parents were bustling into the room with their arms full of boxes and a flat-screen TV. After more introductions, Mason asked if they needed help.

"That would be awesome," Pat said. "We have a carload."

Mason eyed Ali, knowing she needed to head back. "All right," he said. "I just have to walk Ali to her car. I'll grab some stuff on my way back."

"Thanks!" Pat said. "Nice to meet you, Ali."

Mason and Ali were quiet as they walked across the parking lot. She unlocked her car and opened the door to let the heat out.

"Thank you again for *everything*," Mason said with the crooked half smile Ali loved. "I really don't know what I'd do without you."

"Oh, you'd manage," she teased, laughing. "Wing and a prayer, right?"

"Right . . ." he said, searching her eyes, "but usually with your help."

Ali smiled. "Oh! I meant to ask you—did you send a friend request to your . . . I mean Maeve yet?"

"No, not yet. I was going to last night, but after going to the car cruise, I forgot."

Ali nodded. "That was fun. Everyone loved your car."

"It was fun . . . and it was really nice of your parents to treat,"

Mason said, remembering how Mr. and Mrs. Harrison had insisted on paying for their cheeseburgers and milkshakes at the diner—they'd even paid for Jeff's and his wife Holly's dinner.

"My parents loved it, too. My dad said to remind you that if you need someone to go over to the house and start the engine, or even take it for a spin once in a while, he's your man."

"I know," Mason said, laughing. "Jeff said the same thing, and I might just take them up on that. It's not good for a car to sit."

Ali nodded. "My mom also said the preemies are going to miss you."

Mason smiled. "I'm going to miss them, too."

"Well, anyway, don't forget to send her a friend request."

"I will. . . . I mean, I won't."

Ali rolled her eyes. "Promise?"

Mason nodded, smiling at the idea of yet another woman making him promise. "Yep, tonight. I promise."

"Okay, good, because I think she would really—" But before she could finish her sentence, Mason leaned down and softly kissed her.

"Wow," she whispered. "Where'd that come from?"

"I don't know," he said innocently. "Was it okay?" he asked, smiling shyly.

"It was more than okay," she murmured, kissing him again. Then she pulled back. "You better go help Pat and his parents unload their car, or they'll be all done."

He nodded. "Text me when you get home."

"You'll be in your meeting."

"Text me anyway," he said, and then he kissed her again.

"Okay," she murmured, feeling slightly breathless.

"Promise?" he said, walking backward.

"Promise," she said, laughing, and then he turned and trotted toward the dorm, but before he went in, he turned again and waved.

Ali smiled and waved back, her heart swelling with the possibility and promise wrapped up in his sweet kiss.

# 48

"How was your snickerdoodle?" Maeve asked, as she walked down the empty porch, picking up napkins and glasses and putting them on her tray.

"It was delish," Bud said, leaning back in his chair. "I had two!"

"I saw that," Maeve teased. "I hope you saved room for dinner."

"I did," Bud replied, "but I have to agree with Gladys: 'Meatless Monday is B.S.!'"

Maeve laughed. "Oh, it's not that bad. Sal makes a mean veggie lasagna."

"I don't think those two words belong in the same sentence, never mind in the same baking dish." As he said this, he leaned down to pick up a napkin that was under the chair Aristides had been sitting in, but which was now occupied by Tallulah. He set it on the pile on Maeve's tray. "Any updates on Ivy?" he asked.

She sat down next to him. "Her son came by to pick up her hearing aids and he said she opened her eyes."

"Wow! That's great!" Bud exclaimed.

"It is," Maeve agreed, "but he said she's not out of the woods yet. I wanted to ask him about the other boy in the photo, but I didn't think it was the right time . . . at least, not right now." She paused. "He must've been important to them, though, if they kept the photo all these years."

Bud nodded. "I was trying to remember more about him. That

photo was taken in the summer of 1941 . . . the summer before Pearl Harbor, and after *that*, every young man I knew either enlisted or was drafted. I'd be willing to bet Will was no different."

"Do you think Ivy got pregnant . . . and he was the father?"

"It's possible—like *you* said, there must be a reason that photo is so important to them, but I think they should've cropped *me* out," he added, laughing.

"Do you remember the circumstances of the photo?"

"Oh, we were all just having fun—there was a whole group of us kids, and Will and I had just competed in a back-and-forth contest . . . kind o' like Gage and I did the other day."

Maeve nodded. "I wonder what happened to him."

Bud pressed his lips together. "We lost a lot of good men in that war."

Maeve shook her head. "That would've been incredibly hard for her back then—getting pregnant, possibly out of wedlock—and raising her son all by herself."

Bud nodded. "Takes a lot of courage to do that." He eyed her thoughtfully. "I hope you don't mind me asking, Maeve . . . and please tell me to mind my own business if I'm stepping over the line, but that boy who showed up here on Friday—Mason . . . is he your son?"

Maeve smiled. "He is. But, unlike Ivy, I didn't have the courage to raise him on my own."

Bud nodded. "Everything happens for a reason, Maeve. God has a plan."

"It does . . . and He does," she agreed.

"So what does your handsome beau—as Gladys calls him—think of all this? Did he know about Mason?"

Maeve shook her head. "He didn't know."

Bud nodded but didn't say anything.

"And he's not my beau anymore," she added.

Bud frowned. "Oh," he said softly. "I'm sorry."

"His dad just died, too . . ."

Bud shook his head. "When it rains . . . it pours." He paused. "Are you going to the service?"

Maeve shook her head.

The porch was oddly quiet with everyone inside, and Maeve looked up at the slate-gray sky, not ready to go back inside. "What happened to the sun?" she asked, and then a sudden gust of wind swept down the porch, rocking the chairs and fluffing Tallulah's fur. The little orange tiger cat opened her eyes, and sensing the storm, hopped off her chair and sauntered down the porch toward the door. "She knows," Bud said, smiling, "but that breeze feels good after this hot day." He looked out at the giant old willow tree next to the pond, and Maeve followed his gaze, watching its long, wispy branches dancing in the wind. "That big ole willow has seen a lot of storms in its lifetime," he said, "but its roots are deep and strong. It'll lose some branches in this one, but if Jim doesn't pick 'em up, they'll take root and become new trees. That's how willows are—resilient. They just dance in the storm."

Maeve nodded. "I wish I was more like a willow."

Bud looked over at her. "I know it's not my place, Maeve, but if it's not too late, I think you should go to the service. You may think that boy o' yours doesn't want you there, but I'll bet anythin' he wishes you were."

Maeve looked up in surprise, remembering Jen's sermon about hearing God's voice, and as she considered Bud's words, she felt an odd peace fill her heart. She'd been praying for guidance and praying that she wouldn't lose Gage, and suddenly, it was crystal clear: she loved Gage with all her heart—and whether he got along with his dad, or not, it was still his *dad*! She looked back at Bud. "But the service is tomorrow morning . . . in Tennessee!"

Bud leaned forward in his chair and eyed her solemnly. "Then you better get going, missy."

# 49

When the bell of the old alarm clock went off early Tuesday morning, Gage practically jumped out of his skin. "No wonder Cale and I never overslept," he grumbled, fumbling to turn it off. He felt something heavy on his leg, looked down, and realized Gus had curled up next to him sometime during the night and now had his head on his leg. "Hey, pal," Gage said softly, flopping the dog's ear back and forth, "mind moving your head so I can get up?" Gus opened one eye, made a guttural sound of contentment, and closed it again. "Hey," Gage said, nudging him, and the dog rolled onto his back for a belly rub. "Uh, sorry! No time for that today. I have to hop in the shower." Gage managed to extricate himself from under the sheet, grabbed the towels his mom had brought in the night before, and shuffled sleepily down the hall to shower and shave.

An hour later, after downing a cup of black coffee, he was standing in the downstairs bathroom, trying to tie his tie, when Chase walked by.

"It's crooked," his little brother teased, peering into the bathroom, "and there's a button in the back of your collar that needs to be buttoned."

Gage reached back to button it, but the buttonhole was too small and he couldn't push it through. "Damn!" he muttered. "Can you get it?" he asked, turning so his brother could reach it.

Chase tucked the tie under the collar, secured the button, and then eyed the knot his brother had tied. "Who taught you to tie a tie . . . Dad?" he teased.

"Who else?" Gage asked.

"Well, a Windsor knot is a little fancy for a funeral. You should use a four-in-hand or a half-Windsor," he offered. "I *never* use a full Windsor."

Gage groaned. "I don't have time for a tie-tying lesson. Mom and I are picking up Dutch."

Chase nodded. "It'll only take a second," he said, quickly untying the tie and deftly retying it with a simple half-Windsor. "The trick is tightening the knot as you bring it up," he said, as he slid it up and cinched it into a tight, neat knot close to his brother's collar. "See?"

Gage turned and looked in the mirror. "Nice," he said, lightly touching it. "Thanks!"

"You're welcome," Chase said. "Now you look almost as sharp as me."

"Not quite," Gage said, eyeing the slim tailored suit his brother was wearing. "You always look cool as a cucumber," he said, smiling—it was a phrase they'd often heard their mom use. "Is your eulogy all written?" he asked.

"It's up here," Chase said, tapping his temple, "and in here," he added, patting his heart.

"No way," Gage said, eyeing him. "You didn't write it down?!"

"Nope," Chase said.

"You're a lot braver than the rest of us," Gage said.

"Or more foolish," Chase quipped with a grin.

Libby hurried into the kitchen and eyed her sons suspiciously. "How come you two look like cats who ate canaries?"

"I don't know," Gage said innocently, and then changed the subject. "Are you ready?"

"Almost," she said, brushing away a tear as she stuffed a wad of tissues into her purse.

"You okay, Mom?" Chase asked, frowning.

She nodded. "Are you?"

"Yes," he replied.

She looked at them as if she were seeing them for the first time. "You both look nice."

"Thank you," Chase said. "So do you."

"Thank you," she replied, nodding. "So, you and Liam are going over early to make sure everything's ready?"

Chase nodded. "Yes, we're leaving shortly . . . so don't worry about a thing."

"Thank you so much, hon," she said, giving him a hug, and then, it suddenly dawned on Chase that the last thing his mom needed to do before her husband's funeral service was go to the nursing home to collect her wheelchair-bound, memory-challenged father. "Mom," he said, frowning, "how come you didn't have Uncle Mike pick Dutch up?"

"Because I want to see what kind of day he's having," she replied, "and decide if he should go."

Chase nodded. "Maybe he *shouldn't* go," he suggested softly. "You have a lot on your plate today."

"Maybe," she said, "but if he's up to it, I'd like him to be there."

Chase raised his eyebrows and eyed Gage—who nodded in understanding, suddenly struck by his younger brother's gentle compassion and sensitivity to their mom's needs.

"They said they'd have him dressed," she continued distractedly, and then she looked up at Gage. "Ready?"

"Ready as I'll ever be," he said, mustering a smile.

# 50

The stars were sparkling in the night sky when Maeve looked out the window at 2 A.M. She'd gone to bed early and then proceeded to wake up every hour, on the hour. Now, she was afraid she might oversleep if she fell asleep again, so she got up.

On her way home from work the night before, she'd stopped at Macey's to pick up the white blouse her sister had borrowed a month earlier. "You know, the summery one that doesn't require ironing and will still look halfway decent when I get there," she'd said.

"I can't believe you're driving all the way to Tennessee," her sister had said when she came through the door. "Why didn't you think of this before? You could've gone today and stayed in a hotel."

"I don't know why I didn't think of it before, but I've been praying about it, and earlier today, I had an epiphany," she said brightly, "and I'm just glad I had it before it was too late!"

Macey nodded. "I'm glad, too. How long does it take to get there and what time are you leaving?"

"I looked online and my phone app says it'll take around six and a half hours, and since the service is at eleven, I'm planning to leave by three thirty in the morning, so I can allow time for traffic or stopping for a bathroom, which we both know I'll need to do . . . at least twice!"

"Not if you don't drink coffee," Macey said.

"Mace, I'm getting up at 3 A.M. I will *need* coffee."

Macey nodded. "Well, it's good you're going. Ben wishes he could go, too, but with Gage not around, they've been under the gun, trying to stay on schedule."

"That reminds me," Maeve said. "Can you take care of the chickens?"

"Why does 'under the gun' remind you of the chickens?"

Maeve shook her head and sighed. "I don't know, but it did . . . so can you?"

"Of course," Macey said. "Just one more thing for us to do on the first day of school."

"Oh, that's right! I'm sorry," Maeve said. "I completely forgot it was the first day of school! Well, on the bright side, you can take a photo of Harper surrounded by her favorite hens—that would make a cute first-day picture—you could even post it on Facebook."

"Mm-hmm," Macey said, sounding unconvinced. "Not a fan, remember?"

Maeve rolled her eyes. "Harper's gonna have a Facebook page soon, and then you'll have to reactivate your account so you can keep an eye on her."

"I'll let her aunt keep an eye on her. . . . Then I won't be accused of snooping."

Maeve laughed. "Well, I won't be tattling," she teased. "Oh, and don't leave the gate open," she reminded. "There's no free-ranging—I don't want anything to happen to them while they're in my care. . . . And help yourself to eggs."

"Got it," Macey said.

"Thanks. I owe you one."

"You don't owe me anything," Macey said.

"Okay, well, I better go," Maeve said, giving her sister a hug.

"Okay. Safe travels. I hope it goes well. Tell Gage we're thinking of him."

"I will," Maeve said, "if he's talking to me." And with that, she'd hurried out to her Jeep.

Now, wide awake at 2 A.M., she opened her laptop, clicked on her Facebook page, and realized she had a new friend request. Curiously, she clicked on it, and then smiled in surprise—it was from Mason. "Absolutely!" she said softly, clicking *confirm*. Then she scrolled through his page, smiling at the photos of him at all different ages, and with different friends—especially the pictures that kept popping up of him with a cute blond-haired girl who seemed to have been a fixture in his life since childhood . . . and who'd been tagged, revealing her name: *Ali Harrison*. "Hmm," she mused thoughtfully, wondering if she was the friend he'd talked about. There were also photos of him running cross-country . . . and of him with Laurie, the wonderful woman he called *Mom*. His Facebook page was like a window into his life, and she was beyond thankful to be invited to look in. When she finally looked up from his page, though, she realized, in alarm, that half an hour had slipped by. She closed her laptop and hurried down the hall to shower.

Seven long hours later, Maeve slipped into the last pew of a little white country church, overflowing with mourners, and looked up at the tall mullioned windows. Her drive had been uneventful, and even though she hadn't had much coffee, she'd still had to stop. She looked around the simple sanctuary now, wondering if it was the same church Gage had attended when he was a boy. She checked her phone for the time, texted Macey that she'd made it, turned off the sound, and slipped it back in her pocket. She'd briefly considered wearing a dress, but the idea of driving seven hours and stopping at rest stops in a dress and nylons was a little daunting, so she'd opted for something simple—gray slacks and a white blouse with a light blue silk scarf tied loosely around her neck. She reached up to touch both her ears to make sure she hadn't lost an earring and then slid the clasp of her necklace back where it belonged—at the back of her perspiring neck.

Even with the windows open, the church—which obviously had no AC—was very warm, and when she noticed everyone around her fanning themselves with their bulletins, she picked hers up and studied the image on the cover: it was a beautiful photo of a field with a setting sun behind it, and over the image were the words *Well done, good and faithful servant*. She opened it, and read the title, *A Celebration of the Life of John (Jack) Matthew Tennyson*, and then quickly scanned the page, looking at the different readings the family had chosen, and the names of speakers. She noticed the minister's name listed across from "Reflections by the Minister" was Melinda Keck. She continued to study the bulletin, looking for Gage's name, but wasn't surprised when she didn't see it. She did see Chase's name, though, across from the traditional reading from Ecclesiastes . . . *and* across from the eulogy.

Promptly at 11 A.M., the church bell began to toll high up in the steeple, and a pretty, middle-aged woman wearing a long, black robe with a beautiful purple stole opened a door in the front of the sanctuary, and the whispering and murmuring in the church grew quiet as the Tennyson family walked in. Maeve peered over the heads in front of her—looking for Gage—and was surprised when he appeared first, pushing a wheelchair with an older gentleman in it. A slim, graceful woman with silver hair followed him, and behind her walked a man with salt-and-pepper hair—who looked like the photo she'd seen of Dutch—and then, three more of Jack Tennyson's tall, blond-haired sons, their wives, and a host of tow-headed grandchildren emerged. Coming through the door last were Liam and Chase.

Maeve took a deep breath and reached into her purse for a tissue—the service hadn't even begun and she already had tears in her eyes. She watched Gage maneuver the wheelchair to the end of the first pew, adjust the light blanket on the man's lap, and sit down next to him. The rest of the family filed in, too, filling two entire pews. Finally, the minister stepped up to the pulpit, and with a warm smile, welcomed everyone, and then invited them to stand—if they were able—to sing one of Jack's favorite hymns, "The Old Rugged Cross."

# 51

As the first notes of the old hymn drifted out, Gage opened his hymnal and offered it to his mom, and even though Libby knew the words by heart, she held her side of the book and sang softly, trying not to cry. Soon, the collected voices of the congregation swelled, along with the music from the organ, and Gage looked down and realized his grandfather's weathered face was radiant as he mouthed the words, too. Gage nudged his mom so she would see her dad singing, and she shook her head, and whispered, "He's having a really good day—seeing you has made such a difference." She motioned to her brother, who nodded and smiled, too, and soon the entire family knew Dutch was singing. When the hymn ended, Gage gently squeezed his grandfather's shoulder, and the old man reached out his gnarled hand shakily and patted Gage's knee.

Meanwhile, up in the pulpit, Melinda closed her hymnal, set it to the side, and looked up. "I will never forget the first time I met Jack Tennyson. It was my first week as the new minister here, and a tall gentleman walked into the office. 'Welcome, pastor,' he said. 'I never thought the search committee would go through with it, but they surely did!' And after some pleasantries, he left, and I asked Jeannie—our faithful church secretary—what he'd meant, and she laughed. 'I think he meant he didn't think they'd ever hire a woman!'

"'Oh!' I said in surprise.

"Not long after, I learned that Jack was the patriarch of a family with six sons and the proprietor of a famous nearby farm with over five hundred dairy cows—or as Jack would say, 'five hundred head of cattle,' and I thought, holy cra . . . cow! That's a lot of sh . . . manure!" Her words immediately broke the somber tension in the room and everyone chuckled. She smiled and continued, "But I also learned that, above all else, Jack Tennyson was a man of God . . . *and* a man of his convictions; he was always willing to lend a hand, no matter what the task . . . or how busy he was—whether it was serving communion, drying dishes, or . . ." she looked up and smiled—"donating *and* serving his family's ice cream at our church suppers.

"In fact, whenever there was a project, Jack was the first to volunteer . . . the first to arrive . . . *and* the last to leave. He was every minister's dream in a parishioner and in a fellow servant." She paused and searched the faces of his family. "But that isn't to say Jack was without some faults . . . because he was also definitely old-school. Jack's interpretation of the Bible was literal, and he would defend his position by quoting countless verses from both the Old and New Testaments. But this didn't mean that Jack couldn't evolve . . . because he did! God threw some hard lessons Jack's way, and through it all, he kept the faith, learned from those lessons, and persevered. He was the proverbial, pliable clay, and he allowed *his* master craftsman to mold him into the man we all loved so much." She smiled. "Jack Tennyson was indeed a great man . . . and no one knows that better than his family." She eyed Chase and smiled. "Now, I'd like to invite Jack's youngest son up to read from scripture and share some memories that only a Tennyson boy would know."

Chase—who was sitting on the far end of the second pew—smiled and stood up, and all the other Tennyson boys breathed quiet sighs of relief, thankful that their brother had been willing to take on this task. Gage watched Chase bump fists with Liam, and he was thankful that their mom had insisted Liam sit with the family, and then a sudden ache washed over him as he realized she would have insisted Maeve sit with them, too.

Chase strode to the pulpit, and as he adjusted the mic, he looked out at the congregation, his kind smile warming their hearts. "Even at six feet, I'm still the shortest Tennyson boy," he joked, "but I'm a little taller than Melinda." At this, the congregation chuckled and immediately felt at ease.

Chase scanned the page of the open Bible and then looked up. "The reading my mom chose for this morning is from the book of Ecclesiastes, and although it's often read at memorial services, I feel like it's especially appropriate for my dad—whose life *and* livelihood depended on the seasons." He proceeded to read the well-known words, and when he finished, he looked up.

"Well, I can absolutely attest to what Melinda said—my dad *knew* his Bible verses! But what most people don't know about him is that his knowledge *and* his interpretation of the Bible were rooted in the fact that his *own* dad—our grandfather"—he looked at his brothers as he said this—"was also a minister, and John Tennyson Sr. wasn't a kind, gentle soul like Melinda. Reverend Tennyson was a fierce, Bible-thumping, fire-and-brimstone, true Southern Baptist minister—a stern man who insisted that his two sons memorize countless Bible verses and Psalms and sit through endless church services. In recent years, when I found this out from my mom"—as he said this, he looked down and smiled at the woman sitting next to Gage—"I began to see my dad in a new light, and I began to understand the influences that had shaped his thinking.

"When I was little, sitting on my dad's broad shoulders—with him holding tightly to my ankles—I was on top of the world. Nothing could hurt me. My brothers would all traipse along after him, but I got to ride on his six-foot, four-inch frame . . . and I always knew, without a doubt, that he loved *me*.

"Growing up in the shadows of my mischievous fun-loving

brothers, I watched as rules were set and broken, and as storms rolled in . . . *and* out, but peace—thanks to our mom—always seemed to prevail. My brothers paved the way, and by the time I came up through the ranks, I got away with just about anything." He paused and looked at Liam. "Even being gay.

"As you might imagine, this revelation didn't go over well in our house. My dad—whose faiths and beliefs, as Melinda said, were *old-school*—had a very hard time understanding and accepting this news, but when he started quoting the Bible to prove his point, I pulled some Bible verses out of my own back pocket. I reminded him that every time he planted his corn next to his alfalfa . . . or wore a silk tie with a cotton shirt, he was sinning . . . because in Leviticus 19:19, it says that you shall not plant your field with two kinds of seed . . . or wear clothes woven from two kinds of material." Chase smiled. "This revelation set him back on his heels because the Bible really *does* say that—and this is certainly an outdated commandment—I mean, who made up such rules? Was it really God that said that? Or was it some self-righteous Pharisee? So, we talked at length about the change in thinking that happened after Jesus came along, and how the New Testament was about love . . . and not about rules and vengeance.

"As Melinda said, God *did* throw some hard lessons my dad's way, but he *was*—as we all *must* be—pliable . . . and he *did* change." Chase looked at Gage and smiled. "And I wasn't the only free-range chicken that went off the farm." Everyone chuckled at this and Chase grinned. "Just one of the many colorful and politically incorrect phrases our dad liked to use when he was characterizing people he thought were making risky decisions. But I wasn't the only son who forced our dad to grow and change, and to consider life from other perspectives." He paused and eyed his brothers. "We *all* did, in one way or another . . . because you can't raise six sons without having a little hell break loose!" At this, everyone laughed, and then Chase's face grew solemn as he continued.

"Another hard lesson came our dad's way when, on a beautiful summer day—much like today—tragedy struck our family. When Cale died, it seemed like everyone in town was mourning, but no one mourned more than our parents . . . and especially, my dad . . . because he blamed and never forgave himself for what happened." Chase looked up. "No parent should ever bury a child . . . and even though this tragic accident changed our dad, he kept his faith.

"So, this past weekend, my brothers and I . . . *and* our sweet mom . . . had the amazing opportunity to spend quite a bit of time together, reminiscing about the old days, remembering our dad. Although he seemed to always be serious—'as serious as four heart attacks and a stroke,' another saying he liked to use when he wanted to express the gravity of a situation—he also had a sense of humor and a smile that could move mountains. My brothers, Gage and Matt, recalled the time Dad and Dutch took them—and Cale—up to Bristol Motor Speedway to see a NASCAR race, and how Terry Labonte—who'd stopped for fresh tires with just five laps to go—had taken the lead, when Dale Earnhardt Sr. came up behind him and—as he so loved to do—bumped into him and spun him around so he could take the checkered flag for himself. . . . And as great as it was for my brothers to see their favorite driver win, what they remember most about that moment was seeing their ever-reserved dad pumping his fist in the air and shouting, 'Woo-hoo! Bump and run, baby! Bump and run!'"

Chase smiled. "Now, Dad's up in heaven, reunited with Cale . . . and maybe even meeting Dale! After this weekend, I think we all have come to realize what an amazing person our dad was—a giant of a man who loved his family, and who, I learned, as I sat beside his bed, was also a hopeless romantic . . . because his last words to our mom came from their wedding song, 'Bridge Over Troubled Water.' Before he closed his eyes for the last time, he smiled at her, squeezed her hand, and whispered, *Sail on, silver girl*." Chase's eyes glistened visibly as he looked at his mom and smiled. "Sail on, Dad."

Gage put his arm around his mom and watched Chase give Melinda a hug before stepping down from the pulpit, and as they stood to sing the next hymn, "How Great Thou Art," tears spilled down his cheeks. His brother's wise words and open heart made him feel ashamed of his own closed mind and hardened heart, and they rendered him unable to speak, never mind sing. *Why hadn't he tried harder—or tried at all—to make amends with his dad?* His mom had begged him to come home, but he'd stubbornly resisted, harboring resentment and pride, and not only hurting his dad, but also hurting himself . . . and now it was too late. His dad had loved *all* his sons with *all* his heart for *all* his life. Even Chase had found a way to understand their father and forgive him . . . but *he*—after one disagreement that had been rooted in his father's concern for him—had never found it in his heart to forgive. Instead, he had pushed aside all the wonderful childhood memories he had of him and, for eighteen years, allowed resentment and anger to fester in his heart. *Oh, God, how wrong he had been!* And now, he realized, his inability and stubborn unwillingness to forgive his dad had hampered his own ability to move forward, and he wished with all his heart that he'd come home sooner to tell him, in person, that he forgave . . . *and* loved him, and always would.

Libby looked up, saw her son's head bowed in sorrow, and reached up and gently brushed away his tears.

# 52

Maeve dabbed her eyes with her last tissue, thankful she'd had the presence of mind—at 3 A.M.—to put on water-resistant mascara. Then she tearfully gathered her things and followed the stream of people making their way downstairs to Fellowship Hall, but when she spied a ladies' room, she ducked in to use it, and then listened as two women talked about how moving the service had been.

"That Chase Tennyson always was the cute one," one of the women said. "I can remember when he was little, riding on his daddy's shoulders, but I had no idea he was gay!"

The second lady chimed in. "It's always the cute ones," she said, as if those in the LGBTQ community were from another class of people. "So eloquent and well-spoken, though," she added, briefly redeeming herself. She then whispered, "Do you think that dark-haired young man is his boyfriend?"

Maeve tried to block out their conversation as she washed her hands and splashed cool water on her puffy eyes and tear-stained face. She dried her hands, slipped from the room, and stood resolutely in the hall—her stomach rumbling with hunger as the line to greet the family inched forward.

Twenty minutes later, as she neared the front, Chase saw her, and his face lit up with a smile.

"Oh, Chase," she said, "I'm so sorry about your dad. Your eulogy was amazing and so heartfelt."

"Thanks, Maeve," he said, smiling.

"Did you have it written down? I never saw you look."

He shook his head. "No, I knew what I wanted to say.

Maeve shook her head. "I could never . . ."

Chase smiled, and then looked puzzled. "How come you're in *that* line and not this one?" he asked, gesturing to the receiving line. He frowned. "Does Gage know you're here?"

"I don't think so," she said, and then she eyed him. "You know we broke up, right?"

"No," he said, shaking his head in disbelief. "Has he lost his mind?!"

"That's what I'm thinking," she replied, laughing.

Chase smiled. "C'mon. You don't belong here, and besides, I know someone who wants to meet you."

Maeve started to protest. "I'll lose my place . . ."

But it was too late. Chase had pulled her out of the line waiting to give their condolences to the family and guided her toward the woman she'd seen sitting beside Gage during the service. "Mom, do you know who this is?!"

As Libby searched Maeve's face, a warm smile crossed her own. "You must be Maeve!" she said. "Oh, my goodness! I've been looking forward to meeting you for such a long time!"

"I've been looking forward to meeting you, too. I'm so sorry about your husband."

Libby nodded solemnly. "Thank you." And then she pulled Maeve into a hug. "I'm so glad you came. Did you get in last night? Because you should've called and stayed at the house."

Maeve shook her head. "I drove up this morning."

"You did? You must be exhausted."

"A little," Maeve said, "but I'm really glad I came—the service was beautiful."

"Thank you," Libby said, and then she looked down the line of family members and frowned. "Chase, where is Gage?"

Chase followed her gaze. "I don't know. Dutch isn't here, either."

"Well, would you mind seeing if you can find them?"

"I wouldn't mind at all," Chase said, glad to be released from the receiving line. "Just a second. . . ."

Maeve watched Chase walk over and say something to Liam, and when he came back, he said, "I think I know where he is."

They walked across the parking lot, and Chase gestured to a stone wall behind the church. "This is Memorial Garden—it's where the ashes of church members are interred. My brother is buried on the farm, and my dad will be buried next to him, but other family members are here, including my grandmother on my mom's side, and I'll bet that's where Gage and Dutch are." He smiled. "Gage hates crowds . . ."

"Don't I know it," Maeve said, feeling her heart race at the prospect of seeing him.

As they reached the garden, Maeve realized it was more than just one long wall—it was a courtyard of walls with more walls in the middle. They were all capped with heavy blocks of slate, and many had metal placards engraved with names and dates of loved ones.

Chase stopped when they reached the first wall, and pointed, and Maeve saw Gage sitting on a stone bench next to a wheelchair. "That's where my grandma is interred—she died two years ago—which is also when Dutch's own health took a downward turn. I'll let you take it from here," he said with a gentle smile.

"Are you sure you don't want to come?" she said.

"I think you can handle it."

"All right," she said nervously. "If you say so."

Chase smiled, and she watched him walk back to the church, and then pressed her lips together, gathering her resolve and courage. As she walked to where Gage was sitting, she thought she could hear music, and as she drew near, she realized it was coming from his phone.

Hearing footsteps, Gage looked up, and then stood in surprise. "Maeve! What are you doing here?"

She swallowed. "I came for your dad's service."

Gage bit his lip. "I didn't expect you . . ."

She nodded. "I know. I'm really sorry about your dad, Gage. Chase's words—they . . . they were so moving. I almost felt like I knew him."

"He did a great job. I could never . . ."

"I couldn't, either." She looked over at Dutch and smiled. "Is this your grandpa?"

Gage smiled. "Yeah, this is Dutch." And then he knelt in front of the old man. "Dutch, I want you to meet someone," he said softly. He pulled her over. "This is Maeve—the girl I've been telling you about."

The old man looked up, his blue eyes seeming to smile as he nodded. Then he looked back at his grandson. "Is this the one you're goin' to marry?"

Gage bit his lip as tears filled his eyes. "Yeah, she's the one," he said, and then he looked up at Maeve. "But I've been a bit of an ass lately."

"Well, I could be an ass, too, in my day. Maybe she'll forgive you, eh?"

Gage nodded as his tears spilled down his cheeks. "I hope so," he whispered.

"Well, why don't you stop your blubberin' and ask her, for Pete's sake . . . and then we'll both know."

"To forgive me . . . or to marry me?" Gage asked.

"Aren't they the same thing?" Dutch asked, his eyes sparkling with wisdom.

Gage nodded again and bit his lip again, feeling his heart pound. "I guess they are. . . ."

He turned to Maeve. "I'm so sorry for how I've behaved . . . and treated you, Maeve. I *have* been an ass . . . and listening to Chase talk about our dad today made me realize what a fool I've been. It broke my heart to finally realize I'd let the opportunity to make amends with someone I love slip away . . . and I don't ever want that to happen again."

Maeve pressed her lips together and nodded. "It's okay, Gage. I know you've had a hard time."

Gage shook his head. "No . . . it's no excuse. Everyone has difficult things happen . . . and the things that've happened to me don't even compare with what other people have been through."

Maeve nodded as tears filled her eyes. "You're going to make me start crying again," she said softly. "You Tennyson men sure know how to make a girl cry."

Gage smiled and held her face in his hands, and with his thumbs, he gently brushed her tears away. "I've missed you so much," he said. "I wanted so badly for you to be here."

"I'm here," she said, mustering a smile.

He nodded and searched her eyes. "I'm really sorry, Maeve. I now realize what a surprise—what a wonderful surprise—it must've been for you to have your son come back into your life . . . and I—I was so selfish to act the way I did. Can you ever forgive me?"

Maeve pressed her lips together, recalling everything she'd thought about when she'd been driving here—everything Gage had been through when he was younger . . . and how she'd known the minute she met him at Ben and Macey's picnic—by the way he'd scooped his sweet, sleepy puppy into his arms . . . and talked about listening to the loons at night when he was a boy, even knowing their calls—that he was shy and old-school. And how it absolutely didn't surprise her that he'd kept all his painful memories—from having his heart broken to feeling like his dreams were being dismissed by his father, and from losing his favorite cow to tragically losing his brother—tucked deep in his heart, never wanting to share them. It was just like him to press on, trying to do his best and make his way in the world . . . *because isn't that what we all do when we're hurting?* Gage had been doing the best he could, not wanting to burden others with his troubles, but at the same time, wanting to trust and love . . . and *be* loved. *How could she* not *forgive him?* "I already have," she said.

Gage shook his head. "I don't deserve you." He paused, looked around at their surroundings, and realized Dutch was watching them. He turned back to Maeve and searched her eyes. "I already talked to your parents . . ."

"You did?!"

He nodded and smiled. "They gave us their blessings . . . and I already have a ring, too, but I don't have it with me," he added. "And this"—he gestured around him—"isn't the setting I had in mind, but . . . Dutch is here, and that is probably the best setting I could ask for, so . . ."

He knelt down in front of her, and Maeve's heart raced—this was not at all what she had expected to happen *today*, or *right now* . . . or maybe *ever*—and she suddenly felt as if it might beat right out of her chest.

"Maeve, I can't imagine my life without you in it," Gage said softly. "I love you with all my heart . . ." He glanced back at his grandfather and then looked at Maeve, and in a clear voice he was sure his grandfather could hear, he said, "Maeve Lindstrom, will you marry me?"

"Yes," Maeve said, tears spilling down her cheeks. Gage grinned and pulled her into a hug and then held her face in his hands and softly kissed her, and Dutch smiled, his eyes twinkling, and reached out and rested his old gnarled hand on the wall next to him.

# 53

*One month later*

The drive from Savannah to Atlanta always reminded Maeve of her college days and all the times she'd driven back and forth to Emory, especially that one long ride with her dad after she'd given her son up for adoption. That day, when he'd picked her up, it had taken everything she had not to cry. Now, as she looked out the window at the old familiar landmarks, her mind drifted back over everything that had happened in the month since Gage had proposed.

The entire Tennyson family had been thrilled with their news. They'd welcomed her with open arms—and hearts—especially Gage's mom, who'd said it had made a very sad day a happy one, and was further proof that the joys and sorrows of life *do* walk hand in hand. She had also said she hoped they would consider having the wedding at the farm—after all, she'd added with a smile, barn weddings were all the rage right now, and it would give them a reason to paint and refurbish the big barn, a project that was long overdue.

After sharing their news, they'd stayed to see Jack Tennyson's ashes interred beneath the boughs of the giant oak tree next to his son. The sun had been setting and the Tennessee sky had been on fire with every shade of pink and orange, washing the fields and barns in an ethereal golden light. Later, after a quick bite, they'd said good-bye, and as they'd driven past the field again, Maeve had looked up at the solitary oak tree standing in the dusky shadows, and suddenly caught her breath. She'd stopped her Jeep and Gage had pulled over behind her, and they'd both climbed out and watched as a line of cows walked slowly up the hill to stand solemnly under the tree's long, gnarled branches. Gage had pulled her close, and they'd watched the scene in amazed silence. Afterward, they had followed each other home, stopping only once for a bathroom—and a tree for Gus—finally arriving at the cabin at one in the morning.

They'd walked in and Gage had clicked on the light over his table and noticed a new drawing on it, and the likeness of its subject was uncanny—it was *him*. In the bottom corner, the artist had signed her name: *Harper Samuelson* with a small heart next to it—her insignia.

"Wow!" Maeve had said, looking over his shoulder. "I think she's gotten the hang of using that kneaded eraser you gave her . . . *and* I think she has a crush on you."

"You think?" Gage had said, smiling. Then he'd turned and pulled her into his arms. "Too bad I'm taken," he'd murmured.

"It's good you're taken," Maeve had said, leaning into him. "Besides, she has Sam."

"Sam?" Gage had said, frowning. "I thought they were just 'friends'?"

"That's what she *says*," she'd said, laughing, "but I've seen the way she looks at him . . . with his wispy hair and 'eyes that look like pieces of moorland sky.' By the way, did I tell you Sam's mom released the baby fox back into the wild?"

"No, you didn't," Gage had said. "But that's great . . . so long as she didn't release him around here . . ."

"She and Sam and Harper took him to Skidaway Island State Park, and they said as soon as they let him go, he caught a mouse!"

Gage had smiled, and then he'd moved the framed photo of

Dutch on the shelf above his drawing table, revealing where he'd tucked the black jewelry box—between the back of the frame and the easel. "The jeweler taught me all about the four *Cs*," he'd said with a slow smile, "*and* he helped me pick out a very sparkly one because, he said, that's what girls like." He'd opened the box, revealing a gorgeous diamond in a delicate setting.

"Oh, my! It's beautiful," Maeve had whispered, staring at it as he slid it onto her finger, and after admiring it on her hand, she'd pulled him toward the bedroom. "By the way," she'd said, "you never told me you knew how to play the fiddle!"

And he'd smiled as he wrapped his arms around her. "I'm a man of many hidden talents, remember?" he'd teased, as he'd backed her against the wall and softly kissed her.

"Indeed you are," she'd murmured, and although it had been late, and she'd been up for almost twenty-four hours straight, and they both had to work the next day, that night between the sheets had been well worth the weariness she'd felt the next morning.

Maeve held out her hand now, admiring her ring again, and Gage glanced over. "Still like it?"

"Like it? I *love* it!" she gushed, and then she recalled how all the residents at Willow Pond had reacted when she'd showed them. Up and down the porch, everyone had wished her well. "Congratulations!" and "Blessings!" came from all the ladies—including Gladys, who added, "You caught yourself a hottie, missy!" The men had all given her hugs, too, and Aristides had said with a grin, "I tol' you, you weren't gonna be an old maid!" Then it had been Bud's turn. "God always has a plan, Maeve. We may not see it when we're in the middle of the raging river, but *he* does."

Later that day, Ivy's son had stopped by to pack up his mom's things. He'd reported that she was doing much better and that he'd secured a bed for her in the new memory care facility in Savannah. Maeve had peeked into her room a little later when he was packing and told him all about his mom clapping and tapping her feet to the fiddle music on the porch, and she'd suggested he try playing some of her favorite music . . . and making sure she put her hearing aids in. He'd said he would, and then she'd finally asked him about the boy in the photo. Will had told her that the boy was indeed his dad and that he'd been killed in World War II before he'd had a chance to marry his mom. He'd also said he couldn't believe that Bud was the other young man in the photo and said he was eager to meet him.

"A penny for your thoughts," Gage teased as they neared Atlanta. "You've been so quiet."

She smiled. "Oh, I was just thinking about Bud and Ivy again, and what a small world it is."

He nodded, squeezing her hand.

"Sooo, are you ready for this?" she asked, changing the subject.

"Ready as I'll ever be," he said with a grin.

"Chase said it's a very prestigious gallery, and you should be proud."

"I still can't believe I got in, never mind *Best in Show*!"

"*I* can believe it," Maeve said. "That drawing of Dutch—with all its intricate detail—the wrinkles, wisps of white hair . . . and those eyes—that see right through you! The judges probably took one look at them and heard him warning them: 'You better pick my grandson!'"

"Maybe," Gage said. "He does have a way of getting *his* way."

"I'm so glad I got to meet him . . . and everyone in your family."

Gage looked over. "I'm glad, too. I know they loved you . . . and Dutch definitely approves."

Maeve smiled. "We'll have to have the wedding soon so he can be there."

Gage nodded. "I'm going to be busy getting ready for the show—the gallery wants to have it in the spring—so I don't know when I'll have time to plan a wedding."

"You have a lot of pieces already," she said, "and they're going to take care of all the framing—which is nice."

"It *is* nice, but I'd like to do some new drawings, too."

"You'll have time," Maeve assured him. "And between *your* mom, *my* mom, and Macey and Harper, we can plan the wedding, and you'll just have to stay up late, drawing, and not fooling around so much."

"But I *love* fooling around," he teased, squeezing her thigh.

"Well, which do you love *more*—fooling around . . . or having a one-man show in a prestigious gallery in a hip section of Atlanta?"

"Both," he said, laughing.

"Oh, well, you can't have everything," she teased.

"I can't?" he asked, sounding wounded.

Maeve smiled. "Chase did an awesome job with your website, too."

"He did. It's very professional."

"I bet it'll get a lot of traffic after today."

"Maybe," he said, as he turned off the highway.

"Ben's gonna have to start looking for a replacement for you."

"Yeah, right," he said, laughing. "That's not happenin' for a while. Speaking of Ben, are they still coming? It's an awfully long ride . . ."

"They are, but Harper had a soccer game this morning. They were going to have her go to the game with a friend, but she said she'd rather miss her game than *your* opening."

Gage nodded and looked over curiously. "Did you two ever start your new book?"

"We did," Maeve confirmed.

"Which one did you pick?" he asked, knowing they'd been considering several titles.

"Harper chose *My Side of the Mountain* . . . so we're leaving ten-year-old, strong-willed female protagonists behind and embarking on the wilderness frontier with a fourteen-year-old boy named Sam," Maeve reported with a smile.

Gage nodded approvingly. "I read that trilogy when I was younger. What does she think so far?"

"Well, she's an animal lover so she thinks it's *awesome*, of course."

Gage laughed. "Hopefully, she doesn't decide to set off into the wilderness looking for a peregrine falcon."

"I hope not," Maeve said, chuckling.

"Did they ever make a movie from that book?" he asked, looking puzzled.

"They *did*," Maeve confirmed.

"Maybe I can watch it with you since I already read the book."

"Maybe," Maeve teased. "We'll take it under consideration."

Gage laughed. "Okay, so who else is coming *today*?"

"Everyone," she said.

He frowned. "*Everyone?*"

"My parents are on their way home from vacationing in Virginia, Chase and Liam are bringing your mom, and Mason and Ali are coming, too . . . since they both go to school right there."

Gage nodded. They'd all had the chance to meet Mason and his girlfriend at a cross-country meet two weeks earlier, and Gage had been impressed by Maeve's son—especially when he had learned he was in the ROTC program and planning to go into the air force.

"It's funny how everything has fallen into place," Maeve said, remembering how, when Gage had finally gone through the mail after being in Tennessee for several days, he'd found the letter informing him that his entry into the art show, which he hadn't told her about, had won top honors—and how the gallery hoped he would be able to attend the opening.

"It is," Gage said, knowing, deep down, that the lyrics of the Garth Brooks song that had always made his grandfather cry had also been inspiration for him to enter—*he'd definitely chanced the rapids . . . and dared to dance the tide!*

"I wonder if your dad is pulling some strings in heaven," Maeve mused.

Gage looked over and smiled. "I bet he is—it would be just like him."

# WITH HEARTFELT GRATITUDE . . .

To my editor, Rebecca Raskin, and my agent, Elizabeth Copps, for their thoughtful guidance, positive critiques, and patient encouragement. I couldn't do it without you!

To the entire Harper Perennial team, who have all worked so hard to make *Promises to Keep* the best it can be.

To my husband, Bruce—whose wonderful, funny, loving traits are the inspiration for so many of the male characters in my books; and to our sons, Cole and Noah, and our lovely daughter-in-law, Leah, who fill our hearts with joy, and who endlessly cheer me on. God truly blessed me when he gave me *all* of you!

To the Wonderful Women of the Congregational Church of Brookfield, with whom I have the privilege of spending every Monday morning. Together, we learn, inspire, share struggles, celebrate joys, and pray in earnest.

To all my family, friends, and fans, who faithfully buy, read, and enthusiastically spread the word about my books. It's your support that makes it possible for me to follow my dreams.

To our noble, solemn black Lab, Finn, who I can always count on to make sure I don't spend too much time sitting at my desk and get plenty of fresh air and exercise.

And to my heavenly Father above, who continues to bless me beyond measure!

## About the book



## About the author



## Read on



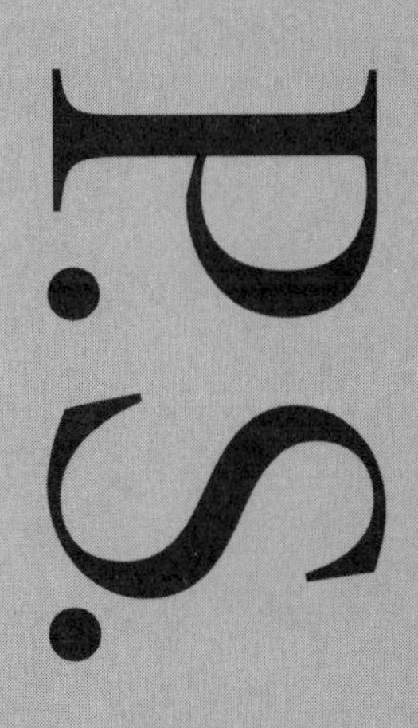

Insights,
Interviews
& More . . .

# Maeve's Chocolate Chess Pie

**Ingredients**

1 cup sugar
4 Tbs. unsweetened cocoa powder
1 5-oz. can evaporated milk
¼ cup softened butter
1 tsp. vanilla
2 beaten eggs
¾ cup chopped pecans (optional)
9-inch unbaked pie crust
Confectioner's sugar, for dusting
Whipped cream, for serving

**Directions**

1. Preheat the oven to 325 degrees.
2. Over medium heat, mix together the first five ingredients until the chocolate is blended and smooth.
3. While constantly stirring the eggs in a separate bowl, slowly add ½ cup of the hot pie mixture. When blended, add the egg mixture into the pot, continuing to stir. It will thicken immediately.
4. Blend in the pecans (if desired) and pour into the prepared pie shell.
5. Protect the pie crust with foil or a metal pie crust shield, and bake for one hour or until set.
6. Let cool for another hour and sprinkle lightly with confectioner's sugar. Serve with whipped cream. Yum!

About the author

# Meet Nan Rossiter

*New York Times* and *USA Today* bestselling author Nan Rossiter loves to weave together stories about the complicated relationships to which all readers can relate—motherhood, sisterhood, friendship, marriage, and romance. She draws from her own life experiences to create authentic situations that mirror the trials and triumphs we all face. Compassionate, real, and funny, her books take readers on emotional journeys that often include heartbreak and joy, but also include threads of faith, a furry friend or two, and an uplifting ending. Nan's books have been highly acclaimed by reviewers from *Publishers Weekly* to *Booklist*. Her novel *Summer Dance* was the 2018 winner of the Nancy Pearl Award.

Nan is a graduate of the Rhode Island School of Design and began her writing career in the world of children's books. Along with her many contemporary fiction novels, Nan is also the author/illustrator of several books for children, including *Rugby & Rosie*, winner of Nebraska's Golden Sower Award, and *The Fo'c'sle: Henry Beston's "Outermost House."*

Nan lives on a quiet country road in Connecticut with her husband and a solemn black Lab named Finn, who diligently watches her every move and can be roused from a slumber in a distant room by the sound of a banana being peeled or a cookie crumb hitting the floor. Nan and her husband are the parents of two handsome sons who have struck out on life journeys of their own.

For more information, please visit www.nanrossiter.com, where you can sign up for her newsletter, or follow her on Goodreads, Facebook, Twitter, and Instagram @NanRossiter.

# Have You Read? More by Nan Rossiter

**THE GIN & CHOWDER CLUB**

*Set against the beautiful backdrop of Cape Cod,* The Gin & Chowder Club *is an eloquent, tender story of friendship, longing, and the enduring power of love.*

The friendship between the Coleman and Shepherd families is as old and comfortable as the neighboring houses they occupy each summer on Cape Cod. Samuel and Sarah Coleman love those warm months by the water, the evenings spent on their porch enjoying gin and tonics, good conversation, and homemade clam chowder. Here they've watched their sons, Isaac and Asa, grow into fine young men, and watched, too, as Nate Shepherd, aching with grief at the loss of his first wife, finally found love again with the much younger Noelle.

But beyond the surface of these idyllic gatherings, the growing attraction between Noelle and handsome, college-bound Asa threatens to upend everything. In spite of her guilt and misgivings, Noelle is drawn into a reckless secret affair with far-reaching consequences. And over the course of one bittersweet, unforgettable summer, Asa will learn more than he ever expected about love—the joys and heartaches it awakens in us, the lengths we'll go to keep it, and the countless ways it can change our lives forever.

*"Eloquent and surprising . . . I loved this story of faith, love, and the lasting bonds of family."*

**—Ann Leary, author of *The Good House***

*"Nostalgic and tender . . . summons the passion of first love, the pain of first loss, and the unbreakable bonds of family that help us survive both."*

**—Marie Bostwick, *New York Times* bestselling author**

## WORDS GET IN THE WAY

*From the author of* The Gin & Chowder Club *comes an exquisitely heartfelt and uplifting novel that explores the infinite reach of a mother's love—and the gift of second chances.*

The modest ranch house where Callie Wyeth grew up looks just as she remembers it—right down to the well-worn sheets in the linen closet. But in the years since Callie lived here, almost everything else has changed. Her father, once indomitable, is in poor health. And Callie is a single mother with a beautiful little boy, Henry, who has just been diagnosed with autism. ▸

**Have You Read? *(continued)***

Returning to her family's quiet New Hampshire community seems the best thing to do, for the sake of both her father and her son. Even if it means facing Linden Finch, the one she loved and left, for reasons she's sure he'll never forgive. Linden is stunned that Callie is back—and that she has a son. Yet in the warm, funny relationship that develops around Henry and Linden's menagerie of rescued farm animals, Callie begins to find hope. Not just that her son might break through the wall of silence separating him from the world, but that she too can make a new start amid the places and people that have never left her heart . . .

*"Rossiter's second novel is an intimate portrayal of a family in crisis, with good character development and a bucolic setting."*

***—Publishers Weekly***

**MORE THAN YOU KNOW**

*Bestselling author Nan Rossiter weaves a poignant, empowering novel in which three sisters gather to celebrate their mother's life—and find new inspiration for living their own.*

Losing their father on the night Beryl Graham was born could have torn her family apart. Instead, it knitted them together. Under their mother's steady guidance, Beryl and her older sisters, Isak and Rumer, shared a childhood filled with happiness. But now Mia Graham has passed away after battling Alzheimer's, and her three daughters return to their New Hampshire home to say good-bye.

Swept up in memories and funeral preparations, the sisters catch up on one another's lives. Rumer and Isak have both known recent heartache, while Beryl has given up hope of marriage. But surprising revelations abound, especially when they uncover Mia's handwritten memoir. In it are secrets they never guessed at: clandestine romance, passionate dreams, joy, and guilt. And, as Beryl, Rumer, and Isak face a future without her, they realize it's never too late to heed a mother's lessons—about taking chances, keeping faith, and loving in spite of the risks.

*"A gripping story of three sisters, of love lost and found, and of a family's journey from grief to triumph. A sure winner."*

**—Debbie Macomber,**
**#1 *New York Times* bestselling author**

*"Rossiter's patient, deliberate pacing makes this one a perfect bedtime read."*

***—Publishers Weekly*** ▸

**Have You Read? *(continued)***

*"Rossiter's writing style is compelling. The setup of the novel provides a number of passages that tug at the reader's heartstrings, and the situations evoke realistic compassion."*

***—Houston News***

**UNDER A SUMMER SKY**

*Bestselling author Nan Rossiter transports readers to Cape Cod with a warm, compelling story of family, new beginnings, and finding the courage to love honestly and well.*

The old Cape Cod house that Laney Coleman shares with her minister husband, Noah, and their five boys is usually brimming with cheerful chaos. There's nothing fancy about the ancient kitchen or the wooden floors scuffed by the constant parade of activity and the clicking claws of their two Labrador retrievers. It's a place to savor the sea breeze wafting through the windows, or sip coffee on the porch before another hectic day begins. This summer, life promises to be even busier than usual, because Noah's younger brother, Micah, wants to hold his upcoming wedding on their property.

Although thrilled that Micah has found happiness after past heartache, Laney is apprehensive about having her home turned upside down. She has other concerns, too—her youngest son is being bullied at school, and Noah's father is not the robust patriarch he once was, in mind or body. As the bride's and groom's large, close-knit families gather, there will be joyful celebration but also unexpected sorrows and revelations, and a chance to store up a lifetime of memories during the fleeting, precious days of summer.

*"The setting, with its sea breeze and quaint charm, is immediately inviting, adding to the overall sense of familiarity that the author so beautifully evokes. . . . [T]o read this book is to feel like you've come home."*

**—John Valeri,**
***Hartford Books Examiner***

**NANTUCKET**

*From bestselling author Nan Rossiter comes a tender, moving story of rekindled passion, set amidst the timeless beauty of Nantucket.*

More than twenty-five years ago, Liam Tate and Acadia McCormick Knox fell in love. It was summer on Nantucket, and seventeen-year-old Liam knew that wealthy, college-bound Cadie was way out of the league of a local boy who ▸

**Have You Read?** ***(continued)***

restored boats for a living. Yet the two became inseparable, seizing every chance to slip away in Liam's runabout to secluded spots, far from the world that was trying to keep them apart. After Cadie returned home to New York and discovered she was pregnant, her parents crushed any hope of communicating with the boy she'd left behind. Unanswered letters and calls couldn't change Liam's heart, but over the years he's settled into a simple, solitary life in his rambling beachfront house. Now he's learned that Cadie is returning to Nantucket for the opening of her son's art show. Over a weekend of revelations and poignant memories, Cadie and Liam have an opportunity to confront the difference time can make, the truths that never alter, and the bittersweet second chances that arrive just in time to steer a heart back home.

*"There are moments of pure gold in the story that will undoubtedly touch readers' hearts. With wonderful characters and a charming idyllic setting,* Nantucket *does pack an emotional wallop along the lines of a good Kristan Higgins book."*

***—RT Book Reviews***

**FIREFLY SUMMER**

*Bestselling author Nan Rossiter's touching new novel reunites four sisters at their childhood vacation spot on Cape Cod—where they uncover the truth about a past tragedy to find their future as a family.*

The close-knit Quinn siblings enjoyed the kind of idyllic childhood that seems made for greeting cards, spending each summer at Whit's End, the family's home on Cape Cod. Then comes the summer of 1964, warm and lush after a rainy spring—perfect firefly weather. Sisters Birdie, Remy, Sailor, Piper, and their brother, Easton, delight in catching the insects in mason jars to make blinking lanterns. Until, one terrible night, tragedy strikes.

Decades later, the sisters have carved out separate lives on the Cape. Through love and heartbreak, health issues, raising children, and caring for their aging parents, they have supported each other, rarely mentioning their deep childhood loss. But one evening, as they congregate at Whit's End to watch the sunset, the gathering fireflies elicit memories of that long-ago night, and a tumult of regrets, guilt, and secrets tumbles out. ▸

Poignant yet hopeful, *Firefly Summer* is an uplifting story of the resilience of sisterhood and the bright glimpses of joy and solace that, like fireflies after rain, can follow even the deepest heartaches.

**SUMMER DANCE**

**Winner of the 2018 Nancy Pearl Book Award**

*Bestselling author Nan Rossiter brings together characters from her acclaimed novel* Nantucket *in a powerful, heartwarming love story that bridges past and present.*

When Liam Tate was seven years old, his Uncle Cooper opened his heart and his Nantucket home to the boy. In the intervening decades, Liam has found both love and loss on the island and, since learning that he has a son, Levi, a new kind of happiness. Yet one piece of his family history remains elusive—the long-ago romance between his uncle and Sally Adams. Now Sally makes a revelation that sets the whole town abuzz: she's publishing a book about what happened during the summer when she and Cooper first met, painting a picture so vivid it feels like yesterday.

In 1969, recently discharged veteran Winston Ellis Cooper III landed on Nantucket with only a duffel bag and a bottle of Jack Daniel's. He found a sparsely furnished beach cottage, about as far from Vietnam as he could get. But even here, Cooper couldn't withdraw from the world entirely—especially once his eyes met Sally's in the flickering lights of a summer dance. The effects of that fiery affair can still be felt decades later. As the story unfolds, there are new lessons for all to learn about life's triumphs and heartaches, and about loving enough to let go.

**PROMISES OF THE HEART**

*Can the course that they've set for the future handle a slight detour . . . ?*

Macey and Ben Samuelson have much to be thankful for: great friends, a beautiful—if high-maintenance—Victorian house on idyllic Tybee Island, and a rock-solid marriage. The only thing missing is what they want the most. After her fifth miscarriage in six years, Macey worries that the family they've always dreamed of might be out of reach. Her sister suggests adoption, but Macey and Ben aren't interested in pursuing that ▸

path . . . until a three-legged golden retriever named Keeper wags his way into their home and their hearts.

Harper Wheaton just got kicked out of another foster home and it won't be the last if she keeps losing her temper. She's not sure why she gets mad; maybe because no family seems to want a nine-year-old girl with a heart condition. She loves her caseworker, Cora, but knows that staying with her forever isn't an option. Will she ever find a family to call her own?

As a physician's assistant, Macey meets lots of kids. Harper Wheaton's a tough one, but Macey knows the little girl has already struggled more than most. It gets Macey and Ben thinking about all the children who need homes. Then Harper goes missing, and one thing is suddenly crystal clear: life is complicated—but love doesn't have to be.

*"A multileveled, beautifully written story that will glow in readers' hearts long after the last page is turned."*

**—Kristan Higgins, *New York Times* bestselling author**

# Reading Group Guide

1. Maeve and Gage have both kept long-held secrets about events that have shaped their lives, and even though they happened long ago, Maeve feels their unwillingness to be forthcoming with each other has put a wall between them. Why does she feel this way?

2. Gage stoically internalize his heartaches. How does this affect his outlook on life and his ability to move forward?

3. Mason seems unwilling to commit to a promise his mom wants him to keep. Why is this? When did you figure out what the promise is?

4. Maeve has a wonderfully upbeat personality that all the old folks at Willow Pond seem to love. How do they respond to her? Who is your favorite character there and why?

5. How does the death of the fox foreshadow the future?

6. Gage is very angry when he learns about Mason. Is his reaction justified or over the top?

7. Gage and Mason both deal with the pending loss of a parent. How do their responses differ? ▸

**Reading Group Guide** ***(continued)***

8. When Mason loses his mom, his grief is overwhelming. When Gage loses his dad, he feels numb and empty. Why do you think this is? How do they each come to terms with their loss and move on? In what way(s) does Mason honor his mom?

9. Maeve is crushed when Gage breaks off their relationship. She prays for guidance. How does she receive it? Have you ever received God's guidance through a friend or mentor?

10. Gage finishes his pencil drawing of his grandfather (Dutch) and enters it in a contest. How does this symbolize his willingness to take a chance as well as the resiliency of human nature? How does the resulting opportunity show that life often comes full circle?

11. When Gage and Maeve head home after the funeral, they stop in amazement and wonder to watch the cows standing solemnly under the ancient oak tree. Do you think the animals understand what has happened?

12. Throughout the book, many promises are made and kept. What are some of them?